One New York Christmas

Mandy Baggot

EBURY
PRESS

First published by Ebury Press in 2018

1 3 5 7 9 10 8 6 4 2

Ebury Press, an imprint of Ebury Publishing
20 Vauxhall Bridge Road,
London SW1V 2SA

Ebury Press is part of the Penguin Random House group of companies
whose addresses can be found at global.penguinrandomhouse.com

Penguin
Random House
UK

www.penguin.co.uk

A CIP catalogue record for this book is available from the British Library

ISBN 9781785039256

Typeset in 10/13.75 pt Adobe Caslon Pro
by Integra Software Services Pvt. Ltd, Pondicherry

Printed and bound in Great Britain by Clays Ltd, Elcograf S.p.A.

Penguin Random House is committed to a sustainable future for
our business, our readers and our planet. This book is made
from Forest Stewardship Council® certified paper.

MIX
Paper from
responsible sources
FSC
www.fsc.org   FSC® C018179

For Rachel, who virtually propped me up with encouraging words as I wrote Christmas in a UK heatwave. Bad-ass, baby!

Praise for Mandy Baggot

'A sizzling seasonal read from the Queen of Hot Heroes!'

Heidi Swain, *Sunday Times* bestselling author

'I absolutely love Mandy's books'

Milly Johnson, *Sunday Times* bestselling author

'Magical, heart-melting fiction at its best!'

Samantha Tonge

'There's brilliant chemistry ... such a fun read'

Bella Osborne

'Mandy creates characters that are full of life and absolutely delightful. I thoroughly enjoyed this book'

Jenny Hale

'This is fun, flirty and heartfelt romance at its very best'

Annie Lyons

'A gorgeous hug-of-a-book'

Zara Stoneley

Mandy Baggot is an award-winning romance writer. She loves the Greek island of Corfu, white wine, country music and handbags. Also a singer, she has taken part in ITV1's *Who Dares Sings* and *The X Factor*.

Mandy is a member of the Romantic Novelists' Association and the Society of Authors and lives near Salisbury, Wiltshire, UK with her husband and two daughters.

Also by Mandy Baggot:

Single for the Summer
One Christmas Kiss in Notting Hill
Desperately Seeking Summer

One

Appleshaw Market Square, Wiltshire, UK

It was raining hard, close to freezing, and the windscreen wipers on Lara Weeks's articulated truck were proving no match for the so-very-British winter weather. A mile. They had *one* mile to go before they reached the market square of her village, the every-second-house-is-a-thatch Appleshaw. Then the festivities could begin.

Turning up both the heat on the windscreen and the music – Taylor Swift singing a rendition of 'Last Christmas' through the Bluetooth connection – Lara focused on the road, blowing icy breath out into the cab. The 'they' encompassed the two Weeks Haulage trucks driven by her and Aldo. Aldo, her almost-brother, was in the lead vehicle carrying a huge, decoration-festooned evergreen complete with glittering lights of gold, red, green and a little out-there damson Mrs Fitch had had on special offer at the garden centre. Beneath the tree sat the whole tableau: Mary, Joseph, two sheep – who would be getting soggier by the second – the local MP's pet goat Milo, a shepherd and three wise men. The three wise men were Mrs Fitch's triplet grandsons who now, at thirteen, looked decidedly less than happy at being dressed in gold lamé.

But this was Aldo's big night. The eighteen-year-old had been waiting almost his entire life to drive a Weeks Haulage lorry in the annual 1 December parade and finally he was getting his chance. He had passed his HGV test a few months before and it was Lara who had taught him everything he knew. Except maybe what to do when you had Baby Jesus rocking in a crib and it started to hail ... Why didn't it snow instead? That's what it was supposed to do in December. A light sprinkling over picturesque Appleshaw to make it more festive Christmas cake rather than simply quintessential chocolate box.

'Keep your speed down, Aldo. Just crawl along. There's no rush,' Lara said to herself, reaching to turn Taylor Swift back down. She eyed the CB radio on the dashboard. No one else she knew used CB except her dad Gerry's haulage company. He'd got two brand-new trucks – Lara had called hers Tina – after a good spell of trading, but had insisted on keeping the old-style communication going. *It's tradition*, he'd said. So here they were, handsets that looked like they belonged in a museum, alongside USB ports and built-in satnav. Lara took the walkie-talkie from its housing and put it to her mouth.

'Aldo, do you copy, over?'

The handset found her lap, as she put both hands back to the wheel, visibility growing worse. She couldn't remember a parade having weather quite as bad as this before. Perhaps no one would even be out to watch ...

'Lara? Is that you?'

Lara shook her head at the sound of Aldo's surprised voice. As well as lorry-driving, she had also taught him to use the CB. The problem was, Aldo didn't retain information very well, unless, like with the HGV driving, he was absolutely passionate about it. Trucks, football teams and anything Marvel was about the extent of it. And lately, martial arts. If that obsession kept up she might need to suggest he slimmed down his growing Bruce Lee collection, perhaps focus on lighter kung-fu, like *The Karate Kid* …

'Aldo, yes it's me. You need to keep your speed down, over.'

A crackling sound commenced, like someone was crunching up tin foil, and Lara eyed her mobile phone, currently playing the music through the speakers. She could phone him … but what were the chances that Aldo would *reach* for his phone instead of going hands-free?

'How do I keep my speed *downover* again?' came Aldo's reply. 'I don't remember that from the test, Lara.'

She forced in a deep breath. She was being overly cautious. Aldo would be fine. They were less than a mile away, going no more than fifteen miles an hour, and she was right behind him. What could possibly go wrong?

Suddenly Lara's phone lit up and a side-eye to the screen showed a photo of her boyfriend, Dan. It was a picture of him in the summer, pulling a face, when she had made him suck on the biggest slice of lemon after a shot of tequila. She smiled, hitting the button on the steering wheel to answer safely.

'Is everyone there or are they all hiding in the pub until the hail stops?'

'What?' Dan asked. It sounded like he was in a car. Either that or the ban on traffic through the centre of Appleshaw while the parade came through had gone awry.

'I'm literally half a mile from the square now. Aldo and I are about to lead the procession through the town. Have you got a good spot? Is there anyone else there? It might be a great time for Mrs Fitch to sell those golf umbrellas.'

'Is it the parade tonight?'

Lara laughed. He did like to tease her about the village's quirks. 'Very funny! Because it's not like it's always on the first of December or anything.'

There was no response. Just the sound of ... motorway traffic?

'Dan,' Lara said. 'Where are you? Because you know it's my work's Christmas party tonight too, right? You're having melon, turkey and chocolate roulade.'

Still there was nothing. She would have thought the line was dead if it hadn't been for the constant roar of an M-road. 'Dan, did you hear me?'

'Listen, Lara, I'm not going to make it tonight.'

She bit her lip. This was the third time Dan hadn't been able to make it to something that was important to her. He hadn't made the fun day at the haulage yard when he'd said he was going to help with the barbecue and he hadn't come to Aldo's eighteenth birthday party at the social club before that. There had been a disco that night, a killer darts competition and Aldo had drunk cocktails from a bucket he'd also needed to be sick in later on. Lara's best friend Susie was a relationship guru, and she had told Lara how to handle these sorts of moments. *Play it cool. No one likes Little Miss Shrink-wrap.*

'Oh, well, that's a shame but ... never mind.' She swallowed. It felt unnatural. She was annoyed with him. Angry even. And it felt very alien to hold that frustration in. She didn't do holding in emotion very well ... not keeping a lid on it had almost earned her points on her licence last year. A car had pulled out in front of her lorry and she had blasted the horn and shouted some choice expletives. Then, at the next set of traffic lights, she had screeched Tina to a halt, leapt down from the vehicle and confronted the driver ... who happened to be a policeman in an unmarked car. 'You got my text about Christmas though?'

Susie said always follow up the let-down with something positive. *Make plans*. Remind him, *and* yourself, of all the other good stuff you have coming up. It was a case of keeping things fresh and not being complacent. They had been together two years. Things weren't exactly Interflora and Thornton's. They were more garage carnations and Dairy Milk. But that was fine. That was normal. What mattered most was they loved each other. And Dan was her window to the world, with his job in hot-tub sales that took him all over Europe. She'd ask him about these trips when he got back, and he would tell her about the little pavement cafes in Paris, the canals of Amsterdam and the buzz of New York's Manhattan. As much as she loved the cosiness and quaint charm of Appleshaw, she loved to hear stories of a different real life going on in every corner of the globe.

'Lara ... I thought you'd been at home now,' Dan replied.

'No,' she answered. 'It's the first of December so I'm driving a truck. Like I've driven a truck on the night of the first of December since I was eighteen.' Six years ago, it had been *her* first time leading the procession and she'd almost jack-knifed on black ice. 'So, anyway, Christmas Eve, Aldo wants to do Chinese and a film, Christmas Day we're going to Mrs Fitch's for lunch and Boxing Day I thought we could—'

'Lara, I'm sorry ... I can't do this any more. I ...'

'Dan ... I think you're breaking up,' Lara called, adjusting her position slightly, trying to listen hard while maintaining a hard visual on the back of Aldo's lorry.

There was a sigh, then: 'Yeah,' Dan replied. 'Something like that.'

'Dan ... I don't think I'm hearing you properly.'

'Lara, I don't know about Christmas. I think … I think I need some space.'

She hit the brakes hard, the hissing sound rising up like a hundred angry cats had all started fighting with each other. There was a definite shifting of her load and she instantly regretted the action. On the back of Tina were the Second Appleshaw Scout Troop, and their depiction of Christmas Through the Ages included a tableau of the various John Lewis adverts. There were boys and girls in penguin suits, snowmen, large full moons and a collection of boys dressed as wizened old men.

'I … don't think I heard what you said,' Lara stuttered. The hail was hammering at her windscreen now as she sat stationary, Aldo's back lights rolling away from her.

'Lara … I think we should go on a break.'

She racked her brain for a Susie-style interpretation of this. What was the best thing to say? What did he mean? *Think! Think! Something positive and plan-making! Quick!*

'We should get away,' Lara blurted out. 'We haven't been away since … the camping trip.'

'Lara …'

'We could go camping again. It was fun, wasn't it? Sitting around the fire, toasting marshmallows, drinking that awful cider, feeding the rabbits the horrible chips from the chip shop …'

'It's December,' Dan said.

'I know but … we could go in Tina.' She felt hope spark in her chest. Her lorry was full of all the modern trucking conveniences, including heating. 'I'm sure Dad wouldn't mind, just for a few days. It'll be cosy. It's got the bed and we could fill the cool-box with beer and find a great band to go and watch and then we could—'

'I need to get away for a bit,' Dan stated. And then there was an out-breath. 'And ... I think we should have a time-out.'

A time-out. It sounded like something you gave a naughty child as punishment. Lara was desperately thinking for an alternative explanation but right now it sounded like Dan was breaking up with her.

'I'm going to Scotland for Christmas,' he said quickly.

'Oh.' What else was there to say? This felt all wrong.

'A friend has booked a lodge up there and—'

'Which friend?' Lara asked. 'Derek?'

'No.'

'Smooth Pete?'

'No.'

'Then who?'

There was a throat-clearing that sounded nothing short of guilty. 'You know Chloe ... from the golf club.'

Chloe from the golf club! *Cleavage* Chloe. Her boyfriend was spending Christmas in a lodge in Scotland with Cleavage Chloe! This couldn't be happening. Lara held her breath and closed her eyes, only coming to with the sound of questioning voices coming from the back of her rig. The scouts. The Advent Parade. Her almost-brother, Aldo. She was in the middle of a very important job. She put the lorry back into gear and put her foot to the accelerator.

'There's others going too. Sam and Fiona. Darren and Amanda—'

'But not me,' Lara said. 'You haven't invited me.'

Why hadn't he invited her? Scotland at Christmas sounded romantic. It was bound to snow. There would be log fires and single malt whisky, tartan rugs and ... kilts. Dan in a kilt. He had such great legs ... and now those legs would be in Scotland for Christmas along with the rest of him ... and Cleavage Chloe.

'I think we need to ... think about things ...'

'Well, what things? Tell me what we need to think about and we'll think about it,' Lara said. 'We can think in Appleshaw, can't we? I know I can. Why do you have to go to another country to think?'

'I need a bit of space and time—'

'Why?' Lara said. 'I don't understand what for.'

'To work things through.'

'What things, for God's sake?!'

'To work out if—'

'Dan! I'm seconds away from the Appleshaw Silver Band's rendition of "O Holy Night".'

'To work out if ... I still love you.'

It was at that second that Aldo's back lights became visible again ... and so close. So close that Lara wasn't sure she was going to be able to stop in time. Her options were limited now she had reached Appleshaw's centre. She either smashed into the back of the vehicle containing the Messiah, his parents, the Magi and the villagers' livestock or she took out the soup stall ...

'Lara,' Dan spoke over the phone. 'Lara, are you OK?'

Two

Appleshaw Social Club, Appleshaw

'Best bit of driving I've ever seen, Doug. I'm telling you, my girl could do that truck racing they have at Thruxton.' Gerry Weeks ate another mouthful of turkey and stuffing before carrying on. 'Skewed that unit in double quick time, missed the soup stand by inches and not one of them scouts lost a woggle.' He let out a hearty laugh and slammed his hand down onto the table. Aldo copied him, gravy splattering up from his plate. 'Lara, you might have to re-enact that move in the yard. Teach the other drivers,' her dad concluded.

Lara said nothing. Tonight was supposed to be the first night of the beginning of her favourite time of year. She might have avoided disaster in the square but, after Dan's words, there had been no festive joy in the proceedings for her. Usually Dan would be there, teasing her about the trad-itions – Mrs Fitch selling her Christmas pudding woollen hats, Flora giving out her home-made mince-pie whisky, the school children determined not to let anyone go home without purchasing a zip-lock bag of 'reindeer food' (basically Quaker Oats and glitter). But he *hadn't* been there. Wasn't here now. Would be spending Christmas in the Hebrides. Wanted to go on a break …

Lara picked up her second pint and took three good gulps. When in doubt, turn to probably the best lager in the world. Except it wasn't quite hitting the spot. She wasn't in the mood for a party. She felt like going back to her barn and crying like her heart had been ripped out … which it had. She hadn't even gone home to get changed before coming here. She had planned black trousers and a Christmas vest top stating 'It's the most wonderful time for a beer' but instead, while everyone else was sparkling in new shirts or dresses, she was still in her jeans, Dr Martens and Slipknot T-shirt. As was normal, the social club heating was belting out at full blast so her hoodie was on the back of her chair. It was hail-soaked anyway and needed to dry out. A bit like her hair. She had shoved her short, dark crop under the hand dryer in the ladies' toilets but it was no Dyson Blade and her hair was still wet-wipe damp. And Susie hadn't turned up yet either.

Lara's best friend Susie Maplin was a hairdresser at Appleshaw's Cuts and Curls. She had moved to the village from London with her parents five years ago, fresh out of hairdresser training. Mr and Mrs Maplin were fed up with the rat race and were looking for a little bit of English countryside peace and quiet. To begin with, Susie hadn't been enamoured by the slow pace and far too many shampoo and sets but, when Wendy had given her total control over colour, extensions and basically anything twenty-first-century mane, Susie had come into her own, bringing a whole new wave of waves to the high street.

Lara looked at her phone and the background wallpaper. Her and Dan standing in front of her new, beloved, thankfully unscathed Tina. She needed to call him back. She needed to tell him going to Scotland was a mistake. That they should spend Christmas together. Maybe she could go with him to Scotland. Granted, she could think of nothing worse than being in a cabin with Cleavage Chloe, but being there was certainly preferable to being in Appleshaw, knowing your boyfriend was in a cabin with a femme fatale. And she *was* a femme fatale. There were divorcees in the village who called her the Mantis.

'Don't you want your chicken, Lara?' Aldo asked from across the table.

She looked up from her phone to her almost-brother. He was red-cheeked and grinning, his thatch of tightly curled Justin Timberlake hair showing all its ginger under the bright bulbs of the social club. He had added a bow tie to his plaid shirt, just like her dad.

'It's turkey, Aldo,' Lara reminded him.

'Don't you want your turkey, Lara?' he asked. 'Or the sprouts. I really like the sprouts.'

She pushed her plate across to him. 'Don't eat all the sprouts though. You might end up being blown to Amesbury by the end of the night.'

Gravy drizzling down his chin, Aldo looked a little confused. He wasn't the best at picking up subtle humour. Lara looked back to her phone as the first few bars of 'Step into Christmas' began from the disco.

'I am sooo sorry I'm late!' Susie threw herself down into the chair next to Lara, unwound a fake-fur scarf from her neck then removed a matching hat. The coat was next. 'This woman comes into the salon at a minute to six – and I mean a *minute* to six – and wants her hair glitterised.' She picked up Lara's pint of lager and downed half of it. 'Sorry ... I'll get us some more drinks in a minute. Anyway, so I'm half-tempted to send her to the garden centre for that spray we coat the outside plants in at Christmas but then I notice what she's wearing: face-cheek to butt-cheek in designer. I'm talking Victoria Beckham jeans, Prada top and one of those very I'm-leading-the-fox-hunt Barbour jackets,' she said breathlessly. 'So, I look at Wendy and Wendy looks at me and I'm already deciding what I'm going to do. Well, to cut a long story short, I create this amazing fusion of pinks and purples and a little of that mermaid-blue Demi Lovato favours every now and then, then I roll her hair up into these two unicorn-horn-shaped cones and I cover the entire thing in this diamond dust I bought at that conference in Italy.' Susie grinned. 'She Insta-ed before she was even out of the chair and she has over two thousand followers! I'm hoping they're all from the polo set, or at least members of the golf club.'

At the mention of the golf club, Lara's delight at seeing her best friend waned absolutely.

'I'm so sorry I'm late though, Lara. But I've heard all about the close shave with the soup stand – Flora caught me up on the way in – and it doesn't matter that I missed the melon course, melon's basically water, I'll get some water when I get the next drinks in.' Susie looked around the table, giving a feasting-on-sprouts Aldo a little wave. 'Where's Dan?'

Lara felt the hurt and rejection crush her chest like she was pinned to the wall by an out-of-control forklift. And she knew how that felt because it had actually happened once. Tears were welling up before she could keep herself in check. What did she say? What could she say?

'Lara?' Susie asked, putting a hand on her arm. 'What's happened?'

'Dan ... he ... doesn't know if he loves me any more. He wants to go on a break.'

Her words had tumbled out the very second the DJ had messed up mixing into the next tune and the function room plunged into silence. Suddenly, the inquisitive eyes of every partygoer were on her.

'With Cleavage Chloe,' Lara said.

The whole room inhaled.

Three

'I'll pulverise him!' Gerry declared. Aldo, next to him, threw a karate chop into the air. Everyone in the Weeks Haulage team were crowding around Lara at the bar in a show of solidarity. 'When I've finished with him he'll need physio to learn him how to smile again.'

'Dad,' Lara said, touching his arm. She hadn't wanted this to come out tonight. Her dad worked hard every year organising the party. It was their big annual celebration. She didn't want it blighted by her relationship drama.

'I've a good mind to go round there now. Give him a piece of my fist.'

'Dad, no,' Lara stated hurriedly. She knew Gerry was at least three pints down already, and there was a quarter-drunk flagon of Flora's mince-pie whisky on the Weeks Haulage table. 'Honestly, it's fine.'

'I wouldn't say it's fine,' Susie interrupted. 'I'd say he's being a complete dick.'

'Dick!' Aldo shouted angrily.

Lara closed her eyes for a second. They were all being so nice but equally they were angry, mad on her behalf, but she wasn't feeling anything like fury. She felt desperately, desperately sad. This was her fault. Her and her small village mentality had lost her Dan. Cleavage Chloe might work at the golf club, but Lara knew she travelled. She saw more than the inside of a truck and didn't holiday at Haven campsites. Chloe probably had interesting things to say about sunsets over Santorini and eating tabbouleh. Lara *was* hungry for more than Appleshaw, but Appleshaw was the centre of her universe. Her dad, her job, Aldo, they needed her as much as she needed them. Her mum had left the village, and it had taken her dad a long time to pick himself and a six-year-old Lara up. Appleshaw was who she was. It, and the people in it, had helped raise her. But apparently Dan was done with it. And done with *her*.

'We'll excommunicate him,' Gerry declared. 'And that company he works for.' He held his hand in the air like he was the preacher from *Damnation*. 'Let it be noted down this night. As from the first of December 2018, Dan Reeves is not to be spoken to, written to, or communicated with in any way … and neither is Spa South.' Gerry drew in a long breath, his bald head going bright red. 'Let's see how they transport their hot tubs now.'

Lara couldn't listen to any more. She snatched up her hastily poured tumbler of Flora's special brew from the bar area, almost knocking over the tinsel-draped charity pot, before retreating to a table in the corner of the room. It was the furthest seating area away from the fallout of her life and the disco, that seemed to be playing an early erection section starting with 'When a Man Loves a Woman'.

'Oh no you don't.'

Susie was at Lara's heels, nudging her arm before she could take a chair.

'I'm fine,' Lara snapped.

'No, you're not,' Susie replied. 'And I don't blame you one bit. Not only has Dan done a really, really shitty thing to you on one of your favourite nights of the year, but you've got your dad and Aldo and the rest of the drivers turning all biblical talking about burning at the stake and ostracising.'

She still didn't know what to say. What was there to say? When your heart was breaking in half and you didn't even know how to go about making it through the next few hours, let alone the rest of your life.

'So, in order for me to help you I need to know *exactly* what Dan said to you.' Susie sat down, slurping at her glass of mince-pie whisky.

'What?' Lara asked, suddenly coming to a little.

'Well, you said that he said that he wants to "go on a break". In my experience, that's man-code for "I'm having a bit of a pre-thirty crisis, am worried about my age, my attractiveness to women, my ear hairs and my risk of prostate cancer versus how many pints it's acceptable to drink on a weekend".'

'It is?' Lara asked.

'It's classic, almost-thirty behaviour,' Susie confirmed. 'Remember Ruby at the Appleshaw Inn and her bloke, Trigger? He bought a motorbike *and* shares in a speedboat then said he was going off to "find himself". Absolute classic case. And Dan is the same. He's heading off to Scotland for Christmas because he thinks it's different, new and exciting. It's not playing Scrabble with your dad, Aldo and Mrs Fitch, not that there's anything wrong with that but ...'

The home-made whisky was starting to numb Lara's senses a bit. 'He knows I wouldn't want to leave the family at Christmas,' she began. 'But he still made his decision on this lodge without even talking to me ... and then why didn't he say he was going there for Christmas and he'd see me for New Year? Why this "break" stuff as well?'

'Pre-thirty crisis, like I said. So, what did he *actually* say? Word for word.'

As Lara thought back to that hands-free conversation in her truck, the sound of Christmas crackers being pulled filled the air, together with comments about the arriving dessert. Her group were making their way back to the table, but she didn't want pudding. Right now she wanted to fill her system with as much booze as she could get her hands on.

'He said he needed space ... to go on a break ... to have time out, no, to *have* a time-out.' Saying the words out loud was making her feel sick. How could this be happening? They were good together, solid, comfortable ...

Maybe that was the issue. Maybe she had got too comfortable. She had started leaving the door unlocked when she was in the shower. Dan often came in to clean his teeth. They hadn't gone so far as using the loo in front of each other but ... she had thought about it when he had been in there for more than half an hour and she was at bursting point.

'Well,' Susie said, triumphant. 'None of that sounds like the end to me. It sounds like he wants to assert his control over the relationship. Remember? I told you that's what men do, what they feel they *have* to do ... to feel like men.' Susie gritted her teeth and made a noise like a horny Viking. 'Despite all the grooming products and apps that can do anything, they're always going to act stone age. It's written in their DNA.'

A tiny flicker of hope burnt a little brighter inside her. 'Do you really think so?'

'Absolutely. I mean, Chloe, she's ...'

'Hot.'

'No ... well, a bit, I suppose ... if you like that sort of thing.' Susie took a swig of her whisky. 'Do you want me to stop doing her hair?'

'You do her hair?'

'I do every Appleshaw resident under-sixty's hair! She has highlights and lowlights and colour … it's a good couple of hundred quid every six weeks or so.' Susie put a hand on Lara's arm. 'Anyway, you're hot too. Super-hot. With that petite frame that says vulnerable and needs looking after, mixed with the feisty attitude that says you definitely don't need propping up by anyone. Killer eyes. Fantastic hair – you're welcome – and the funniest person I know, except for me.'

Lara swallowed. 'He said he needed to work out if he still loved me.' She looked to Susie for the next piece of relationship advice. A silence descended as the music went back to Slade.

'But he must still love me now, right? To want to do the working-out-if-he-does bit.'

Susie's flat expression was making anxiety trampoline in her chest. This was bad. This could go from being a break to a break-up. What was she going to do? What the hell was she going to do?

Lara stood up, her hand at her chest, feeling overwhelmed. She couldn't catch her breath. She couldn't focus. The room was beginning to spin, all its Christmas finery blurring into one big, glittery melting pot.

'Lara,' Susie said. Her voice sounded tinny, like she was standing from far away. 'Lara, sit down.'

What did she do in December if it didn't involve Dan? There would be no dressing the barn and falling into bed halfway through. No taking it in turns to write the office Christmas cards and seeing who got the septic tank company this year – she always fixed it so Dan did – Merry Christmas from us to poo. She felt sick and sweaty …

'Sit down!' Susie ordered, grabbing her arm and forcing her into her seat. 'This is not happening. Do you hear me? Dan is not going to make you fall apart like this. Lara. Lara, are you listening to me?'

She was trying to. Really trying to. She looked directly at her best friend, attempting to take in every subtle detail of her appearance. Her subtle mousy curls that had somehow survived both the freezing hail of the night and her hat, her honest green eyes, her lips slicked with a rose-coloured gloss … slowly Lara's breath stopped catching, rolled over into a full exhale. She was getting back in control.

'OK?' Susie queried, still holding her arm.

She managed a nod. 'Yes.'

'Right then,' Susie said decisively. 'There are two courses of action open to us now. You need to answer one question.'

'What?' Lara asked, blinking determined tears away.

'Do you want to make this work with Dan?' Susie asked. 'Do you love him?'

'I think that was two questions,' Lara answered gingerly.

'Well?'

'Yes,' Lara said immediately. 'Yes, of course I love him. Of course, I want to make this work.'

Susie clapped her hands together and rubbed them like she might start a fire with her hot palms. 'Right then, I know just what to do.'

Four

Seth Hunt and Trent Davenport's apartment, West Village, New York

'I can't do it! I cannot do it! This is nuts! Literally nuts!' Trent put his hands in his short, blond hair and pulled. He made gorilla noises and thumped his chest as he strode around the open-plan apartment like he was caged.

From his seat at the diner-style table, Seth watched his friend in full-on meltdown mode. He should really video it. Despite the expletives falling from Trent's lips, it would make a great comedy reel … Maybe he'd thank him for it later. 'What's up?' he asked.

'I swear to God I am gonna sack my agent! Get this!' Trent turned to face Seth, iPhone gripped in his hand. 'He wants me to turn up to an audition today, like in an hour's time, for a commercial. For nuts! Nuts!' Trent screamed. 'It's nuts!'

'What kind of nuts?' Seth asked, pushing his glasses up his nose.

'Seth! Man, are you for real?!' Treat grabbed hold of the still-bare spruce they had installed in the apartment last night. They'd both been a little buzzed from drinks at Jimmy's Corner in Midtown, seen the tree-seller on the way back in the cab and made the driver stop while they purchased a fir that was no way going to fit in the taxi with them. Carried across the city to home in the West Village, it had been left to Seth to find some sort of vessel to prop it in – currently the bowl from the kitchen sink. He would ask his mom if she had a pot they could borrow when he caught up with her later. He looked to the notepad in front of him, the blank page he was supposed to be filling with questions …

'Well,' Seth began as Trent altered the position of the Christmas tree's branches. 'Nuts, pulses and raw diets of that stuff are big business these days. And Gwyneth Paltrow does it.'

'Do I look like Gwyneth Paltrow to you?' Trent asked, hands on hips, a study of pent-up frustration.

'I don't know,' Seth said, angling his head a little. 'Perhaps with a dress and a weave …'

'OK, man, you can laugh but what auditions has your agent lined up for you this week?'

Seth put his pen down. 'Trent, I wasn't laughing. The total opposite. The nut commercial, it's a chance for cash, right? We all need cash. It pays for this apartment and the cab fares to the auditions that matter.' He sighed. 'Plus, you know, it's *nuts*. It's something you can … crack … without breaking a sweat. The job's yours already.'

'Unless Junior Benson's there again. God! That guy!' Trent thrashed his arms out, fighting to unbutton his cuffs and roll up his sleeves. 'No matter how hard I try I can't look as urban as him. Every single audition and he's there in his *dope* clothes, snapback on his head, breathing cool-hood like he invented it.'

'Urban is a phase,' Seth said, getting to his feet. 'And nuts, they're … sophisticated, they're cashews and macadamia and—'

'Monkey,' Trent interrupted. 'The brief said they were monkey nuts with shells you can eat, coated in cinnamon and honey.'

'Jeez,' Seth said. 'How have they made shells you can eat?'

'I don't know! And I don't care!' Trent sniffed. 'This is beneath me. It was only a few months ago I was in a film with George Clooney!'

'And that will come again,' Seth told him, slapping a hand to his shoulder. 'Soon. But until then … I'd take a chance on the nuts.'

Trent sniffed, finally seeming to calm down a little. He pointed at the neon sign that hung on the bare-brick wall of the kitchen area. 'There's a light out on the coffee mug.'

'I know,' Seth answered. 'I'm gonna get to it this morning.'

'Haven't you got anything on today?' Trent asked. 'I bet *your* agent has a whole stack of great things lined up.'

Seth didn't reply. The truth was there was nothing. Not even a commercial for nuts. 'Not really,' he answered finally.

'What about the Netflix series screen test you did?'

'I've not heard back.' And he'd had flu. He'd sweated a fever out all night while trying to learn the script and delivered the lines completely through his nose. *He* hadn't even understood what he'd said.

'But you've followed it up, right? Your agent has told them you're gunning for the gig and you're good to go whenever they are.'

'I … don't know.'

'Come on, man. I got nuts! You've got—'

'Nothing,' Seth answered. 'I got nothing.' He let out a sigh and walked back to the table. He was beginning to get that creeping feeling he'd had just before he'd decided to try and make it as an actor. Disillusionment. Fear. The constant thought that his time playing Dr Mike on *Manhattan Med* might have been the pinnacle of his career ... and he'd gone and thrown that fame and regular salary away for a chance that hadn't come off.

'Listen, man, I might be feeling a little off about the nuts thing but that's because I know I'm better than that,' Trent stated. 'And I'm not too stupid to know that I only have *half* your talent.'

'Get outta here.' He waved his friend's claim away.

Trent cleared his throat. 'Pardon me, but you got down to the final casting for Christian paddles-are-my-weapon-of-choice Grey, did you not?'

Seth shook his head, a hint of a smile on his lips. 'I can't trade on that indefinitely. And the world knows I didn't get the part.'

'I blame your ass,' Trent said with a long inhale. 'When you do your squats at the gym you really gotta pull it on in. Suck that core to momma.' He began a demo, crouching down in pants that didn't look like they were going to withstand too much thigh-straining.

Seth brushed back his dark hair, then picked up the pen again, holding it over the notebook. He should have done this last night instead of going out with Trent. Now he only had a few hours before lunch with his mom and he wasn't nearly as prepared as he wanted to be.

'Listen, Seth, you've gotta get back out there,' Trent said, raising one knee to his chest then the other. 'Get your agent to get on to Netflix. Get on to the other studios. Big things, man.'

'Yeah,' Seth replied. There was little conviction. The reality was he was scraping by with what he had left from *Manhattan Med.* Just yesterday he had considered applying for a job at the little coffee shop down the street. He might even accept part-payment in their melt-in-your-mouth bagels.

Trent pointed at him suddenly, his eyes wide. 'I know what you need!'

'Do not say another shot of JD.'

'You need some publicity,' Trent continued. 'Get yourself under the public eye and into the news. It will give your agent something to really hang your hat on when he makes those call-backs.' Trent pulled up the chair opposite and slid the notepad towards him. He took the pen from Seth's hand before he could do anything about it. 'What kooky humanitarian projects are going on right now? How's your Twitter looking? You do use a management system to grow your account, don't you?'

'Trent, it's ten thirty in the morning.'

'And you're out of the game, buddy. Come on, this needs to change.' Trent put his hand out, fingers beckoning. 'Gimme your phone. We'll do a search. See if we can't find something Christmassy and heart-warming to put *Manhattan Med*'s Dr Mike back on the map.' He held up a finger. 'How about the zoo? People love animals. There must be some ailing critters that need a bit of attention. I can see it now … *Manhattan Med*'s Dr Mike brings meerkats back to life.' He paused. 'How about your mother's cause?'

Seth shook his head. 'No.'

'OK …'

'I don't know, Trent. All that stuff is more your thing than mine.' Seth wasn't stupid enough to think he could be an actor without social media, photo opportunities and promotion but it was his least favourite part of the role. One of the reasons he got into acting to begin with was because he delighted in having the chance to be someone else. It was so much easier than facing head on where he had really come from – and that was starting today ... if he went through with it.

'Listen, man, do you want the nut job? Because if you need a shot of something right now, I'm thinking it's confidence.' Trent smiled. 'And you could sell anything to anyone with those eyes.'

Seth smiled. 'Trent, do not say anything like that in a bar, in company, like ever.'

Trent laughed. 'Come on, man, humour me. Let's hook you up with a cause.'

Five

Lara Weeks's barnpartment,
Appleshaw, UK

'There can't be *nobody*,' Susie slurred, dropping her body down onto the rustic leather sofa. The seating was tan, worn and reminded Lara of saddles and cowboys. It smelt a bit like that too. Probably because the whole area was still barn-like despite the conversion that had taken place when she had decided to move out of the main house.

'I know everyone in Appleshaw,' Lara replied, stumbling a little as she headed to the tiny kitchen area for some glasses. She had hijacked the flagon of Flora's mince-pie whisky and left the party as soon as the DJ had played 'All I Want For Christmas Is You'.

'Well … what about Ian from the fish and chip shop?'

'Susie!'

'What?'

'He looks about twelve!'

'But he's got to be over sixteen, because he's been working there full-time for at least two years now.'

Lara poured the dark brown fragrant liquid into two over-sized tumblers and sat down next to Susie. 'I know, but sixteen is way too young and … I don't fancy him.' She took a swig, before cradling the glass in her hands and folding her legs up underneath her, sitting back on the settee. 'And at a certain angle he looks a bit like a fillet of haddock.'

'You don't have to fancy him!' Susie exclaimed. 'Dan just has to *believe* you do.'

'Well … he won't.'

'Why not?'

'Because I fancy *Dan*.' Lara sighed. 'We *do* talk to each other you know. And he knows who I like and who I don't. We *have played* Kiss, Marry, Avoid.' She had admitted to a slight girl crush on Jennifer Lawrence and Dan had concurred. They had laughed then, drunk more beer, ate peanuts and both pledged to avoid Keith Lemon at all costs.

'There has to be *somebody* you fancy besides Dan.' Susie spilt a little whisky down her shirt and patted her hand on her boobs to get rid of it. 'It's natural to look and admire and think "yes, if I wasn't with him, I definitely would".'

Lara smiled at her friend. 'And who do you look at and think that? Because it's been half a year since David.' Susie's Spanish boyfriend was as crazy as she was. They had met at a hairdressing conference and it had been lust at first undercut. Susie had spent alternate weekends travelling up to London to be with him and David had returned the favour, visiting Appleshaw and falling a little in love with Mrs Fitch's attempt at tortillas. But a massive opportunity had seen him jet off and Lara knew her friend was finding the added distance difficult.

'David and I are still very much together,' Susie responded a little tightly.

'He moved to New York,' Lara reminded.

'I'm well aware.' Susie sniffed. 'We FaceTime all the time, when we're both not busy.'

'But you haven't seen him in six months.'

'New York is a long way away and I just said, he's busy and I'm busy and everyone is really, really busy.' Susie swigged at her drink again. 'Besides, we weren't talking about me and David, we were talking about you finding someone to make Dan jealous.'

Lara shook her head. She didn't really want her life turning into some half-arsed challenge from a reality TV show. She shouldn't be needing to make Dan jealous. Dan should be with her now. They both should be at the social club, making fun of the giant paper Christmas ball that had been hanging there, apparently since the 1970s.

'What am I thinking?' Susie said suddenly, bounding up from the sofa, eyes wild with alcohol and whatever had just come into her head. 'We need to look further than Appleshaw.'

'Salisbury?' Lara shook her head again. 'Oh no, Susie, not the guy from Prezzo who always gives me extra olives.'

'Not Salisbury,' Susie replied. She grabbed Lara's laptop from the coffee table, opened the lid and sat back down with it on her knees. 'Celebrity.' She started to type. 'The world.'

'What?'

'There was this woman – it was in one of my magazines – she tweeted with her favourite celebrities and posted all the replies on Facebook and Instagram in a bid to make her husband jealous.' Susie drew in a breath, fingers still flying across the keyboard. '*He* was having a relationship with Byron Burgers, apparently he would rather spend time with a double bacon cheese than her ... anyway, it worked.'

'What d'you mean it worked?' Lara leaned forward a little. Not that she was interested in this ridiculous idea. 'You mean people like ... Tom Hardy tweeted her back? I don't believe it.'

'Obviously not all A-listers ... although she did get a response from Zayn Malik.'

'I'm not sure I'd call him A-list.'

'The point is, she got replies and she got his attention. And that's what we should do with you and Dan.' Susie's fingers ran over the trackpad of the laptop. 'Let's log you in to Twitter and get going.'

'I don't use Twitter to stalk celebrities,' Lara said. 'I use it to find out about the world.' It was one of her favourite pastimes. Pick a country and type it into Twitter and see what she could learn. When her day consisted of loads of farm feed or fertiliser, it was a chance to travel outside the village in her evenings. From her laptop, she could walk down any street in the world. And she had. In her head, she had eaten tacos in Mexico and drank limoncello in Venice.

'Let's start with Ed Sheeran. He seems like a nice guy—'

'Susie, stop.' Even with her head being addled by the whisky and her stomach full of Christmas fayre this didn't seem right. She should talk to Dan, properly – not hands-free before an Appleshaw parade. She put a hand on the edge of the screen of her laptop. 'How is this going to help?'

Susie straightened up but in no way relinquished control of the device. 'You told me that Dan is going to Scotland for Christmas with Chloe from the golf club.'

'I know.' Her friend saying the sentence made Lara's chest ache again.

'We need action! He needs to see that the love of his life, the girl of his dreams, is going to make this break permanent if he doesn't hurry up and get his act together. *You* are going to be in demand … *you* are going to be Ed Sheeran's … Appleshaw Amour … OK, it's not quite "Galway Girl" but you get it, right?'

She didn't want to get it. She didn't want to be having this mad conversation. She wanted to be undressing Dan, listening to a Christmas classics playlist, the faint snoring of the goats from the farm next door making her feel warm, content and December-y ... except Dan was who-knows-where with who-knew-who ... or Chloe.

'Thinking down to about D-list,' Susie said, 'who was that actor you had a crush on?'

Lara shook herself and reached for the flagon of whisky. 'Narrow it down a little. There's been a few. I even had a crush on John Simm once.'

'Younger than him. Hotter than him ... oh God, what was the name of that show? He was a doctor ... all moody and broody and a little bit punchy when there was a drug-addict mother and a newborn baby ...'

'Dr Mike,' Lara said. 'From *Manhattan Med*.' She still watched it, although it wasn't the same without Dr Mike. He had been a glorious piece of eye candy to while away an hour or two when Dan was travelling for work. And she was picky – hence the rejection of local potential jealousy-making suitors.

'Yes! We'll tweet him too,' Susie announced, eyes back down on the screen.

'And Dan does know I liked him,' Lara admitted. 'He even didn't shave one weekend when Dr Mike was going through his stubble stage.'

'See!' Susie exclaimed. 'Now we're getting somewhere. So, what is Dr Mike's real name?'

'Seth,' Lara answered, moving closer to Susie. 'Seth Hunt.'

'Seth Hunt,' Susie said as she typed the name into the Twitter search bar. 'Let's see what you've been up to since you left the fictional hospital.'

Six

Dominique Bistro, Christopher & Gay Street, New York

Seth checked his watch again then poured some more water into his glass, adjusting the cuffs of his thick red-and-black plaid shirt. Pushing his glasses up his nose he checked out the other diners in the restaurant. All of them seemed to be engaged in animated conversation, as if the French vibe here was rubbing off on them. It was cold, some people were still wrapped up in scarves, coats unfastened but not removed, acclimatising before they shrugged them off. None of them appeared to be nervous like he was. Nervous about meeting his own mother. It was crazy. And then he saw her.

Running through the front door, a whirlwind of dark curls, a bright carrot-coloured scarf at her throat, already slipping off her thick winter coat as she came in on the breeze. Now his heart surged with nothing but love and admiration for Katherine 'Kossy' Hunt.

Seth went to stand up, wave a hand, but she knew where he'd be sitting. They always sat at the same table when they came here to eat – the one at the end of large windows displaying the street outside, next to the shelves filled with vinyl records, corks in a glass jar and a rustic, wooden pumpkin.

She headed towards him, hands at her neck, unwinding the scarf.

'Hey, listen,' Kossy began. 'Before you say anything, I know I'm late, but you will not believe the morning I've had.'

Seth smiled. Almost every one of his conversations with his mom began this way. He hugged her tightly and she gasped as if the contact was unexpected. Perhaps he held on a little longer than normal. She kissed his cheek, then held his body away from hers, eyes roving over his frame as if she was doing an inspection.

'Are you sick?' Kossy asked firmly. 'Because if you're sick you really need to tell me before I order the ravioli. Ravioli is my happy food here and if it's accompanied by bad news then ...'

'I'm not sick, Mom,' Seth reassured her.

'Well,' Kossy said, hanging her coat on the back of the wooden chair. 'I might have acted all cool and nonchalant on the phone when you fixed up this date, but don't think your father and I didn't discuss the reasoning behind it before I left for work.'

Seth's conviction was leaving him. He didn't want to worry his parents. He never wanted to worry them, but he had been working up to this for a few months now and he'd made himself a promise: on 1 December, before things got too sentimental and snowy and sugar-coated, he needed to ask the question.

'Your dad wants to know if you're gay.'

Seth knocked the water glass with his elbow and it was enough to make a few droplets splash onto the dark wood table.

'I told him a mother would know that already. I'm right, right?' Kossy continued.

He mopped up the water with his napkin. 'I'm not gay, Mom.'

She seemed to study him again, as if checking he wasn't kidding around. 'I can't help feeling a little disappointed. When your dad said it, I had visions of us getting front row seats for *Hello, Dolly!*'

'I don't have to be gay to do that with you,' Seth told her.

Kossy grinned then, nudged his arm and laughed out loud. 'I know, I'm playing with you, Seth.' She reached out and pinched his cheek. 'Can we order? I've spent the whole morning watching my guests creating penises out of clay.' She rolled her eyes. 'They were meant to be making pots.'

His mom was one of life's great people. She worked at a shelter, making sure at least some of the city's homeless population got food, drink and somewhere safe to sleep. She also campaigned heavily to the city administrators for more funding for other centres just like hers and tried to not give the needy just the bare necessities, but also to attempt to enrich their lives too. Her latest project was getting the homeless – she called them her guests – to make things, explore the arts a little. It was all about empowerment and building self-worth. The idea didn't work with every case but most, after a little Kossy-coaching, enjoyed having their day made productive with the promise of a clean bed to sleep in. And his mom being a wonderful, hard-working, caring, beautiful person made what he was about to ask her feel so much worse.

Kossy had already beckoned a waiter and ordered the ravioli with wild mushrooms and ricotta she loved so much. Seth had something different every time they came, preferring to work his way through the dishes, making a new discovery to try again one day, or never eat again – although he had never found anything he had truly detested.

'The North Atlantic salmon for me.' He passed the menu back to the waiter. 'And shall we have a bottle of wine?'

'Wine with lunch and I'll be eating those clay pots *after* they've been fired,' Kossy replied. 'I'll have a club soda.'

'Can I get a glass of the Malbec, please.' He needed a touch of alcohol to smooth things along.

'So,' Kossy said, leaning over the table a little and clasping her hands together, thumbs making a steeple. 'Do you have another role yet?'

'Not quite yet,' Seth admitted.

'Not *quite* yet,' Kossy repeated. 'Is that Actor Code? Does it mean you have an amber light on something and are waiting for the green of go? Come on, Seth, talk to Momma. Do you need money? Is that what this is about?'

'No.' Although the real answer was probably almost yes if this role drought carried on. He shook his head. 'We ... hadn't had lunch in a while. I thought ... it would be nice.'

'Yeah, not buying that,' Kossy replied. 'Either you're in trouble or someone you know is in trouble. Whatever it is, Seth, you can tell me. You can tell me anything and everything. Haven't we always had an open door at home? Didn't we both sit and listen and try not to laugh when your father admitted he wanted to make a replica racing car out of spaghetti?'

Seth couldn't help but smile. He knew he could tell his mom anything – she would be honest and upfront with him – but this was different and he still felt uncomfortable. He had never raised the issue in sixteen years despite being given every opportunity to do so. It had been he who had insisted he didn't want to know. He didn't really understand why he needed the information now, apart from a nagging feeling he'd had since an audition he'd done a month ago.

'We should wait for the ravioli,' Seth answered softly. Or at least the red wine, so he could have that first lick of velvety alcohol on his tongue.

'I told you. Now I've ordered ravioli it can't be bad news or it's gonna screw up my dining here for all eternity.'

'I wouldn't do that to you,' Seth said.

'Have you got a role in a biopic? You know how much I hate biopics ... except the one about Winston Churchill.' She gasped, hands to her mouth. 'Has someone offered you something ahead of Gary Oldman?!'

'No.' He shook his head. If only ...

'Seth, come on, tell me, baby, I'm getting all strung out here.'

He cleared his throat. He had to stop doing that. It smacked of a lack of confidence and that was bad form for an actor. 'Mom ...'

'Stop pausing and start talking, Seth. You're doing that thing you did when you played the patient with anxiety. I bit through all my fingernails and almost started on your father's.'

'I want you to tell me where I came from.'

He watched his mom drop her hands down from the table and her pallor curdle. This was what he had been afraid of. It had been too long – his whole life – he had left it so late she had thought he was never going to ask at all.

'Mom, have some water.' He filled up her glass.

'I'm fine,' Kossy said, not sounding fine. 'I'm good.'

'Mom, listen, I know, years ago, I said I didn't wanna know but—'

'Seth,' she said, reaching for the water glass. 'We're good here. *I'm* good here. Honestly. Wow. I wasn't really expecting you to say that. I went through all the scenarios because I was worried but ...'

Part of him wanted to take back what he'd said, but the other half of him was standing firm. He had, after all, been thinking about this for a reasonable amount of time. 'I know I've sprung it on you but … I went for this part, this really great part I haven't heard back from, and the character was this guy called Sam and he was adopted and … *I'm* adopted, and I should have felt more resonance with the character somehow and … I didn't.' He took a deep breath. 'And it started me thinking. How could I really understand Sam if I don't really understand me.'

He saw the tears forming in his mom's eyes and he quickly reached for her hand. She batted it away, instead drawing a Kleenex from her sleeve and dabbing at her eyes. 'I'm good. I shouldn't have let you feel like that for so long. It's my fault.'

'I haven't felt like that for long and it isn't your fault,' Seth insisted. 'It was my decision.'

'Something you said when you were sixteen. I should have brought it up again. Every year to make sure you were sure …'

'Mom …'

'I'll tell you everything.' Kossy looked directly at him. 'Of course, I will tell you everything.' She sighed. 'Everything I know, at least.'

Seth felt suddenly lighter, like a cloud had moved from blocking the sun.

'But, Seth, promise me one thing.' Kossy looked serious.

'Anything.'

She took his hands, squeezing them tightly in hers. 'Promise me you'll keep in mind … that it isn't where a person begins that's important, it's where they end up.'

He squeezed his mom's hands, looking straight into her warm, honest, brown eyes. 'I promise.'

Seven

Lara Weeks's barnpartment, Appleshaw

'Lara!'

'Lara! This is crazy! Aldo, will you get off my arm!'

'Lara, can I dojo Dan?'

'You do that, Aldo, and I'll take back the car magazines I gave you.'

'Lara says once you give someone something you can't ask for it back. It's a present. Lara! I'm going to use karate on Dan now.'

Lara's head felt like it had been split in two by a rather ropy woodcutter and was hanging by a few splinters while it decided whether to drop to the floor or not. She unlatched the window and a freezing cold draught of winter air whipped around her hangover. She held her breath and, eyes closed, poked her face out over the scene below, put her hands over her ears and yelled: 'Stop shouting!'

Despite muffling her scream, it still hurt and gingerly she opened her eyes to survey what was going on below her in the yard. Aldo was holding Dan in a martial arts death grip *she* had taught him after he'd got bullied at another yard when he was delivering. Dan was struggling even to squirm.

'Get off me, Aldo! Lara, this is mad! Tell him to let me go!'

'Why are you here?' She had to play this cool. She couldn't seem too excited that he had come by, early, the morning after he had said he needed a break. Slow and steady won the race ...

'I think I left my grey jacket here,' Dan called out.

He was coming to collect stuff, not to see if she was OK. Nothing could soften the blow of that. 'It's not here.' She didn't know if that was true, but right now she felt terrible. It was a good job she wasn't driving today. She pulled her head inside, untroubled as to whether Aldo kept him contained or not. She swallowed. But what if Aldo hurt him? Or *he* hurt Aldo? No, Aldo was a lot stronger than he was clever ... and she was maintaining a degree of aloofness. And it was that very sentence Susie had struggled to say after copious amounts of alcohol last night.

Taking a breath, Lara surveyed the devastation of the open-plan living area. Her scatter cushions were most definitely scattered – all over the bare-board floor. There were packets of beef jerky and Kettle chips on the coffee table, together with tumblers and ... a completely empty flagon of whisky. Had they really drunk the *entire* contents? It would definitely explain the depth of her hangover ...

And then her eyes went to her laptop. *Twitter! Celebrities!* Now she felt sick. Susie's mad idea about making Dan jealous ... Just *what* had they done? *Who* did they tweet? Cautiously, pulling down the hem of her T-shirt that stated 'Fcuk Yeah', then buttoning up her cardigan, she approached the computer. Touching a key, the screen came to life and after one-finger in-putting her password there were three tabs open. *How to make mince pies without mincemeat. Hot male musicians under thirty. Twitter.* Lara wasn't sure which open window scared her the most. She clicked on Twitter. *Four notifications.*

Her heart almost stopped. She had never had four notifications at once before. A couple of likes of her photos of lorry Tina against a great British countryside scene or a retweet of something she'd written about an episode of *Silent Witness* and ... that was it. No one really tried to converse ... only the occasional highly decorated widowed military man.

She pressed to reveal the correspondents.

@edslefttoe Saw your tweet to Ed Sheeran. Sorry about your boyf. Ed doesn't use his Twitter account at the moment but you can follow him on Instagram. Good luck!!

Oh God. Susie *had* tweeted Ed Sheeran. Maybe she should see exactly how many people her friend had told about the disaster of her relationship before she looked at the replies.

@realappstitude Having relationship problems? Download our free app and one-click your way to a new you ... and a new two.

This was getting worse.

@dailyhardon *laughs* I think you might have been looking for Tom Hardy's account ... but we can meet ... maybe you AND a friend! #allthekinks #tomhardy #hotandhard

Lara felt suddenly grubby. She took her hands from the keyboard and wiped them on her cardigan. How had her life degenerated to sex-tweets?

The sound of banging and crashing from down below the wooden staircase made her shift quickly from her position over the computer. And then the door flew open, bringing in a freezing wind that whipped up the stairs and into Lara's loft-space faster than Dan who was sprinting towards her, Aldo hot on his heels.

'You tricked me!' Aldo bleated, grabbing hold of Dan's jumper and pulling hard. 'Lara, he said he had more football cards for my album!'

'Get off my jumper! This is a Pringle!' Dan exclaimed, trying to mount the last step without having his pullover stretched like an elastic band.

'You're tricking me again!' Aldo exclaimed, tugging even harder on Dan's outerwear. 'I know what a Pringle is!' He rolled a chunk of the jumper around his arm. 'Once you pop you can't stop.'

'Aldo, it's OK,' Lara said with a sigh.

Aldo still held on fast.

'Aldo! *No* dojo!' she ordered.

Immediately, Dan was released, and Aldo stood back, folding his arms across his chest.

Dan looked aghast at Lara. 'What the hell was that? Are you turning him into some kind of guard dog now?'

'Hey!' Lara exclaimed angrily. 'Aldo's right here you know!'

'Right here,' Aldo repeated.

'We have a code now,' she continued. 'Since I taught Aldo karate.' She sniffed. 'And I said your grey jacket wasn't here.' She pulled at her T-shirt again, wishing she was wearing something better. Why wasn't she wearing the really nice woollen Christmas-tree-print top she'd bought last weekend? The laptop screen had already shown her that her usually manageable-in-any-weather-or-life-condition short hair was unusually shit this morning too. She looked at Dan in his skinny jeans and box-fresh Nikes, canary-yellow polo shirt underneath a now stretched-out-of-shape black designer jumper and her heart ached. He was showered and dressed early on a Saturday morning and he smelt of woodland and mandarin …

'I know,' Dan said, a little calmer. 'But, after yesterday …'

He did care! Susie was right. *This wasn't a break-up!* She needed to give him his space. Honour his needs.

'Tina's fine.' Lara smiled. 'Not a scratch. Dad says he's going to be talking about my pro-driving at the truck convention.'

'You were almost up on one side!' Aldo announced excitedly, dropping his arms from his chest and doing actions. 'Sliding away from the crowd until … whoosh! Back under control.'

'Does he have to be here?' Dan said.

That was a bit mean. Lara quickly smiled at Aldo. 'Aldo, could you go and see if the hens have left any eggs by the fence this morning?'

'All right,' Aldo replied, giving Dan a glare. 'If you're sure, Lara.'

'I'm sure,' Lara answered, ushering him down the stairs towards the front door. She watched him all the way, making sure he didn't catch his size 12 feet on any of the steps or get his Mr Tickle style arms stuck in the banisters. She didn't realise she was holding her breath until the moment the front door closed behind him.

'He doesn't get any better, does he?' Dan said, blowing a breath onto cupped hands. 'Is your heating on? It's freezing in here.'

'It's the second of December,' Lara stated.

'And it's freezing,' Dan said again.

Had he really forgotten? She never put her heating on until it was twelve days before Christmas. They did it together. They went out to Cactus Jacks, the Mexican restaurant in Salisbury, ate enchiladas, drank beer then came home, full of spicy food, to a beautifully snug *barnpartment*. She should remind him of this … but then again, he might take that as a slight. When someone was having a pre-thirty crisis – or whatever it was – you needed to be supportive, not pick at their faults.

'I'll put it on a bit later.' She didn't know what to do. She was standing opposite the man she had shared a life with for so long and she didn't even know how to *be*. How should she stand? How should she stand to look *comfortably alluring*? Did she need to offer him a seat on the couch they usually had sex on? It all felt so awkward, so unreal. One hands-free phone conversation had changed everything. 'D'you want a drink?'

'No,' Dan replied. 'Thanks, but … I'm going out. I wanted to see if my jacket was here and … to see how you were.'

She was itching to ask where he was going. With who. For how long. But that would make her sound like Control Freak Girlfriend and that was the total opposite to Self-Confident Girlfriend, which was her current aim. Why did she remember the relationship website Susie had read aloud better than her best friend tweeting celebrities? Why did her brain choose to recollect only *some* of the memories after too much alcohol? Surely it should be all or nothing.

'I'm fine.' Lara nodded firmly. Apparently, a self-assured nod could speak a thousand words. 'Just a bit tired after the Christmas party. It was a really good night. You should have come – that isn't a criticism, by the way – just that the disco played Clean Bandit and Sia rather than the usual Steps and Kylie.'

'I bet they played plenty of Michael Bublé though?' There was a slight smile on his lips.

'Oh yes. Obviously.' Lara rolled her eyes.

'So, what I heard at the Co-op wasn't true then,' Dan said, slipping his hands into the pockets of his jeans.

'What wasn't true?' Did the village somehow know what she and Susie were googling late last night? She knew the grapevine was impeccable, but she didn't believe Mrs Fitch had the ability to be able to use a webcam as a spying tool. And even Lara had trouble pressing the right buttons for a screenshot ...

'You left early,' Dan stated. 'Because you had some sort of panic attack.'

'Ha! What?! Is that what they're saying?' She blew out a breath, cardigan-wrapped arms coming up and down like she was a frightened Christmas turkey. She had had a moment, that was all, one wobbly moment while she was in crisis. 'We all got a lot drunk on Flora's whisky.' Lara darted for the coffee table and lifted up the empty flagon as evidence just as her mobile phone pinged to indicate an incoming message. 'And you know what they're like at the Co-op. Even Lance gets high on After Eights at this time of year.'

'So, it's not true?' Dan asked. 'Any of it?'

'Me and Susie left at gone one, she came back here, we listened to *Rock Bands Do Christmas* on Scuzz, we drank, we ate crisps and Aldo walked her home.' Why had she given him an entire rundown of what she did. *Being quietly and confidently aloof gives you power.*

'OK,' Dan replied, blowing out a breath.

'OK,' Lara answered, trying desperately to ignore her hammering heart. *He was here because he was worried. He was here because he felt guilty* … She swallowed, her eyes scanning the room. 'I really don't think your grey jacket is here.'

'OK,' Dan said softly. Then, like a different person had inhabited his skin, 'OK. Right. Good. So, I'd better go.' In two long strides he was at the top of her staircase. He was going. As quickly as he had arrived.

'So, will I … see you before … you know … Scotland.' She couldn't bring herself to say anything about 'the break'. And while she was saying 'Scotland' out loud, she was thinking 'Chloe'.

'I'm not going to Scotland until a week before Christmas.' He continued down the stairs.

'I know, I mean … I guessed because of work and holiday and …' She sounded so pathetic. Susie would implode if she could hear her now. 'So … will I see you … before then?'

Dan finally stopped at the step two up from the slightly straw-covered floor and turned to face her. 'I haven't changed my mind about the break, Lara.'

Of course he hadn't. It had only been one night. No one made a decision, delivered it and then took it back the next second. Not when it was something as monumental as this.

'Listen, I know this is hard. It's hard for me too. But I think it's for the best.' He smiled at her. 'OK?'

OK? Was that a real question at this moment? It felt like he was trying to settle down an elderly temperamental aunt. But she had to remain in self-belief mode, totally optimistic about the outcome of this scenario.

She managed a half-smile. 'See you at the pub, maybe.'

'Sure,' Dan answered. 'See you at the pub.'

He pulled at the door, letting in another harsh draught and then his Pringle jumper, his nice legs and the rest of him was gone.

With no whisky left in the house Lara wanted to crawl back into bed and recommence dying from her hangover, but the pinging of her phone started up again, indicating that more than one message had arrived. She headed back to the coffee table and plucked her phone up. The messages were all from Susie.

Is your headache as bad as mine?
Are you sitting down?
?
Reply!
??
Pack your bags!
We're going to New York!!!!!!
And ... check your Twitter!!!!!!
You've got a reply from Seth Hunt!!!!!!!

Eight

Cuts and Curls Salon, Appleshaw High Street

Lara had phoned Susie after the text messages, asking what exactly she meant. She'd had to hold her phone away from her ear as the high-pitched squealing like her best friend had won a game show had not helped her hangover. A mention of flights was all she could glean from the squawking over a hairdryer. It had been necessary to dress, swallow as many paracetamol as was allowed and walk to the high street to get more, hopefully less screechy, information.

Appleshaw High Street was Christmas ready after the Advent opening and there were strings of glittering lights adorning every shop front. Even the butcher's had their glowing, slightly bloodied knuckles of ham lights swinging from their awning. The towering tree – donated by Appleshaw Landscaping – was decked in the usual multitude of colours, nothing matching, some of the tinsel looking like it came from biblical times. Beneath the lower boughs sat costumed members of the Scouts and Brownies creating a twelve-hour Jesus-in-the-manger-tableau that alternated around wee breaks and egg sandwiches. She had been Mary once, until Russell, who was playing the back end of the donkey, tried looking up her dress. After that she had always been a shepherd and insisted on wearing dungarees.

She stepped out of the cold and into the warmth and lacquered ambience of Cuts and Curls. Susie was busy setting Ruby from the Appleshaw Inn's curlers. Two teenaged twins – the new Saturday girls – were in the middle of the window display fighting with a Christmas fir that was far too big and threatening to knock over the stand of expensive products Lara knew Susie had ordered in from America.

'We're going to New York, Ruby,' Susie gushed, expertly rolling as she edged around the chair her client was sitting in.

'Oh, I've heard it's very busy there,' Ruby replied.

Susie laughed. 'Everywhere's busier than Appleshaw.'

'Are you going in the spring?' Ruby asked.

'No,' Susie said. 'Next week … or the week after. It depends on flights.'

'Goodness!'

Ruby turned her head and looked at Susie as if there was no way in the world such a thing could happen so quickly. The barmaid did have a point …

There was a scream and one of the twins fell to the floor, the spruce landing on top of her. Lara dashed to help, pushing the tree back up and holding on to it while the second twin did something creative with wool to try and secure it to the venetian blinds. Twin-on-the-floor got up and dusted pine needles from her clothes.

'I know you're at work and everything,' Lara called, still taking the full weight of the tree. 'But we need to talk.'

'About what to take to NYC?' Susie asked, bubbling with so much enthusiasm it was evaporating off her and into the peroxide-tinged air of the salon. 'It's cold there at the moment. Really cold. Minus-figures-in-the-daytime cold. Too-cold-to-snow cold. Woolly-hats-and-gloves cold. Bagels-and-cream-cheese cold. Ice-cold-beer cold …'

'Hot-chocolate cold,' Ruby added with a beam.

'I can't go to New York,' Lara blurted out. This was crazy.

'What?!' Susie exclaimed. 'Why not?'

'Because I've got no money until I get my Christmas bonus – if Dad gives everyone a Christmas bonus this year ...'

'I told you on the phone, David can organise the flights. He *wants* to organise the flights. He told me he gets tips that can pay for flights. Tips! And he misses me. We talked for hours last night when I got in.' Susie looked at Ruby. 'Not that I'm too tired to function or anything.' She drew in a breath. 'So, you need some dollars, or a couple of credit cards, to spend up on Fifth Avenue ...'

'And money for somewhere to stay,' Lara added. 'You said David shares an apartment smaller than Harry Potter's cupboard under the stairs.'

'He does,' Susie said, more to Ruby than Lara. 'I've seen photos. He has to tuck his legs up a certain way to even get into bed.'

'So, we can't stay there,' Lara concluded, still holding on to the tree while one of the twins performed a cat's cradle with the wool. 'So, we need money for somewhere to stay.' She had no idea why she was even talking this through. She had work. The haulage company was busy at this time of year. Dan might change his mind about 'the break' before he went to Scotland and she needed to be around if he did ...

'David's going to find an Airbnb for us. There's loads near him and they're not that expensive.'

'Define "that",' Lara said, folding her arms across her chest. The tree listed sideways but held. Both twins clapped their hands and delved into a box of decorations.

'Let me finish Ruby's rollers, set her under the dryer and we'll have a coffee,' Susie said, still buzzing. 'I can't believe I'm finally getting to go to New York. I mean, I've been to America before, but that was Atlanta and I didn't really see much outside of the conference centre … apart from a really good bar called the Ping Pong Emporium.'

Lara headed for the back of the salon and the kitchen.

'Give me one good reason why you can't go to New York.'

'I have a job.'

They were sitting on the cream pleather sofa that was squeezed into the corner of the small kitchen area at the back of the salon. It was well worn and the confidant of many hairdresser secrets. It was the place Susie's client from the manor house, Fion Charles, had broken down and admitted she was pregnant with triplets and wasn't sure how she felt about it, even after so many failed tries at IVF. And it had been a bed to Diego, a barber from Mexico, who had been hired last summer when the village started wanting their beards trimmed – even Mrs Hopkiss.

'Give me two reasons.'

'Aldo.'

'Come on, Lara, Aldo isn't your responsibility.'

Except he was. A bit. When her dad had offered to take him in, Lara had pledged her support. Orphaned after a fire claimed his parents and then cancer had claimed his Aunt Peggy, Aldo had been just ten when he'd been left with no one. Lara remembered how it felt to be left. Except *she* hadn't been alone. She'd always had her dad. She also knew Aldo wasn't the sharpest tool in the box. His learning difficulties meant he needed extra support, love and a firm family unit to lean on. The Weekses had given him all of that and more.

'He's my brother,' Lara said. 'I can't leave him.'

'You won't be leaving him,' Susie said. 'Your dad will be here.'

'I know, but—'

'When was the last holiday you had.'

Camping with Dan. Snuggling up together in a tent. She wanted to cry.

'You need a break,' Susie told her.

She wanted to cry even more now the 'b' word had been mentioned.

'I can't,' Lara said.

'This is to do with Dan, isn't it?'

She couldn't eke out a reply. She knew her expression was saying everything.

'Has he been round to see you?'

'No,' Lara said hastily.

'He bloody has, hasn't he?' Susie blew the steam off the coffee cup she was cradling. 'Let me guess: he heard everyone at the Co-op talking about you having that little moment at the party last night.'

'What?!' Lara exclaimed. 'Did you hear that too?'

'You know what the village is like.'

'I know, but I thought the fact I saved the soup stand with my superior driving might have been more interesting than me ... needing to take a few deep breaths.' She took a swig of her coffee and it burnt her mouth.

'We talked about this last night,' Susie reminded her. 'We had a plan. And you got a tweet back from Seth Hunt!'

'And a direct message,' Lara stated with a sigh.

'What?!' Susie exclaimed. 'What d'you mean a direct message?!'

The tweet had said:

@laraweekend Keep smiling. Happy is a place under your control. Your boyfriend does not know how lucky he is!

It was nice. It had made her shiver a little bit when she read it because she remembered Dr Mike saying the 'happy' line to student doctor Iris before they eventually got together in season four. But it was a line. And anyway, it had probably been delivered by his social-media manager. Still, it had made her feel a little better for five minutes after Dan had left.

But then she noticed he had also followed her back and she had a direct message notification ... and that was from Seth Hunt too ... or his social-media manager. She had to keep this real.

'Show me!' Susie stuck her hand out for Lara's phone.

She got her device out of her jeans pocket and gave it over. Within a second Susie was on Twitter and read aloud:

'"Hey, Lara ..." Oh that's so sweet!' Susie cleared her throat. '"I just wanted you to know that I've totally been there with the whole break thing and it sucks. I feel for you." Oh, I love him! I love him! "But you have to be stronger than him and you can be, even if you don't feel it right now." Oh my God, Lara, he sounds like the most perfect, perfect—'

'Actor?' Lara offered. 'A perfect actor.' He was good. That's why she had watched *Manhattan Med* so much. She had believed in Dr Mike wholeheartedly.

'"Honestly, if you think I can help then I would like to." Oh, sweet baby Jesus! Is this real?'

'Probably not,' Lara answered.

'"I see you're based in the UK so I kinda don't know how much help I can be, but if you're ever in NYC send me a DM and I'll do what I can. Seth." Lara! Lara! Are you hearing this?!'

'Yes,' Lara answered. And she had read it earlier. Twice.

'This is it! This is your big chance! It's really happening! This is definitely him and not any managerial team!' Susie leapt out of her chair, spilling coffee on the well-weathered sofa. 'We're going to New York and you're going to make Dan jealous by posting loads of photos of you and Seth Hunt on social media.'

Lara clicked her fingers in front of her friend's face. 'And the hypnotist says, "come back into the room on my count … one, two, three … awake".'

'Listen,' Susie said, a calmer voice overriding the hysteria. 'I know you love Dan. I'm not suggesting you come to New York and sleep with Seth Hunt – although, if I wasn't loved up with David and dying to get my hands all over his hot Latino body because it's been *months*, then I definitely would do that – I'm just saying …'

'What?' Lara asked. 'What are you saying?'

'You *do* need a break. A break from your job. From Aldo. From Appleshaw.' Susie put her coffee down on the edge of the kitchen worktop. 'Lara, I know how much you want to travel, and I know you think doing it via Google is enough for you but … it's really not.' She reached out and took hold of Lara's hands. 'This is a big opportunity to get out of Appleshaw and to see the Big Apple. New York City! Nearly at Christmas! The whole place will be alive with Santas and lights and ice skating and … clothes stores!'

Lara smiled at Susie's last remark. Her friend did love retail therapy. She missed the designer shops and independent boutiques of London. And Susie was right: she did want to see all the places she looked up online … one day … but she thought she would visit them with Dan. She swallowed. Lara went to reply.

'Wait,' Susie said. 'Don't say anything yet. Let me talk to David again, make sure his tips really can cover both our flights, see how much an Airbnb place would be and, while

I'm doing that, you can be thinking about it.' She squeezed Lara's hands. '*Really* thinking about it.'

'For you,' Lara said.

'No, Lara,' Susie replied. 'For *you*.'

Nine

Blind Tiger, Bleecker Street, NYC

Seth put down his glass of Pilsner and exhaled. All around him were people winding down after work, either before going home to their significant other or they were already with that significant other, getting ready for a big night in the city. From his wooden bar stool, the roaring fire in the grey stone hearth warming his back, he could see the dark sky, bright Christmas lights on the buildings across the street, traffic backing up, yellow taxis at a crawl, the noise muted by the warm air, music and chatter in the bar room.

His mother was a prostitute. He closed his eyes and repeated it again, a whisper on his lips, trying to make it more real. *His mother was a prostitute.* And he, apparently, was some sort of intolerant prude who had crazily thought that his birth mother might have been a hard-working Catholic shop girl who loved her boyfriend, had got caught out and had a father with strong values. Instead she had been a hooker, working the street near his mother's shelter. He had wanted the truth and he had got it. So, what now?

'Jeez, man.' Trent had returned from his trip to the bathroom. 'You've drunk that beer already?'

Seth looked at his glass, nothing but a layer of froth on the inside. He hadn't even tasted it. 'I'll get us two more.'

'Just a half for me, bud,' Trent answered. 'I've gotta sell peanuts tomorrow, remember?'

'You went to the audition,' Seth said.

'And I got the job,' Trent replied. 'Just like you said.'

'That's terrific.'

'How about you? Did you call your agent?'

'Almost.'

'Seth, that's not an answer. What are you holding off for?'

'I've got a little on my mind.'

'A little or a lot?'

He wasn't ready to share. He didn't know why. He just wasn't. But Trent would need some kind of answer. He was like a New York rat with leftover meatballs and spaghetti.

'I'm thinking of getting another agent, maybe,' Seth blurted out. He wasn't. Although he did need to have a conversation with Andrew about the call-backs, or rather the lack of them. When his mind wasn't on the fact his birth mother was a call girl.

'I think that's a great idea, bud,' Trent said, nodding as he sipped at his beer. 'It's December, it's the perfect time for new beginnings.' He slapped a hand to Seth's shoulder. 'Most people are waiting for the ding-dong of midnight and January, but it's right to strike now. And I have a proposal for you.' He unbuttoned the collar of his aqua long-sleeved cotton twill shirt, the fire doing its job in the room.

'Don't tell me,' Seth started. 'They need someone else to sell nuts on camera.'

'Listen, I'm too good for nuts, but things are kinda sparse right now. *You, you* are definitely too good for nuts and I'm gonna make sure you never have to work another commercial again.'

'I've never had a problem working commercials, I just ... I mean ... things aren't ...' He had been preoccupied with needing to find out who had conceived him. 'Can we get two more Pilsners, please?' he asked the barman.

'Let me take over your management,' Trent said firmly.

'Trent, you don't have to do that.'

'I want to do it. And, being completely upfront with you … I think I can do a fucking great job,' he stated with all of his usual bravado and then some.

Seth couldn't help but smile at his friend's confidence.

'Listen, bud, hear me out. I know that on paper I don't have Andrew's experience. But I've been at this game for years, just like you. I've got contacts. I know people who've got contacts. And there's absolutely no catch here. I will give my services for free for the entire month of December and, if I don't land you a decent role in that time, you can go find someone else.'

'Trent, you're a great actor,' Seth said.

'No,' he replied, a sigh coming out with the word. 'I'm an average actor. You're the great actor— uh, uh, uh, before you interrupt me. I'm cool with that. I know I'm not gonna be biting at the heels of Leo DiCaprio any time soon. I gotta take what I can get if I wanna stay in this industry.'

'Trent, I—'

'Give me this chance, bro. Let me work some magic over your career. Sprinkle a little Davenport dander over your lack-lustre résumé.'

Seth had seen most of Trent's dander around their shower tray. The barman set down their drinks in front of them. What did he have to lose by giving Trent a month's trial? Andrew seemed to be focused on other clients. Perhaps it was time for a shake-up.

'I'll get Andrew to waive his notice period too.' Trent picked up his beer glass.

'I signed a contract,' Seth reminded.

Trent waved a hand in the air like it was of absolutely no significance. 'I know his barber.'

'And that helps because?'

'Don't *you* tell your barber everything? Confess all the little indiscretions you've had in elevators of hotels with actresses who should know better? *Married* actresses?'

Seth didn't tend to tell anyone anything. And he wasn't really the indiscreet type ... at least the him he had known all these years wasn't. Who knew what the son of a prostitute could be capable of ...

'OK,' Seth announced before taking a sip of his beer, a little froth coating his top lip.

'OK?' Trent said, eyes lighting up like the Christmas tree at the Rockefeller Center. 'I'm gonna be your agent?'

'For a month,' Seth said. 'We'll see how it goes.'

'Woo hoo!' Trent hollered, air-punching his fist upwards. 'You won't regret it, man, I promise.'

He slapped Seth's back hard, nearly making him fall off his stool as his mouth again hit the foam of the beer.

'Right, well, now I'm officially heading up Team Hunt we need to get you back in the game real quick, so I am completely taking over your social-media management. Have you checked it at all today?'

He hadn't even looked at his phone apart from to answer Trent's call about meeting here for drinks. 'No, but I can take a quick look now,' Seth said. 'Post a photo of our drinks on Instagram? People still like beer and food photos, right?'

'They do,' Trent agreed. 'But leave all that to me. I have your logins. I'm already working an angle on Twitter that should get great press attention if it comes off.'

'You have my logins?' Seth queried. 'You've been my acting agent for sixty seconds.'

'And already I'm more prepared than Andrew, right?'

'I'd say.'

'So, two things. Next week you're doing a photo shoot as one of the new celebrity faces for Stand for Wildlife, supporting the fundraising at Central Park Zoo.'

'What?'

'You like animals, Seth, you did that short artsy film where you spent the entire nine minutes in a closet with a monitor lizard.'

'It was sedated!'

'Lemurs,' Trent blurted out. 'I've got you lemurs. They're gonna set up a Christmas scene, you're all gonna be wearing cute little Santa hats, you and the other celebs, not the lemurs, and Katherine Langford might be coming. You know, she played Hannah Baker in *13 Reasons Why*.'

'Might be?'

'It's either gonna be her or the chick who plays Judy Robinson in the reboot of *Lost in Space*.' Trent nodded as if completely satisfied. 'I know, right. Win-win.'

'Trent ...'

'Second thing. Lose the glasses.' Trent plucked them from Seth's face and put them in the pocket of his pants.

'Hey! Give them back! You know I can't see now, right?'

'What's with the glasses anyhow?'

'I've been giving my eyes a break, and I haven't had a minute to pick up my contacts from the optometrist.'

'Make time,' Trent ordered. 'Before the lemurs.' He picked up his beer glass. 'Now, where shall we go eat tonight? I'm thinking how about where the rich and famous go. Tarantino's Korean joint?'

'I guess we *have* already paid the rent this month,' Seth said.

'We've paid the rent this month.' He slapped a hand to Seth's shoulder again. 'And the city's alive with Christmas spirit. Let's get out in it. Did you find a pot for the Christmas tree?'

'My mom is gonna find something.'

From inside the pocket of his pants Seth's phone began to vibrate. Trent immediately held his hand out.

'I don't get to answer my calls now?'

'Is it business?' Trent inquired.

He checked the display. It was Andrew.

'Andrew,' Seth informed his friend.

Trent plucked the phone from Seth's hand. 'Seth Hunt's phone, Trent Davenport here ... Andrew! Wow, it's good to hear from you, man. Tell me, how long has it been? Because I'd say weeks ...'

Seth watched Trent prowl towards the door of the bar, looking for a quieter space to take the call. Maybe more of what Trent had planned was just what he needed.

Ten

A week later ... East Village, NYC

Lara stepped out of the yellow taxi and looked up into the first light of a morning sky. The ground underneath her Dr Martens was crunchy and crisp, a mix of light snowfall combining with frost. The air was freezing, and her bomber jacket was in her case, but right now she didn't care. She sniffed hard, breathing in New York City – the *real* New York City – not the stale scent of the airport terminal where immigration had kept them for what felt like hours, scanning their hands and eyeballs. She could smell the river, a slight dampness, steam and griddled meat ... At that last thought her stomach turned, reminding her she hadn't eaten since the meal on the flight ... and a tube of Pringles Aldo had insisted she take in her rucksack.

Aldo had looked so forlorn when she'd told him she was going to New York. He'd asked her if she was going to be back for that Sunday's dinner, like she was just driving ten miles into Salisbury. Her dad's reaction had been slightly different. Gerry had come up with a list of twenty things not to do in New York, including not standing in the middle of the sidewalk, not dressing like a tourist and not taking a taxi. That was one black mark already. But, after his initial worry had passed, he had thrust her Christmas bonus at her – in dollars – and demanded she take lots of photos. Then, right at the last moment, just before Susie's dad arrived to take them to Heathrow, Lara had almost bailed. Travel was something she craved and feared in equal measure. She'd had her passport since she was supposed to drive Tina to France with a delivery, but when the day arrived she'd feigned sickness. Travelling via Google had given her expectations. She didn't want to be disappointed. Also, there was the flipside. What if her research expectations *were* met. Appleshaw had been everything for so long. What if she got into the wider world and didn't want to come back? Like her mum …

'Oh, Lara! Look at this place!' Susie exclaimed, climbing out of the cab and expertly putting a chic fur hat on her head. 'It's like an advert for the most Christmassy Christmas ever!'

Lara swallowed. Susie was right. The decorations here put Appleshaw's to shame. There were glowing, coloured lights hanging from restaurant canopies – Italian and Japanese she could see across the street – decorated fir trees outside hotels and bars and ambient lighting coming from windows of three- and four-storey townhouses, the city seeming to come awake. It was just like in the movies. And Lara was in the very thick of it. She should be feeling thrilled, but instead she felt like little balls of apprehension were blocking every receptor.

Susie put an arm around her friend and pulled her close. 'I know what you're thinking.'

'What time they roll the food trucks out around here?' Lara responded with half a smile.

'Has he done it yet?' Susie asked, her voice a little flat.

Lara immediately knew what she was referring to. When she had told Dan she was going to New York, he had told her that if she thought the crowds at the Appleshaw summer fete were something else, then NYC was going to be over-whelming for her. And before she could reply, say that they had found a cute little (cheap) apartment to rent in East Village, that David was going to show them around a little when he wasn't working, that apparently one of the best places to buy jeans was the Brooklyn Denim Company, Dan had said he was going to change his relationship status on Facebook. She had been floored. Still was.

'I haven't checked,' Lara answered.

'Do you want me to?'

'No.' Lara shook her head. 'I'll do it later.'

Susie nudged her with her elbow. 'While we're posting photos of you and Seth Hunt at the zoo.'

Lara still wasn't quite sure how she had gone from ordinary, hard-working village girl to being in the Big Apple, on the verge of being dumped by Dan, having been invited to Central Park Zoo that afternoon to meet someone she had watched season after season on her TV in her barnpartment. And she still had no idea why Seth Hunt was communicating with her. Over the past week he had chatted to her about Christmas and parties and told her he was a Gemini ... and then, when she said she was coming to New York, he had invited her to the zoo. And she was equally unsure what photos of her with a hot actor were really going to do to help her relationship with Dan ... *if* she still had a relationship with Dan. Just what was he going to change his relationship status to? Single? It's complicated? Nothing at all? She wasn't sure which one of those was worse.

'Hey, I'm still right here and your luggage is on the side-walk.' It was the cab driver and Susie turned around with a squeak, apologising and dipping a hand into her bag for her purse.

Lara gazed up at the building in front of her. It was five windows high, the first row at street level, the second a little higher, those ones arched, the paint around them white. On the ledges were planters, a little snow on their edges, filled with snowmen in varying poses – one brandishing a candy cane, one smoking a pipe, one wearing a red hat – all with glowing bellies. She hoped their apartment wasn't at basement level. She hoped she got to look after the snowmen. Aldo would have liked the snowmen. Straight away, a little guilt invaded her consciousness. She had never been so far away from her family. Now she was halfway across the world.

Lara yawned. 'Maybe we should go to bed for a bit.' She could do with a sleep as she hadn't done much of it on the plane. And hopefully she could nap right through the time of this zoo thing. In the cold light of day, the whole thing seemed rather pathetic.

'You're not serious!' Susie grabbed the handle of her four-wheeled suitcase. 'We're in *New York*!' She pushed Lara's case towards her, a little snow getting caught in the wheels. 'The city that never sleeps … where we can ditch our vagabond shoes and … buy several other better pairs in Saks.'

'I know but—'

'No buts,' Susie said firmly. 'We came here to remind ourselves we are strong, independent women who can jump on a plane and grab an opportunity as it comes at us, like a well-aimed snowball.'

'You came here to sleep with David,' Lara responded.

'And to remind *him* that I am a strong, independent, *hot* woman he'd better not forget while he's over here surrounded by all the temptations of the city.'

'So, we don't need to go to the zoo today then,' Lara stated.

'Oh, Lara, why not? This is Seth Hunt! Dr Mike! Who asked *you* to come to his personal appearance for *charity*.'

All Lara could think about was how long it would be before Dan was moving into the golf club, and how many bedrooms this lodge in Scotland had. Why hadn't she asked that very question? Perhaps she could google it later.

'Well, *I* want to meet him. Maybe I'll tell him *I'm* Lara,' Susie suggested. 'Seeing as your profile photo is slightly more truck than you.'

'And how will that help you with David and explaining the "temptations of the city"?'

'Good point,' Susie said, walking towards the steps to the entrance. 'So, you need to help me out and be you.'

Be me. She drew in a breath of the freezing air and wished her long-sleeved Panic! At the Disco sweater was just a little thicker. She knew exactly who Lara Weeks was in her safe, cosy south of England village, with Dan, her dad and Aldo. She wasn't sure who she was on her own in big city New York.

'Come on,' Susie said, running up the steps, case wheels banging against each and every one. 'Let's check out our place, dump our luggage and find an authentic place for bagels!'

Bagels. Proper New York bagels, fresh from the oven, not just pictures on Pinterest. Lara's insides applauded and messaged her boots to get walking. 'We should have pumpernickel,' she called after Susie. 'I've always wanted to try pumpernickel.'

Eleven

Central Park Zoo, NYC

'Look happy,' Trent whispered to Seth while maintaining a perfectly fixed blissed-out expression on his own face.

'This *is* me looking happy,' Seth answered, waving at the crowd gathered ahead of him. They had been waiting in the freezing cold for over thirty minutes while a speech was given about the importance of the Stand for Wildlife campaign. It was a great cause. He had looked it up, despite Trent telling him he needn't bother. Central Park Zoo was doing everything it could to advance wildlife conservation and promote the study of zoology. He just wasn't too sure about holding a lemur …

'Seth, you are an A-game actor. If that's you looking happy then you need to work on your motivation.'

He smiled harder. When had smiling become a problem? When had ignoring a phone call from his mom been a thing too? Last night, Kossy had called him and the second he saw her photo on his cell-phone screen, he knew he wasn't going to answer and he didn't really know why. All she had done was tell him what he had asked and yet, now he knew, he was more confused than ever. What happened next? Did he act on the vague information he had and try to find his birth mother? Was that what he really wanted? Maybe Kossy had found something out. Perhaps that had been the reason for her call. They hadn't spoken since their lunch last week. He really should have picked up. He should call her back.

'Wait for your cue,' Trent hissed. 'Remember what we talked about. You have to get on the stage first. Grab the best position in the centre, make for the smallest, cutest lemur with the biggest eyes.'

'You sound insane.' As much as he loved animals, to Seth the lemurs looked like a cross between a racoon and a large, angry-looking squirrel.

'And stay away from the Santa Claus,' Trent continued. 'The rumour is he's *exactly* like that gnarly character he played in *Basement One*.'

'Is there anything I *can* do?' Seth queried.

'Yes,' Trent answered. 'Smile more.'

'... so, everybody, let's hear it, let's all show our appreciation for the talented, famous faces, lending their support to our Stand for Wildlife campaign this Christmas.'

'Oh my God, Lara, there he is!'

They had eaten bagels at Tompkins Square Bagels – the Grav Deluxe which consisted of gravlax (cured salmon) with sundried tomatoes, capers, onions and avocado on pumpernickel – then Susie had forged on to Fifth Avenue for a first look at those shops she craved. Kate Spade had been today's main attraction, Susie comparing bags like her decision was as important as the Brexit negotiations. Lara had never been a bag person. Everything she needed was on Tina's dashboard or in her coat. She didn't understand why anyone would want to pay hundreds of dollars for one. She'd said this out loud when Susie was weighing up whether to plump for a tote or a satchel and it had earned her a rather disgusted snort from a woman next to them. Susie had decided not to buy in the end. Apparently, there were hundreds of handbag stores in New York. The gorgeous Christmas decorations had been worth seeing though, icicle lights dripping down from the ceiling, giant red baubles made into seats …

Now here they were at Central Park Zoo and it was as if someone had lifted up a toy safari park and placed it right in the middle of this wintry metropolis. Low-rise animal enclosures and open spaces were surrounded by towering glass and concrete skyscrapers. It was a little like something Aldo might have made from Lego when he was younger. They had already photographed the famous clock and listened to one of its festive tunes – two monkeys looking cheeky by the bell – and now they were standing around the sea lion enclosure, between leafless trees and snow-covered wooden benches, surveying the people standing on a winterscape stage scene. There was someone dressed as Father Christmas, two elves dancing, a sleigh full of gifts and, making his way onto the stage, was the man she had been in correspondence with. Seth Hunt.

'He's tall,' Lara remarked. 'Taller than I thought he would be.'

'He's hotter than I thought he would be,' Susie said with a sigh.

'Even in the elf hat,' Lara agreed.

'Especially in the elf hat.'

She desperately wanted to hear him talk. As Dr Mike he had the most wonderfully velvet tones, a voice both sexy and trustworthy. But that was his role. In reality, he might squeak like Mickey Mouse. She moved herself forward a little, inching closer, until the woman in the crowd ahead of her looked round like Lara might be about to pick her pocket. Pickpockets had been on her dad's list of things to avoid in New York ... and Brownsville. Maybe she *did* need a handbag.

'Hey, everybody, it's so good to be here with you today supporting this fantastic cause, Stand for Wildlife. Please, if you can, give a little towards ensuring these animals continue to be expertly cared for here and at our other great parks.'

Velvet. Sincere. *Gorgeous*. But, of course, just a means to an end, for her to take photos with. To remind Dan that she was a strong, self-reliant woman, *his* strong, self-reliant woman, who was now grabbing life by the baubles.

'We need to get closer,' Susie said, pushing through the crowd. 'Did he say where you should meet him?'

'No,' Lara said. 'I don't know. I didn't take the invitation *that* seriously. And people say things they don't really mean all the time.' *Like Dan, when he said he loved me* ... She swallowed. 'I expect he started off being kind – or drunk like we were that night – and then he didn't know how to get out of it when we responded saying we were going to be in New York, and so he picked this very public place knowing there would be no real chance I'd get anywhere near him.' She swallowed again. 'That's what I would have done.' Although they had discussed star signs and he had made her laugh out loud ...

Suddenly Lara felt a twinge of disappointment. This was definitely down to the jet lag. Her mind wasn't in a sane place. She was surrounded by Christmas, a time she loved, a season she usually spent nesting in her barnpartment, readying it and herself for two weeks of traditional food, drink and family. Instead she was at a zoo. In New York.

'I don't believe anyone with a voice as chocolatey as that is going to deliberately mislead anyone.' Susie sniffed. 'It's an impossibility that Dr Mike could ever do such a thing.'

'But Dr Mike isn't real,' Lara reminded her, running a hand through her hair.

'Come on,' Susie urged. 'I want to meet him even if you're claiming not to be bothered.' She shifted left with a loud 'excuse me' as she nudged other spectators.

'Susie,' Lara called. 'Susie, wait!'

Twelve

Seth was wearing a bright green-and-gold embroidered elf hat with a bell on the end that tinkled every time he even so much as breathed. And now there were lemurs being brought into the mix, and he had to keep smiling when he didn't feel like smiling. Add in the fact he was also freezing his ass off because Trent wouldn't let him layer up in a coat and, if Seth didn't get a strong coffee very soon, there was a real danger that his new agent might be given notice before the day was out.

Hoping for some sort of sign this was all going to be over very soon, he looked over to Trent who was standing offstage. Instead he was met with more animation than an episode of *Dance Moms*. Trent had his fingers inside his mouth, pulling the skin wide, leaping up and down and doing crazy eyes. If Seth hadn't been caught in the middle of all this he would have fallen apart laughing. He interpreted the actions as meaning he obviously still wasn't looking happy enough.

'Hey there, which one would you like to hold? We have Cyrus here on the left or we have little Jax.'

Seth observed the two lemurs in the arms of one of the zoo employees. They were both staring at him like he was food. Up close they were built like miniature kangaroos, all large limbs and a furry striped tail that looked like it could go boa constrictor at any minute, wrap around his neck and suffocate him to death. At least he wouldn't die cold.

'The cute one!' came the very loud stage-whisper from Trent. 'The one with the big Amanda Seyfried eyes!'

Seth stared at the ring-tailed lemurs. Was he really looking into their pools of yellowness and deciding on cuteness? Did his profile really need raising this desperately?

'Little' meant cute, didn't it? 'I'll take this one,' Seth said, opening his hands towards the animal the woman had called Jax.

'Ok, just let me soothe him for a quick second.' The keeper began smoothing her hands over the lemur's head, buffing his ears a little until his eyes took on a look of someone who had been hypnotised. *This lemur needs to be soothed before he's handled by a non-professional.* Right now, he was so glad Trent hadn't got him the grizzly bears ...

'Does he bite?' Seth asked, as he felt his manliness depleting by the second.

'Do you?' the handler asked before being taken over by a laughing fit Seth was surprised didn't split her uniform.

He managed a nervous smile before the creature was handed to him and he frantically tried to work out the best place to put his fingers in order to grip the squirming animal securely, as well as avoiding any orifice that might emit bodily fluids – or solids.

'Be calm,' the keeper instructed. 'No sudden movements or sounds.' She grinned. 'He might be little, but we didn't name him after the lead in *Sons of Anarchy* for nothing.'

Seth held still, forcing a rather inane expression, really wanting to maim Trent. Jax emitted a growl.

'I don't think he likes animals,' Lara remarked to Susie. They were only a few rows back, behind a large group of teenagers who seemed to have their phones fixed on a twenty-something onstage along from Seth Hunt, who had been introduced as a country music star. 'He doesn't look very comfortable holding the lemur.'

'Give the guy a break,' Susie said. 'Have you ever held a lemur before? Anyway, I'm not particularly interested in his animal-handling skills. Instagram-worthiness, that's all that matters.' Susie adjusted the hat on her head. 'And he has that by the bucket-load.'

'It's going to wee any minute,' Lara remarked.

'How can you tell?'

'Any minute now ...'

She watched Seth release the underneath grip he had of the lemur, as liquid began to squirt from its bottom, drenching his dark jeans. It seemed to be just enough distraction for the animal to seize its chance and it leapt from Seth's arms, down onto the floor, scooting off the platform and heading for the crowd.

'Oh God! It's escaped!' Susie exclaimed. 'This is awful! Aren't they endangered or something?' Then, more worried: 'Do they carry rabies?'

Zoo employees were trying to calm down the other animals being held by celebrities, while others tried to get down into the throng to pursue Jax. Lara tracked the animal, its tail making him easy to spot as onlookers either shied away from him, or tried to grab him. Instinctively, she knew where the animal was going to go. Living next to a farm had its advantages. As the first few bars of Frank Sinatra singing 'I'll Be Home for Christmas' began, Lara headed out of the crowd on a mission.

'Lara!' Susie called. 'Lara, where are you going?'

'Seth! Jeez, buddy! You dropped the freaking lemur!' Trent rushed onto the stage. His body language said 'pissed' – a bit like Seth's pants – yet his face was still calm-camera-ready.

'I did not drop the lemur,' Seth insisted, shaking his pee-covered hand. He whipped the elf hat from his head and wiped his hands with it. 'The lemur, who, incidentally, is named after a bad-assed motorcycle gang member, kicked me in the ribs and made a break for it.' He wanted to rub his eyes. Wearing the contact lenses again was making them dry and irritated but with fingers covered in lemur urine ...

'This is gonna turn into the worse profile-raising stunt ever ... unless we can get it on one of those blooper shows, or ... you go and rescue it.'

'Rescue it? Trent, I couldn't even hold it.' He looked to where the crowd were training their smartphones. They were all now *not* looking at the country music star but instead focused on the trees at the side of the park. He swallowed. 'There are professionals here,' he stated. 'I'm sure they'll have the situation under control in minutes.' He looked back to Trent. 'Do you think I should say that, maybe on the microphone?' He dropped the hat to the stage.

'I think you need to get over there and catch it,' Trent ordered, giving his shoulder a shove. 'Or at least look interested! You are one of the faces of Stand for Wildlife now.' He lowered his voice. 'Eke out some tears, if you can.'

Thirteen

Lara had been in New York just half a day and she was up a tree looking at the backside of an angry lemur who she was pretty sure was about to let off a fight smog. She'd looked up Madagascar once – not the movie – the real place. The garden centre cafe had ended up with a job lot of coffee from the island thanks to White Van Ron – Mrs Fitch had learned not to ask too many questions – and Lara had been intrigued. Where in the world was it? What was there? The answer had been white sand beaches and rainforests. Blue skies and humidity. A different world. She'd mentioned it to Dan and he said someone at work had been and said the all-inclusive hotels were good. Except Lara hadn't searched 'luxury' when she'd investigated. She had looked at cabins and hammocks and nets and sprays to stop bugs sucking the life out of you, bars with vine canopies and rats running up the walls ... and lemurs who fought by inflicting a stench on their predators.

Lara whistled, attracting the lemur's attention. 'Listen, it's my first day here and I really didn't think I'd be up a tree in the middle of a zoo.' Why was she talking to it? Her? Him? She didn't know – or want – to find out. 'But don't tell my friend Susie that being up here is preferable to shopping for handbags.'

And what was her plan? She knew the lemur would go up the tree, she had headed up after it, but what came next? Apart from everyone filming her and possibly uploading her eventual demise to YouTube. She was cold, the wind numbing her bare fingers as she gripped onto the trunk with one hand, the other reaching up for a branch nearer to the lemur. Three branches down there had been tinsel and fairy lights, now all there was were boughs devoid of foliage to shelter her from the elements. She needed to do something. The animal obviously only understood French or Malagasy. She didn't know either.

'Ma'am, step away from the animal! We have specialist equipment coming to ensure the lemur remains unharmed.'

With the PA announcement ringing in her ears, Lara turned her head to the crowd. This was great. This was the thanks she got for going up here after the creature. Well, now she was up here she was going to make sure she got him/her/it down. She reached out for the bough above her head.

'Hey,' a velvet-coated tone said.

Lara missed the branch and clawed for the trunk, hugging it tight. Seth Hunt was only one bough below her, looking every inch Instagram-worthy and then some. She suddenly felt sick for so many reasons. The pumpernickel started to repeat.

'Hello,' she responded.

'OK,' he said. 'That totally explains what you're doing up here.'

'What does?'

'You're British.'

He did not recognise her. Maybe Susie was right. Perhaps she did have far too much of Tina in her profile photo and not enough of her actual face.

'And that means what?' Lara answered. 'I don't think you're in any position to be rude when you're the one who dropped a lemur.'

'I wasn't being rude. I just meant, out of all the people here, people who aren't British and people in uniforms, you were the only one brave enough to go up a tree.'

She couldn't help but smile. 'Not the only one,' she answered. 'You're up here now. And you don't look at all comfortable.' The wind blew harder. 'And you have no coat.'

'All completely on-point observations,' Seth answered.

'And you're covered in lemur pee.'

'That I am.'

He reached up then, pulling his rather lithe frame from the lower bough to the one opposite her. From here, if she hadn't been totally focused on not falling and recapturing the lemur, there was an amazing view of the whole of Central Park, its wide open spaces spotted with a little snow.

She should tell him who she was. The girl he had tweeted with across the ocean. The girl who wanted to use him to help make her boyfriend jealous to win him back. Well, actually, the girl whose best friend had persuaded her in a moment of drunken weakness she should use him to help make her boyfriend jealous to win him back. It sounded even more ridiculous when she was perched precariously up a tree.

'Any ideas how we get him down?' Seth asked her. 'Cos I know I'm up here and all, but I really don't know what happens next.'

And if the city's cameras hadn't been recording every second since he set foot *Santa*-stage, Seth would definitely not be up here now. He had clambered up to escape Trent more than for any other reason. Plus, the dark-haired woman with an air of a kick-ass Margot Robbie about her seemed to be a lot better at looking natural while tree-hugging than he was.

'Do you have any food?' the woman enquired.

'Here?'

'No, in your kitchen at home.'

'I don't know. Maybe a Bento box of leftover Chinese food and some cereal.' He looked straight at her. 'You meant here, didn't you?'

'Yes, I meant here!'

'No, I mean ...' Did he have any gum? He took one hand off the tree to check the pocket of his jeans. He drew out a stick of Trident. 'Gum?'

'For the lemur?' she stated, shaking her head. 'I'm not sure you've got the hang of this Stand for Wildlife thing.'

'Again, completely correct.'

'They eat fruit,' she said, reaching up for the branch above her head as if preparing to move. 'And leaves. And sometimes tree bark.'

'They seem to be taking some time to come with their specialist equipment,' Seth remarked.

'We don't need specialist equipment,' she replied.

He watched her hoist herself up another bough, the branch quavering a little under her weight. The crowd below them gasped. She stepped again, swinging herself up until she was within an arm's reach of the escapee.

'I didn't have any specialist equipment when I rescued the feral cat and her kittens from the roof of the combine shed.'

'No?' He had no idea what a combine shed was.

He watched her reach into the pocket of her short, padded coat and draw something out from its depths. He tried to focus, while scrambling up another bough. 'Is that ... a Pringle?'

'Shh!' the girl ordered.

'Listen,' Seth began in quieter tones. 'I want to save this thing, of course I do, but, if the worst comes to the worst, and it doesn't make it out alive, I'd like it to be a tragic accident rather than a poisoning.'

'Speaks the guy who was going to give it gum. I'm not going to let it eat it, just tempt it enough to grab it,' she answered.

'It's not that happy with being grabbed,' Seth called to her. 'But it does like to be soothed ... you kinda ruffle its ears.'

'I'll let you do that when I bring it down.'

Taking one last step to the highest branch Lara had anticipated thick enough to take her weight, she boosted herself up, balancing carefully, trying her best not to think of anything but the task in hand. Focus on the now. Just like when she had avoided the soup stand, even though she had been swamped with shock and hurt over Dan's admission.

She took a breath, willing fearful feelings away, then slowly, inch by inch, she held out the snack towards the lemur just as the music changed to Dean Martin's 'Let it Snow! Let It Snow! Let It Snow!'

'That's it,' Lara whispered. 'This is a real Christmas treat. Much better than tree bark and fruit. Come on, come and get it.'

She really, really wanted to get this lemur down. Despite it looking mean, she knew it was probably just as scared as the hissing feral mother of kittens had been back in the summer. She also knew although it could bite, it had nails not claws, almost certainly incapable of gouging out an eye ...

'Come on, little one, just a little bit closer ...' If anyone from the organisational committee shouted over the microphone now she would be seriously pissed off.

'I think he's gonna take the bait,' Seth whispered, somehow his voice right at her shoulder now.

'Shh,' she shushed as directly but quietly as she could. The very second the animal reached out for the Pringle she was going to take her chance ...

Gingerly, its hand crept out. Lara didn't wait a second more. She dropped the Pringle, grabbing the lemur securely, but hopefully not too hard, and swung it towards her, clasping it into her body and steadying her weight against the trunk of the tree. From the ground came excited applause she hadn't expected at all. It felt a little surreal.

'Wow,' Seth stated, sounding impressed. 'Way to go.'

'Now I have to work out how to get down again with this one in my arms,' Lara said, fighting to hold onto the lemur as it began to howl.

'Shall I call for the specialist equipment?' Seth suggested.

'Don't you dare.'

He smiled, cautiously beginning his descent of the tree. 'I'm Seth, by the way. Seth Hunt.' With one hand wrapped around a frost-covered bough he held the other hand out to her.

'I know,' Lara answered. 'You were up onstage getting owned by a lemur ... and I think that hand you're offering me is still covered in its wee.' She hugged the animal tight with one arm, then used the other to follow Seth's path through the trees.

'Are you always right about everything?' Seth wiped his hand on his jeans. 'Lemurs, my inability to perform with lemurs ...'

'I'm pretty rubbish with reading my boyfriend right now.' Lara sighed, swinging onto the next length of branch. 'But you know that already.'

'Here he is! Here he comes! With the lemur! Everybody! Seth Hunt saved the lemur! Let's hear it! Let's get a chant

going! Seth Hunt saved the lemur! Seth Hunt saved the lemur!'
It was a blond-haired guy in a tight suit.

'God! This was a mistake,' Seth groaned. 'This whole thing
was a mistake.'

'Who *is* that?' Lara queried, as the group around their tree
began to grow, every arm extending a mobile phone, every
TV-style camera pointing in their direction.

'Trent's my ... new agent,' Seth admitted. 'My *very* new
agent. He's a little excitable.'

'I think he really wants you to take the lemur.' Lara eased
the creature away from her abdomen for a moment, much to
its delight.

'Oh, no. No, no, no, you have totally got this,' Seth said
immediately.

Lara laughed. He was funny, as well as really having that
rich, chocolatey voice she'd enjoyed when listening to him
deliver sexy but professional bedside manner as Dr Mike.

'And I'm gonna make sure that everyone who doesn't already
know, realises that it was *you* who rescued this critter and not
me,' Seth concluded.

'Seth! Seth, take the lemur! Take the lemur and hug it all
the way in to you!' Trent called. 'Can you cradle it? Rock it
like a baby?'

Suddenly, Lara's foot slipped as she tried to plant her boot
on the last bough before the three-foot jump to the crisp
paving. A firm hand grabbed onto her arm and she was quickly
able to adjust her footing, the crowd gasping a little, zookeepers
appearing.

'Are you OK?' Seth asked her.

She caught her breath, the cold air beginning to burn her
lungs a little. 'Yes,' she answered, recovering. 'Can't have a tragic
accident when we're this close to safety.'

'Listen, I'll jump down first and then I'll … catch you both.'

Seth had no idea why he had said that. His catching skills were average at best, and that was with a baseball, not a woman carrying a primate. But he had done practically nothing to help this rescue.

'I can jump down,' Lara called to him. 'I jump down from my cab every day.'

'With an animal?' Seth asked, preparing for his descent.

'I had to do it with a pig once.' She coughed. 'It was my … brother's fault.'

Seth braced himself a little then jumped, hoping to land in the space the zoo employees were trying to move onlookers from at the base of the tree. He landed, knees jarring a little, then hurriedly turned around to stare up at his branch companion.

'Why didn't you grab the animal?' Trent was at his shoulder, looking red-faced and sweaty despite the minus temperatures. 'Let's get it down in your arms for a photo. We need to limit the damage the escape might have caused.'

'Trent, there's a woman still up a tree right here.'

'Yeah, buddy, I know that,' Trent answered. 'And right now, her Jungle Jane routine is costing you feel-good column inches in the first article that gets published about this gig.'

Seth turned away from him and held his arms out towards the first upper boughs of the tree. 'Listen, I promise you, I've totally got this.' He clapped his hands together, blew into them and then offered them back up. 'You jump and I'll catch you both.'

'Hey, I said *the animal*, not both of them,' Trent said. 'You drop a girl *and* an endangered species then you can kiss goodbye to any positive press.'

'I don't need any help,' the woman shouted from above him. 'Just for you to move out of the way.'

'Let's get a ladder over here,' one of the keepers suggested. 'I'll go up and get Jax and—'

Then, suddenly, the woman above him started falling through the air.

Fourteen

Lara landed perfectly next to Seth, like it was a dismount she'd done many times before. The lemur had wrapped its black and white ringed tail around her neck and the keepers swooped in, desperate to get the beast into a secure box.

'Is he OK? Is he injured? Did you feed him something?'

'I don't think so ... and no.'

The lemur was wrenched from her and she was suddenly left wide-eyed and bewildered, cameras trained on her.

'I think we should give her a little space, don't you? She's been through quite an ordeal,' Seth began, stepping closer as a wailing Jax was put into a carrier.

'God, Lara, are you all right?' Susie came rushing in.

She *was* all right. She was. It was just that somewhere between jumping out of the tree, hitting the slightly ice-smeared ground and feeling the weight of the crowd all around her, everything had all swelled up like a rising snowdrift. She took a breath, focusing on her friend. 'I'm fine.'

'What's your name, ma'am? What made you decide you needed to rescue the lemur here today? Have you done anything like this before?'

A woman in a dark, woollen coat had stuck a microphone under Lara's nose and the crush of people were starting to ease forward, inch by inch, enclosing the area around her.

'I think we need to back up a little here, everyone,' Seth ordered. 'Trent, can you make a little room?'

'Nice touch,' Trent replied, smiling. 'Chivalrous.' He put his hands into the air. 'Back up, ladies and gentlemen, let's let the hero of the hour head back to the stage.'

'Heroine,' Seth stated. 'The heroine of the hour.'

'I really don't want to go on any stage,' Lara said, propelled along by the crowd.

'Don't listen to Trent,' Seth replied. 'We'll just let him shout and make some space and then we'll get out of here.'

'I'm Susie,' Susie said, hands adjusting her hat as Trent seemed to start succeeding in his parting of the throng.

'Seth,' Seth replied. 'Seth Hunt.'

'We know who you are, Dr Mike,' Susie continued. 'Season after season of dipping Doritos while you cure the ills of Manhattan and solve a few mysteries too.'

'Well …' Seth began.

'Wasn't he great?' Trent said, turning his head as he moved them along past a towering Christmas tree, flanked by sparkling rotating angels blowing trumpets.

'Completely great,' Susie agreed. 'And I think it's also really completely great how you're helping Lara here.'

'Susie …' Lara began. Seth not recognising her, she had decided, was a good thing, a *great* thing. She could forget it ever happened. Christmas wasn't that far away and when Dan got back from Scotland everything would go back to normal. Why shouldn't it?

'I mean, what Dan is doing to her is downright cruel. He's wanting his Yule log and eating it, keeping her hanging on, not knowing whether he's going to swing one way or the other, changing his mind, mixing his signals, it's so unfair.'

'I'm not sure I understand,' Seth answered.

Lara sighed. Now an explanation *had* to be given. 'I'm Lara,' she said. 'Lara Weeks.'

Seth stopped walking, his expression still a little confused. 'Have we met?'

Lara shook her head. 'Not in person.' She sighed. 'Susie, this is silly.'

'No, it's not,' Susie countered. 'She's laraweekend.'

Trent span around then, the force of his turn almost making an ornamental candy cane tree topple over. 'Laraweekend!' Trent exclaimed. 'You're laraweekend?' He grabbed Seth by the shoulders, shaking him. 'Seth! This is laraweekend!'

Now Seth felt like he had a major part in a sitcom he hadn't ever seen the script for and everyone was looking at him waiting for some sort of reaction. And Trent was acting like he was a winner on *Wheel of Fortune*.

'Oh, laraweekend, Seth ... has told me so much about you,' Trent declared.

Seth went to ask for clarification, but a harsh slap to his back came down between his shoulder blades, then Trent grabbed him forcefully.

'Wow ... this is ... really so wow ... isn't it wow, Seth.' Trent's head nodded up and down like it was attached to a Slinky spring.

'It's a wow from me,' Seth managed to reply. He was looking at Lara now, desperately trying to recall her. Where had he met her? Was she an actress? Had he worked with her on a film? She had mentioned a pig when she was up the tree, hadn't she? Had he done anything with pigs ... ever?

She was petite, perhaps five five, her short brown hair cool rather than boyish and only serving to accentuate her large chestnut eyes ... and there were curves under that short jacket. If he had met her he was sure he would have remembered her. He was usually so good with faces.

'So, laraweekend, you're here in NYC and you've met my buddy Seth and you've ... wow, you've saved a freaking lemur!' Trent laughed loud and hard then reached out, grabbing the nearest journalist in the crowd. 'You! You should really take a photo of these guys right here. Standing for wildlife! Woo! Go lemurs!'

'Trent ...' Seth began.

Trent pulled him close, like he might want to start slow-dancing with him if Dean Martin kept the Christmas waltz vibe going. 'I'll explain everything later, I promise, just ... act like you're Wikipedia.'

'What?'

'Act like you know everything. Pretend you know exactly what I'm talking about. And trust me. This could turn into something special, particularly after today's events.'

'Trent ...'

'Laraweekend, you stand here and Seth, you stand next to her – a little closer, man, I don't think she's gonna bite – grr!' Trent laughed out loud and performed a hand claw in the air while the journalist set about taking photographs.

'I am so sorry about this,' Seth said to Lara.

'You must think I'm crazy.' Lara blew out a nervous breath.

'Given that we've both climbed up a tree chasing something from Madagascar, we're about equal in the crazy stakes.'

She smiled at him. Where could he possibly know her from?

'So, you should definitely come tonight. Both of you,' Trent said, parting the crowd again and moving them through the melee. 'It was Sally, right?'

'Susie,' the other girl answered, sounding a little put out.

What was tonight? Where was Trent inviting these virtual strangers? 'Tonight?' Seth queried.

'Excuse my friend who seems to have lemur brain ...' Trent put his mouth to Seth's ear. 'It's your mom's Christmas open house for the shelter. The annual winter cook-out and half the guests stealing the silverware.'

Seth gasped. He couldn't believe he had forgotten one of his mom and dad's most important dates in the calendar. Every year Kossy and Ted invited the regular shelter users, plus the fifty others who turned up on the day of the event, to a winter party at their own home. There was food of all kinds from Italian through to Creole to all-American barbecue. Unlike the Christmas fundraiser for the shelter, which was a couple of weeks closer to Christmas and about making money to keep the centre open, this was about feeding the hungry and making them feel a little bit more human, even if just for one night. And that was probably why Kossy was trying to call him. To tell him what to bring. Just how self-focused was he?

'Tonight we're meeting David for dinner, aren't we?' Lara said to her friend.

'I have no idea who David is,' Trent began. 'But David can come too. It's quite the party.'

'Trent, I—' Seth started.

'I can have dinner with David and you can go to the party,' Susie said as they finally broke out into a bit of space, near to one of the entrance gates of the zoo.

Susie was making the kind of expression that said one of two things. Either she was severely constipated, which was a possibility if her body was reacting to pumpernickel like hers was. Or she was channelling a very excited anime character with a secret to keep. And, at the very first opportunity, as had been one of Lara's New York holiday concerns, she was being palmed off. Susie and David were a duo. No one wanted to make a triangle when a couple hadn't seen each other for six months, unless you were into that sort of thing already. She shivered.

'David and I can meet you there,' Susie continued, nudging a sharp elbow into Lara's ribs. 'What time and where?'

'Crowds have ears,' Trent whispered, looking over his shoulder at the group of people now refocused on the country star onstage who seemed set to sing. 'I will …' He cleared his throat. 'I mean, Seth, will message you the address. Seven thirty. And don't dress up, and, if you can, dress *down* … like way, way down. Most of the guests don't have much, and last year someone wore Givenchy and never saw it again.'

'We'll be there,' Susie said. 'Thank you. See you tonight.'

'Come on,' Trent said to Seth. 'We need to get you back onstage before the next Tim McGraw there takes over everything.'

'See you later!' Susie said with over-the-top enthusiasm.

'It was nice to meet you both,' Seth replied. He sent a smile their way before he was pulled by his shirt towards the front of the festive display.

Susie turned to Lara, giddy, eyes unfocused like she had been drinking more of the mince-pie whisky. 'I can't believe this is happening, can you? Seth Hunt! Dr Mike! You and a lemur! The press taking photos! Never mind posting a few selfies on Insta, you're going to be all over the news!'

Was she? Lara wasn't sure that was a good thing. She felt the same way about this party tonight too. OK, so Seth Hunt was a celebrity, but she didn't *know* him. How could Susie line her up with an evening with someone she didn't know at an as-yet-undisclosed address that was who-knew-where in New

York City, a place she was finding was a lot bigger and more disorientating than Birmingham. And, now she was down from the tree, the only thing on her mind was checking Facebook to see if Dan had gone through with changing his status ... and to what?

'I'm happy to stay in the apartment while you go to dinner with David.' Lara kicked her boot at a small pile of ice as they walked towards the exit. The sky had clouded over, the temperature a little over freezing, spelling snow.

'Stay in the apartment.' Susie said the words like Lara had suddenly confessed she was going teetotal.

'Yeah,' Lara said with a nod. 'We've only been here half a day and I'm really jet-lagged and I know you want to eat with David, and then eat David himself probably, so I can cosy up in the apartment and—'

'Pine over bloody Dan?'

'I was going to say watch TV.'

'Like you do at home.'

'It's only Day One,' Lara reminded.

'Exactly!' Susie exclaimed. 'Day One of our NYC adventure and I am *not* leaving you in the apartment on your own to watch *Law & Order*.'

'Not even *Chicago PD*?'

'You've met Seth Hunt!' Susie grabbed hold of her arms and shook them. 'Seth Hunt! Your dreamy Dr Mike!'

Lara rolled her eyes. 'He isn't *my* dreamy Dr Mike.'

'No, back in 2016 he was *everyone's* dreamy Dr Mike and Most Sexiest Star on TV, according to a Facebook poll I looked up.'

'I'm not saying that he isn't attractive.' Or nice. He was very nice. And funny. And he really *had* looked like he was willing to catch her if she needed help getting down from the tree. 'But ... it doesn't feel right.'

'OK,' Susie said. 'I'm going to get completely serious with you now.'

Lara swallowed as Susie's tone took on an edge of *Marcella*.

'Dan has told you he's changing his FB status.'

Lara knew she wasn't going to like what was coming next. She looked down at her Dr Martens and the ground as it went from zoo to sidewalk and they left the attraction.

'Dan is going to Scotland with Chloe for Christmas.'

It sounded as if Susie was giving their relationship the last rites.

'Dan has told you he wants a break.'

Yes. All three of those things were correct. Ugly and hurtful but undeniably true. Lara raised her head.

'Now, personally, I would be ditching his sorry arse very publicly with every single dodgy photograph I owned of him filtering out at all the most opportune times on social media – ad break for *Coronation Street*, five minutes before News at Ten, seven a.m. to accompany everyone's first morning coffee – but I know you don't want to do that. So …' Susie heaved in a long breath. 'You *have* to take the other route. You have to *appear* happily disconnected. You have to try and *forget* what Dan is doing and concentrate on enjoying *your* life as it stands right now … your holiday here, with me … and your chance to go to a party with Seth Hunt.' Susie grinned and shook her head at the same time. 'I can't believe I said the words "go to a party with Seth Hunt".'

Susie was right. Lara knew that. All she was doing by going over everything in her mind was moping. Far better to stop moping and engage in ridiculous fantasy with an actor you used to have a crush on …

Lara pulled her phone out of her coat pocket, the screen covered in crumbs of Pringles.

'Ugh! God, what's all over your phone? That coat should come with some sort of health warning. Have you ever washed it?' Susie sniffed then, stopping and propping her behind up against a fire hydrant. 'What are you doing?'

'I'm doing what I should have done the second we landed.'

'Phoning Aldo?'

'I messaged him.'

'Phoning your dad?'

'Aldo will tell him I messaged him. Probably half a dozen times.'

'You're checking Dan's Facebook.'

Lara nodded then pressed at the onscreen icon with pure determination. Super-quickly she searched for 'Dan Reeves'. It took mere seconds for her to have her answer.

'Dan Reeves is apparently ...' She handed Susie the phone.

Single. It said *single*. The tears were right there, in her eyes and sliding up into her throat but she bit them back. She wasn't going to give him the satisfaction, especially not here in vibrant New York. Not when there were gorgeous golden, sparkling fountain-shaped lights on a high-rise she couldn't even see the top of across the street and a newspaper seller dressed as a penguin. Sirens wailed and traffic honked horns and she felt so small but so suddenly awake ...

'I should go to the party, shouldn't I?' Lara said, blinking away the hurt and looking straight at her best friend.

'Yes, you definitely should,' Susie replied.

Fifteen

Gramercy, NYC

'I tried to call,' Seth began as Kossy threw open the door of the partly ivy-covered three-storey brownstone he had once called home. 'And I left three messages.' He proffered two large paper grocery bags. 'So, I got some beers and I got sausage and potato salad and plenty of chips and guacamole ...'

Kossy, hair wild and around her shoulders, apron over a long-sleeved, pale-yellow dress, grabbed the bags, dumped them down by the doorstep, then gathered Seth up into a fierce hug before pinching his cheeks. 'I thought you weren't coming. I said to your dad, "Seth isn't coming because I haven't heard from him since the ravioli" and then we're making jambalaya and we've got the TV on and there's all these cameras at the zoo ... and there you are, with that great new country singer and you're holding a monkey!' Kossy let him go and slapped her hands to his face. 'You holding a little monkey and saying all those great things about the zoo we first took you to when you were four and you tried to feed the seals.'

'It was a lemur, Mom,' Seth answered.

She waved a hand dismissively. 'I'm betting they're more slippery. Come in! Come in! Everything's under control in here with thirty minutes before the coach arrives.' She scooped up the groceries and pounded inside.

He smiled as he stepped into the chaotic but welcoming space, every bookcase, sideboard and chair – and there were plenty of all of those – covered with memories of his mom and dad's life together. Random pebbles, plants – some clinging to life, others thriving – photographs, ornaments – some missing body parts – gadgets – some from the eighties and broken – and appliance leads no one knew the origin or purpose of. There seemed to be hundreds of strings of tinsel to add to the disorder now too, swirling around the banisters of the staircase, pinned to corkboards, wrapped around china dolls and taxidermy birds … Seth followed his mom towards the hub of the home, the kitchen-cum-diner-cum-lounge that led out onto a deck and their patch of grass in the city.

'D'you like my trees? You like my trees, right?' Kossy said, bustling into the kitchen and stretching her arms to indicate two fat spruces that were far too big for the space.

'I—' Seth began.

'Your dad says they're too big, but I told him that was insulting. Can you imagine if he says that to me one day? "Kossy, you're too big." What do I say to that? "Buy me a bigger house?" Can you see that happening, Seth? I ask you!'

'Where is Dad?' Seth asked, watching his mom get sucked back into the organised mess of kitchen operations.

'He's out back,' Kossy replied. 'Do not disturb him. He's halfway up a ladder trying to get all the Christmas lights to work. What's the party of the year without Christmas lights on the outside?'

Seth's phone pinged.

'Do you want a coffee, Seth? Or shall we go all out and open the Jose Cuervo? You know, just the one, to help us through Party Prep Central.' Kossy held up the bottle of tequila and swung it in her hands.

'I'll have a coffee, if that's good with you,' Seth answered, drawing out his phone. It was a message from Trent.

So before the party you need to know @laraweekend is someone you're helping get over her loser boyfriend. This is gonna be so great. I'm thinking we push this out for an exclusive ... maybe an interview with Ellen. Hitting the nice-guy-does-good angle, grabbing all the feels with the twenty-somethings AND their mothers. I know, I'm a genius. BTW it's a no from the last Netflix audition. IMO I think they're gonna give it to Michael Fassbender. Sorry, bud!

'Fuck,' Seth exclaimed dropping his phone to the counter and putting his hands into his hair.

'Seth! You're dropping an F-bomb in my house right in front of me!' Kossy said, putting a flour-covered hand to her chest. 'Have we regressed to the year 2000?'

'Sorry, Mom.' He picked up his phone and slipped it back into the pocket of his clean jeans. 'Sorry.'

'Is it bad news?' Kossy asked.

'I ...' He really had quite wanted the Netflix series, maybe not as much as he wanted the character of Sam in the upcoming Universal film *A Soul's Song* but all he could think about was the girl up the tree with the lemur and the fact Trent had pimped him out for the idea of something to sell to the press. And everything looked like it had come from him. Why had he let Trent control his social media? 'I didn't get a part, that's all.' His mom really didn't need to know how messed up his life had gotten recently.

'The part you told me about?' Kossy enquired. 'The guy who's adopted?'

He shook his head. 'No … I haven't heard back about that one yet.'

'And we haven't had a chance to talk any more about Candice.'

Seth's body bristled at the sound of his birth mother's name. He hated himself. What was wrong with him? He swallowed, desperately trying to regroup as he picked up an ornamental Santa Claus that was holding toothpicks to distract himself.

'I spoke to Bernadette in the kitchens and she says Candice's last name was Garcia. I am ashamed that I never even knew that.' Kossy stuck her hands into something that looked like dough. 'We're trying to check through the records but it's all a bit up in the air at the centre coming up to Christmas.'

'Garcia,' he said. 'Spanish?'

'I guess she kinda had that air about her. Although, great dark hair can be achieved even with cheap products, it doesn't have to come from the gene pool. Not that I know anything about that.'

'Do *you* think she was Spanish?' Seth enquired. Was that where he got his hair colour from? His skin wasn't particularly olive toned. Seth Garcia … unbelievably it sounded more Hollywood than Seth Hunt.

'I don't know,' Kossy answered. 'I told you. I only knew her as much as you *can* know people who stay at the shelter. Some treat it like their home, others you see once and never again. Candice came for perhaps four months, on and off, and then she was gone.'

'And she left me with you,' Seth stated.

Kossy nodded, hands churning up the mixture in the bowl. 'But I know, if she could, she would have kept you and taken care of you and—'

'Mom,' Seth said, interrupting quickly. 'You don't need to make this heart-warming and uplifting. She was a prostitute, working the streets.' He paused, the words coming out stiff and uncomfortable. 'How was she gonna keep that job going looking after a baby? The reality would have been she'd have left me in a drug den and I would have got ill or died from neglect or—'

'I don't think she was ever into drugs,' Kossy insisted. 'You see things, you look for these things. She was not someone I had pegged as a user.'

'But the people she associated with—'

'We all have associations with people from all walks of life.'

'Now you sound like Dad.' Ted was a school counsellor who had perfected the hard art of being both friend and adviser to the local youth community. In this day and age of total equality for all, with no 'ism' being acceptable, *he* was usually the King of Politically Correct.

'Do you want to try and find her, Seth?' Kossy asked. 'Because, when we were at lunch and after my ravioli had gone cold, you still didn't say if you wanted to try and find her.'

'I know.' Seth didn't know the answer to that question. He knew he wanted to know who she was and where she was from, but he didn't know if he wanted to take that next step.

Kossy stopped kneading the dough, ran water in the sink and dived her hands underneath it before wiping them on a festive hand towel. 'I will do everything I can to help you find her. If that's what you want.'

'I know,' Seth said again. 'I need to sit with it a little longer. Is that OK?'

Kossy smiled. 'Of course it's OK. Whatever you want is OK. Just ... tell me what you want me to do and I'll do it.'

Seth took a breath. 'Maybe, if you can ... are there any photographs at the centre? So I can see what she looked like.'

'I can't promise. Like I said, mainly they're in and out and not exactly pouting for the paparazzi, but there might be something. I'll look out everything I've got.'

Seth smiled. 'Thanks, Mom.'

'Whoa!' the excited whoop came from outside and drew Seth's attention to the patio doors to the deck. There were now more lights shining in the backyard than at a Pink Floyd concert.

'I don't believe it,' Kossy said, striding out from behind the worktop and surveying her garden. 'He promised me this year's lights were gonna be something special, but I was sceptical.' She breathed in, watching the dancing laser lights. 'I was actually a lot more than sceptical.'

Within a few seconds the pinks and purples began to spin faster, hitting the back fence with an array of colour before swirling up to the cloud-laden sky and back again. Then suddenly, poof! They were gone and a loud disappointed grunt filtered through the double-glazing.

'As I was saying,' Kossy said with a heavy sigh, 'sceptical was pushing it.'

'I'll go and see what I can do to help,' Seth said, pushing at the door.

'Wait,' Kossy said, bustling towards him. 'Not before you do up your coat.' She fussed around him, zipping up his jacket like he was three years old. 'It's freezing out there.'

He smiled, then leaned forward to kiss her cheek. 'Thanks, Mom.'

Sixteen

Lara looked at her phone and the text she was composing to Aldo.

> Today in New York I ate a pumpernickel bagel and I rescued a lemur from a tree at Central Park Zoo. You would love lemurs. They're like the feral cats but less bitey with longer tails. I think they also like Pringles. Don't forget to help Dad put the bins out tomorrow and remember it's 20% Day off at the garden centre. Xxx

She deleted the last line as the taxi pulled up outside a row of neat-looking townhouses. She didn't need to remind Aldo about the bins or the garden centre discount. He didn't forget, she always assumed he would. She needed to stop assuming he was incapable, or she would end up *making him* incapable. Everyone else always assumed Aldo wasn't able to do anything himself. She had always tried to teach him that with practice and patience he could achieve whatever he put his mind to.

The cab driver cleared his throat like his entire windpipe was full of a thick winter stew.

'Sorry,' Lara said in response, sitting forward in the cab. 'Are we here?'

'Here we are, lady,' he answered. 'It's the one with the door wide open and people drinking on the steps like it's the middle of summer. What sorta party you been invited to?'

'I have no idea,' Lara replied, reaching into her jacket pocket for her purse.

She and Susie hadn't really had much time to talk about it as David had arrived at their apartment early before whisking her best friend out to dinner. David had obviously really missed Susie while he had been half a world away and they had both had a starry-eyed look of adoration in their eyes. A little part of Lara felt envious, but it also served to remind her that actually she couldn't remember the last time Dan had acted anywhere near as amorously.

Paying the cab driver, she opened the door of the taxi and stepped out onto the pavement as the first flakes of snow began to fall. She took a deep breath of the cold air and looked towards the houses. They were all similar but yet also individual. Some were brown brick, others had cream-coloured masonry, all with some element of greenery despite the season. Ivy stretched over walls, firs and other hardy plants sat in pots on doorsteps and provided interest in small front gardens. Every house also had an element of Christmas – strings of golden lights in the window or a soft glow of cosy life going on behind the curtains – none more so than the building she was destined for. The one with half a dozen people in mismatched hats, coats and scarves sitting on the steps, some wearing shoes that showed all their toes. She stepped towards it.

'Hello,' she said to the first man on the third step up. 'Merry Christmas.'

'Don't eat all the pie!' the man barked. He had a beard that stretched down to the step he was sitting on, crumbs and things that looked alive nestling in the folds of hair.

'OK.'

'Don't eat anything,' the man snapped. 'I want there to be more.'

'Shall I ... get you some more?' Lara offered.

He shook his head. 'There's only more when Kossy says there's more.'

'Oh, OK,' Lara said. 'Sorry.' What was this party?

'Don't mind Earl,' said a young girl with dreadlocks. 'He hasn't eaten all week to make room for tonight.' She touched Lara's arm with bitten-to-the-quick nails. 'And, just so you know, there's *always* more.'

Lara smiled.

'You have no idea what this party is, do you?'

'It's that obvious?'

'We're all here for Kossy. She runs the centre we all try and go to to get a bed for the night and a warm shower. She's the best woman I've ever met. Tonight is her Christmas treat. Food, drink, laughs, no judgement. We get to feel like we live in this part of town, like we *could* live in this part of town.' The girl smiled. 'I hope you're hungry.'

Lara went to speak, to say she was starving. Then she closed her mouth. She had no idea what real starvation was and there was no way she was going to claim that she was in front of people who looked like they did. Was this a fundraising thing Seth supported?

'This is your first time, huh? Rubbing shoulders with the unclean,' the girl stated with a laugh.

'No ... well ... here in New York maybe. But there's a whole lot of ... unclean at the truck stop cafe I go to for sausage sandwiches back in England.' She swallowed. 'Not that I'm saying you're unclean or that anyone is unclean.'

The girl laughed. 'You're cool ... and it's OK. I'm good with being dirty. It reminds me why I chose this life. Being dirty on the outside allows me to feel cleaner on the inside than I ever had the chance to be where I came from.' She stuck out her hand. 'I'm Felice.'

Lara took hold of her hand and shook it. 'Lara. It's nice to meet you.'

'You too.' Felice picked up a bottle of beer and took a swig. 'So, I'm guessing, you're one of the good people who has come to show us that the world isn't full of shits who wanna take you for a ride.'

'Well, I was invited by ...' Was she really going to say she was invited here by Seth Hunt? It sounded ridiculous. But it *was* the truth and her social media had seen a real flurry of activity since Susie posted a photo of her and Seth at the zoo and tagged her in it. No response from Dan, as yet ...'Seth Hunt invited me.'

'Ah, the hot son.' Felice smiled.

'Son?' Lara queried.

'Seth is Kossy's son. He's inside helping with the barbecue. They've got sausage if you wanna *partake in a sandwich*.' Felice's English accent was pretty much spot-on.

'Don't have more than one!' Earl shouted up to them.

'Dad, these sausages are almost at the point of burning,' Seth stated, frantically moving them from the bottom shelf of the barbecue to the top.

'I'd leave them another couple minutes,' Ted replied, cool as a cucumber as he flashed off some steaks in a pan, throwing a little brandy over them and igniting a blue flame.

'Another couple minutes and we're gonna be dealing in charcoal,' Seth answered. Although a light flurry of snow was coming down from the sky, he was sweating. His mom had filled the garden area with patio heaters, chimeneas and old-school oil barrels. People were standing around, warming their hands over the flames, others were toasting marshmallows. Old Eddie, who had to be close to eighty, was playing his mouth organ along to the Christmas music blasting from the oldest-looking boom box Seth had ever seen. It was vibrating on the table so much the plastic ketchup and mustard bottles had been gradually bouncing across to the edge.

'After all these years of this cook out, you still don't understand the importance of not getting sued for food poisoning?' Ted served his steaks up onto plates and, quick as a flash, they were gone, whipped away to be devoured by the hungry.

'Seriously, Dad, you think anyone here is gonna try and sue you? You're doing a good thing here.'

Ted waved his spatula in the air. 'And we don't do it naively.' He lowered his voice. 'You think everyone here is needy and starving?'

'You told me *I* was needy since I was five and asked for a fire truck for Christmas ... and if I don't get a sausage soon ... what can I say?'

'There's always press here, Seth,' Ted continued. 'Every year they want to report on the crazy do-gooders who open their home to the city's destitute, hoping someone will hold us at knife-point or set a fire or steal our worldly goods.'

'People do sometimes take stuff,' Seth said, thinking of the Givenchy dress.

'Of course they do,' Ted answered. 'They have nothing. And if they want to steal your mother's God-awful dust-collecting ornaments to sell for a couple of bucks I'm not gonna stand in their way.'

'But ...'

'There's nothing your mother and I have that we wouldn't give away in a heartbeat, except you.' He slapped a hand on

Seth's shoulder. 'We have memories.' He tapped the side of his fair-haired head. 'It's all the times that are important, not the gadgets ... although I have seen a new drill I'm hoping Santa might bring me.'

Seth smiled at his father, drinking him in from his beige chinos tucked into thick winter boots to his reindeer jumper, sleeves rolled up. He was such an honest, hard-working man who had always been there when he was growing up, for every moment from the loss of his first pet – a snail he'd picked out of the garden – to his first film premiere. Then he jumped. 'The sausages! Dad! They're gonna be ruined!' He started taking them off the heat and putting them on paper plates.

Ted laughed. 'So, in answer to your first question about law suits. I overcook the sausages so the press don't get food poisoning. If they wanna report my bad barbecuing skills that's up to them.' He helped Seth move the food. 'But if you think handling the tongs on blackened wieners is going to harm *your* career then you can drop them any time.' Ted smiled. 'Just like that lemur.'

'Hey, that's a low shot,' Seth replied.

The house was as full of people as it was things. Photos and paintings adorned every inch of wall, but they were almost covered by guests – some standing, others sitting or propped up against furniture. There was a cosy living room off to the right Lara had looked into, but it was packed with people gathered around a table playing cards for what looked like sushi. She had moved along, into a dining room-cum-kitchen where two enormous Christmas trees dominated most of the space. Music and laughter filled the air as well as the chink of glassware and bottle tops popping. She felt a little out of place, a bit apprehensive and totally overwhelmed.

She was in New York completely on her own in a house full of strangers. She stopped in the kitchen, nestled next to one of the Christmas trees and slipped her phone out of her jacket pocket. She called up the text she hadn't sent to Aldo yet.

Today in New York I ate a pumpernickel bagel and I rescued a lemur from a tree at Central Park Zoo. You would love lemurs. They're like the feral cats but less bitey with longer tails. I think they also like Pringles.

How to end it? Not with an instruction. Maybe a suggestion. Something nice.

If you want to open my Advent calendar while I'm away and eat all the chocolates then you can. Xxx

'Hi there. I'm Kossy. Can I get you something to drink?'

Lara looked up from her phone and into the face of a beautiful fifty-something woman with impressive, slightly curly, long dark hair, slightly speckled with grey, she knew Susie would kill to get her hands on.

'I ... don't know if I'm going to be staying very long.' That hadn't been what she wanted to say at all and it had sounded so rude. 'Sorry, it's just, I'm not homeless or starving, and I feel bad, if I have a drink or something to eat ... I don't want to take it away from ... everyone else.'

Kossy laughed out loud. It was rich and full-bodied, somehow sounding of the deep, dark texture of figgy pudding lightened with a touch of whipped cream. 'I like you! You're crazy!' She slipped an arm around Lara's shoulders. 'I'm not homeless either, or theoretically starving, but one thing I've learned is *everybody* needs to eat and drink and no one is gonna deprive anyone of anything in this house. Beer?' Kossy asked. 'Or shall I open the tequila?' She lowered her voice. 'I've been dying to open the tequila since it was five o'clock.'

'Beer would be good,' Lara admitted.

'One beer coming up,' Kossy said, taking hold of Lara's arm and guiding her through the guests to the kitchen island. 'Two if you tell me all about yourself and England. You know the Queen personally, right?'

Lara smiled. 'I'll settle for one for now.'

'Ha!' Kossy exclaimed. 'A mystery lady.' Then she let out a gasp, hands going to either side of her face. 'I know you! I know you! Wait a minute, it will come to me! You've been in something on TV with my Seth ... was it *Manhattan Med*? Were you that student nurse he was mildly involved with in season four? I thought they could have done much more with her character.'

Lara shook her head. 'No, that wasn't me. But I wish it had been. She had really good skin.'

'She did have good skin ...' Kossy popped the top off a beer bottle and handed it to Lara. 'But you're an actress, right?'

Lara smiled. 'No. I drive a truck.'

'Get away! With looks like that?'

She blushed. Not many people commented on how she looked in a positive way. She was mainly just Lara. One of the drivers. Or, when delivering elsewhere, the token eye candy who couldn't possibly have a brain. She swigged her beer. 'Are you saying cute girls can't drive lorries?'

'God! I think I almost did! I will definitely be going to hell! Come on, put me out of my misery. What's your name and where do I know you from?' Kossy opened the bottle of tequila and poured herself a small measure.

'I'm Lara,' Lara informed.

'And she starred with me on the news channels today. Up a tree at the zoo.'

Seth had appeared alongside Lara without her even knowing and was looking casually hot in dark jeans, a shirt and jumper, coat hanging from one arm, a plate full of sausages in the other. Before he could even put the food down on the worktop, guests were helping themselves.

'Hello again,' Lara said, feeling like she should not be here at this party. This was obviously his parents' home and she was invading an important event ...

'You know they're naming it Saving Primate Ryan, right?' Kossy said. 'Bernadette called me earlier and said it's bending on Twitter. Is that right? It doesn't sound quite right.'

'Trending, Mom,' Seth told her. 'And the lemur's name was Jax. Hi, Lara. Want a sausage?'

She watched his face colour up the second the suggestion hit the air.

'So forward, Seth,' Kossy said with a laugh. 'That sounded very much like something Dr Mike might say. Take a sausage. Take anything else there is. I'll go and get some more buns.'

'Really, it's fine,' Lara said, helping herself from the platter Seth was holding. 'This is fine.'

'Believe me, there's absolutely no chance of not doing what my mom says in this house.'

'She's so nice,' Lara said, biting into the sausage. God, it was good.

'Has she managed to get your life story from you yet?'

'She said I can have a second beer if I give her that.'

'You are officially screwed.'

'No,' Lara said, taking another bite of the sausage, grease oozing out and drizzling down her chin. 'I'm officially at a great party in New York eating the finest sausage and realising just how lucky I am.'

'I'll get you that second beer,' Seth answered with a smile.

Seventeen

Having looked at his Twitter mentions in between barbecuing and handing out drinks, Seth was surprised he could look Lara in the eye. Her initial tweet had been a little out there, but he sensed the sincerity of the quest. She obviously loved her boyfriend and felt she needed to do everything humanly possible to save the relationship. Trent's responses posing as him had made his insides coil like fancy Christmas gift ribbon. He would never have repeated a corny line from *Manhattan Med*! He wouldn't even had replied in the first place. He didn't really *want* to use Twitter, it was more a business necessity. And he never read direct messages, that was where the real crazy people ended up. So, after he had finished this dance with Mad Maggie – it wasn't an insult, everyone called her Mad Maggie, including Maggie herself – he was going to take Lara Beer Number Three and confess that Trent had been the one managing his social media, his friend thinking he was doing the right thing – perhaps 'the right thing' was a bit kind – and that although Seth felt for her, he wasn't really the ideal person to work through this with her. He knew all too well he was no one's Alex Pettyfer. And he was in a weird place at the moment, hanging onto his career by a thread, cosseting the news of his parentage. He was distracted. He felt like he was on an emotional see-saw. He looked across the garden to where Lara was talking with Earl. Earl usually had little to say unless it was about how much food everyone was depriving him of …

'When you gonna be on the big screen again? The last film you were in your mama got a projector and we all sat on the floor and ate popcorn,' Mad Maggie said, staring up at him, all big bloodshot eyes and missing teeth.

'Actually, I'm going to a premiere real soon, Maggie.'

Until he'd looked at his calendar, after checking Twitter mentions, he had barely remembered. How did you forget you had a film premiere to go to? Except he had made the film over a year ago and it had been held back from its original release because its themes coincided a little too closely with real world events. He had done a couple of interviews for smaller magazines about the upcoming launch, but he wasn't one of the shining stars. In fact, compared to Mark Wahlberg he was basically just a fading flashlight, with rather weak batteries. But he still got to go to the premiere and the cash injection had helped cover the rent this month.

'Red carpet and champagne?' Mad Maggie sucked freezing air in through her teeth. 'I can't remember the last time I had champagne … or even saw carpet.' She sniffed. 'It's bare boards in the rich houses as well as the squats. Everyone wants to live like they got nothing. It's kinda funny!' She laughed loud and hard, squeezing his arms with strong hands.

'Girls like you shouldn't drink beer,' Earl stated, Christmas cake crumbs leaking from his lips and falling into his beard.

'Girls like me?' Lara queried. 'That's very judgemental of you, Mr Earl. You don't know a thing about me.'

'I know you're pretty … and you're not homeless and you've had four sausages too many.'

Lara put a hand to her chest in mock horror. 'Earl, do you make a mental note of what everyone eats?'

He got a little closer to her then, his beard tickling the side of her face, a little body odour mixing with the grilled meats, cold air and scent of winter. It was still snowing but the flakes floated down like gentle feathers, caressing the guests and outdoor furniture rather than making them too cold or damp.

'Some people are known to take advantage,' Earl whispered. 'See that guy over there?' He tilted his head a little to the right, indicating a middle-aged man wearing a red woollen hat standing near the barbecue. 'He doesn't even come to Kossy's shelter. He's from the other side of the city.' Earl shovelled from cake into his mouth. 'He's a professional shelter-crasher.'

Lara wanted to laugh at the absurdness of the suggestion. 'Like a wedding-crasher?' she asked. 'You're telling me he goes around to the best shelters taking what they have to offer?'

'You got it, kid.'

'But if you know that, why don't you say anything?' Lara asked. She couldn't really believe anyone would go around pretending to be homeless to take from the people who needed it most.

'Kossy welcomes everyone here,' Earl told her. 'Good, bad, ugly, uglier still … this whole place is a den of liars, thieves and people who would kill for the last burger on that grill.'

Lara swallowed, looking the old man in the eye and trying to tell if he was serious or not. Then, just like that, he laughed hard, his expression going from felon in an interrogation room to children's TV presenter – albeit a slightly scruffy one.

'This is New York, kid! Get used to it!'

'Hey, Earl.' Seth joined their group. 'Mom says if you want more cake she's about to cut up another one.'

'Gotta go,' Earl said to Lara. 'And go easy on that beer.'

'Yes, sir,' Lara answered, taking another swig from her bottle. She hadn't seen much of Seth since he'd got her the second beer earlier. He had been called to put out a small fire on his dad's barbecue, then had to get up a ladder to refix the garden light show, followed by dancing with everyone who asked, including a woman who looked at least ten months pregnant and he'd had to hold at arm's length to accommodate her bump between them.

'I hope Earl was playing nice,' Seth said.

'He was telling me I eat too much and apparently can't drink beer because I'm a girl.'

'Whoa,' Seth replied. 'Did you tell him you rescued an endangered species today?'

'I think that would have impressed him less than the beer-drinking.'

He laughed. 'You know him real well already.'

She smiled. This felt easy. This whole night had felt nice. Low key. Familiar, almost. If you washed the guests a little – but not much – got out some straw bales, changed the city backdrop for trees and put her dad and Aldo in the middle of it, it could almost be an Appleshaw party. Her apprehension about being here without Susie and David had lessened some-what since the Christmas music had been turned up louder and she was two Coors Lights down.

'Do you wanna sit?' Seth put both beer bottles he was holding into one hand. 'We ... haven't really had a chance to talk.'

No, they hadn't and in a lot of ways she was glad. Somehow, it had been easier to find her newly single feet as a stranger in the middle of an event where there was no expectation from anyone about anything, rather than someone knowing she was here because she had sent a stupid tweet to one of her favourite actors when she was drunk …

'Come on,' Seth said, leading the way. 'There's two of the sturdier chairs under the heater over there.' He looked back to her as he moved. 'When I say sturdier, I mean they've been fixed up by my dad, so *you* should be fine, but I might have to sit on one side a little.'

She smiled, suddenly nervous. There were going to be questions. About why she was a needy, crazy stalker whose neediness and craziness had probably lost her the attentions of Dan in the first place. But she was ready to tell him it was all really Susie's mad plan and there had been rather a lot of mince-pie whisky involved. Just looking at the Christmas cake on Earl's lips had caused an ugly flashback.

She sat carefully on one of the blue-painted wooden chairs and it wobbled significantly. So much so she had to make a grab for the wrought-iron bistro table on top of which was a glowing Santa face tea-light holder, the empty shells of about a hundred monkey nuts – or so it seemed – and a branch of spruce in a glass, a silver ribbon tied around it.

'You OK?' Seth reached out and steadied her arm with his free hand.

'Yes, sorry. I wasn't expecting it to move quite that much.'

'I think he used glue instead of screws,' Seth said. 'My mom had kinda asked him to fix them for about six months straight and he grabbed the nearest thing to make the harassment stop.'

Lara laughed. 'A quick fix.'

'Yeah.' He handed her one of the two beers. 'So, is that what you're hoping for with your boyfriend?' He slowly lowered himself onto the chair next to her.

'Ouch. I walked straight into that one, didn't I?'

'Listen, Lara, I—' Seth started.

'I know what you're going to say and I agree.'

'You do?'

'A hundred per cent. I would say a hundred and ten per cent like everyone seems to say these days, but I've always thought that's complete bullshit because it isn't a real number.'

'OK,' Seth replied.

'You think, particularly after I got up a tree in Central Park when I'd only been in your country for a few hours, that I am a total pillock. A total, crazy, stalker pillock who you felt you had to invite to this party to be nice, because you *are* nice and really you wish you hadn't wasted your time replying to my insane tweet in the first place. I'm betting that you completely wish you were Ed Sheeran.' Lara took a swig of her beer. 'Did you know he's not on Twitter right now? Not because I tweeted him ... well, I did, but only because Susie suggested it. She suggested Tom Hardy too, but she cocked up his handle.' Another swig of beer was consumed. 'God, that sounds totally filthy.'

Seth watched her, body nervously moving on the chair, fingers in the spray of spruce, flicking over the ribbon, then going to the Santa Claus candle, her thumb grazing his shiny red nose. He was also wondering what the word 'pillock' meant.

'Not that I want you to think you were the bottom of the list. Because you weren't. You were very much the first person I thought of ... but not because I'm an obsessed fan or a member of the *Manhattan Med* fan club ... I only know there *is* a fan club because I signed up for a new season alert and well, once you've done that, and Cambridge Analytica have your information, they can basically send you anything they like, and they do – frequently.'

Was it best to interrupt her now? It was apparent she was struggling with this scenario, like he was. Under false pretences was never a comfortable place to rest. He opened his mouth to speak—

'So, I'm happy to forget the whole thing. Forget I ever contacted you. Forget the unhinged scenario of us hanging out creating fodder for my Insta. I mean, you're so famous and I'm just—'

'I believe the press are calling you "Lemur Girl",' Seth interjected. 'If Marvel get a hold of you there could be your own film deal coming and a whole heap of merchandise.'

'See,' Lara said, smiling. 'You're too nice. You're being reasonable and understanding and bringing me beer – Earl is going to tell you off for that later, because believe me he will know how many I've consumed – and it was so lovely of you to invite me here tonight and I'm having the best time, even though I wasn't sure I would have the best time because I came on my own and it's New York and not Appleshaw and it's scary as well as exciting … and you probably have a hundred better things to do than make photos with me.'

'A hundred and ten,' Seth replied, smiling back at her.

'Now, you said like that it's a real number,' Lara stated, pointing at him with her beer bottle.

'Lara,' Seth said, daring to relax back in his chair a little. 'I need to tell you something.'

'You've called your security team. They're on their way with tasers and if I go quietly they'll be no charges and I'll be able to re-enter America again someday, if I can ever afford it a second time. I could barely afford it this first time and I'm not quite sure how I feel about air travel. It's only been half a day and I'm caught between feeling exhilarated and thinking I should probably google "how aeroplanes stay in the air" because everything looked and felt quite heavy, like gravity-law-defying heavy.'

'This was the first time you flew?' Seth exclaimed.

'This is the first time I've been out of England, because the Isle of Wight doesn't count, apparently.'

'That's … wow, I'm not sure I've met anyone who's never travelled before.'

'Except most of the people here?' Lara indicated the dancing, laughing, warming-their-hands-by-the-fire guests around them. 'Maybe that's why Earl and I get on so well. Maybe we gravitated towards each other because we love sausage and we haven't toured.'

Seth shook his head. 'Believe me, Earl mightn't say that much but there's times he'll come out with something no one else in the room knows, with real authority, like he's lived it, you know.'

'Or he's a very good actor,' Lara suggested.

Seth laughed. 'Sure. I guess that's a possibility.'

'So, tell me, how long do I have?' Lara asked.

'Before what?'

'Before the security team arrive.'

'You definitely have time to finish your beer.' He laughed, shaking his head.

'That wasn't what you were going to tell me?' Lara asked him.

'No.'

'Then what *were* you going to tell me?'

Here was his opportunity to tell her Trent was behind his corny tweet. That, up until late this afternoon he hadn't even known who she was. But what would it achieve? It could destroy her self-confidence at a time when it appeared her boyfriend was already doing just that. And it wouldn't make him feel good either. In fact, right now, it would make him feel like a real, uncaring ass towards someone who had saved his. Jax had been reported to be happily munching whatever lemurs munch all day – didn't she say fruit and tree bark? – and had come to no harm following his escapade.

'I'm ...' he began. 'Really not that famous.' He smiled, putting his beer bottle to his lips and drinking, watching her reaction. She was looking at him with fresh eyes, probably wishing she had persevered with Tom Hardy ... and why was he even remotely concerned about that? He had so much on his plate already, or he hoped to, if he ever got another call from Universal or decided if he wanted to meet his birth mother ...

'Bollocks!' Lara exclaimed with a laugh. 'You're Dr Mike! Everyone knows who you are. And you don't get invited to be an ambassador of Central Park Zoo if you're not famous.' She sniffed. 'But I get it. And it's a good get-out. Telling the crazy English girl you're not famous enough for this making-Dan-jealous scheme for it to have any chance of working. And you're right. Even if I posted photos of me and Jennifer Lawrence naked together, I doubt that Dan would take any notice.'

Seth tried to stop his eyes from performing a detailed reconnaissance of her body. He knew where the curves were already. He wasn't blind or immune to the fact she was every kind of gorgeous, and the mention of nakedness was quirking his insides ... or maybe it was the charcoal-coated offerings from the barbecue he'd consumed. No, he was pretty sure it was her. And he couldn't remember the last time a woman had quirked anything of his ...

'Not now he's defined himself as "single",' Lara finished.

'Oh,' Seth replied.

'Definitely a break ... almost a break-up ... and on its way to being completely broken,' Lara said with a sigh.

This Dan had to be a complete jerk, but there were two sides to every story. Nothing was ever black and white. But Lara seemed genuine. A good person. A good person who had asked for his help – and got Trent instead. He couldn't tell her that.

'Listen,' Seth said, leaning forward in his chair and receiving a creaking reminder that collapse could be imminent. 'My life isn't really that interesting, but I am between jobs, so I have a little time.' He did and he didn't, but it was the right thing to do. And it definitely had nothing to do with Trent's need to get an appearance on *Ellen* on his résumé. 'How about I take you to a couple of great places this week, show you and your friend around New York a little? We can take a whole lot of great photos … us at the Empire State … us in Times Square …' He shrugged. 'If you think it's gonna help.'

He watched her lips shape into the most radiant, whole-hearted smile that lit up her whole face. 'You'd really do that for me?'

'I think it's the very least I can do for Lemur Girl.'

Then suddenly she was almost in his lap, her arms around his neck, a sweet scent of cotton candy, mulled fruit and notes of pine flooding his senses as the warmth of her body melted into his.

'Thank you,' she breathed. 'This means so much.'

'You're welcome, Lemur Girl,' he replied, holding her close. 'You're welcome.'

Eighteen

'They're gone!' Kossy exclaimed, her hand on her forehead. 'Not that I don't like and respect every last one of them, but when they started playing Jenga with the empty beer bottles I knew it was gonna be testing.' She slumped down onto one of the garden chairs and it collapsed beneath her, sending her sprawling onto the snow-kissed ground.

'Mom, are you OK?' Seth asked, jumping up and going to her aid. He took her hand.

'Ted!' Kossy scrabbled to her feet with Seth's help. 'Are these the chairs I asked you to fix in the summer?'

Ted bent his head a little as if he was analysing the seating before he made any attempt at answering. He scratched his now-hat-covered head. 'I'm not sure.'

'Don't you lie to me, Ted Hunt. You and I both know these are the chairs you were supposed to fix this summer.'

'And I did,' Ted answered.

'With that freaking glue gun! Not with nails or screws like any sane person who wants a repair to last more than a freaking New York minute.'

'Have you been drinking tequila?' Ted asked.

'What?' Kossy bit back. 'Why would you ask that?'

'You said "freaking" twice in that last sentence.'

'So freaking what? Oh, that means I'm drunk on tequila now, does it?'

'Usually, yes.'

Seth laughed out loud, watching the face-off between his parents like he had so many times before. This back-biting was like a constant courting ritual, part of the fabric of their relationship he knew neither one of them would be without. He was almost glad his dad never mended things well. If everything in his parents' life was perfect, there would never be anything for his mom to get crazy about.

'I don't know what you're laughing so hard about, Seth. You're on toilet-cleaning duty and you know how the shelter-goers love a proper toilet.' Kossy smiled, carefully sitting down on another chair before picking up her mug of hot chocolate. 'You think it's only food and drink they come here for?'

'Mom, jeez ... didn't I do toilets last year?' Seth asked.

'I'll do the toilets,' Ted said, putting his hand in the air before sitting down next to Kossy and passing Seth another bottle of beer.

'I want them done properly, Ted, with products. Not just water and a wave of the toilet brush,' Kossy ordered.

'I've got some industrial-strength bleach in the garage.'

Seth smiled. His parents were like many in NYC, non-car owners. His dad's garage was only ever filled with tools, products he had bought from TV shopping channels and books Kossy had banished from the house that he couldn't bear to part with.

'So ... I think your father and I need to hear a little more about Lara,' Kossy said, sitting back in her chair and blowing at her hot chocolate. Steam rose into the air and mingled with the light snowflakes still dancing around in the dark.

'I like her,' Ted added. 'She likes beer.' He sucked in a breath then looked into the middle distance. 'What was the name of that girlfriend you had who would only drink carrot juice?'

'God, what was her name?' Kossy interjected.

'Rosie,' Seth said. 'And we only had a couple of dates.'

'You brought her here.'

'I knew you would have a lot of carrots,' Seth replied.

'So,' Ted said, thoughtfully. 'Did you bring Lara because you knew I would have a lot of beer?'

'I didn't bring Lara. She came here in a cab.' And she had left the same way too, dismissing his offer of escorting her back to the apartment she was staying in in East Village. They were meeting up tomorrow afternoon, at the Empire State Building.

'You're being evasive, Seth,' Kossy said. 'Don't you think, Ted?'

'I'm losing the eye contact too,' Ted answered.

Seth shook his head and pointedly looked at both his parents. In that moment he realised exactly how lucky he really was. To have been taken on by this wonderful couple, just like half the needy in the city, except that he had been kept for life, not just for Christmas.

'Thank you, guys,' Seth said softly. 'You know, for not freaking out when I asked about my mom.' He cleared his throat. 'My other mom.'

'Wow, there's a whole lot of use of the word "freaking" tonight,' Ted commented. 'It almost feels like I'm back at school.' He put a hand to his nape then took a drink.

'Have you decided?' Kossy asked, somewhat tentatively. 'If you wanna …'

'No … I mean … I wanna know more about her, like I said earlier, see what she looks like, see if she looks like me … I don't know. Is that stupid? To wanna know about someone but not know if you wanna meet them?'

'No, sweetheart, of course it isn't.'

'And it might not be just her,' Ted said. 'There's the whole maybe you've got a brother or sister aspect too. It's a lot to take on.'

'Ted ...' Kossy said.

Seth took a breath in, drawing the cold night deep into his lungs. 'I know there's a possibility she's got a whole new family. I mean, why wouldn't she?' He sighed. 'And I'm not into Disney enough to think she ended up marrying my blood father and I'm gonna be reunited with this perfect family. I mean, I have the perfect family right here. I don't need anyone else. I just ...'

'No,' Ted said. 'I meant the other hat next to you in the box.'

Kossy got to her feet in a hurry. 'Shall I make more hot chocolate? Seth, you'll have one, won't you? Start curdling up that beer and smoothing over the cancer-causing carbon that was all over half the meat on the grill.'

'Have I missed something?' Seth said.

'You didn't tell him about the hat, did you?' Ted said. 'Kossy, you said you'd told Seth everything.'

'I did. I was going to ... when the time was right.'

'Kossy, he's twenty-eight years old and he came to you with this. For answers. For the honesty you've always promised him and usually given him.' Ted shook his head. 'This isn't who we are at all.'

Seth watched his mom sink back into her seat, now unconcerned for the stability, her head down, eyes on the smear of snow on the ground. 'Could one of you please tell me what's going on?'

'Kossy?' Ted said.

His mom just shook her bowed head, white flakes collecting in the middle of her dark and grey crown.

'Seth, when you were left at the shelter, there were two little hats. One on your head and one right next to you.' He sighed, then reached for Seth's hands, holding them in his own. 'Now, it could well be that it was just a spare hat meant for you, or, it might mean ... you weren't the only baby.'

Seth swallowed, his heart pounding against the wall of his chest. This was not something he had been prepared for. This was almost unbelievable.

'I always thought ... *we* always thought ... that maybe there's a chance you were a twin,' Ted said.

Nineteen

Lara and Susie's Airbnb apartment, East Village

With the window of the apartment wide open, Lara sat on the ledge, filling her lungs with the new morning air New York City was serving up. From her vantage point, past the three snowmen she had named Harry, Ron and Hermione, she could see right into the heart of East Village.

Already it seemed to be filled with the world's most on-trend individuals. There were coats of all varieties – long and leather, pink and fluffy – coupled with an eclectic mix of clothing peeking out underneath – ripped jeans and plaid, shorts and trainers, business suits and leather shoes, a Santa Claus on a skateboard … All were buzzing into coffee shops, talking into their mobile phones, commuting any way they could on bikes, buses or rollerblades. It was noisy, nothing like Appleshaw, but Lara found if she closed her eyes, the constant hum was almost soothing and just watching this new world going by was making her feel part of something bigger.

'Morning.'

'*Buenos dias.*'

Lara turned around to greet Susie and David, having seen nothing of them since they'd left for dinner the evening before. She wouldn't have known they were in the apartment at all, except someone used the toilet in the night and she had assumed it was one of them and not an intruder. Her dad would probably have plumped for intruder if he were here. He believed the Big Apple was just like it was portrayed in the movies.

'Morning,' Lara replied, spinning out of the window seat she'd made and standing up.

'Aren't you cold?' Susie asked, taking hold of the window and pulling it closed. 'It's cold in here. I'm not sure the heating's working and they definitely promised heating on the Airbnb description.'

'Hey, baby, are you trying to say I didn't keep you warm enough last night? Because that would put a real dent in my pride after not having seen you for so long.' David hung himself over Susie almost as if she were a clothes horse and he was a dressing gown, slightly damp and in need of airing.

'I wasn't warm last night,' Susie said softly, turning around in his tangle of arms, legs and bare chest. 'I was hot … scorching hot … chestnuts-roasting-on-an-open-fire hot … rich-thick-gravy-being-poured-over-the-Christmas-turkey hot …'

'OK,' Lara said. 'Can you stop because I don't want to know what you're going to say when you get to Christmas pudding.'

'Brandy butter,' Susie said, licking her lips. 'Poured all over—'

'Shall I make more coffee?' Lara asked, making for the kitchen area. 'They might not have proper heating but they have a really good coffee machine.'

'Never mind the coffee,' Susie said, extricating herself from her dark-haired Latin lover and following Lara to the kitchen. 'How was the party with Dr Mike last night?'

'You would have known if you had actually turned up.' Lara sniffed a little like she was put out. She wasn't really put out, because the party had been so much fun, and given that her best friend hadn't seen the lust of her life for months she hadn't truly expected they would leave dinner early and slip out of their cosy couple bubble. 'And don't keep calling him Dr Mike. He has done other stuff you know.' He'd told her a little about the films he'd been in, some of them she thought she had heard of, but didn't think she'd seen. She was sure she would have remembered if he had graced her Friday nights in front of the TV wearing something other than his *Manhattan Med* white coat.

'That was my fault.' David stretched his arms in the air, elongating his lithe torso. 'We found this little Spanish restaurant in West Village and they served *pisto* like my grandmother makes and I got talking to the owner and he brought us pigs' feet and—'

'Pigs' feet!' Lara exclaimed. 'And I thought some of the burgers on the barbecue last night had sketchy origins.'

'They were quite nice.' Susie sat up on one of the bar stools. 'I hadn't tried them before.'

'It's not even something Mrs Fitch has had on the menu at the garden centre cafe and she's had some odd stuff,' Lara said.

'But her tortillas! They were so good!' He smiled. 'Anyway, I completely, totally take all the blame. Am I forgiven, Lara? For taking your gorgeous, sexy best friend away from you for an evening?'

Within seconds, David was lolling over Susie like he was performing a contemporary dance routine. Lara had forgotten how hands-on he was. It was nice, if you didn't need to breathe.

'Go and have a shower,' Susie ordered, palming his cheek and giving him a playful push. 'Don't you have clients this morning?'

'Not until ten thirty,' David answered. 'I moved them back a little, so we could have time together while you're here. And, my first client today is my prince.'

'Go and have a shower,' Susie ordered again.

'What?!' David announced, hands going down onto slim hips. 'I tell you one of my clients is a prince and you don't want any more details?'

'I want to hear about Lara's party. I'm sure the prince can wait until after you're showered.' Susie smiled. 'Aren't princes meant to be dutiful?'

'He *is* beautiful. Because I style his hair,' David answered, beaming.

'Shower,' Susie ordered. 'Get *yourself* on-point.'

'I love the way you boss me around. I have missed that, baby.' David blew Susie a kiss before galloping from the living space in the direction of the bathroom.

Lara started up the coffee machine and it began to fill up the mug she'd set under it. The delicious smell of dark roasted beans permeated the air. Just the thought of another cup of coffee was making her feel warm.

'So, tell me all about the party and Seth. Leave nothing out because I was starting to worry when you didn't tweet or Facebook any photos. I mean that's what you're supposed to be doing to wind up Dan,' Susie reminded her.

Lara didn't want to wind up Dan. She wanted to do the very opposite of winding up Dan. She wanted to make him see that she was here in New York with the world at her feet and a gorgeous someone by her side, because she was interesting and fun and so much more than just previously untravelled Lara Weeks who drove a truck in Appleshaw. But perhaps Dan announcing he was single had changed the game-play a little. Had he posted any photos since he'd altered his status?

Perhaps *he* was somewhere with the world at his feet and a gorgeous someone at his side ... Cleavage Chloe. 'It wasn't a photo opportunity kind of party,' Lara answered, swapping mugs over and putting the full one in front of Susie.

'Every party is a photo opportunity kind.'

'Not this one.'

'Well, who was there? Anyone else famous? Affleck? Tatum? Diesel?'

'Earl was there and a cool girl with dreadlocks called Felice.'

'What shows have they been in?' Susie asked, sipping at her coffee. It was only at that moment that Lara realised her friend was wearing David's animal print shirt, leopards with pink roses between their teeth.

'They weren't actors. They were homeless.'

'What?'

It took Lara only as long as the second mug of coffee took to fill to tell her about Kossy's shelter and the Christmas party she laid on every year for the people living on the streets she tried to aid.

'So,' Susie said as Lara sat on the bar stool next to her. 'Seth was there looking all dark and dreamy serving up hot dogs to the vagrants of NYC while the paparazzi took lots of heart-warming shots for the papers this morning? Did you get in any of them?' Susie waved a hand in the air, mouth full of hot coffee. 'Did you know everyone's calling you Lemur Girl.'

'I had heard.' And she had seen a few tweets. Someone had been less than complimentary about her breasts – or lack of them – and she hadn't read any more. She took a sip of her drink, letting the foam coat her top lip. 'But it wasn't a paparazzi kind of party. Although there were apparently some press in disguise. It was kind of like ... the barn dance we had in the summer. Casual, everyone enjoying the food and drink and the music ...'

'And Aunt Flora's summer fruits punch ... that has nothing on the mince-pie whisky though.'

'Agreed.'

'So, how did you get on? If you didn't take any photos is it a no-go with creating a bit of a social-media stir? Did he get cold feet?' Susie asked. 'Did you?'

Lara shook her head. 'I just told him it was all a stupid idea, and really all *your* idea and I had somehow entered into an alternate universe, like that German show I watched on Netflix ... and after I'd finished going on and on and on some more about what a pillock I'd been he said ...'

'Yes?' Susie said, looking like she was waiting for news of a Love Island contestant pregnancy announcement.

'He said he was between jobs and he had a bit of time if we wanted to be shown around the city, taking a few snaps here and there, if I thought it would help.'

'Oh my God! Dr Mike is going to show us round New York! Lara! This is huge! This is the hugest news ever! It's going to blow Dan and his stupid, super-cold, super-silly Scottish lodge out of the Hudson River or whatever one of the rivers in Scotland is called.' Susie stopped talking and looked at Lara who was hugging her mug with both hands. 'Why aren't you excited? This is what we wanted! This is *more* than what we wanted. He's giving up time to tour us around his town. There will be oodles of opportunities for photos.'

'I know,' Lara said quietly. Last night she had been under the influence of beer and the cinnamon and nutmeg smells from Kossy's baking and the scented candles, feeling she wanted to strike back at Dan's status change. Today, she was more reserved. Today she was wanting this trip to be very much about her rather than anyone else. Was that selfish? She wasn't sure she had actually ever been selfish before. Was this what it felt like?

'Listen.' Susie put down her coffee and slipped an arm around Lara's shoulders. 'This is Fate. This is deity-given karma falling into your lap and it's my job to not let you waste it.' She tugged at a strand of Lara's hair. 'We should get David to put in some lowlights *or* he could let me into his workspace and I could give you a makeover. We could Christmas it up a little. What about some silver streaks? It's really in at the moment.'

Lara pulled a face. 'When people do that it just makes them look old.'

'Red then?'

'I don't know ...'

'Come on, Lara. A whole new you while you're in New York.'

Lara's phone made a noise and she retrieved it from the back pocket of her jeans.

'Is that Dan?' Susie asked, eyes narrowing.

'No, it's Aldo.' She shook her head as she read the text.

I ate all the chocolates in the calendar. Dad said I was meant to only open one window each day until Xmas. Sorry.

'Is he OK?' Susie asked.

'Yeah,' Lara said, smiling. 'He's fine.'

Twenty

Seth Hunt and Trent Davenport's apartment, West Village, New York

'No carbs today or tomorrow!' Trent spat as Seth came over to the kitchen island, a plate full of toasted bagels in his hand.

'What?' Seth asked, swallowing. He was starving. Despite the amount of barbecue he'd consumed he still needed something solid to soak up the beer, and the whisky he had settled into when he'd got back to the apartment. His mom had cried and said she had let him down and he had just stood there watching the snowfall thicken, stunned and shocked by the fact that he could have a brother or sister. The exact same age, perhaps with the exact same face, and no one seemed to know about it. He'd said very little – not knowing what to say, not wanting to spoil what had been a great evening, not wanting to say lots of things he might regret – and he'd got a cab back to West Village. His mom had called him several times already, but he just couldn't bring himself to pick up yet.

'I have got you a fast-track audition for a biopic based on the life of David Hasselhoff.'

'What part am I going for?' Seth sat down and poured himself coffee. Trent snatched the pot away with one hand

and pushed the orange juice carton towards him with the other.

'Is that a joke?' he asked. 'The Hoff, obviously.'

'Trent, I'm not sure it's really me and—'

'You'd be going for the role of David when he was in his twenties and had rock-hard abs, hence no carbs. And you'd better do a couple of sessions at the gym. You're still a member, right?'

He was. But he hadn't done anything other than swim for quite some time. He preferred to jog around the city, taking in the fresh air and ambience of the New York he loved. But he hadn't really done that for a while either. Sit-ups and squats to keep his tone had lately been done in front of a box set of *Friends*.

'Trent, I know you're trying to pull out all the stops here and I know, believe me I *really* know, I can't pick and choose if I want to keep living in West Village, but …'

'This is playing The Hoff,' Trent said, looking at him with an expression usually worn by a newsreader giving dire news with global consequences. 'Not advertising nuts.'

'I get that,' Seth said. 'Really, I do, but …' What could he say? That what he really wanted was a second chance to read for the character of Sam in *A Soul's Song* now he knew his mother was a prostitute and he might have a twin? He could dig deeper with that reference point, he just knew it. And he felt right about the film. It had a Nicholas Sparks vibe to it and what actor in their right mind didn't want to be part of a Nicholas Sparks adaptation? 'I want that Universal film. *A Soul's Song*. Do you think we should follow it up?'

'You mean call them?' Trent asked, eyes almost bulging out of his head. 'Call the casting director and … *hurry them along?*' Trent had said 'hurry them along' like he had suggested walking up to the White House front door and inviting the president for coffee.

'I just … I don't know … I would hate to hear that someone else had got the role when I don't think I gave the best of myself in the first round.'

'You don't wanna appear too keen. It's not a good look,' Trent said, picking up one of Seth's bagels and biting into it.

'I know, but … I don't know … I really feel that part should be mine.' Did that sound completely egotistical? Who did he think he was? He wasn't exactly Matt Damon.

Trent pointed a finger at him, nodding. 'This is good. This is positive. I haven't seen you looking this positive for quite some time. But …'

'But?'

'Let's not hang everything on one part. Isn't that one of the first rules of acting?'

'Yeah, I know.'

'So, let's cover our bases and our asses,' Trent said, pouring himself a coffee. 'How long has it been since you auditioned for that part?'

'Two weeks and three days,' Seth replied.

Trent sucked in a breath that sounded like Seth had as much chance of getting a call-back as he did of stopping the onset of Christmas.

'I know it's been a while but it's gonna be a great movie, a *big* movie. They take longer to make decisions, don't they? Come on, Trent, you know they do.'

'I got a "no" phone call after thirty-six minutes once.'

'But that was a "no". No news is good news. It has to be.' That's what he wanted to believe. And it was what was keeping him going. The chance at another part he really wanted. That hadn't come along since he'd left *Manhattan*

Med, if he was really honest. And it would be something to work towards that wasn't the messed-up madness of his family life.

'OK,' Trent said, speaking through a mouthful of bagel. 'I'll tell you what I'll do. You get prepared for The Hoff audition and you get me the details of the director and producer of *A Soul's Song*.'

'Are you gonna call them?' Seth asked, interest significantly piqued.

Trent waved a hand. 'That's old school. These days the best business is done on the fly, which is why I didn't make the party last night.' He bit into another bagel. 'I would say sorry, but an evening eating Vietnamese with the casting director for *Knight to Bay – The David Hasselhoff Story* should not require an apology.'

'Thanks, Trent,' Seth replied, meaning it.

'So, how did it go with laraweekend? I see social media has called her Lemur Girl. It couldn't have gone better ... well, unless they had started calling you Lemur *Boy*, but frankly I'm glad they didn't. It's not quite as cool as *Deadpool*.'

Seth had completely forgotten how mad he had been with Trent for creating this social-media incident with Lara. He had enjoyed himself so much last night and that had mainly been down to her company. He swallowed, not really knowing what sort of emotion was going to come out.

'You should have told me about her the second you saw the tweet.'

'And what would you have said?' Trent asked him. 'No, you don't have to tell me. Because I know you would have just ignored it. If you had even seen it at all. And poor laraweekend would be here in New York, alone and heartbroken, when Dr Mike could be soothing her troubled soul.'

Seth shook his head. 'I know what you're doing and I'm having no part of it. She's nice. I'm not gonna use her for publicity.'

'Er, hang on a second, bud. I think it's *her* trying to use *you*, unless her plan's changed.'

Trent had a point. But it hadn't felt like that at the party. Having spent the evening with Lara – who he was never going to refer to as @laraweekend – he didn't see her as the publicity-seeking kind. He believed this was a genuine case of her wanting to show her boyfriend she was strong, whether she really felt it or not. And Seth was just the prop she had plumped for, somewhere in between Ed Sheeran and Tom Hardy.

'Come on, Seth, what happened at the zoo was as golden as it gets! It won't hurt to hang out with her for a couple of hours and tweet a few photos. Lemur Girl and the new Stand for Wildlife campaigner. Tag the zoo – are there animals in the film you want? If there are then tag Universal. Keeping in the public eye with feel-good PR is the way to go, and there's nothing more feel-good than animals and almost-doctors treating broken hearts. And it's getting closer to Christmas every day, man! All those Hallmark movie feels ... that reminds me, we should send your reel out to them ready for 2019.'

Should he tell Trent he was meeting Lara this afternoon? He didn't see why. Any photo-taking they were going to do together was most definitely going to be on *her* terms. He didn't care for maintaining his actor brand with anything that wasn't authentic. There were limits. He wasn't sure Trent knew this, but his friend *was* under *his* employ. Seth was the boss. He needed to be better at remembering that.

'When's the fast-track audition for The Hoff?' Seth asked, swerving the conversation.

'This afternoon. Two. I'll message you the details.'

His heart sank. It was right when he was supposed to be meeting Lara at the Empire State Building.

'Get down the gym,' Trent stated. 'Focus on your core. I don't know what they're gonna make you do, and I know you can't grow a chest thatch in a couple of hours, but let's give it our best shot, yeah?'

Twenty-One

Macy's, W 34th Street

'Look at that!' Susie's voice was rich with enthusiasm. Lara suspected that if her friend breathed out in too much of a rush she would cover the street in glitter, such was her sparkling joy.

Macy's was the tallest, brightest, shiniest shop Lara had ever seen – in reality or on the internet. It shot up from pavement to sky in one extraordinary extravaganza of colour that looked pretty impressive now in the afternoon but would surely appear twice as glorious at night. There were huge green, red and gold Christmas wreaths at every second window, the other windows curtained in red with gold flashing stars at their centre. It was like every girl's fantasy doll's house ... but super-sized.

'What do they sell here?' Lara asked, her neck aching from gazing up at the frontage.

'Lara!' Susie exclaimed, her mouth gaping, her look saying that knowing the answer to this question should be as common knowledge as the dance moves to cha cha slide.

'What? You know I'm not exactly a shopper.' She smiled. 'Do they sell rock band T-shirts?'

'Macy's is a department store. The biggest store in the world,' Lara said. 'They sell pretty much everything I'm interested in.'

'Shoes?' Lara asked, trying desperately not to wince.

'Handbags too, and jewellery, and men's things. I need to get David a Christmas gift.'

Christmas was ever present here in New York, from the sparkling decorations adorning every building to pavements with choirs clinging to the snowy kerbs treating the constantly bustling city to renditions of 'Twelve Days of Christmas' and Mariah Carey classics. Lara usually loved Christmas, and had a festive agenda, starting with dipping into the After Eight mints followed by pâté on toast every day for breakfast from around the fourteenth. But here she felt completely removed from Appleshaw and everything that had gone before this break – the Dan one and the aeroplane one – and feeling so detached from the galloping on of December was another hangover of that. She would be back before Christmas Day. She had to think what to get her dad and Aldo for a gift. She wasn't sure there would be anything for either of them in Macy's.

'I was thinking of something leather,' Susie remarked as they headed towards the entrance.

'Macy's even has one of "those" sections?' Lara answered.

'A bag,' Susie elaborated. 'Nice, leather, professional. He can keep his scissors, combs and brushes in it. Maybe I could even get it monogrammed. What do you think?'

'I think, after your PDAing this morning, he would probably prefer the leather thing *I* was thinking of.'

'We haven't seen each other for six months,' Susie reminded her. 'There was a lot of catching up that needed to be done.'

She couldn't deny that David's affection for Susie was nice. Except it was hard not to feel a little bit envious because Dan had never draped himself all over her like he never wanted to let go. Who knew who he was draping himself all over right now? Perhaps, instead of looking for Christmas gifts for her dad and Aldo, she ought to have a look at Facebook. Mrs Fitch always said forewarned was forearmed – or something like that. If she was about to start posting photos of her and Seth Hunt she should see what Dan was posting, purely to get an idea of any impact that might occur after *she* posted. Would he engage with a picture of him out and about, enjoying his new single-for-the-holidays status? Or would he retreat and not post anything? Would he press like? Would he angry-face? No, angry-facing wasn't Dan's style and he didn't really have anything to be angry about seeing as *he* had made this situation.

'Are you coming?' Susie asked, standing over the large star dominating the doorway.

'If Macy's has everything, am I going to be able to find something for Aldo in here?' Lara enquired, catching up.

'God, Lara, I said *everything*, but they don't sell miracles.'

'That's not even a little bit funny.'

'Come on,' Susie urged. 'Maybe we'll find something else for you to wear when we meet up with Seth.'

'It's not a date, it's a photo opportunity.'

'I know. But wouldn't it be nice for Dan to see you wearing something he hasn't seen you in before?' She reached out, past Lara's partly zipped-up jacket to the top beneath. 'One without a stain from the Emperor of India on it.'

'It's one of my favourite tops,' Lara protested. 'And what do they put in curry these days that *makes* marks like that?'

'It's probably best not to think about it,' Susie said. 'But come on, we've only got a couple of hours!'

The inside of Macy's was just as spectacular as the outside. It was like stepping into one never-ending Santa's grotto that rolled from floor to floor, seamless in its twinkling, sparkling display. There were real Christmas trees – smelling so fresh and piney – making it like being in the middle of a deep, dark, festive forest. And there were crystals on everything – suspended from the ceiling, rising up from the ground like stalagmites, fastened to mannequins possibly as an accessory suggestion – creating an ambience of *Frozen* meets disco ball. Susie was in her element, dancing through the aisles, fingers fondly fondling everything in her path.

'You need a bag! Look at this one! This is so on trend this season. It's a muted tangerine – perfect for Christmas – and it's a classic hobo with a professional edge.' Susie whipped the bag from the rail and pressed it to Lara's jacket.

'When would I need this?' Lara edged away from the bag as if it contained novichok. 'I drive a lorry.'

'And that comment just proves how much you're limiting your life thinking like … like …'

'A lorry driver?' Lara suggested.

'Just hold it.' Susie inched the handbag a little nearer. 'Feel it between your fingers and imagine it helping you to carry all your necessary items around each day.'

Lara eyed the bag that could possibly fit in a whole week's worth of clothing … for a family of four. She carried her phone, her keys, her debit card and maybe a bit of cash. There was no justification for a satchel that could help someone move house. Susie's eyes were shining with admiration, fingers curling around the bag's handles.

'I get it,' Lara said, smiling. '*You* want to buy the bag.'

'No,' Susie said quickly. 'No, I think it would be perfect for you.'

'Why don't you buy it?'

'Because I don't need another bag … and it's perfect for you.'

'Well, I don't need it either and I don't want it.' Her eyes went to a section of sunglasses. Weren't designer ones supposed to be a lot cheaper here than they were in the UK? Aldo kept losing his and, even in the middle of winter with the sun low, you needed them most days when you were driving a truck. It could make a nice Christmas present.

'You should treat yourself,' Susie said, trailing after Lara as she moved away from bags to Ray-Bans.

'I am,' Lara replied. 'I scrabbled together enough cash to be able to eat three meals a day while we're here.'

'I meant buy yourself something nice.'

'I will,' Lara answered. 'Pizza, as soon as we can. Can we not spend too long shopping? Do they have a food court here?'

'They have everything here!'

'Even something for Aldo!' Lara picked up some sunglasses and tried them on. She smiled at her reflection. 'See, miracles do happen.'

'Please look at Facebook,' Susie said suddenly.

'What?' Lara exclaimed.

'I know you haven't because you haven't been active on there for *hours* and I need you to be active on there for thirty seconds, so I don't have to keep not saying anything since I saw it this morning.'

'Saw what?' Lara asked, swallowing.

'Please, Lara, please look at it and then we can discuss it.' Susie dropped the handbag to the ground. 'And *I'll* buy the pizza.'

Her phone felt like a big, fat elephant in the pocket of her jeans. She knew she should look. She had talked herself into looking before she met up with Seth. But now the looking issue was being forced, it felt difficult. Plus, there was obviously something on social media that was going to adversely affect her ability to function if Susie was ready to buy pizza, and that meant it could only be to do with Dan.

'I think he's a shit, by the way. A complete shit who doesn't deserve you doing everything you can to make this relationship work.'

Lara drew out her phone and pressed the blue 'F' icon. She had Dan set to 'see first' so whatever was griping Susie was going to be quickly revealed ...

Dan Reeves: Christmas shopping ☺

There wasn't much going on with that info update, but then Lara noticed the check-in location and that someone was tagged in the post. Her heart fell, as if it had just slipped off an escalator and someone was kicking it down to ground level.

'He's at the Salisbury Christmas Market.' Lara had to force the words out. 'With Chloe.'

Susie threw her arms around her, holding her as tightly as if Lara had been out overnight in Icelandic conditions and she was trying to stop her from developing hypothermia. 'I know, I know. It's horrible and cruel and I can't believe he's done it so publicly. I mean, first a single status and now flaunting another woman.'

'We always go to the Salisbury Christmas Market together,' Lara stuttered. 'He always has mulled wine and I always have German sausage.' They wrapped up in almost every layer they owned and would spend the afternoon visiting each and every one of the little wooden chalets that speckled the city's market square. There were bands in a small rotunda, the scent of winter spices in the air and handmade pleasures you couldn't buy anywhere else. It was always full of smiling faces, crowds joining in with Christmas songs and that feel-good run-up-to-the-big-day vibe.

'I know,' Susie said again.

Upset was quickly turning into something else. Anger. Annoyance. With Dan and with herself. What was she doing, close to tears in New York, when he was swanning around Salisbury, festive shopping with the village femme fatale?

'How dare he do that!' Lara blasted. 'How dare he!'

'This is good,' Susie said as Lara wrenched herself from her embrace, flapping her arms in the air and almost getting tangled up in pearlescent baubles. 'Perhaps it's time to get angry.'

'He said it was just a break!' Lara exclaimed.

'I know!'

'He said it was just a time-out and now this!'

'I know!'

'Well, I can't stand by and take it, can I? I mean, honouring this break was one thing, but letting him have this mini-split so he can work through how he felt and what he wanted, should not involve him calling himself single on Facebook or going Christmas shopping with another woman, should it?'

'Absolutely not!'

'Right then!' Lara exclaimed, with as much panache as if she were Emma Willis announcing the next *The Voice* contestant.

'Right then!' Susie repeated with as much vigour.

'I'm ... going to buy something!' Lara declared. 'Something I wouldn't normally buy.'

Susie grinned in pure delight, retrieved the designer handbag from the floor and presented it like she was centre stage on *QVC*. '*Voila!*'

'No,' Lara said, eyes sweeping around Macy's, trying to pick out anything and everything all at once. 'I need ...'

'Shoes? I saw some beautiful boots with a wedge heel in a mink colour? Or maybe a coat. It's set to get colder here and that jacket of yours has seen better days and—'

Then a thought suddenly struck Lara, and she looked directly at her friend. 'Take me to the scarf section.'

'Ooo yes,' Susie said, pushing the handbag back onto the first available shelf and clapping her hands together. 'Something in hot pink or cranberry-red for the festive season. I saw a beautiful one, in foulard, so probably not expensive. This way!'

Twenty-Two

The Empire State Building

As the snow began to fall from the sky of pure white clouds above New York, Lara looked into her Macy's shopping bag, regarding her purchases like a proud mother hen admiring her clutch of newborn chicks. She was now the happy owner of a dozen scarves in an array of colours. She had let Susie go wild, plucking from a golden Christmas tree display a dozen woollen hats in every shade you could imagine. There were also sunglasses for Aldo's Christmas present and a set of sterling silver golf tees for her dad her credit card had winced at.

'Put one of the scarves on.' Susie bobbed up and down to keep warm. 'The bright yellow one. It's going to really pop on Instagram.'

'What's the time?' Lara asked.

'Nearly two o'clock,' Susie said. 'He'll be here soon.'

Lara looked at her watch. It wasn't nearly two o' clock, it was nearly ten past. Seth wasn't coming. She took a deep breath, then turned around and looked up at the magnificent building they were standing beneath.

It was one hundred and two storeys high and built of concrete, limestone and granite with a steel frame — she had looked up the details on her phone earlier. And those one hundred and two storeys stood one thousand four hundred and fifty-four feet, going up in tiered stacks, to the tip of its lightning conductor. Looking at it now, the point of its peak seeming to touch the clouds, she couldn't imagine being at the top if it *did* get struck by lightning. The images Google had pulled up of the inside of the structure were nothing short of opulent. She was expecting all kinds of grandeur she hadn't ever seen in Appleshaw, where the grandest thing in town was the tea set Mrs Fitch got out for pensioners' scone afternoons at the garden centre.

'We should go in,' Lara said, eyes going from skyscraper to Susie.

'What? But we're waiting for Seth, aren't we? Didn't he say right outside? Here? Where we're standing?'

'He did. But he's probably had to go somewhere else.'

'Maybe he messaged you. Have you checked your Twitter?'

'No, but—'

'Check it!'

'Let's just go in.'

Susie put her hands on her hips and looked all arse-kicky. 'I am not moving from this spot until you've checked for a message.'

Seth was late, and he had glue on his chest that was making his shirt stick to his body. Every time he broke into a jog it was ripping at his skin. Why the casting director had needed to see all the auditionees with a chest wig on as they read the lines, he didn't know. He was quite certain he didn't want the part, despite the niggling reminder that he had rent to pay in one of the most expensive areas of the city. He checked his watch again. Almost quarter past two. He hated being late and Lara was going to think he wasn't coming.

He quickened his pace as much as he could, but the streets were packed with tourists walking slowly and photographing everything, more hot dog vendors per square metre than was necessary, fire hydrants he seemed to have to swerve for every few metres, plus a layer of snow on the sidewalk hampering his progress, with more falling from the sky.

His mom had called just before the fake hair was pressed to his chest. He couldn't answer while he was being glued to death, so he had let it go. He'd listened to her voicemail before he descended into the subway, which had been full of apologies about the previous evening, as well as the news that Kossy had found a photo of his mother. That information had knotted his insides. He was about to see what his birth mother looked like. Was she going to resemble him? Would he gaze into the photo and feel some sort of connection? He texted back, saying he would drop into the shelter. And he would. After he had gotten over feeling scared to death about this whole scenario.

Thirty-fourth Street. He was here. He rushed towards the entrance of the Empire State, hoping that Lara was still there. Despite this odd set-up – Twitter, a lemur up a tree, drinking beer in broken chairs – he felt a strange thrill about showing this British girl the sights of his city. She had never been to the US; she had never been out of the UK. And here she was in this metropolis for her first overseas trip. NYC wasn't perfect by any means, but it was, in his opinion, one of the coolest places to be on the planet. And he was interested to know if she would feel that way too. He liked her. He hadn't taken to someone as easily or as quickly in … possibly forever.

He heard Lara's voice. 'No message. Direct or otherwise. Can we go in now? Before my pizza-high wears off?'

Seth smiled as he approached the two women. Susie noticed him straight away and he waved a hand.

'Lara,' Susie said.

'What? You want me to check my Snapchat now? He doesn't have my Snapchat ... or my Facebook, or my mobile number or—'

'Hey,' Seth said, stepping into Lara's line of vision.

Lara slipped back into the path of a boy on a scooter and the boy skidded, sliding towards a lamppost. Seth reached out quickly, getting a hold of the boy's coat and straightening him up before he toppled. 'You OK?' he asked the tween.

'Yeah,' the boy replied, with the almost-teenage attitude that Seth had possessed at that age, before scooting off with the line of pedestrian traffic again.

'Are *you* OK?' Seth asked, turning his attention back to Lara who was stamping her boots to the concrete as if to remove stubborn balance-altering snow.

'Yeah,' Lara said, quickly, her cheeks pinking up a little. 'It's slippery around here with the ... snow and everything.'

Seth nodded, smiling. 'That's New York in winter.' He clapped his gloved hands together. 'I'm real sorry I'm late. I was being David Hasselhoff.'

'Really!' Susie's eyes lit up.

'I echo the really,' Lara said.

'Really,' Seth said. 'I swear to God. I have body glue stuck to my chest and everything.'

'Oh my!' Susie said. 'Can we see?'

'Susie!' Lara exclaimed.

Seth laughed. 'I can't say I'd recommend it. I didn't quite make the gym this morning despite Trent's orders, so I'm a little out of shape.'

'Oh, I doubt you're as out of shape as half the population of where we live,' Susie stated. 'The only decent pecs in Appleshaw belong to the chickens.'

'It's more *Countryfile* than fitness,' Lara answered. 'Um, *Countryfile* is a TV show about ... the countryside.'

'It sounds nice,' Seth said. 'There's not a whole lot of green around here. Apart from the parks. Which we'll have a great view of from up there.' He pointed a finger skywards. 'Shall we go in? Get outta the cold?'

'Yes!' Susie agreed quickly. 'But first we need a photo, don't we? You and Lara outside the entrance of one of the Big Apple's landmarks.'

'Sure,' Seth said, looking to Lara. Susie had given her a shove and she was suddenly propelled next to him looking a little awkward. 'You OK?' he asked her.

She nodded, giving him a small smile. 'She took me shopping in Macy's. I made her buy pizza to help me over the trauma.'

'Look this way!' Susie shuffled backwards like she was trying to create space in the ever-flowing sea of New York's walking population – no easy task.

'Your friend seems happy today,' Seth remarked, his eyes on Susie's camera phone.

'She spent the whole night getting no sleep with her boyfriend.'

'Oh,' Seth said. 'Totally got the vibe now.'

Lara laughed. 'TMI? As they all seem to say on Twitter.'

'No, I think you explained it perfectly.'

'Can you get a little closer?' Susie shouted above the honking of New York cabs. 'You know, perhaps seem like you're standing in the same block? Otherwise it's going to look like a desperate fan photo and that's not the look we're going for at all.'

Seth moved in tight to Lara, putting his arm around her shoulders. He felt her flinch a little.

'I'm really sorry about her,' Lara said. 'About this. If you want to turn around and run down the street then ...'

'Hey, if I start running anywhere, this glue is gonna be pulling out every fibre of my shirt.' He hugged her into him. 'It's gonna be fun. The Empire State is so cool. I want to show it to you.' He smiled at Susie, camera-ready. 'Call it a thank you for Saving Primate Jax.'

He watched her smile then and loosen up a little.

'He *was* a beast,' Lara replied.

'If I wasn't now part of Stand for Wildlife I would probably never feel the need to look at another lemur again.'

'Don't look at the arse again,' Lara replied. 'I think he fogged me. I can't seem to get the smell of animal out of my hair.'

Seth laughed out loud, then winced as the movement of his chest made glue stick to material again.

'That's perfect!' Susie exclaimed, hopping up and down. 'Perfect!'

Twenty-Three

'Wow!' Lara exclaimed, bursting through the doors and down the ramp towards the fenced outer edge on the eighty-sixth floor.

'Lara, hang on,' Seth called, rushing after her.

'You won't be able to stop her,' Susie said. 'One thing she's definitely not afraid of is heights. You think the tree in the zoo was impressive? She's a regular roof scaler if something needs rescuing from the farm next door.'

'I can hear you, you know!' Lara called out. She sucked in the cold air as it buffeted her face. It was windy, and the wild force was steeped with icy snowflakes. The inside of the Empire State had been everything she had hoped for. It was wall-to-wall art deco luxury with a touch of Christmas. From the spectacular lobby with its sparkling twin Christmas trees to the almost chocolate marble-and-gold coloured walls, each level gave itself over to near-majesty and told the tale of its concept right through the construction to completion – with a little dash of movie moments – *King Kong* had been Lara's favourite. But it was *this* that she had wanted to see the most. The scene from here, the outside view. Not the very top – where it was enclosed – but the expanse of city from this vantage point with the winter weather circling around her. And it was breathtaking.

Lara dropped the Macy's bag to the ground and wrapped her fingers around the metalwork, pressing her face into the gap, wanting to get as close to the view as she could. Here you could see everything. Other skyscrapers that looked so monumental from the ground were now dwarfed by the Empire State's stature. Steam was mingling with the winter weather and there were small squares of snow-dappled green in between the slender heights of steel and glass. It was so far removed from Appleshaw. It was busy and vibrant and buzzing with energy, and Lara felt completely alive in the midst of it.

'Susie,' she called, not taking her eyes off all that was in front of her. 'You have to come and see this.'

'Oh no.' Susie's voice told Lara she was a least a few metres away. 'I can see fine from back here. It's beautiful. Lots of buildings.'

'Come on, Susie! You can't see anything from back there! You have to come closer!' Lara finally turned to find her friend, Susie's eyes apparently fixed on the iPhone in her hand. 'What are you doing?! There's this amazing view of New York and you're—'

'Googling medication I can take for vertigo.'

'You don't have vertigo!' Lara said. 'Vertigo isn't really a fear of heights, you know, it's an inner ear imbalance.'

'It will be more than my inner ear that's imbalanced if I go anywhere the edge,' Susie replied. 'I'm going to go and get coffee. Do you want one?'

'Not really,' Lara answered. 'I want to rip down this fence and get a better look at the Hudson River.'

'Seth? Coffee?'

'No, I'm good,' Seth replied.

'You're not scared of heights, are you?' Lara asked as Seth arrived next to her.

'Lara,' he said. 'I thought you were a real *Manhattan Med* fan. Don't you remember the scene on the roof of the hospital? When I stopped grouchy Dr Crowther from spiralling to his certain doom?'

'Of course I remember it. I just assumed you'd had a double for that scene.'

'What?' Seth put a hand to his chest like she had delivered a heart-stopping blow. 'So while I was scaling dizzy heights, you thought I had a stunt double? I'm appalled.'

'Actually, I thought it was a fake rooftop. Something about the skyline didn't look quite right.'

Seth nudged her arm with his elbow. 'OK, I confess.'

'Fake rooftop?' Lara asked.

'Fake rooftop. But I'm not afraid of heights. I also wanna move the fence and breathe in the city.'

Lara watched him close his eyes for a second, taking a lungful of the snowy air before opening them up again and looking out at the scene falling away below them.

'So how does it feel?' Seth asked. 'Your first trip to America. Your first trip anywhere.'

'It feels ...' Lara began. How *did* it feel? Scary? Thrilling? There was a whole mixture of feelings currently going on inside her and all of them were unprecedented. How did you choose words to describe that? 'How did *you* feel the first time you came up here?'

'Well, I'm told the very first time I came up here I was one and I sat inside one of those baby backpack things. My dad walked the eighty-six flights up here and I barfed in his hair.'

'No!' Lara exclaimed, putting a hand over her mouth.

'The first time I *remember* coming up here I was seven and I had to do an art project for school. I carried this giant notepad and coloured pencils up here and it rained for about an hour.'

'So, you couldn't draw anything?' Lara guessed.

'No,' Seth said. 'I was kind of a determined kid. I watched the rain and I drew and I realised it was a waste of time bringing up those coloured pencils. I sketched the city in different shades of grey and I got the best mark of my whole class.'

'Show off,' Lara said with a laugh, eyes going back to the view, snow dashing past her vision.

'And now are you gonna tell me how it feels to be up this high, in a foreign country with the snow hitting your cheeks?'

It should have felt completely alien. Being here was so far out of her comfort zone. But instead she felt both deeply content and stimulated beyond belief. This was New York City and she, Lara Weeks, truck driver from Appleshaw, was bang smack in the centre of it.

'I feel like I'm ... not standing still,' Lara began, eyes roving over the cityscape. 'Like I'm flying, or paragliding or freefalling or something.' She took a breath. 'Like I'm floating over everything, but not in a frightening way, like I might crash to my death at any minute, in a kind of totally in control way.' She smiled out into the city. 'I want to shout at the top of my voice. I want to say, "Hey, New York! I'm here! And ... I want to be a part of it!"' She laughed out loud. 'And everyone would think I'm a crazy girl from England and they'd look into their coffees and wish me away.'

Seth swallowed, unable to take his eyes from her. She was beautiful to watch. There was an energy coming from her that he'd never seen in anyone before. She was coming to life right before him, completely uninhibited, free, sucking up NYC like it was the most glorious place she'd ever been.

'Do you think I'm crazy?' Lara asked, turning to look at him.

'No,' he said. 'I wish everyone who came up here really looked at things the way you do.' He took a breath. 'And I think we should shout.'

'What?'

'I think we should do it, just like you said.' He grinned at her. 'We should shout out, "Hey, New York! I'm here! And I want to be a part of it!"'

Lara laughed. 'Now I think *you're* crazy.'

'It was your idea.' He nudged her arm with his.

'I know but I said I *wanted* to do it. I didn't say I was *going* to do it.'

'Why wouldn't you? If you want to then you should,' he told her. '*We* should.'

'But ...'

'What's holding you back?'

'Everything my dad told me about being seen and not heard.'

'And have you always done what your parents have told you?'

'Paren*t*,' Lara corrected.

'Your mom passed away?' Seth asked softly.

'No,' Lara said, shaking her head. 'She left. Probably because I did too much of the "being heard" part.'

'I don't believe that.'

'My dad says I used to sing the instrumental parts to songs at the social club and it drove everyone crazy.' She sighed. 'Who knew nobody likes a lip-saxophone solo.'

Seth lowered his voice. 'Well, all those people are thousands of miles away now.'

She smiled at him. 'That's true.'

'OK then,' Seth said. 'Let's shout it out together. Let's hold onto the fence and speak to the Big Apple.'

He watched her put her fingers around the metal of the barricade and take a steadying breath, hair buffeting around her cheeks.

'After three,' Seth said. 'One ... two ... three!'

They shouted in unison. 'Hey, New York! I'm here! And I want to be a part of it!'

She laughed, looking at him with wide, excited eyes, her hot breath expelling into the cold air, snowflakes in her dark crop of hair. He smiled. 'That felt pretty good to me.'

'Me too,' she answered. 'Really good.' She looked over her shoulder, to the other tourists taking in the sights. 'And no one's called the NYPD yet.'

'No,' he replied. His heart was doing something a little out there as he looked at her. Could it be that the chest wig glue had seeped through his skin and was causing a cardiac event? His thoughts and feelings were rushing through his veins like they desperately needed to come out. Why now? Why here? With Lemur Girl?

'I'm adopted,' Seth found himself saying.

'Oh! Wow! I didn't know that,' Lara responded immediately. 'Did *you* know that?'

'Yes ... I mean, my parents – Kossy and Ted – they told me when I was twelve and I was cool with it. Kind of cool with it. After I'd gotten into the idea. But after I auditioned for this part, I found I wanted to know more.'

'And do you?' Lara asked, looking at him with an intrigued expression. 'Do you know more? Are you going to find out who your real parents are? Do you already know? Are you going to meet them?'

'I ... don't know.' He still didn't.

'Oh.'

'I'm not sure how much I want to know. I'm a little apprehensive.'

'Scared, you mean?'

'Maybe,' he admitted.

'What of? Not looking for them isn't going to change who they are. It's just going to stop *you* knowing who they are.'

She made it sound so simple. The clarity she brought to things was totally refreshing. No one talked straight in his world, not agents or casting directors, definitely not Trent, and, it seemed, neither did his mom.

'My mom, Kossy, she found a photo of my birth mom at the shelter.'

'Well, what are we waiting for?' Lara asked, stepping away from the vista. '*I* want to see what she looks like, so you must be bursting to!'

'Yeah,' Seth admitted. 'I am.'

'Well, let's go,' Lara ordered. 'Plus, this bag right here is full of scarves and hats. Susie thinks they're all for me but there's something for everyone I met last night. The orange is going to look so great on Earl and there's this turquoise one I got for Felice and one with sparkly bits for Mad Maggie.'

Seth shook his head. 'You bought everyone a gift?'

'I know they hate charity … but I'll tell them it was to stop Susie from making me buy a handbag I didn't need, which it was.'

'Are you sure you're done with the view?' Seth asked her.

'Done for now,' Lara admitted, taking one last lingering look. 'I want to get back down into the heart of it.' She grinned. 'And be a part of it, remember?'

'You're going to regret not having coffee!' Susie called, as she walked over to join them, large paper coffee cup warming her fingers as the snow fell around her. 'This one has chocolate pieces and caramel.' She stopped short of the fence and its view. 'I'll drink it from here.'

'We're going down now,' Lara told her. 'Seth is going to take you to meet some of the people I met last night.'

'Oh really?' Susie said.

'You didn't really think I bought all these scarves and hats for me, did you?'

Twenty-Four

The Chapel Shelter, W 40th Street

The shelter was an old church. Lara hadn't been expecting that. She didn't know quite what she *had* been expecting but it wasn't the large, slightly tired, ecclesiastical-looking building they had entered, leaving the snowy streets behind. Inside was pure upheaval. There were Christmas decorations being fixed up around the main part of the room – people on stepladders tussling with tinsel and strings of stars – another group painting at easels while an instructor issued directions and there were three men lying, seemingly asleep, on crash mats in one corner. Lara swallowed, a little overwhelmed by the scene. She was half glad that Susie had turned down the shelter visit to hook up with David instead. This place was no Macy's.

'You OK?' Seth asked.

'Yeah, of course,' Lara answered. 'It's … thriving.'

Seth laughed, leading her purposefully past the chaos of decorating and would-be artists. 'This is quiet,' he replied. 'It's the evenings when it really picks up. People come in for the bed ballot.'

'The bed ballot?' Lara queried.

'This is one of the larger centres in this area, but there's still not enough beds for the number of people who need them.' He sighed. 'Names go in a hat, people drawn out get a bed.'

'That's … no fun.' She didn't really know what to say.

'Yeah, it still gets to my mom every single day.'

'Remember, everybody,' the instructor at the head of the room announced. 'I'm not looking for just a tree. I am looking for the tree's true essence!'

Lara looked at the easels as she walked by. She wasn't sure where she would begin in drawing the essence of a tree. Most had drawn Christmas trees with bright baubles and stars at their top, one woman had drawn a dancing hot dog, while a man no taller than three feet had sketched a frighteningly good caricature of Hillary Clinton.

'Want to join the art class?' Seth asked her.

Lara shook her head. 'We don't all have skills with pencils.'

'Come on,' he urged. 'Let's take Mom the scarves. She'll know where everyone is.'

Seth led her through a door at the end of the hall and down a corridor into another space that looked like a canteen. There were people eating at long wooden tables, still dressed in their coats and hats, most shivering, noses dripping, coughing in between mouthfuls of what smelled like chicken soup. Behind a wire mesh with a padlocked door was a kitchen area, two people in hats and plastic gloves tending to giant pots on the stove. Then, passing across that room, they went along another corridor, finally reaching a bright red door. Seth knocked before opening it.

'Hey, Mom.'

'What are you doing here already?' Kossy leapt up from her desk, knocking over a stack of paperwork, of which there was plenty. The whole room looked like one big filing tray with piles of papers on every surface.

'I—' Seth began.

'I told you to text me when you were coming. I bet they haven't finished the Christmas decorations, have they? I bet the essence of tree pictures aren't done either. And it's … wow, almost four p.m. I don't know where the day's gone. Do *you* know where the day's gone?' Kossy finally stopped talking just as she got out and around from her desk. She exclaimed, hands going to her mouth. 'Lara!'

'Hello, Mrs Hunt.'

'Kossy. Just Kossy, honey, I don't want to appear older than I already feel. Everyone calls me Kossy, don't they, Seth?'

'Except me,' he admitted.

'Yes, well, that's different and I'm not sure I'm deserving of the mom mantle right now …' Kossy stopped talking a little abruptly and Lara watched a look pass between mother and son.

'It's OK, Mom,' Seth said. 'I told Lara about … Candice.'

'You did?'

'We went to the Empire State Building,' Lara said. 'And howled at the city.'

'Well, everybody needs a good howl every now and then. Especially when you have three staff off sick and more guests than ever.' She made it sound like she was in charge of a luxury hotel.

Lara held up her Macy's bag of goodies. 'I bought some stuff. Something for Earl and Felice and Maggie and anyone else who needs it.'

'You did?' Kossy said, stepping nearer to Lara. 'From Macy's!'

'Well, it's a long story, but it's a credit card purchase I had to make for so many reasons.'

'OK, then,' Kossy said. 'Let's get you two some coffee and we'll see who's around. Just so you know, we never see Earl before dark. He plays a ukulele for change in Lower East Side. And Felice has a new boyfriend.' Kossy raised her eyes. 'I'm not sure he's the best influence, but I'm not her mom so ...'

'Did you say coffee?' Seth asked.

'Without caramel and chocolate bits, if I could,' Lara said.

'Honey, the only time you'll get caramel and chocolate bits in here is unintentionally ... probably outta someone's beard.'

'Great,' she answered. 'Thanks. Not a fan of extra toppings of any sort, unless it's pizza then anything goes.'

'Atta girl. You can come over again,' Kossy replied, putting her arm around Lara's shoulders.

Twenty-Five

Seth couldn't quite believe he was looking at the woman who had given birth to him. Sitting in the main room while someone gave a class on contraception, he held the old photo a little closer. He really did need to go back to wearing his glasses. The dark-haired woman in the picture seemed so young, so not ready for motherhood, which of course she hadn't been. He ran a finger over her dark hair. She was standing alongside three other people, two other women and a man, who were smiling at the camera with their lips *and* their eyes. If he hadn't known this photo was taken at a shelter he would have thought they were just young people getting ready for a night out. Candice's clothes weren't shabby or worn. She was wearing a maroon velvet dress and high stiletto shoes. The outfit of her trade, he guessed. He swallowed.

'You OK?' Kossy sat down into the seat next to him.

'Yeah,' he answered quickly. He wasn't, not really. He was as mixed up as a person could be. His whole existence up in the air and unknown.

'I couldn't believe it when Bernadette found this photo almost straight off. You know the state of things around here. So much paper. Not enough time.' Kossy looked at the picture herself, taking a deep breath in. 'She was pretty, don't you think?'

He didn't know what he thought. It was so hard, looking at this young woman knowing that she was his mother. He knew she would be older now, perhaps looking more mom-like, but here, back in time, she was so much younger than him, a teenager. It felt odd knowing that sometime, maybe only a few months from when this photograph was taken, she had had a baby. Him. And, maybe someone else too ...

'She has dark hair.' Was that all he could muster up to say?

'Yeah,' Kossy answered. 'And your eyes.'

This felt so difficult, he was uneasy. Why was he uneasy? This was what he had decided he wanted. But seeing her image made it all the more real. She was a person now, not just a name ... and she apparently had his eyes.

'I don't know what to say.'

'I know.' Kossy took his hand. 'If it helps, and I'm sure it doesn't, I don't know what to say either.' She paused. 'Particularly after last night ...'

'Do you really think there could have been another baby?' Seth said bluntly. He raised his head from the photo to look at his mom.

'I don't know.' Kossy's voice wavered a little. 'After she ran off, after I realised the other hat was there, I checked the garbage, the alleyways either side of here and there was nothing. I called child protection services. I did all the right things, Seth, I promise you.'

'I know you did.' Seth never had any doubt of that. His mom did the right thing. She always had. 'You think, if there was another baby, that she took it with her?'

'No,' Kossy said immediately, but he caught her swallow. 'No, I don't think that.'

'But it's possible. I mean, maybe it wasn't that she couldn't cope with a baby. Maybe it was she couldn't cope with two babies.'

'Seth ...'

'No, it's OK. I mean ... I don't know anything about her. *You* don't know that much about her either. We're hanging on guesswork and maybes.' And that would always be the case unless he did something about it.

'So, what happens next?' Kossy sounded almost scared of how he would answer.

'I don't know,' he admitted, sighing. 'I'm still kinda processing.'

'OK,' Kossy said. 'But, Seth, you know, I'm here for you. Whatever you need.'

'I know,' Seth answered. He put the photo down on the table.

'And I see Lara is too.' Kossy nodded to the other side of the room where Lara was chatting to Felice. The homeless girl was toying with a turquoise woollen beanie. 'What's happening there?'

'We are ...' Seth started. How did he begin to explain it to his mom? 'She is ... that is ... I'm showing her a little of the city while she's over here from England ... her and her friend Susie, who was with us but had a date with her guy so ...'

'OK,' Kossy said, her eyebrows raising. She got to her feet. 'Take her to Bryant Park.'

'The Christmas market?'

'It's a shopper's paradise and there's the ice skating. It's the true New York at Christmas.'

At that second, his phone vibrated, and he quickly drew it out of the pocket of his pants. It was a message from Trent.

You should be loving me right now. The casting director for *A Soul's Song* has a dinner reservation at Cafe Cluny tonight at eight. Do not ask how I know this. I can't

come with you I have filming for the nuts ad involving
a gorilla. If you want this ... make it happen!

'Bad news?' Kossy asked.

'No,' Seth said at once. 'It could be good news.' If he
managed to down a shot of bravery.

'Take the photo,' Kossy said, pushing it towards him. 'And
I'll do my best this afternoon to find any other information
we hold in the shelter.' She nodded, like she was finally, truly
accepting the situation.

'Thanks, Mom.'

'So, this hat,' Felice said, inspecting it with her fingers, almost
as if she didn't believe it was real. 'Is this because you're rich
and I have nothing?'

'Oh, Felice, get over yourself,' Lara said with a laugh. 'I'm
not rich and I hear you've got a boyfriend.' That was more
than *she* had right now. Her boyfriend, if he was still her
boyfriend, was festive shopping with someone who ate men
for breakfast and probably brunch too ...

'He plays guitar,' Felice said, finally putting the hat on her
head.

'In a band? What band? I'm loving the Brothers Osborne
at the minute.'

'He just plays, you know, for people, on the street.'

'He and Earl should make a band.'

'Earl can't really play the ukulele, you know.' Felice used a
nearby window as a mirror, going on tiptoes to see her reflection over the inch of snow settling outside on the ledge. 'He
just plucks a few strings and people feel sorry for him.'

'At least he's doing something,' Lara said.

'What?'

'Well, in the city closest to my village we have some home-less people and they just make a nest out of blankets and sit there. At least Earl's trying to be productive even if he isn't any good.'

'Wow,' Felice said. 'You really do tell it like it is.'

'Doesn't everyone?'

'OK, so you're real fresh and ready to be taken advantage of by everyone.'

'I just think that you have to make the best of things, no matter what your situation. We all have shit times, don't we?'

'Oh yeah,' Felice agreed. 'This morning I was so hungry I ate something that smelt real bad from the alleyway behind a Chinese. What did you eat today?'

Now Lara felt guilty. 'Pizza,' she answered. 'At Macy's.'

'Yeah, now who's having the shit time?'

Lara put her hands to Felice's hat and adjusted it slightly. 'Well, now you have a new hat and it isn't a pity present, I actually bought it to entertain my friend, and it's gone on my credit card which is perilously close to never being able to be used again.'

'First world problems.' Felice yawned. '*And* you're hooked up with that god over there.'

Seth had got up from sitting with Kossy and was helping a short woman wind Christmas lights around the top of a bookcase.

'We're not hooked up,' Lara said. 'We hardly know each other. We just ...' How did she explain it? 'I have a sort-of boyfriend in England.'

'What's a sort-of boyfriend?' Felice asked. 'Like, you had sex with him one time and you still WhatsApp?'

'No ... nothing like that.'

'Then what?'

'He's called Dan,' Lara answered simply.

'And why didn't he wanna come with you to New York?'

Lara swallowed. 'He had to work.'

'Yeah, first world problems again,' Felice said with a heavy sigh. 'Come back and talk to me when you've eaten rotting Asian food.'

'Do you like the hat?' Lara asked, watching Felice still admiring her reflection in the glass.

'Yeah,' she answered roughly. 'I like the hat.'

Twenty-Six

Times Square

'This is a little like Piccadilly Circus in London,' Lara commented. 'But taller and shinier ... and there's more traffic and ... noise.' She had shouted the last few words as she took in everything about one of New York's most famous landmarks. The towers were towering and, because of the number of pedestrians and queues of cars, it all felt slightly enclosed and hectic. Wide neon billboards flashed, buskers played music in any available street space – there was so much going on it was difficult to decide where to look first. It was then, when Lara was pushed a little into the stream of the crowd, she realised Seth wasn't next to her. Her heart started to pick up pace as the sea of people forced her along. Should she stop? Should she keep going? Suddenly, her arm was pulled, and she was, at last, out of the moving tide and standing in the porchway of TGI Friday's.

'Hey,' Seth said, looking a little concerned. 'Are you OK?'

'I ...'

'It isn't like your little village, right?'

She had told Seth a bit about Appleshaw as they'd walked here. The snow had stopped briefly, and the sun had come out, lifting the frozen chill just a touch. As they'd strolled through the city's streets she had talked about where she lived, the people she loved and recounted the incident at the 1 December village parade. Seth had looked both amazed and alarmed – no wonder he was so good at acting – but also appeared to be really interested. However, thinking about Appleshaw had made her think about *not* being there, not being with Dan and being overseas and completely out of her comfort zone.

'Tell me more about your almost-brother,' Seth said softly, putting a hand on her shoulder. 'Aldo.'

An image of the lanky, curly haired man-boy came to her mind and immediately she smiled. 'He has … learning difficulties. No one really knows why, or even if there *is* a reason why, but having his whole family die on him wasn't the best start.' She took a breath. 'Everything fazes him,' she said. 'But also, *nothing* fazes him.' She thought about those words. It was true. 'He's kind of trapped but also completely free. I think he'll forever be somewhere between twelve and eighteen, but he doesn't know any different and what does it matter? He is who he is, and who he is is simply kind and loving.'

'I'm guessing he's never been overseas either.'

'He gets a nosebleed when he has to drive to Manchester.'

Seth laughed out loud then held his hands steady on her shoulders, a bit firmer, stronger. 'You good?'

Lara took a deep breath in, filling her lungs with cold. She did feel better. 'Yes,' she answered. 'I'm good.'

'So, you think this place is busy now? You wanna see it at New Year's.' Seth stepped out onto the sidewalk again and she tracked his movement, this time sticking close.

'I've seen videos,' Lara said.

'It's crazy. There are bands and fireworks and thousands of people and—'

'A big glittery ball.'

'And a big ball,' Seth confirmed, nodding. 'And forty-eight tonnes of trash to clear up after ... Now isn't that a great eco-friendly way to start a new year.'

'Wow,' Lara replied. 'That's a lot of rubbish. In Appleshaw we usually get the paper doilies Mrs Fitch puts under the cakes flying about and the occasional crown from one of the three wise men. One of them always loses a crown.'

'Your village sounds really great,' Seth said, looking at her.

He thought Appleshaw was great? Despite her wonder about what happened outside of her rural bubble, Lara thought it was great, but she also knew Dan didn't think much of it at all. He preferred the city of Salisbury. Thinking about it, lately he had almost seemed to begrudge the village events she loved so much. Like his non-attendance at the advent parade ...

'Well, *I* think it's great,' Lara admitted, the beginnings of an a capella rendition of 'Silent Night' filtering into the air from a choir across the street. 'But New York is cool too.'

'New York *is* cool,' Seth agreed. 'I've lived here all my life.'

'But you've travelled?'

'A little.'

'Ha! Even a little is more than me.' She was aching to know where he'd been and what he'd seen. 'Tell me where you've visited.'

'I've been to Italy.'

'Wow.' She was probably going to be saying 'wow' a lot in this conversation, but Italy was one of the places she had looked at longingly on the internet. Ornate fountains with statues that spurted water, gorgeous piazzas to eat pizzas in, the Mediterranean weather ... Dan had been there for work, delivering bespoke hot tubs to a big hotel. She'd asked him about the Colosseum and he'd laughed, nudged her arm and said he didn't know there was a spirit called that, but he had drunk a lot of limoncello.

'Did you drink a lot of limoncello?' The words were out of her mouth before she could stop them. She breathed in, frost, along with the scent of sizzling hot dogs and caramelised onions wafted up her nose.

'A little,' Seth answered. 'I was there for a couple of months working on a film. It was in the fall, so the weather was mixed. Some days it was non-stop sunshine, others it was rain and storms. But I loved it. And we got to see all the ancient buildings up close in the days we had off, be like tourists, you know?'

No. She didn't know. Not after only two days in New York.

'Sorry,' Seth apologised.

'Don't be sorry. Tell me more! Have you been to Paris?' Lara asked, stopping as they reached a crossing, the street sign hung with festive lights.

'I have.'

'Was the Eiffel Tower amazing? Did you walk all the way up? Was the view as cool as the view from the Empire State? Did you eat frogs' legs? Is the coffee really as good as everyone says it is?'

Seth didn't know what the Walk/Don't Walk sign was currently displaying because he was focusing on nothing but Lara. She was bubbling with energy, spilling over with questions and curiosity, so different from a few minutes earlier when she had been disorientated by the bustle of the city. But now she was back to being bright, enthused and eager. She was this wonderful, enigmatic, contradiction. And now she was staring back at him because he had made no reply to any of her questions.

'Oh … sorry, I did see the Eiffel Tower, half of the steps, the elevator the rest of the way. No to the frogs' legs but I did eat a lot of croque monsieur and the coffee really is good.'

'Wow,' Lara replied, gazing up at him in awe. 'I can't even begin to imagine what Paris would be like.' She smiled. 'I'd want to drink all the beer from those fancy little European glasses and Susie, she'd want to spend the whole time shopping.' She sighed. 'It's meant to be so pretty there at Christmas.'

'What would your boyfriend like to do if he went there?' Seth asked. Immediately, like someone had prematurely dropped the Times Square New Year ball, the joy went out of her eyes and he wanted to kick himself for even mentioning him.

'I don't know,' Lara said simply. 'Maybe see if he could get tickets to one of the football matches?'

'He's into sports?' Seth asked.

'Not *playing* them, apart from golf, but I think he does that just for the social aspect or to sell more hot tub products. He's more of a spectator.' She hesitated, as if a little unsure. 'Do you play sports?'

'Dr Mike played sports,' Seth said with a grin, beginning to cross the street.

'He played basketball with the street kids,' Lara reminded him. 'It wasn't actually a proper game.'

'Hold up! You wanna try playing with those kids. The couple minutes they put in the episodes was nothing! Sometimes we were out there for hours getting those takes.'

'So, Seth Hunt doesn't do sports,' Lara said, laughing.

'I didn't say that.'

'You seemed to be saying you got out of breath playing basketball with kids.'

'No one said anything about out of breath ... actually, I run. Not marathons or even half-marathons, just run, kind of for fun. It's a good way to burn off some energy, gather my thoughts, learn my lines ... and see the city.' He looked at her. 'What do you do?'

'I dance to loud rock music in my barnpartment and I clamber over roofs saving farm animals.' She slapped her jean-covered ass with her hand. 'It seems to be enough to make up for the sitting on this all day in Tina.'

'Tina?'

'My truck.'

'It has a name.'

'*She* has a name.'

'Pardon me.'

'It's not that weird. Everyone names their cars. Why can't I name my truck?'

Seth held his hands up. 'No judgement here.'

'Susie does think it was a little mad to name the snowmen though.'

'Snowmen?' Seth asked as they reached the other side of the street, traffic immediately beginning to move again.

'They're plastic and they glow! They're sitting in the window box outside our living room where we're staying in East Village. There's three of them.'

'Let me guess,' Seth said. 'You called them Harry, Ron and Hermione or something?'

Lara stopped walking and looked at him, eyes wide like she'd just discovered ice cream for the first time. 'Did Susie tell you?'

'What?'

'The snowmen!'

He laughed then, suddenly catching on. 'You *really* called them Harry, Ron and Hermione?'

'What's wrong with that?' Lara asked, scowling a little.

'Absolutely nothing. Obviously, I would have called them the very same thing.'

A bleeping broke the moment and Lara stopped walking, pulling a cell phone from the pocket of her jacket. He stopped next to her, people beginning to walk around them.

'It's Susie,' Lara stated, reading a message. 'She says she's back at the apartment, but David's invited us to a hair show tonight. I suppose I should go.' She sighed. 'God, what's a hair show?'

'A show where they show hair?' Seth offered.

'Dr Mike was clever. Seth Hunt … not so much.'

'Hey!'

'God, I really don't think I want to go to a hair show,' Lara said, looking up from her phone to the street around them as if contemplating her whole life. 'It sounds like there will be lots of people watching a lot of—'

'Hair?' Seth interrupted.

'Genius,' Lara said shaking her head. 'Oh well, I'm sure it will be different and different is why I'm in New York.' She pulled in a breath. 'Different … and taking photos of me with a hot, albeit quite stupid, actor.'

She'd called him hot. Did she think he was hot? Something made him tighten his core, stand a little taller. The media called him 'hot' on occasion, women he was interested in … well, there hadn't been any women he was interested in for quite a while. He cleared his throat. 'I'm joyously free though, living in my stupid bubble,' he joked. And then he knew exactly what he wanted to do. 'Listen, if you don't wanna go to the hair show then—'

'I could get some takeaway? Watch Netflix?'

'You could,' Seth agreed. 'But, see, there's this thing I have to do tonight … and it kind of loosely involves France, you know, if you wanted to experience a close-to-the-real-thing coffee.' He hadn't explained anything at all in that sentence except the coffee part. Why was he behaving like the class nerd asking the odds-on favourite for Prom Queen for a date? Not that this was a date, because Lara had a boyfriend and he wasn't in the right head space to get involved. At that moment his mother's photo in his pocket felt not like photographic paper but weighty like a bag of sugar.

'I don't want to take up all your time with my mad, probably hopeless and frankly quite ridiculous social-media crusade.'

'No, I know, and I don't think that.' What was he trying to say? He cleared his throat again. 'There's this film I really, really want to be in and the casting director is having dinner at this French restaurant tonight. I was gonna go there and—'

'Stalk him?'

'No.'

'Poison his water glass then be there with a quick antidote?'

'What?'

'I come from near Salisbury. Believe me, anything is possible.'

'No,' he said. 'I was just gonna, you know, talk to him, reintroduce myself, make sure he knows how much I want the part so I'm at the forefront of his mind when he thinks about making the call-backs.'

A taxi blasted its horn and Lara jumped, bumping into him. He reached out to steady her. 'You OK?'

'This countryside girl is only used to loud mooing and the occasional tractor.' She smiled at him. 'OK.'

'OK?'

'Show me a little bit of France here in New York,' Lara agreed. 'It sounds like there will be plenty more photo opportunities there than at a hair show.'

He smiled. 'Great! I mean, good ... yeah, photos of frogs ... their legs, I mean, and ... coffee.' He stopped talking before the apparent mix of excitement and apprehension turned into an unworkable fusion of words.

'Well,' Lara began. 'As long as it isn't too expensive, I was thinking beer in one of those European glasses.'

He smiled at her. 'I like your thinking. Good plan.'

Twenty-Seven

Lara and Susie's Airbnb apartment, East Village

'You know David said he was cutting the hair of a prince this morning.'

'Mmm,' Lara answered.

'He wasn't lying.'

'Did you think he was?'

Lara was sitting in the window seat again, legs curled up underneath her, composing a text to Aldo. She had received one from her almost-brother earlier indicating that he had let a couple of animals from the farm into their house because they looked cold. A quick text to her dad and Gerry had replied with a quip about the time difference, then confirmed that the shire horse and the alpaca were safely back in their own home. Her dad had then reiterated his concerns about the safety of New York and said she should also avoid somewhere called Hunt's Point.

'I don't know. I just thought that maybe he had made his job and New York sound just a little bit too fantastic, that it couldn't really, seriously, be quite as amazing as it all seemed. I mean, when he said he paid for our flights with tips I thought he'd maybe ... borrowed the money or ... put them on his credit card.'

'How do you know the prince is real?' Lara asked, still focusing on her message.

'I googled him, obvs! He's from Saudi Arabia but he has an office here for his oil business in New York – well, it would be oil, wouldn't it – and my David cuts and styles his hair! Asks for him personally!'

'Who cut his hair before David came to New York?' Lara asked, typing more.

'What?'

'Before David joined the New York salon. Who cut the prince's hair?'

'I have no idea. Why?'

'Well, there must be a reason the prince got David when he hasn't been there that long.'

'Because David is an excellent stylist.'

'I know,' Lara answered. 'I just wondered …' She looked up from her phone and finally took in Susie's appearance. 'Whoa!'

'What's the matter?' Susie asked, blinking back at Lara, then looking down at her outfit of a long, stylish, figure-hugging red skirt teamed with a cream jumper, a crystal embellished robin on both sleeves.

'Your hair!' Lara remarked. 'It's …' She desperately searched for the right word. 'Extraordinary.'

Susie grinned and moved closer to Lara, using the window as a mirror. She carefully poked a couple of escapee strands back into the huge spiral of hair forming a solid mass that stood up about thirty centimetres. 'It's supposed to look like the Guggenheim.'

'God!' Lara exclaimed. 'It really does.'

'Do you think?'

'Really,' Lara said, admiring her friend's appearance. 'I don't know how you do it.'

'Well, I don't know how you drive a truck or … put up with Dan.' Susie looked at Lara, hands at her mouth. 'Sorry … I'm sorry, I shouldn't have said that. I wasn't thinking.'

'It's OK,' Lara answered with a determined nod. 'I know what you meant and, of course, you're right really.'

'Any more posts from the Salisbury Christmas market?' Susie asked, lowering herself onto the seat next to Lara.

'I haven't looked.'

'Come off it.'

'I haven't!'

'Lara!'

'OK ... I did look, once.' She sniffed. 'But there was nothing else. Just some of his stupid friends from work commenting on the photo.'

'What did the hot tub morons have to say?'

'Nothing much. Just being moronic.'

'Lara, if you don't tell me I'll just look myself. He's still my friend on Facebook – for now.'

She took a deep breath. One particular comment *had* hurt. She knew it was pathetic, a remark made by Johnny, one of Dan's most laddish, very-inflammatory-after-the-sixth-pint friends, but it had scorched.

'Johnny Warren said, "nice upgrade".'

'What?' Susie leapt back off the seat, Guggenheim hair wobbling precariously.

'Stop! Susie! Slow down, your hair might collapse!'

'Johnny Warren will be collapsing when I'm finished with him. That bastard! That bastard who will never get the benefit of my highlighting cap ever again!'

'He has his hair highlighted?' Lara asked.

'Sorry, but customer confidentiality comes second to my best friend being attacked on social media! You should report the comment.'

'It's not that bad.'

'It *is* that bad!'

'It wasn't directly directed at me.'

'I know but—'

'Susie, honestly, it's fine.'

'It's *so* not fine!'

'Listen,' Lara took hold of Susie's hand. 'I can't deal with anything while I'm here. He asked for space. I gave it to him. He made himself single. I can't stop that. I just need to stop looking at what he's doing and focus on what we're doing.' She paused. 'What *I'm* doing.'

'Is that what your horoscope says?' Susie asked seriously.

'No, it's the new law according to Lara Weeks.' She straightened herself up, unfolding her legs and planting her feet on the floor. 'And I'm not staying in while you go to the hair show. I'm going to a French restaurant. With Seth.'

Susie clapped her hands to the side of her face, looking as astounded as someone who had just been told that black was the new black. 'A date! You're going on a date!'

'It's not a date,' Lara said immediately.

'It's a French restaurant! *That* says "date" to me.'

'I'm not single,' Lara reminded her.

'Dan says he is,' Susie countered, adopting a cross-looking expression.

'Seth might not be single either,' Lara answered. Did Seth have a girlfriend? She didn't know. She hadn't asked. What sort of a sightseeing companion had she been if she didn't even know the basics about him! Although she did know he was a Gemini.

'He doesn't,' Susie informed her, sounding like an authority of Seth's status. 'He broke up with someone last year but even that didn't appear to be serious. She's some neutron shake fanatic. Does some of that weird body toning stuff with kettle bells and hula hoops … not the crisps.'

'He said he wasn't keen on sports, but he did say he runs,' Lara remarked, recalling their earlier conversation.

'There we go. Not compatible with Little Miss Raw Food.'

'It's just dinner and he wants to impress some casting director who's going to eat there.'

'OMG, he's involving you in his life.'

'I think I'm a prop, so he isn't eating on his own if the guy doesn't turn up.'

'A prop who's going to eat fancy French cuisine with Dr Mike.'

'If you weren't wearing a famous New York museum on your head I'd trade places and style it out with David at the hair show.'

Susie grinned. 'No, you would not.'

'No, you're right,' Lara agreed. 'But can you please help me? I've looked at the menu and I'm trying to find the least fancy thing there is because you know, for me, fancy is having mustard on my hot dogs instead of ketchup.'

Susie laughed and came back to sit down. 'Come on, Lara. This is your first trip anywhere. Live a little!'

'I am.' She swallowed. 'I'm trying … just not with Mussolini.'

'What?'

Lara clicked onto Safari and showed Susie her phone, displaying the menu choices for Cafe Cluny.

'God! You're going to Cafe Cluny?!' Susie exclaimed. 'Now I really might have to reconsider the hair show.'

'You want to nosh Mussolini that badly?' Lara asked, still none the wiser.

'No, but this restaurant … loads of celebrities go there. Bradley Cooper's even been there several times.'

'Really?' Lara said.

'Really,' Susie said, eyes excited. 'And mousseline is just a light sauce. The chicken sounds great. And you really like chicken.'

'Do you think I should get changed?' Lara pulled at her Ramones sweater.

'What?' Susie exclaimed. 'Yes! Yes, I do think you should get changed! Bradley Cooper might be there and you're on a date with Seth Hunt! Come on! Before David's bounding in here like an excited giraffe and I have to go!'

'It's not a date,' Lara reminded, as much for her own sake as for Susie's.

Twenty-Eight

Cafe Cluny, West 12th Street

Seth was nervous. Stupid nervous. This wasn't an audition. This was dinner. And a cleverly contrived meeting. He had to be *himself*. He had to be articulate in getting over how much he wanted this role. He wasn't going to sound desperate or needy. His bank balance was a pinch above desperate and needy ... just. He was going to sound positive and impassioned ...

'Stupid, bloody tights! Argh! What is the point of you?! If a woman was supposed to have nylon over her legs, then surely we would have evolved that way!'

Across the street, pounding through the inch of snow on the sidewalk was Lara, her hands on her thighs, fingers pulling at their covering. She was still wearing her Dr Martens boots and that inadequate-looking short jacket, but the jeans were gone, instead the edge of a skirt was just about visible. Her way was lit by Christmas lights from neighbouring buildings and she almost walked into a rotund Santa ringing a bell and carrying a charity bucket. Seth was suddenly smiling on the inside, all anxiety forgotten. And then he remembered what Trent had texted him earlier.

I tweeted some #LemurGirl stuff today. Be good if you could hook up with her again while you're still hot and she's desperately seeking a distraction. Get some photos of you looking cute together? Cute but just good friends. *The Ellen Show* laps that stuff up. I'm thinking – Dr Mike heals Lemur Girl's broken heart. Let me know how The Hoff went. Are we expecting a call-back?

He hadn't mentioned meeting Lara for sightseeing and, as Trent hadn't been at the apartment when he'd got back earlier, he hadn't seen him to say he was also meeting her tonight. He wasn't on board with working angles at all.

'Lara!' Seth called, waving a hand.

As much as she hated the tights, at that moment, when Lara looked up, she was instantly glad Susie had made her change clothes. Seth looked good enough to be modelling in a hair show: long dark woollen coat, black trousers and leather shoes, his ebony hair, flecked with snow, bouncing over his forehead a little. He was wearing glasses, just plain black frames, but they were the type that made sexy people look ever sexier. He was *so* good-looking. And she was learning he was nice too, really nice, and funny and … absolutely not to be thought of in any of those ways when she was committed to Dan. No matter how uncommitted Dan seemed to be to her at the moment.

What was wrong with her? She had to stop focusing on her gorgeous companion and her heartache and remember she was here in NYC spreading her wings, being independent, untied from Appleshaw. The restaurant looked cosy as well as upmarket. Its exterior all cream-coloured paint and large windows, snow-speckled wooden benches on the pavement and a trio of miniature Christmas trees bearing white lights. It fitted perfectly with the whole West Village vibe she had experienced walking from the subway. Here the streets were chic and slightly leafier than anything Midtown had had to offer. There were uber-cool bars and high-end shops mixing with cosy coffee houses and intimate bistros. Parts of it looked like they were sets from a movie.

'Do the French wear tights?' Lara asked quickly, hands pulling at the hem of her skirt. 'Because I know it's really cold and everything, but I think I might be allergic to elastane. I need to get them off.'

'I'm not sure,' Seth answered.

'If I should take them off? Or if the French wear tights?' Lara asked.

'Both?' Seth said. 'What exactly are "tights"?'

Lara pressed her face up against the glass panes of the door of Cafe Cluny, her breath misting up the window as she observed the interior. It looked so beautiful: ornate cornices, their décor lit by uplighters; fawn-coloured curtains with swags making them bunch and billow in all the right places; matching blinds halfway down the windows and lights that hung down low over tables. There weren't many vacant seats.

'Are you OK?' Seth asked.

'I'm seeing who else is wearing tights … I mean "pantyhose".' She took a breath. 'I don't believe I just said that.'

'Well, hopefully none of the men, unless they're ballet dancers,' Seth answered. 'Lara, I doubt there is anyone here who's French or anyone who cares whether you are wearing hose or not.'

'Really?' she said, looking back at him. 'Not even the chef? Being French, I mean … not caring if I wear … the things we call a different name.' She cleared her throat. 'Susie said Bradley Cooper comes here.'

'If Bradley Cooper's gonna get under the table and look at your hose then I might have something to say about that.'

Lara's breath caught in her chest for a second as his eyes met hers. He was so close, looking so fine and he was going to challenge Bradley Cooper should the other actor be interested in her itchy undergarments. *She wasn't single. She was not single.* She laughed quickly. 'Sorry! To be honest I don't even think Bradley Cooper is all that.'

'No?' Seth asked. 'You didn't tweet him as well as Tom Hardy?'

'Are you ever going to forgive me for that?'

'I might make you eat frogs' legs as a penance,' Seth answered.

'I could manage Mussolini.'

'What?'

Lara smiled and shook her head. 'Never mind. Can we go in?'

'And meet all the New York French people?' Seth asked. 'I can't wait.'

Lara slapped his arm. 'I haven't been to a French restaurant before. Don't make fun of me.'

'Ow!' Seth said, clutching his sleeve. 'With a hit like that I wouldn't dare.'

'Do you think the guy you want to charm is here yet?' Lara asked in a whisper.

'He has a reservation at eight.' Seth pushed open the door of the restaurant.

'And do you know what he looks like?'

'Yes,' Seth replied. 'I've already auditioned for him. A few times, for different roles.'

'But if he knows you already then he should know how good you are.'

'I keep telling you I'm really not that famous,' Seth said, smiling as a waiter came to meet them. 'He probably doesn't remember me at all.'

'Come on!' Lara exclaimed. 'Everyone watched *Manhattan Med*.'

'They really didn't ... Hi, I have a table booked in the name "Hunt".'

'Right this way, sir,' the waiter answered.

'What's the name of the guy?' Lara asked in hushed tones. The tights were still driving her mad. It was like being in a straitjacket for your thighs.

'Toby Jackson,' Seth told her.

Lara turned to the waiter, guiding them into the hub of the restaurant. 'Where is Toby Jackson going to be sitting?'

'I'm not ...' the waiter began, looking a little bemused.

'Can we have a table with a good view of Toby Jackson, please? So if, say, Toby Jackson was sitting here ...' She indicated a table for two by the wall. 'Then could we be sitting here?' She pointed to the only vacant table by the fairy-light-encircled window. 'I believe he has a reservation later.'

'Lara ...' Seth began.

Lara smiled at the waiter then pointed to the table by the window. 'Can we sit here? And ... could you put Toby Jackson over there?' She pointed to the vacant table by the wall. 'Please.'

'Well ...' the waiter started.

'If you could,' Lara said. 'Then we will both sign a menu or something for you at the end of the night. This is Seth Hunt, you know.' She lowered her voice but put more emphasis into his name. '*Seth Hunt* ... you know, Dr Mike from *Manhattan Med*. And I'm Lemur Girl. I got up a tree at Central Park Zoo.' She moved towards the table by the window. 'Here is OK, isn't it?'

The waiter smiled. 'Absolutely.'

'Thank you,' Lara said, putting a hand on the back of the chair.

Seth joined her, taking ownership of her chair and pulling it out for her while shaking his head a little, an amused expression on his face.

'Did you want to sit here?' Lara asked him.

'No, Lemur Girl, I'm pulling it out for you, you know, being a gentleman.' He paused then whispered. 'Like the movies.'

'Why, thank you,' she answered, dropping down into the seat and unzipping her jacket. The view of the street was fantastic. The slight wind was making the trickle of snow dance around in the dark, tickling streetlamps and passers-by in turn. Christmas decorations glowed from awnings and a group of small children were collating a pile of snowballs while their mothers chatted on the corner of the block. She turned her head back to the room. 'We should get the waiter to take our photo.'

'Absolutely,' Seth replied. 'But let's give him a break first and maybe order some wine?'

'Or beer,' Lara said, smiling. 'In a little European glass.'

Twenty-Nine

Lara sipped at her glass of red wine and let the warm, honey, vanilla and cranberry notes coat her taste buds. She had had a beer and that had been nice too, but in the spirit of trying things she wouldn't ordinarily try they had moved onto wine. And, after a delectable starter of something called Hamachi Crudo, made from mushrooms with a tomato jam, and the chicken breast, with the now infamous mousseline, it was getting on towards nine o' clock.

'The wine is really lovely,' Lara commented, putting her arm down and trying to conceal the fact she had looked at her watch. 'I don't know, "lovely" doesn't seem to be enough of a word. Let me think of something better than "lovely". Um. *Delicious*. No, that really should relate to food not drink. *Sumptuous*. No, that's not right. *Divine*. Yes, it's—'

'Lara,' Seth interrupted, his big brown eyes looking at her through the sexy glasses.

'Mmm,' she said, sipping more of the liquid in her glass. 'Divine wine.'

'I know it's nine.'

She let go of a sigh. 'You saw me look at my watch, didn't you? I'm sorry. I'm really enjoying myself, but I just want the guy to turn up and sit where I've placed him, so you can grab that role.'

'This happens,' Seth said with a shrug. 'People make reservations, they change their mind, they get ill, the babysitter doesn't come. It's all good.'

'It's annoying.'

'It's New York,' Seth reminded her.

'It's rude to not turn up,' Lara said. 'Unless he's phoned to cancel.' She turned in her chair, seeking out their waiter. 'Shall I call our waiter and ask if he's phoned to cancel.'

'No,' Seth said. 'It's fine, honestly.' He took a breath, then moved his hand to the pocket of his trousers.

Seth drew out the photo his mom had given him at the centre earlier and placed it on the table, next to bottle of wine between them. He pushed it towards Lara and watched as she picked it up.

'That is my real mom.' He picked up his glass. 'The one on the left.'

'Wow,' Lara said, eyes on the picture in her hand. 'She's so pretty ... not that she wouldn't be, because you've got really good DNA and ... Susie would say she has really nice hair.'

He smiled. 'She does have good hair, doesn't she?'

'Kossy has good hair too,' Lara remarked. 'I would never have known *your* hair didn't come from *her* hair.'

'No,' he agreed.

'She looks happy,' Lara continued. 'And she's wearing a great dress.'

'Without pantyhose, I think,' Seth said.

'Well, it looks like this photo was taken in the summer and it would be a lot hotter than December. No need for tights.'

'Why do you think the photo was taken in the summer?'

'The windows in the background are wide open,' Lara remarked.

He leaned forward a little as she showed him the photo again. She was right. Why hadn't he noticed that? He had been staring at the photo since he'd got it but apparently missing all the details. Did it matter what time of year it was taken? How was that going to lead to him knowing more about the woman depicted in it?

'She was a prostitute,' Seth said bluntly.

'Wow,' Lara said, almost as if he had just told her his mother used to be President of the United States. 'Well, as I said to Felice earlier, at least she was doing something.'

'What?'

'Well, she was working for a living, despite having nowhere of her own to live. She was obviously doing everything she could to try and get out of her situation.'

He hadn't thought about it that way. To him, prostitution had meant 'dirty' and 'trash'. Right then he felt his soul couldn't get any more presumptuous or ugly. Who did he think he was, sitting on his middle-class throne?

'What's her name?' Lara enquired.

'Candice,' Seth said. 'Candice Garcia.'

'Have you looked her up on Facebook?'

'What?' His heart sped up ten-fold. He hadn't even thought about that. Why hadn't he? Because he wasn't ready to pursue it? Because he wasn't ready to even *think* about pursuing it?

'That's what I would do. I mean, there might be thousands of Candice Garcias, but one of them might be your mum.'

'I ...' He didn't know what to say. Lara was right. She was absolutely right. His birth mother could literally be one click away. Maybe even still here in New York. And that thought was making him feel sick. His mouth went suddenly, terribly dry.

'I thought about finding my mother once,' Lara said wistfully.

'You still don't know where she is?' Seth asked.

She shook her head. 'I told you she left. I was six.'

'So, did your parents divorce?'

'Eventually. I don't really know the details. Just that they used to argue about everything. And every time I would go to my bedroom and play with my farm set. Then one day she said goodbye like she always did before she went to work but that night ... she didn't come home.' She sniffed. 'My dad cried a lot for a few weeks and I watched Disney Channel. Then he got it together and we just carried on.' She took a breath. 'But after we took in Aldo I did start to wonder about her. Why she left. Was it because of me? What was out there for her that was more than a haulage business, a husband and a daughter.'

'What did you do?' Seth asked.

'Nothing,' Lara admitted. 'I said I *thought* about looking for her. I finally made up my mind that she had made her choice, left a six-year-old with no contact whatsoever and I knew, no matter what her situation, I was never going to be able to forgive her for that. All those missed birthdays and school stuff and Christmases and just leaving for work like normal and not coming home. It's too much.'

'And that's exactly why I never asked about my parents until now.'

'Why now?' Lara asked, elbows on the table.

Seth took a breath. 'Because of this role. Because of Sam in *A Soul's Song*.'

'The part you want,' Lara guessed.

'Sam, he's adopted, and he's just found out because his adopted parents have just died. He's married, and he and his wife can't have kids so they're wanting to adopt a child them-selves, but the authorities ask him all these questions about himself and he doesn't know any of the answers.'

'So, what does he do?' Lara asked.

She was leaning fully forward now, staring at him with an intense expression on her face, the candlelight casting her face in a warm glow. He leaned a little closer too, remembering the script and feeling that same twist of excitement entering his belly. 'Well, he scours his parents' home ...'

'Obviously,' Lara replied.

'And he finds these letters.'

'To his parents? Who from?'

'Well, I'm gonna be giving you spoilers here. Are you sure you wanna know? You might not wanna watch the movie if you already know the ending.'

'Go on already!'

'They're official letters mentioning a guy called Mo Parker.'

'That's mysterious.'

'Yeah. So, Sam tracks down this Mo Parker and he's a real eccentric jazz musician.' He took a breath. 'I really wanna know who they're getting lined up for that role.'

'Come on! Get to the twist! Mo's his dad, right?'

Seth nodded. 'Yeah, Mo's his dad and Sam realises that quite quickly. But he doesn't tell Mo who *he* is.' He paused, took a sip of his wine before carrying on. 'So, Sam plays the drums, not professionally – he's a horse groom by trade – and he auditions for a spot in Mo's band, which he gets.'

'Obviously.'

'Yeah,' Seth said, becoming more and more enthusiastic. 'Anyway, he spends time with Mo and Mo eventually opens up about having a son, etc., etc., with the only woman he loved ...'

'Sam's birth mother,' Lara said, eyes wide. 'Who is ... a singer ... one of the characters everyone thought was a bit part but is actually only in the movie because they are a *big* part.'

'No,' Seth said, deliberating stopping and waiting until Lara was moving in her chair, waiting for him to reveal all.

'Tell me who it is!' Lara begged.

'Sam's real mother ... is his adopted mother!'

'What?'

'The mother who had raised him *was* his real mother. She was Mo's girlfriend until her parents found out and banned her from seeing him, but then she was pregnant. They made her get the baby adopted. But, and this is the really cool, different part ... she adopted the baby back. Her own baby after she got married to her husband.'

'Is that even possible?'

'I don't know. I guess they've done their research. But it's a great twist, isn't it?'

'And the film means a lot to you,' Lara said.

She could see from his body language that this part wasn't just a job or a chance to get his name a little larger on that silver screen, this meant far more than that. He was genuinely bubbling over with enthusiasm for the project.

'Yeah,' Seth said. 'I really, *really* wanna play Sam. In some ways I *am* Sam. And I knew that the second I read the script. But without knowing who *my* mother was, it all felt a little bit incomplete.'

'And now you know who she is ...'

'I think I could have done my audition better. I think I could have given Sam more than I did.' He took a breath. 'And I want the role more than ever.'

'Be Sam,' Lara urged, picking up the bottle of wine and pouring more in each of their glasses.

'What?'

'Be Sam, for me, now,' she urged. 'Do a practice. Give me the lines you read in the audition. Transform into a horse groom drummer right now.' She smiled.

'You see, he starts off as this quite ordinary guy, enjoying his life, knowing what he wants from it – his wife, children – and then he turns into this almost reckless guy in the pursuit of a truth he already half had.'

'I want to see him,' Lara ordered. 'I demand you show me him.'

'You're crazy,' Seth said.

'I'm taking away your wine until I see Sam.' She commandeered Seth's glass to her side of the table.

He shook his head, but then took off his glasses, placing them on the table. Lara watched as he smoothed down his hair then closed his eyes briefly before adjusting his stance in the chair and looking at her again. Now he had changed into a totally different person, just like that.

'I need to find my real parents.'

Lara swallowed. Was he expecting her to join in? She didn't know the words.

'How can I be a father if I don't know where I really come from?' Seth threw his hands up in the air. 'How can I be a dad to someone, be a rock to someone, be anything to anyone unless I know who I am?'

Lara sat spellbound, completely caught up in the moment as Seth – becoming Sam – suddenly stood up and grabbed the glass of wine she had pulled away. 'Look at this wine,' he said at full volume. 'How it clings to this glass? It's so full-bodied, yet totally, completely dependent on what's holding it up. Without the glass, without *this* glass, it would fall to the floor, spill … spatter … waste.' He thumped the glass back down on the table in front of Lara, a dribble sloshing out onto the wood. '*I'm* the glass, Virginia, and I need to be the glass for our child. But I can't do that until I know how I was put together. Because one day our child is gonna ask where he or she comes from and we are gonna be there with all the answers.' He looked at Lara, tears forming in his eyes. 'I need my truth. I need *my* answers.'

Lara just stared at him, watching as he smiled and turned back into Seth Hunt.

'How was it?' he asked.

Suddenly the entire restaurant erupted into applause, whooping and hollering as Seth put his hand on the back of his chair and prepared to sit back down. It shocked him. He stopped, turned a little to acknowledge them, dipping his head, almost embarrassed. He had no idea he had been being watched. He'd just got right into the heart of the moment.

'I am so sorry,' Seth said to Lara. 'I should apologise to everyone for disturbing their meals.'

'You will not,' Lara ordered. 'That was …'

There were tears in her eyes and it was only when he saw the emotion in her that he felt it flowing out of him. He wiped his eyes with the back of his hand and quickly retrieved his glasses.

'It was potentially Oscar-worthy,' a male voice spoke from just over his shoulder.

Seth turned around and came face to face with Toby Jackson. He felt his cheeks colouring up. He needed to step up, say the right things, this was the opportunity he'd been looking for.

Seth extended his hand. 'Mr Jackson, sir, I'm Seth—'

'I know who you are. And I'm also wondering why you're performing a film that isn't even in the works yet at a restaurant.'

'Sir, I—' What should he say? Had he potentially scuppered everything?

'I made him do it,' Lara got to her feet. 'Hello, Mr Jackson. I'm Lara, from England, and I asked Seth to give me some lines from the film that means the most to him and he told me all about *A Soul's Song*.'

She had whispered the title and was edging closer to Toby Jackson like she was about to divulge secret voting results from *American Idol*.

'It sounds like the most fantastic movie. I can't wait to watch it. Me and probably millions of other people, you know, if you pick the right actors ...'

'You didn't make the call-back list,' Toby Jackson said bluntly, addressing Seth. 'But, after what I just heard and saw, I'm gonna put you right to the top of it.'

'You are?' Seth said.

'Friday,' Toby said, slapping a hand on his shoulder. 'Ten a.m. Same venue.' He made to walk away but stopped. 'Just tell me one thing. Those lines about the wine glass ... I don't remember them from the script.'

Seth swallowed. 'No, sir, I ... made them up.'

Toby smiled then shook his head. 'Goddamn.' He pointed a finger. 'Friday, ten a.m. Don't be late.'

'No, sir,' Seth replied as Toby left to join his dinner companion.

He finally breathed fully, letting his lungs inflate then relax into an out breath of stabilisation. He felt like his heart was going to burst and when he looked at Lara she was still standing too, beaming at him.

'You've got the role!' she hissed excitedly, not that quietly.

'Not quite yet,' Seth said. 'Did you know he was right there? Did you see him come in?'

Lara shook her head. 'No! All anyone was looking at was you.' She squealed. 'You were amazing!' She threw her arms around him and squeezed him tight. And it felt only natural to return the hug, drawing her body into his and holding on. He closed his eyes, feeling her unique energy filling him up, the scent of her – a little bit red wine, fresh winter air, peppermint – surrounding him. This was not meant to be happening but if he held on to her any longer this celebratory hug was going to be turning into something else entirely. As each microsecond ticked by, he found himself thinking about what it would feel like to draw her away from him and look into her eyes right now. How her full lips would feel if he put his thumb to them. How her warm breath might feel on his cheek. What it would be like to put his lips on hers. She was incomparable.

Then she stepped away, her face looking a little flushed, her eyes not meeting his. 'Well … we should definitely have celebratory French coffee so I can … see what all the fuss is about.' She dropped to her seat and picked up the menu.

Thirty

Hudson River Park

There was a fresh layer of snow on the ground and, as Lara walked, her eyes went across the rippling tidal river to the bright buildings displaying golds, reds, ice white and blue. Being here, by the water, with green space and benches and the slower pace of evening city life, it wasn't like being in the middle of a vibrant, sprawling metropolis, it was quieter, calmer. She could almost imagine, in warm weather, New Yorkers lying on the grass banks, cool drinks their companions. There were still joggers, even at this time of night, and people walking their dogs, but everyone was wrapped up against the winter weather. It was still snowing, but lightly, with hardly a breath of wind, just enough to keep the temperature a shade above freezing. And she and Seth were walking in a companionable silence while she tried frantically not to think about the moment they had shared in Cafe Cluny.

The hug had felt so good, so warm and solid, yet soft and honest. A bit like Seth himself. He wasn't one of these actors who adored their popularity, he was almost apologetic for it. He hadn't performed in the restaurant because he'd wanted to be seen. He had acted because this role was running through him. And seeing him like that, sharing the scene and hearing together what Toby Jackson had said afterwards had been so special. So special, as he'd been holding her, she'd got lost in a daydream where he had taken her face in his hands and kissed her, hard and rough and slightly frenzied and then paused and done it all over again only softer, slower, almost tantric ...

'This is Pier 46,' Seth announced. 'It's quiet. No playpark or food outlet, just the view and the artificial grass.'

'I think the piers are really cool,' Lara said quickly, displacing the daydream images. 'We have them in England, but they stick out in the raging sea and have arcades on them, you know, where you shove a coin in the slots and try to win more than you put in.'

'I have no idea,' Seth admitted.

'And some have really old theatres on them or fine-dining restaurants.'

'And no artificial grass.'

'No,' Lara agreed. 'But as they're so old, the wooden planks are really decayed, and you can see the sea through the gaps.' She smiled. 'The last time we went to Bournemouth Aldo got his finger stuck between one of them and I had to waste some of my ice cream sticking it around his finger to get it to come out.'

'Aldo sounds like a lot of fun,' Seth answered, stepping from the main walkway onto the pier.

'Yeah, he's fun all right. Hard work sometimes. But mainly fun. Although not everyone sees that right away.' She thought about how Dan was with her almost-brother. He often treated Aldo like a child. She knew that Aldo was different, but no kind of different should be mocked.

'Sometimes it takes a while for people to understand something or some*one* extraordinary,' Seth stated, putting his hands into the pockets of his coat.

Extraordinary. He had called Aldo 'extraordinary' as if he was special in the best of ways. She looked across at Seth and he turned to her, those eyes finding hers and suddenly all the kissing daydreams were well and truly back.

'And you tell me he can drive a truck too. That's pretty impressive,' Seth replied.

'It took him a little while to learn,' Lara admitted. 'I had to call the pedals after animals to get him to get it together.'

'No!' Seth exclaimed with a laugh. 'What's the gas pedal called? Cow?'

'No, Cow is for clutch, obviously. Bat is for brake and Ant is for accelerator. And I had to use gorilla for gearstick at the beginning, but he's been weaned off that now. It got a bit much saying, "Cow down, shift the gorilla into first and go easy on the ant."'

Seth laughed, a deep, genuine sound that made Lara think of dark, yet deliciously creamy, mocha-infused hot chocolate. She shivered. It was all New York's fault with its film-like setting and the Christmassy vibe to go with it.

'I'm sorry,' Seth said. 'It's just, I can really imagine you saying that.'

'And what is that supposed to mean?'

'That you have this way about you that's so ... unique.'

'That's what people say when they don't like something,' Lara said, sniffing. 'Susie says it all the time when she looks at hair magazines. She's probably saying that right now at the hair show. "Oh, David, look at that woman's hair. It's so ... unique."'

'I think it's pretty awesome,' he told her. 'I think *you're* pretty awesome.'

Lara suddenly felt light-headed. She didn't need him saying things like that when she was having fantasies about his kissing technique and they were strolling the deck-boards like a couple on a date.

'So, tell me about Dan. I think, given that I am now a small part of your New York adventure without him, I need to know what he's like. Find out more about the man who has Lemur Girl's attention.'

Now she felt sick. Because the new truth was Dan had classified himself single and was about to embark on a trip to Scotland with Cleavage Chloe and every time she thought about him lately it made her angry and sad all at the same time.

'He's not quite as tall as you,' Lara blurted out. 'He has dark hair, shorter than yours and he sells hot tubs.'

'OK,' Seth replied.

'His parents emigrated to Spain, so he doesn't see them, and he doesn't have any brothers or sisters. I think that's why he struggles a bit with Aldo. He's not the best space sharer.'

'So, tell me where you met,' Seth asked.

'I delivered some spa chemicals to his warehouse,' Lara said as they arrived at the end of the pier. She took in a lungful of the cold night air. 'One of the other guys there made a derogatory comment about women driving trucks and ... I punched him.'

'Whoa!'

'It was a few years ago now. I'm much more mature these days.'

'I kinda wish I had seen it.'

Lara smiled. 'Dan asked me if I wanted to go out for a drink sometime, I said yes and that was that.'

'And he's the love of your life,' Seth commented, putting his fingers to the metalwork.

She had *thought* he was. But perhaps, like with Appleshaw, she only felt that way because she hadn't *seen* anything else, hadn't *been* anywhere else to *meet* anyone else ...

'Are you going out with anyone?' Lara asked, looking at Seth. 'I mean, dating anyone?'

'No,' Seth replied with a smile. 'It's not much fun dating an actor. We're either working away for months on end or we're out of work and not knowing what to do until we get the next part.'

'But has there been anyone you thought was the love of your life?' Lara asked.

Seth blew out a breath as he looked across the water. 'I'll be honest with you,' he said. 'No.'

'But you've had girlfriends ... or boyfriends?' She put her hands to her face, eyes wide. 'God, I should not assume that just because you played a hospital lothario who chased women that you're straight. I mean pansexual is in, right? Although Susie said something about a girl with kettle bells and—'

'Girlfriends,' Seth interrupted. 'Most definitely girls. But just not the right girl.' Saying those words started a whirlpool in his stomach and he was back to remembering their embrace at Cafe Cluny. *She was involved with someone.*

'I ... don't know if posting photos of me in New York is going to make Dan change his mind about me,' Lara admitted.

He wanted to ask why, but he sensed her reverie. He stayed quiet.

'Well ...' She swallowed, as if speaking was tearing at her heart. 'I told you he changed his Facebook relationship status to "single".'

'Lara,' Seth said, putting a hand on her shoulder. She inched herself back, resting her weight against the barricade.

She shook her head, but he caught the tears in her eyes. 'Well, he's also going to Scotland for Christmas with friends and another woman and … I don't know what I did wrong.'

He put his hand back on her shoulder, firmly, he hoped, comfortingly. 'Listen, I know I don't know the situation, but why do you think you did something wrong?'

'Because that's what always happens to me,' Lara said. 'I gave my guinea pigs potato peelings because I didn't know they couldn't eat them and they died. I moaned that Bill in the office didn't make tea often enough and two days later he handed in his resignation and my dad was stuck with no help at one of our busiest times of the year. And my mum … my mum probably left because I always wanted to wear army combats and jeans and not party dresses and tights!'

She was practically hyperventilating, and Seth turned her slightly, putting a second hand on her other shoulder. 'Hey, breathe …'

'Everyone always leaves me,' Lara said. 'That's why I have to stay in Appleshaw, with Aldo and my dad. Because they rely on me and I'm not going to be the one that leaves like everyone else.'

'Lara, stop,' Seth said.

'Now Dan is gone too, and I don't know why I'm trying to cling on. If he doesn't want me then I should just let him go. He can join the rest of the list of people that have left me.'

'Lara, don't.'

'And I don't even know why I'm telling you all this. I don't tell anyone this. I'm Lara Weeks, unafraid of anything, kicking ass on a daily basis, climbing up trees rescuing zoo animals and—'

'Crossing the Atlantic to meet with me,' Seth interrupted.

'Yes, totally that and I completely apologise for it.'

'I don't want you to,' Seth said, one hand coming off her shoulder and going to her hair. He so wanted to touch her hair, but his hand hovered in mid-air, unsure. 'Lara, I'm having the best time, the coolest time I've had in a long time, and given that I've just discovered my mom is a homeless prostitute that's quite something.'

'You are?'

He nodded, heart palpitating a rough rhythm. He swallowed and put his hovering hand back down on her shoulder. 'I like a girl in jeans and combats.'

'You're just saying that,' Lara said with a laugh. 'Just to make me feel better.'

'I promise, I'm not.' He looked into her eyes. 'Listen, I'm gonna take you and Susie to Bryant Park tomorrow. There's the best Christmas market and ice skating and … do not wear tights under any circumstances. It's definitely a jeans and boots excursion.'

'Seth, what I said about the photos and Dan, it's …' Lara began.

'You're tired of me already. I knew it,' Seth said, letting her go and folding his arms across his chest.

'What you did, replying to me on Twitter, caring to bother … it was a really sweet, lovely thing to do.'

Now his stomach juices started to curdle a little. He hadn't been sweet and lovely, Trent had. And it had only been one tweet – a cheesy TV line. But it had obviously meant a great deal to her.

'Let me take you and Susie to Bryant Park tomorrow,' Seth jumped in quickly. 'Let's take lots of photos of everything NYC has to offer and it's up to you if you post any to social-media channels or not.'

'I know I said I wasn't a fan of shopping, but I do love a Christmas market,' Lara admitted.

'Then it's a d—' Seth stopped himself from saying the word 'date'. 'A deal,' he concluded.

'A deal,' she repeated with a smile.

Thirty-One

Seth Hunt and Trent Davenport's apartment, West Village

'Good, you're up!' Trent clapped his hands together as he entered the kitchen.

Seth had been awake for a few hours, mind churning over everything that had happened over the past few days. His birth mom, the two baby hats, the impromptu audition at Cafe Cluny, and ... Lara. He had thought rather too much about Lara. More than he should have and nothing in the realms of platonic. In the end he'd got up, dressed in sweats and gone running before the city fully came to life. Christmas had been in abundance, decorated spruces pinned to hotel frontages, strings of lights hanging from every lamppost and structure, the scent of sweet gingery spice in the air. The streets had been crunchy with snow, the sidewalks frosted like icing on a cake and working his body through exercise in the fresh morning air had been invigorating.

'Yeah, I've been for a run and then I'm going to Bryant Park.'

'When?' Trent asked, grabbing the orange juice Seth had just removed from the fridge out of his hands.

'This morning. Ten.'

'Oh no, no, no. I've got plans for you,' Trent told him. 'You're opening up a winter wonderland near Washington Square.'

'What?' Seth exclaimed. 'Today? When? And how come this is the first I've heard of it?'

'Well ... they wanted a famous doctor and David Tennant couldn't make it.' Trent unscrewed the cap on the juice and drank straight from the bottle.

'You mean they wanted *anyone* who could make it and you suggested me. It's not got anything to do with your friend Carlson again, has it?'

'Seriously, Seth, do you not think I learned my lesson after the peanut butter incident?'

'It *is* him, isn't it!' Seth exclaimed, taking back the orange juice.

'No,' Trent insisted.

'Trent!'

'OK, yes, but I owe him a favour. He did a good deal for my sister on a car she desperately needed because the school her kid goes to now is in the middle of Nowheres-ville, and this is a new venture for him.'

'It's *his* winter wonderland?' Seth asked. 'Is it gonna be just a car lot with spray snow over the merchandise?'

'The exact details of the wonder in the wonderland are sketchy, but he's got the press coming and there are definitely reindeer for the kids to pet and you're one of the new Stand for Wildlife ambassadors, and my best friend so ...'

'God, Trent!' Seth exclaimed. 'I'm not sure making you my agent was my best move.'

Trent gasped, putting his hand to his chest. 'I'm wounded. You've Nerf-gunned me right here.' He thumped his chest.

There was no way he was going to let Lara down. Bryant Park had been his suggestion and ... he really wanted to see her. He had friended her on Facebook last night for two reasons. Firstly so, if she wanted to, she could tag him in any photos they created and secondly because he really wanted to look at her profile. Except she had yet to accept. And that search bar had been blinking at him for another reason ... suggesting he inputted his birth mother's name. He had got as far as typing 'Candice' and then backed out.

'I met Toby Jackson at Cafe Cluny last night,' Seth told Trent, pouring himself a glass of juice then handing the plastic bottle back to his friend.

'You did? How did it go?'

Seth smiled as he remembered his 'performance' in the French restaurant. How he had become the character of Sam and how much Lara had loved it.

'He told me to come to call-back,' Seth said.

'Oh, my freaking God! No way! That is awesome!' Trent held his hand up to be high-fived and Seth obliged. 'That's what I'm talking about! You and me, the dream team, huh?'

'Well ...'

'OK, so I've got some finishing bits to do on my nut commercial this morning, but I will try and meet you at Carlson's Christmas World at twelve. It'll be easy. Just say a few words, cut a ribbon, stroke a reindeer and you're out of there.'

'Carlson's Christmas World?' Seth said, shaking his head.

'Carlson's Christmas World today, lead role in a Universal picture tomorrow. This season is gonna be epic.'

Thirty-Two

Bryant Park

'I will not be ice skating,' David announced, shifting from one foot to the other as they stood outside the large area given over to what seemed like hundreds of glass chalets filled with Christmas wares. A large golden tree dominated the scene. It was like someone had parted the hard steel skyscrapers and inserted a little piece of village into the mix. It was somewhat more stream-lined than the higgledy-piggledy stalls at Appleshaw events but it all still looked highly seasonal, with an added New York touch.

'Why not?' Susie asked. She put her arm through his and hugged him close. 'You love to dance. We could pretend we're Torvill and Dean doing a sexy rumba.'

'Dancing is fluid,' David said. 'Unless you are a professional ice skater, trying to move fluidly and fluently with metal knives on your feet is never going to happen.'

'Ah,' Lara said. 'But, if you don't ever practise then how can you become professional?'

'Lara, there are some things in life that you're born to do and there are other things you realise you will never be skilled at.' He shook his head, flakes of snow displacing. 'Like me with hair styling.'

'Oh, David, I actually think you're very good at cutting hair no matter what anyone else says,' Lara joked.

David opened and closed his mouth, inhaling snowflakes and looking distraught.

'David, that's just Lara's idea of a joke,' Susie said. 'Actually, she was just saying last night, when I told her about the woman with the hairpiece shaped like a Christmas star, that she fancies a change. And I thought, instead of me giving her a hair makeover, perhaps *you* could do it.' Susie smiled. 'Who wouldn't want their hair styled by someone who looks after a prince?'

'Lara,' David said, sliding into her space, a look of pure joy in his eyes. 'I make you look like Angelina Jolie.'

'I think that might be a little ambitious,' Lara replied. 'Considering her hair is long and she's beautiful and—'

'We can extend!' David said, his fingers in her hair, pulling a little.

'Ow!' Lara stated. 'That hurts!'

'It was all about the new weave last night at the show, wasn't it, David?' Susie remarked, nodding.

'Before new technologies, the hair pieces resemble the backside of a dirty racoon,' David said knowingly. 'This might be OK if you are my great-aunt Luciana, but if you are not then ...'

'I've heard enough!' Lara announced. 'Please, Susie, get the crazy cutter out of my follicles!'

'Hey,' Seth said.

Lara spun around. 'Oh, thank God, someone sane! Help me, the mad hairdressers are trying to get me to sign up to extensions and new looks I'm really not sure about.'

'Well, hello,' David said, giving Seth an approving look up and down. 'I don't believe we've met this side of a TV screen.'

'David, this is Seth. Seth, this is my boyfriend, David,' Susie said.

'It's really good to meet you,' Seth said, holding out his hand.

'You too, *Ese*.' David shook his hand then looked deep into his eyes. 'Have you thought about turning blond?'

'Er, no. I mean, unless it was for a role.'

'Step away, David,' Susie ordered. 'Give the man back his hand and come and let me choose what you can buy me for Christmas.'

Susie tugged at David's coat sleeve and pulled him towards the entrance to the market.

'So,' Lara said, smiling at Seth. 'What's the best thing about this market? I'm thinking there's got to be some great food stalls.'

'There are,' Seth admitted. 'But, listen, before we go in, I have to leave in a couple hours, earlier than I thought. Trent has promised my services to one of his friends and basically, well, I have to open a real bad-sounding winter wonderland.'

'Really?'

'Yeah, really. Sorry.'

'Don't be sorry, it sounds like fun and I'll probably be bored of shopping by then.'

'You wanna come?' Seth asked her, surprised.

'I can't think of anything more fun than a bad-sounding winter wonderland.'

'Cool,' Seth replied. 'Great. Carlson will really appreciate your support and you may even get a car bumper sticker.'

'A Christmas gift for Tina! Result.' Lara smiled. 'Come on, before those two start buying me hair.'

The air was thick with so many fragrances – chilli, mace, sweet candy, butterscotch, chocolate, ginger – and carols and festive songs rose up from every corner. Seth remembered coming here with his parents, buying gifts and donating to the various charity buckets. He'd eaten bagels as big as his head and met Santa. He wondered if that would have all happened if his birth mother hadn't given him up. Knowing who she was had definitely made him start second-guessing quite a bit.

But, the real highlight was watching Lara take in the Christmas market. She'd baulked at yoga wear and fluffy angora sweaters and had tried on a wide solid silver necklace that she claimed cut off her air supply. Then she had toyed with the idea of getting her dad a jar of garlic pickles from Pickle Me Pete. The way she looked at things was so singular. Everything was regarded in so many ways, making it more of an experience than just a product. For him it was like seeing the whole world through fresh eyes. And now, finally, before he had to think about leaving for Washington Square, they were at the edge of the ice rink preparing for skating. David and Susie were still getting boots to fit after David complained that nothing felt quite right. Seth wasn't sure either of the hair stylists were going to get on the ice at all.

'You've skated before, right?' Seth asked her, over the sound of Christmas music and the swish of experienced skaters' blades.

'I will give anything a try,' Lara answered, stepping forward.

'Wait! What?' Seth exclaimed. 'You can't just go and step out on the ice like that if you've not skated before.'

'Why not?' Lara asked.

'Well, it's, you know … not that easy.'

'You mean you think I can't do it.'

'I would never say that.'

'Hmm, your mouth is moving and the words are coming out but I'm not sure I believe you.' She went to step off onto the rink again.

'Lara, seriously, you're gonna give me a heart attack if you just step out like that,' Seth said, taking hold of her arm.

'What's this?' Lara exclaimed. 'Getting all controlling? Perhaps they *should* have given you the Christian Grey role.'

'Very funny,' he answered. 'But, be serious, the first time … it's harder than you think.'

Lara closed her eyes and grimaced. 'I almost feel like I'm having the sex ed talk at school again.'

'And I feel like if I let you stride on out there I'm gonna be taking you to the ER.'

'I don't know which part worries me the most. The bit where you said if you "let" me, or your concern about the ER when you are a virtual doctor.'

'Please, take it slow.'

'Well, slow or not, I'm not going to be able to find out what it's like unless you get off me.'

'You could hold on to me,' Seth suggested.

'Like a five-year-old?'

'Most five-year-olds here skate better than I do.'

'I'm going on now,' Lara said, picking his hand up from her arm and getting ready to step off the firm ground.

'Lara! Lara, wait!' His calls were in vain as she stepped off onto the ice. But, after a few tentative slips and slides and a little arm flailing, she righted herself, found her balance and began moving across the rink almost confidently. He pushed off, his ability taking a few metres of rink before it kicked back in.

'Are you like this with everything?' Seth asked, skating up alongside her.

'Like what?' Lara replied.

'So confident. So unafraid.'

'What doesn't kill you makes you stronger, doesn't it?'

'So, they say,' Seth answered. 'But not everyone is brave enough to live their life like that.'

'I'm not like that with everything,' Lara admitted. 'Practical things like this, like climbing trees and avoiding carnage in my truck at the advent parade, they're all about belief in your own ability. I don't doubt my ability to do things.'

'And you should definitely keep going with that.'

'I just doubt everyone around me,' Lara admitted. 'No, that's unfair, not everyone, not my dad or Aldo or Susie or Mrs Fitch – although she did go a bit weird when she was on the wrong medication – and I thought not Dan but ...'

'You keep your circle close and your world tight because ...' Seth began as they got to the first corner of the rink.

'Because if you trust too much you'll only be let down. That's why I never had a proper boyfriend before Dan. The tom-boy-who-drives-a-truck-and-drinks-beer-and-lives-in-a-barn novelty tends to wear off as soon as they meet my almost-brother. Plus, I'm very picky.'

'But if you lose your faith in human nature and never step outside of your comfort zone with it, then ...'

Seth watched her lift one skate off the floor and balance precariously on the other skate. 'I'm out of my comfort zone. I'm skating on one leg in New York City when I've never been out of England before. I got up close and personal with a lemur on my very first day here and I ate sausages in a garden in the snow and last night I sucked Mussolini ... wait, no, definitely not that ... I ate mousse*line* and chicken in a great French restaurant and watched this amazing actor perform something special just for me.'

She slid effortlessly over the ice, elevated leg stretching out behind her now as she grew in confidence. Shivers spiked down his spine. The novelty of her, as she had called it, was only strengthening in his mind. Then she turned, slipping a little before laughing and making a grab for his arms.

Smiling, she then sighed. 'I just need to strengthen my resolve about Dan and remember all the reasons I never had a boyfriend in the first place.'

'Hey, no,' Seth said immediately, helping her to keep her balance. 'I mean, yes, to the resolve strengthening. But, please, don't think that all men are like Dan.'

What was he saying? This was not his business. He didn't know Dan. After what she had told him he really *didn't want* to know Dan. But it was not his place to comment on anything like that. However, he'd said it and she was looking at him and he wanted the ice rink to melt, turn into water and plunge him into its icy depths never to resurface until he'd learned some better lines.

'I don't,' Lara answered. 'Not all of them. I have my dad and Aldo, remember?' She let go of him and started to skate backwards, very pedestrian but somehow staying upright. 'Come on, less of the chat and more of the moves, Dr Mike.'

He smiled. 'You got it.'

Thirty-Three

Washington Square Park

'I like this one,' Lara said, showing Seth one of the photos Susie had taken on her phone. 'You look like you're about to fall over and I look like an ice-skating goddess.'

They were walking up through the park following sketchy directions to Carlson's Christmas World, which was apparently a block along from Washington Square Park on a piece of scrub land Carlson was renting for the season. Seth was becoming more and more unsure about this being in any way good for his career portfolio.

It was snowing lightly, decorating the ground, the benches and the chess-playing areas with winter white. There were still a few older men, wrapped up warm in coats, scarves and hats, playing chess despite the cold.

'Maybe I should tweet it and add #LemurGirl. I know I wasn't exactly trending, but it might be a cool touch,' Lara continued. 'I mean, I don't want anyone else to be able to grab my title now I have one.'

'No,' Seth said quickly. 'Don't add that.' The very last thing he wanted was for Trent to be gaining any momentum on his plan to pitch Lara's heartache to Ellen DeGeneres.

'Why not?' Lara asked, eyes off her phone and now looking directly at him.

'We should … make it more personal.' What the hell was he saying now? It seemed like today he had total foot-in-mouth disease. 'I mean … we're friends, right? We don't need any more publicity than that.' He meant it, wholeheartedly, but he wasn't sure it made any sense in this context. He wasn't so great at thinking on his feet. His mom always said it was because he was too honest, and she always sounded so proud.

'I accepted your friend request on Facebook,' Lara told him. 'You're now one of the lucky people able to see all my photos from Truck Fest.'

'I cannot wait,' Seth said sincerely.

'So, shall I share this photo of us?' Lara asked him, coming to a stop right at the foot of the arch.

Lara's hand was shaking a little. She was trying to pass this moment off as something of nothing, but it really wasn't. The minute she uploaded this picture to her social media she was making a statement. She was telling the world, including Dan, that she was in New York with Seth Hunt and she was trying to enjoy every second. And when she wasn't actively *trying to* enjoy every second she *really was* enjoying every second. The city, all the fun, unexpected things she had done already were so new to her, yet she'd found them more exhilarating than terrifying. This wide world was slowly being opened up for her, and she really wanted to just embrace it.

'Lara,' Seth said softly.

'Don't try and stop me,' she replied quickly. 'This was the plan, remember.' Her thumb was still hovering over the 'tweet' button.

'Plans can change,' Seth said. 'They can … metamorphise.'

'He won't care anyway,' Lara stated. 'Why would he? He has Chloe now.'

'It doesn't have to be about anyone else,' Seth said. 'It can just be about you.' He paused. 'Do you care that he cares?'

As Lara thought about his question people walked past them, laden down with shopping bags, heads bowed against the snow. Did she care that Dan cared now? After the single status and the Christmas market with another woman …

'No,' she answered positively. 'I don't.' She pressed the button and put the phone back into the pocket of her coat. 'Now, take me to this *real bad* winter wonderland.'

Thirty-Four

Carlson's Christmas World

'Oh my God!' Lara exclaimed, hands over her mouth. Seth could tell she didn't know whether to laugh or cry and he was right there with her. Carlson's Christmas World looked like the most unappealing festive expo you could imagine. He hated that Lara was seeing this and he was *very* glad that Susie and David had declined the offer to come and were instead staying at Bryant Park for more shopping.

At the entrance to the patch of wasteland stood two elves in outfits at least three sizes too small for them – one of them eating a burger, the other talking on his cell phone – and there was a food truck with thick, black, acrid smoke pouring from under the barely staying-in-one-piece awning. Just behind the entrance arch – a wonky structure part-covered in red and white balloons and tinsel – there was a tiny merry-go-round with half a dozen miniature vehicles covered in peeling stickers of Disney characters and some sort of tunnel alleging that it led to Santa's Workshop. Finally, there seemed to be a woman selling glow sticks in front of a line of second-hand cars and a small badly fenced enclosure containing a miserable-looking reindeer.

'I don't know why I thought it wouldn't be this awful,' Seth remarked. 'I'm only surprised that there are actually people lined up to go into this ... mess.'

'Is that a real reindeer?' Lara asked. 'Or someone dressed up?'

Seth adjusted his glasses and focused. 'I think it's real, but it's not moving much.'

'I'm not surprised,' Lara stated. 'It doesn't look like it has room to move. Come on.' She stepped boldly forward.

'Lara, where are you going?' Seth asked, wondering if he should follow.

'To check the reindeer is OK and to get away from all the smoke!' She marched towards the elves.

'But,' Seth started, 'it isn't open yet.' He took a step towards Lara then looked back to see Carlson heading his way. What he really wanted to do was get out of here completely.

'Seth Hunt!' Carlson bellowed as only a New York car salesman could, tramping over the snow towards him. He was only around five feet four, but what he lacked in height he made up for in width. There was definitely a look of Danny DeVito about him. 'Everybody! Just like I promised! The doctor is in the house! Dr Mike from ZKT's *Manhattan Med* is right here at Carlson's Christmas World! And he is gonna be opening the gates in just a few minutes and signing autographs for the whole of the afternoon.'

There was excited murmuring from the gathered crowd and their group seemed to do a subdued surge forward.

'Wait, what?' Seth said. 'Carlson, Trent said I had to cut a ribbon not stick around. I have things to do this afternoon.'

'Trent told me your schedule was clear for the rest of the day,' Carlson said through gritted teeth, somehow maintaining a smile for his audience.

'Yeah, well, Trent doesn't run my entire life.' His gaze went to Lara who was conversing with one of the elves.

'But he's your agent now, right?'

'He's on trial.' And he would make sure Trent literally *was* on trial after this episode. He might even involve *Judge Judy*.

'I don't care if I have to duck under the ribbon that isn't cut yet! I'm going to see that reindeer!' Lara yelled from her position a few feet away.

'Hey, who's the chick?' Carlson asked, his attention going to Lara.

'I'm not seeing any Christmas poultry around here, Carlson,' Seth answered. 'If you mean who's the *lady* over there then that's my ...' He stopped then started again. 'She's ... with me.'

'She looks like she's getting a little Alanis Morrissette with my employees,' Carlson announced. 'Hey! Lady! We're not open yet.' He started to strut towards Lara and the elves.

Seth rushed after him, feeling that this whole interaction was not going to go well.

'Do you have any idea how to look after a reindeer?' Lara asked the tallest elf.

'Do *you*?' he retorted.

'I do as it happens,' Lara replied with a sniff. '*And* I have a brother who is almost an expert on every animal there is.'

'*Do* you?' the elf said again.

'I do,' Lara replied. 'And that's why I'm going in there to see if it's all right. Do you even know what reindeers eat?'

'Do you?' the elf asked.

'Oh my God! Are they the only two words you know?'

'Lara, we're not gonna stay,' Seth said as he arrived.

'What?!' Carlson exclaimed. 'I've got people here! Promises have been made!'

'We have to stay,' Lara said, turning to him. 'We have to make sure the reindeer is OK. I mean, look at this crappy place. It's not a wonderland. It's like something out of a dystopian movie.'

'Hey! I resent that!' Carlson yelled. 'And can you keep your voice down? I need people through the gate. I got a family to feed.'

'What do you want us to do, boss?' the shorter elf asked, his pointed hat drooping as he spoke.

The reindeer let out a discontented bray and that was enough for Lara. Before anyone could do or say any more she had ducked down underneath the festive ribbon and was striding purposefully towards the pen.

'Hey! We're not open yet! And it's ten bucks!' Carlson hollered after her.

Ignoring his protests, she kept marching, waving off the interest of the woman with the glow sticks and the man in charge of the awful roundabout. While she was power-walking, as best as she was able in the snow, she pulled out her phone and hit one of her speed-dials. She still had no idea what the time difference was between here and the UK but at this moment she didn't care.

'Lara!' came the excited voice and there was Aldo, messy curly hair bouncing over his face.

'Hey, Aldo! Just tell me you're not driving at the moment, are you?'

'I don't drive or answer calls without free hands,' he repeated like a mantra. 'I'm at the garden centre. Mrs Fitch has made mince-pie cake.'

Lara's stomach lurched, and she realised then she hadn't eaten anything since breakfast. She would kill for cake right now.

'Do you want to see the cake?' Aldo asked.

'I would, Aldo, but I've got something I need you to help me with.'

'In New York?' he gasped, then gulped. 'I can fly too?'

'No, just help me here, on the phone.' She had finally reached the makeshift enclosure and the reindeer, who wasn't looking happy at all. There was one vague patch of grass that wasn't fully covered in snow and nothing else for him to eat. She switched the view on her phone around and showed Aldo the scene.

'That's a reindeer!' came Aldo's response. 'It's a porcupine caribou. Can you get closer, Lara?'

Lara held her phone nearer to the reindeer, moving it up and down its body and finally stopping at its sad-looking face.

'Are you at a park, Lara?' Aldo asked her.

'Not really,' Lara replied. 'Actually, not at all, if I'm honest. I don't think the reindeer looks very well.'

'He's sad,' Aldo answered. 'His eyes. They are not bright like they should be. Feel his fur, please.'

'Hang on a second,' Lara said, turning the phone screen back around and tucking the device under her chin. 'What am I feeling for?'

'His skin, it should be thick under his fur. If you don't feel thick then he is too thin, and you need to feed him, then take him to the vet.'

She knew calling Aldo had been the right thing to do. Her almost-brother, the almost-vet. Lara touched the reindeer, talking soothingly to it as they went. 'There, boy. There's a good boy.'

'Lara, we are not staying here,' Seth said as he arrived at the pen. 'I thought, that is, I had an idea it might be bad, but this is something else. I can't open this place.'

'Lara, who is the man?' Aldo asked from the confines of Lara's phone.

'The reindeer's skin isn't very thick,' Lara confirmed. 'And he makes a noise when I touch him some places.' She swallowed. 'Not *those* places … just near the back of his back.'

'You think the reindeer's sick?' Seth asked, sounding concerned.

'Lara! Who is the man?' Aldo called again. 'Is the man dojo or no dojo?'

'Sorry,' Lara said, looking into the phone again and giving Aldo her full attention. 'No dojo, Aldo,' she said quickly. 'This is Seth, he's … a friend.'

'Your new boyfriend?' Aldo asked.

'No no, just a … friend-friend.' She had no idea why her cheeks were heating up so rapidly in this cold weather. Perhaps she had caught something from the reindeer. She moved the phone in front of Seth's face to pass a few moments. 'Aldo, say hello to Seth.'

'Hey, hello, Aldo,' Seth said, taking hold of Lara's phone. 'It's good to see you. I've heard a lot about you.'

'You are being nice to Lara?' Aldo barked.

'Yes I think … I—'

'Aldo, I'm fine,' Lara said, taking the phone back again.

'*Dan* is not fine. Dan is *dojo*, no matter what you say.'

'Aldo, I don't want to talk about Dan. *We* need to talk about this reindeer. What's the best thing I can do for it.'

'It needs room to walk around,' Aldo stated. 'Fresh water and hay.'

Lara nodded, her mind already half-decided before asking the question. She looked to Seth. 'Seth, we need to take him to the zoo.'

Thirty-Five

'There's no answer,' Lara said with a sigh. 'It keeps going through to the information hotline and telling me about the size of elephants.'

'Carlson's heading this way with the elves.' Seth swallowed. How had he managed to get himself into this situation? The opening of a tin-pot Christmas whatever-it-was where an animal wasn't being cared for properly. They had made a decision. If the reindeer was sick, then he needed proper attention. Lara was trying to call the Central Park Zoo.

'Come on,' Lara said, opening the gate of the reindeer's enclosure.

'What are you doing?'

'Well, we can't get hold of the zoo so ...' She stepped inside, the reindeer making no attempt to stop her entrance.

'So ...' He wasn't completely following events but Lara's move into the fenced area was worrying. Did reindeers bite? Or stampede? However, from the look of him, any nature-given default to trample seemed to be overridden by general misery.

'We're going to take him there,' she announced, picking up the end of a fraying lead that was getting damp on the cold ground.

'What?!'

'Hey!' Carlson called, stomping towards them, a mad expression on his face. 'What's going on here? Some sort of animal welfare inspection?'

'Something like that,' Lara reacted. 'Because you really need one.'

'Listen, lady, this animal belongs to a friend of a friend and he's in good shape.'

'Who's your friend of a friend?' Lara asked, stepping up to Carlson, the lead still in her grip. 'Bad Santa?'

'Seth, what is this, buddy? All I was asking was for you to cut the ribbon, say a few words and sign your name a couple of hundred times. You don't have to fall in love with the place.'

'Well,' Seth began. 'That's kind of where you're wrong, Carlson.' He adjusted his glasses. 'You see, I'm now an ambassador for Stand for Wildlife at Central Park Zoo, so I can't just come here, where there's an animal, and ignore things if they're not quite right.'

'*Quite* right is pushing it, I'd say,' Lara remarked.

'Come on, man, I need this break,' Carlson said with a shake of his head.

'I can't do it, Carlson. I'm sorry,' Seth told him.

'And we're taking the reindeer,' Lara said, stepping forward, out of the enclosure, widening the gate first with her hip and then using her free hand to open it further.

'I'm not quite sure that's an option, Lara,' Seth said. 'Do you know how far Central Park is from here?'

'No,' she answered. 'But what other answer is there?'

'You can't take him anywhere,' Carlson exclaimed. 'Mickey! Kirk! Stop her!'

The elves moved forward, looking like they were trying to make themselves wider, arms hanging like menacing apes.

'Stop me?' Lara questioned, eyeing up Carlson's little helpers.

'Carlson, look,' Seth said, recognising the fire in Lara's eyes. 'Let us take the reindeer.' He didn't believe he had just said that. 'You avoid an animal health inspection. No one has to know the reindeer came from here. You can carry on with your ...' Seth looked around at what was left to entertain in the 'park'. 'Car sales and glow sticks and ... *Finding Dory* carousel.'

'But the reindeer is my USP. Everywhere in the city has everything else ... and bigger and better.'

'Are you going to get out of my way?' Lara asked the elves. 'Or are me and Rudolph here going to mow you down?'

'Is this some sort of Christmas ruse?' Carlson asked, folding his arms across his chest and seeming to look at the situation anew. 'Are people gonna spring out and start a flash mob?'

'No,' Lara answered. 'We're just taking the reindeer. Merry Christmas.' She strode forward, the dejected-looking creature putting one hoof in front of the other and plodding after her.

'I'm sorry, Carlson. But it's the right thing to do,' Seth said, patting the man on the shoulder then striding to catch Lara up.

'It's almost an hour to Central Park from here, by foot,' Seth stated the moment they were off the wasteland and onto the sidewalk away from the disappointed crowds Carlson was trying to placate with free burnt offerings from the food truck.

'An hour,' Lara said with a gasp. 'Is it really?'

'Yeah,' Seth answered. 'I know the subway makes everything seem like it's right there on your doorstep but ...'

'Well, we'd better make a start,' Lara said, tugging a little at the rope. 'Come on, boy.'

'Lara,' Seth said, following her. 'We can't walk an hour in NYC with a reindeer.'

'What do you suggest?' she asked. 'We've called the zoo, they won't answer. We can't leave him there at that awful place where they'd probably put people on his back for rides or feed him some of whatever was coming out of that food van.'

'I know, but it's New York,' Seth reminded. 'And he's a reindeer ... on a lead.'

'But, newsflash, he doesn't fly! So, what's the alternative?'

There were already a group of people across the street, mobile phones trained on them, laughing, pointing and taking photos. She didn't care. Just as long as they got the animal somewhere more appropriate, somewhere safe.

'We'll walk,' Seth stated. 'For as long as it takes me to get hold of my dad.' He slipped his mobile phone out of his pocket. 'He'll know someone with some kind of transport. OK?'

She took a breath, meeting his gaze and nodding. 'OK.'

Seth shook his head at her, a smile on his lips. 'You really are something else, Lemur Girl.'

She nodded. 'Yeah. I know.'

Thirty-Six

The Chapel Shelter, W 40th Street

'Lara, you're freezing! Come and sit right by the heater!' Kossy began sweeping around, moving boxes that had been made into multi-faith tableaus – some depicting the Christian stable birth scene, others with festive takes on Hanukkah and Eid-ul-Adha. With chattering teeth, Lara let herself be guided towards a long, ancient-looking radiator where a few people were already sat around, their coats still on.

'We ... took a ... reindeer to the zoo,' Lara told her, the words barely escaping her freezing lips.

'I know, sweetheart. Ted told me.' Kossy looked up from helping Lara onto a chair. 'Seth, bring coffee over here. Felice, go get some more blankets.'

'Coffee coming up,' Seth said, stamping his feet on the bare boards and blowing on his hands.

'Seriously!' Felice remarked. 'We sleep out all year round and the princess needs a blanket!'

'She's right,' Lara said, going to stand up. 'I'm fine. I can go back to our apartment and get warm. I don't want to take anything away from anyone here.'

'You sit down!' Kossy ordered in no uncertain terms. 'No one is taking anything away from anyone here. We're a community. All-comers. No judgement.'

'I liked things better when it wasn't all politically correct. Can't a homeless person get any benefit any more?' Felice tutted, but moved towards the shelving housing the blankets.

'That girl has way too much sass,' Kossy remarked to Lara. 'And she's been getting a bed here every night for five years, lottery or no lottery.'

'She can't find somewhere more permanent?' Lara asked.

'Here's the thing,' Kossy said. 'The second I mention that if she stays here too long I'm gonna have to recommend she talks to someone about a transitional housing programme I don't see her for a week.' She sighed. 'And I worry.'

'I worried about the reindeer,' Lara admitted. 'Because my almost-brother was worried about the reindeer.'

'So, you froze yourself half to death trying to walk it through the streets of the city.'

'We only got halfway until Ted and Morris came with the horsebox.'

'Take off this coat,' Kossy ordered. 'It's soaking wet with snow.'

Lara nodded as she attempted to remove her arms from the sleeves. 'I didn't realise New York was so cold all the time. Or that it snows so much.' She sniffed. 'I would have done more research, but I didn't know I was coming almost till I came and—'

'I got it,' Kossy said, nodding as Seth arrived with a steaming mug of coffee. 'And as for you! Are you crazy? Letting her wander around Manhattan leading a reindeer? Wearing something that looks about as waterproof as a club sandwich?'

'Mom, I did say that—' Seth began.

'I don't wanna hear it.' Kossy took the coffee from him and handed it to Lara. 'Go tell Bernadette we need some soup.'

At the mention of food Lara's stomach took flight and she had to swallow to get it to chill out a little. She was starving … no, not starving … just hungry.

'Sometimes I wonder if I taught him any sense at all,' Kossy remarked with a scoff as Felice arrived back with a blanket. Kossy made a show of wrapping the rough, yet warm material around Lara's shoulders, then handed Felice the damp coat. The girl looked at it, holding it with two fingers like it was contaminated, then crossed the room with it.

'It wasn't Seth's fault I got cold,' Lara insisted. 'I was the one who forced the rescue and he kept offering me his coat and I kept saying no and performing lip-trumpet to Camila Cabello's "Havana" to keep warm.'

'Well,' Kossy said, sitting down next to Lara and putting an arm around her. 'You're here now and getting warmer.'

'And the reindeer is safe,' Lara stated. 'They said they would get the vet to check him over, get him somewhere for tonight and then find another zoo with reindeers already to take him.'

'That's good,' Kossy answered. 'Another stray soul saved.'

There was something about the tone of her voice that made Lara realise Kossy wasn't referring to the caribou. 'You're thinking about Seth … and his other mum.'

Kossy immediately shook her head, so fast and furious that eventually, after a good ten seconds of bouncing curls the negative shake finally turned into a nod. 'He told you.'

'Yes,' Lara said. 'And I know it's none of my business, but I suggested, if he wants to find her, he should start by searching on Facebook.'

Kossy continued nodding, tears welling up in her eyes. 'That's good advice.'

'I wasn't trying to put my nose in. I just said it would be the first place I would try if I was looking for *my* mother.'

'You're adopted too?' Kossy gasped, hands going to her mouth.

'No,' Lara answered. 'Just abandoned, by one of my parents at least. But it was a long time ago and …'

'You've never forgotten the loss.'

That hadn't been what she was thinking. In most ways her life felt good, it was just the lack of explanation of her mother's absence that was missing. And as each year passed it became more and more irrelevant to her.

'I know I haven't known Seth very long,' Lara began. 'But I don't think he will ever get up the courage to look for his mum on his own.'

'You don't?'

Lara shook her head. 'I think he wants to. He's just second-guessing his reasons for doing it when he has such a great mum already.' Her teeth chattered. 'But, I think, if someone were to, maybe, look for his mum on Facebook, or find her, by some sort of chance, then it might not be as hard a decision for him to make.'

'You think I should look for her on Facebook?' Kossy whispered, eyes darting around the room as if expecting Seth to be at her shoulder.

'I don't *really* know,' Lara said. 'But I think something is holding him back, despite him wanting to know who she is.'

Kossy nodded, seeming to take on board what she had said. Then she wiped at her eyes and gave Lara a smile. 'I think you know my son well already. I think you must come to our annual fundraiser.'

'Is there beer?' Lara asked with a grin.

'It's nothing like the cook-out at my place,' Kossy told her. 'It's wall-to-wall swanky and involves all the people with money I've courted all year long to donate to the cause.'

'Do I have to wear tights?' Lara asked.

'Do you have to wear what?'

'Never mind,' Lara said with a smile. Her stomach rumbled. 'What flavour is the soup?'

'Well, today actually we have a treat,' Kossy said, getting to her feet. 'It's reindeer.'

Lara's eyes widened as she felt the icy feeling return to her every part. And then she realised Kossy was laughing and shaking her abundant head of hair again.

'It's winter vegetable, sweetheart. What would pull St Nick's sleigh if we ate them all?'

'You know, if you look at her any longer you're gonna have her face imprinted on your retinas for the whole of eternity,' Felice said to Seth.

'What?' he asked, the bowl of soup hot in his hands.

'I mean, each to their own and everything, but you might miss out on looking at Emma Stone or Charlize Theron, or that soup.'

'You want the soup?' Seth asked, offering the bowl to her.

'Hell no!' Felice exclaimed like he had just suggested she eat a New Year's firework. 'I don't take charity. It's not dinner time … and apparently *she's* as cold as Jack Frost.'

'You don't like Lara?' Seth queried, a little confused.

'I don't not like her,' Felice answered. 'I think she's crazy, stupid, weird but I don't not like her.' She took a breath. 'I think she's kinda cool, in a first world kind of way, you know, if you like that sort of vibe.' She sniffed. 'And you obviously do.'

'Felice, I'm getting really lost in this conversation,' Seth admitted.

'Will you take her out?' Felice asked. 'On a date. Because I can't stand to watch you both being like you are with each other and hip-hopping around the fact that what you really wanna do is rip each other's clothes off, and then have a meaningful talk about it like real people do, in real relationships, or in *Manhattan Med*, so someone told me.'

'I …' Seth looked back to Lara then again at Felice, thrown by her straight-talking. 'She has someone.'

'Not according to Facebook.'

'Felice, do you have a phone?'

'No,' she said. 'But I have friends. And this Dan she used to go out with seems like a real a-hole.' She shrugged her shoulders. 'What can I say? I wanna look after the people I don't not like.'

'It's not a clear-cut situation,' Seth said, moving his fingers as they started to warm with the heat of the soup.

'Wake up, Actor Boy, this is life and you're sitting on top with a great view. Don't waste it.'

Thirty-Seven

Waitress, Broadway

'I can't believe we're on Broadway!' Susie exclaimed. 'Going to see *a show* on Broadway!' She grabbed David's arm, looping it through hers and squeezing tight.

Neither could Lara. She had got back to the apartment and was just telling Ron, Hermione and Harry how exhausted she still felt as some sort of reindeer-pulling, ice-skating jetlag combination caught up with her and Susie had burst in with screams of 'Broadway' and '*Waitress*'. At first Lara thought Susie had given up her dreams of hairdressing and was getting into catering, until Susie had told her about a play based on a film and it became clear they were taking in a show at the most famous theatre strip in the world.

'I tell you,' David said. 'You come to New York and I will make all your dreams come true.'

'That's so sweet,' Susie answered with a sigh.

Lara swallowed, moving her gaze from the glowing-with-love couple to the street around her. It was busy despite the spiralling snowfall, the wind a little fiercer than earlier, everything glowing like the bright lights she had seen on films. Whole walls of moving advertising interspersed with Christmas wishes and more festive signage and the sound of the Rat Pack filled the night. She sighed contentedly, but then realised something didn't feel quite right. Something was missing. And, bizarrely, it wasn't Dan. It was Seth. Crazy! Mad! She was still – kind of – in a relationship, the only relationship she'd ever had. She was in a foreign land with a holiday, first-time-over-the-Atlantic, mindset. That had to be it. Except it didn't stop her wishing he was here by her side, telling her a fact about the area or laughing at her naivety about everything.

'Hey.'

Now she was imagining him so hard it looked like he was actually in front of her. She blinked and blinked again as she stopped at the entrance to the Brooks Atkinson theatre. Leather brogues, smart dark blue trousers, thick winter coat, hair perfectly in place, that firm jaw and plush-looking lips …

'You made it!' Susie breathed.

Lara could tell Susie was looking at her, but she couldn't meet her eyes. Susie had said nothing about this trip to the theatre being a foursome.

'When someone offers you great seats to one of the hottest shows in town you don't say no,' Seth stated with a smile. 'I don't know how you did it, David.'

'I have my contacts,' David said, touching the side of his nose with his finger and looking suitably pleased with himself.

'He knows a prince,' Susie added.

'Can we go in?' David asked, ducking under the signage. 'I want to check out the merch stand. I need a T-shirt that says, "It Only Takes Taste" in my life.'

'Do you think they have bags?' Susie asked, rushing to follow him through the doors.

Lara smiled at Seth and shook her head. 'My friend with the bag obsession.' She didn't know what else to say. Her realisation that the event wouldn't be complete without him here had made her feel a little awkward about the fact he *was* here.

'Is this OK?' Seth asked, stepping up to her, snow catching in his hair. 'Me coming along here?'

'I don't know,' Lara admitted as if he could read what was going on inside her mind.

'Listen, I can go, if you want me to, I just—'

He looked nervous. Like he didn't know what his next lines were in this improvised script. As if he could see through her and knew that he was the absent part of the equation she had been thinking about.

'I don't want you to go.' She swallowed. She needed to make her voice sound way less romantic drama and a lot more *Ex on the Beach*. She attempted a laugh. 'I feel I owe you a night on Broadway after I made you rescue the reindeer.'

He shrugged, snowflakes scattering. 'We've almost got our own literal pet project going on, don't you think? First lemurs, then a reindeer, what's next?'

'I'm quite happy if there isn't a next,' she admitted.

'Are you two coming in?' Susie asked, appearing at the doors.

'Shall we?' Seth asked, offering her his arm.

She slipped her arm through his and smiled. 'Fill me in on everything I need to know about Broadway.'

Thirty-Eight

'All that pie!' David announced a couple of hours later. 'It made me so hungry.' He pushed open the doors to the outside.

'Don't tell me,' Susie said. 'You want to go back to that Spanish restaurant and eat more pigs' feet.'

'I would eat any part of the pig right now.'

Lara felt like she was in some sort of musical herself. As she stepped out after Susie, she didn't feel the freezing air on her skin or really notice the thick two inches of snow greeting them on the pavement, she was lost, surrounded by the atmosphere of the theatre, the drama, lights, songs and pure emotion that had bled from the performers. She hadn't experienced anything quite like it before. It was on a whole different level from the Appleshaw Players attempt at *Oliver With a Twist*.

'You OK?' Seth asked softly as she stopped under the canopy, half paying attention to David and Susie's kissing.

'I don't know,' Lara admitted with a sigh. 'Some of me feels like singing and dancing and filling myself with a double chocolate cherry torte and the other bits feel like …'

'Jenna's character really resonated with you,' Seth suggested.

'Yes!' Lara said, turning to him. 'I mean, I'm not saying she *was* me or anything but there were parts of her story that made me think, wow, I can relate to that.'

'I could tell,' Seth replied. 'You wiped some of your tears on my sleeve.'

'Did I?' Lara put her hands to her mouth in shock. 'I'm so sorry! I ... thought it was mine.'

Seth laughed. 'It's OK.'

'Come! There is a food truck just over there!' David said, performing an elaborate sashay and point.

'You hungry?' Seth asked her.

'Bernadette's soup was good but ... yes,' Lara admitted.

'Come on,' Seth said, smiling and following David's lead.

'This food truck is one of the best,' David announced when they were all gathered around the orange and black tiger-striped, Korilla BBQ van. 'I follow it around on Twitter.'

'You mean you follow them on Twitter,' Susie said.

'No,' David insisted. 'I literally follow them around on Twitter.' He grinned. 'They post the location of their van. I go there, you know, if it isn't the whole other side of the city.'

'What type of food is it?' Lara asked, enjoying the fragrance that emanated from the van. There were definite notes of ginger, soy sauce and spiced meats.

'Korean,' Seth answered.

Lara turned to look at him. 'You're a fan of the van too?'

'It's great food,' Seth told her.

'They do burrito or a rice bowl or a salad bowl ... pick a protein, pick a rice ... you choose anything,' David explained as they moved up the queue. 'I like mine with crack.'

'What?' Susie and Lara exclaimed in unison.

David laughed. 'Relax, it's a lime sauce.'

'Usually I'd play it safe and have something I've had before but ...' Lara began, edging forward and trying to look over someone's shoulder towards the van's hatch.

'She's trying new things,' Susie said, aiming the statement at Seth.

'He knows,' Lara replied. 'We talked about Mussolini.'

The benches around the George M Cohan statue were covered in snow, only pigeons brave enough to strut around on the cold, crispy topping. They stood, their hot breath visible in the air. Seth hadn't touched his rice bowl yet, he was too busy watching Lara enjoy her purple rice and Gochujang pork burrito.

'I've never tasted anything like this before,' she said in pure delight, a little sauce at the corner of her lips. 'It's like ... heaven.'

'I told you it was good,' David replied through a mouthful of kimchi. He had ordered two boxes of food.

'It's sooo good,' Susie agreed.

'I've never had Korean food before,' Lara said. 'And I like it.'

'You haven't had much of anything before unless it came out of Appleshaw,' Susie reminded. 'Seth, we have a fish and chip shop that tries to do Chinese as well as Indian.'

'Why aren't you eating?' Lara said to Seth.

'I ...' He definitely wasn't going to say because he was looking at her. He felt his cheeks develop a fever and he dug his fork into his food and put some in his mouth. 'It's great.' It *was* great, but the food experience was definitely secondary to the other internal sensations happening right now ... and he needed to keep himself in check.

'Oh no! That's my phone! That's my phone!' David squealed, dancing around in the snow, as if he didn't know what to do, food cartons wafting around in the air, hot breath coming out in bursts.

'Do you need to answer it?' Susie asked.

'Yes!' he announced, frantic. 'I am on call!'

'On call?' Lara queried. 'Are you a firefighter and didn't tell us?'

'I am a hairstylist to royalty. I am on call twenty-four seven for any hair emergencies. Susie! You must dig deep into my pocket and get it out.'

'Whoa!' Lara exclaimed. 'TMI.'

'My phone! My phone!' David screamed, almost hysterical.

'All right, stop bouncing up and down or I won't be able to get it out,' Susie answered, passing her burrito to Lara.

'Do you feel like we've walked onto the set of a really bad comedy movie?' Lara asked Seth as David and Susie dealt with the phone-answering crisis.

'It's the prince! It's the prince!' David squealed. 'Answer! And hold it to my mouth!'

'Er, now I definitely do,' Seth admitted with a laugh. He put the fork back into his food box and looked at Lara.

'What?' she asked. 'Do I have food on my face?'

'Actually, yeah,' he answered.

'I don't!'

'You do but, hey, who doesn't get food on their face when they're eating a burrito?'

'Well, you should do what they do in the movies,' Lara said. 'You should get a napkin and delicately dab at the offending whatever it is until it's gone.'

His heart was racing because now all he could focus on was her lips, her mouth, the tiniest trace of pimiento at the very corner …

'Or, you know, I could maybe … kiss it away,' he said. Saying it out loud rather than inside his head shocked him and it took every fibre of himself not to retract the statement immediately. But something was urging him on, not just the plain and simple physical desire to feel her mouth on his but something else, something deeper. He edged a little closer ...

'I ... think they had some napkins on the truck,' Lara said quickly. 'I'll go and see.'

And just like that she was gone, moving past him, heading back towards the fast food. He was the biggest idiot. She was not his to kiss.

Lara felt sick and light headed like she had spent a month in a dark cave and suddenly someone had turned on a whole city's worth of Christmas lights and blinded her. Seth Hunt had tried to kiss her. Seth *wanted* to kiss her. And she had run away. She wasn't sure which part of all that she was most affected by. Her first reaction, when Seth had said the 'k' word was one of pure thrill and excitement and, in a millisecond, she was envisaging a silver-screen snog to rival Allie and Noah's in *The Notebook*, minus the rain, but then real life had kicked in, prudence had come calling and she had fled. And no matter what, she couldn't go back without some form of wipe.

But had she wanted to kiss Seth? Taking away the Dan-sized complications, what was the answer? If she was honest with herself, it was a definite 'yes' and it had nothing to do with his Dr Mike persona. He was just the most all-round wonderful, fun, interesting, gorgeous person she had ever met. But she wasn't allowed to think that way ... or, rather, she wasn't allowing herself to think that way.

She was almost back at the truck now, passing people by the dozen, lights and the sound of Christmas music filling the night. Napkins. She had to focus on napkins.

'Lara, wait.'

She froze, literally stopped still, at the sound of Seth's voice behind her. She needed to chill out. Just act like nothing had happened. Because nothing *had* happened. She turned around, smiling at him. 'You want me to get you a napkin too?'

'No, I wanted to ... apologise.'

She swallowed, feeling suddenly like someone had taken all the festive glitter away and replaced it with paper chains made out of the *Financial Times*.

'I shouldn't have said ... what I said.'

She watched him, floundering a little, because he was just being so genuinely lovely and looking completely hot while he was doing it. She could rescue him here. She had the chance to say it didn't matter, that they could forget about it and move on, but she didn't really want to do that either.

'I mean ... I regret saying it,' he carried on. 'You know, out loud.' He swallowed, his hair falling forward a little as he started to gesticulate, as if he needed help to get his point across. 'But, I can't be sorry about thinking it. Because if I said I was sorry about thinking about it then that would be a lie.'

It was time for her to speak up now. To tell him to stop talking. Why wouldn't the words come?

'I really like you, Lara,' Seth said. '*Really* like you. More than I've liked anyone since, I guess, always. And I realise that now makes me sound like some complete, socially awkward nobody but ... I feel more connected to you after days than I've felt ... ever.'

Speak, Lara. Say something! Except she could hardly breathe. A small crowd of people dressed in red sweatshirts had appeared on the corner of the street and had begun singing 'Calypso Carol'. It was one of her favourite festive songs she'd used to sing at school. It never failed to fill her with Christmas spirit but now all it was doing was sending her heart into meltdown as she looked at Seth gazing at her, telling her how he felt.

'Can I take you out?' Seth asked.

Finally, she was able to drum up a word. 'Out?'

'Not a sightseeing trip or a dinner to meet a casting director.' He paused. 'A date.'

The four-letter word couldn't have been more poignant. A date meant *not* platonic. A date meant romance. If she said yes to this, she was saying goodbye to her relationship with Dan and finally accepting that it wasn't a break but a real and final break-up. What did she say? The choir continued to sing, and Lara felt the enormity of being here, half the world away from everything she had ever known. She was seeing things she had only ever dreamed about before … and she was still holding burritos.

'Listen, Lara, whatever you say, even if it's a "no"—'

'Yes,' she said, her voice quivering a little.

'Yes?' he said. 'Yes, I can take you on a date?'

She nodded, as hard as her reticence would allow her. She wanted to. She really wanted to, no matter how too soon it felt. There was guilt there, gliding into the background, threatening to take over the excited effervescence, but when she thought about Dan's Christmas Scottish lodge plans and the festive market with Chloe, those feelings somehow took a bow and left the stage. 'Where are we going to go?' she asked.

He inched a little closer, his eyes matching hers. 'I don't know yet, but I'll make it special.'

Lara swallowed, her body suddenly alive, dancing in moonbeams of excitement under his gaze. She watched him raise his hand and she really longed for him to cup her face, bring their lips together, deliver on that kiss he had obviously been thinking about. She closed her eyes …

'Lara! We've got to go! David has to see the prince!' Susie sounded so close.

She snapped open her eyes and Seth quickly changed tack, wiping at her mouth with his thumb.

'You've got a bit of sauce right there,' he said, cheeks flushing. 'Hey, Susie, we were just—'

'Seeing if we could get a napkin.' Lara swallowed. 'No napkins.' She shrugged at her best friend, then passed Susie's burrito to her.

'Sorry to rush off, Seth, but we'll see you tomorrow? The boat ride up the Hudson and the Statue of Liberty?' Susie asked.

'I ... don't know if I can make tomorrow.' He looked at Lara. 'I've got my call-back and ...'

'That's OK,' Lara said quickly. She knew how important that audition was to him and they had seen each other every day since she had been here. Time alone with Susie would give her a chance to take a breath and maybe put all this into perspective.

'Susie!' David yelled, just visible a few metres away, arms raised to the sky, waving. 'I cannot be late for the prince! He will be at the salon in twenty minutes!'

'Sorry! See you, Seth,' Susie said, turning away.

Lara looked to Seth. She didn't want to rush away after everything they had just said, but she didn't have a choice. With the choir bowing to the crowd's applause as they ended their first song Lara threw her arms around him, holding him tight and relishing how good he felt against her.

'I think you squashed your burrito,' Seth remarked.

'I like them squashed,' she answered, not letting go.

'I'll message you,' he whispered into her ear. 'We'll make that date.'

'Nothing too fancy,' Lara replied, still holding on to him. 'I'm not that kind of girl.'

'Got it,' Seth answered.

She drew away and smiled, holding her tortilla wrap in the air like the Olympic torch. 'Night.'

'Goodnight, Lemur Girl.'

Thirty-Nine

The 11th Street Cafe,
West Village

'Jeez, are you out of your mind?' Trent exclaimed as Seth came back to the table with the drinks the next morning. 'You know it's minus temperatures outside, right? You did feel that when we walked here, yeah?'

'What's the problem?' Seth asked, putting their drinks down and slipping into the seat opposite.

'You've ordered a freaking iced pumpkin spiced latte, haven't you?'

'Maybe,' Seth answered, sheepishly moving the glass towards him.

'It's making me cold just looking at it,' Trent shivered, picking up his hot coffee and cradling it into his chest.

'It's a ritual,' Seth admitted, putting the straw to his mouth and sucking up the sweet, spicy, chilled drink.

'For people to have in the summer!'

'No, I mean, it's *my* ritual. A superstition if you like.' He put the glass down on the table and breathed in the laid-back morning vibe. The 11th Street Cafe was like a second home. The tiny snug of a coffee shop had served him and Trent everything from triple espresso hangover cures to pre-audition light lunches. He was very tempted to indulge in their scrambled eggs with chorizo, onion, potato and pepper. Everything that was coming out of the kitchen smelt so good. And the cafe was dressed for Christmas. Although, given its limited space, it was a real marvel how they had managed to fit in a full-sized real spruce tree, hanging lanterns and stockings on the walls.

'You make your own luck,' Trent stated.

'You sound like my dad,' Seth answered, shaking his head.

'I've always liked your dad.'

'OK, let's not call it a superstition. Let's just say that every audition I've ever been to, when I've had an iced pumpkin latte, I've got the job.'

'Really?' Trent mused, finger and thumb at his chin. 'What about the audition for the *Gladiator* sequel?'

'That film never got made,' Seth answered.

'OK ... what about the part for the Mayans FX series?'

'I had a hot chocolate before that one ... but maybe if I'd known then that I was half Spanish/Puerto Rican/Mexican then I would have worked that part of me a little harder.'

'What?' Trent exclaimed.

Seth swallowed. He'd lost himself there for a minute. He had forgotten that he hadn't told Trent anything about his birth mother. And, with Trent, there would be no backtracking now he had had a sniff of something.

He shrugged. 'I found out my birth mother is called Garcia.'

'Whoa! You found your mom! Shit, man, when did that happen?' Trent said at a volume where the whole cosy cafe could hear over the coffee machines.

'I haven't exactly found her. I just asked my mom ... my mom, Kossy ... and I got a name and a photo.' He had looked at the photo again this morning, wondering what Candice looked like now, twenty-eight years on. How old was she in that photo? How old would she be now? Was she even still alive?

'And what did you do next? Look her up on Facebook?'

Why did everyone else think of this next step so naturally? He swallowed and shook his head. 'Not yet.'

'God! Why not?! Let's do it now!' Trent said, getting his phone out of his jacket pocket. 'What's her first name?'

'No,' Seth said immediately.

'Come on, Seth. This is your birth mother we're talking about. If I was in your shoes, sitting in front of that colder-than-Manhattan drink, I'd be wanting to know what she looks like now. Where she lives. If she's got more kids. What they look like. Who they are. I mean, theoretically, you could be passing any of them in the street every day and not know you share the same biology.'

He had thought about that himself. Whether it was his twin or someone younger, part of his mother's new life. His eyes went to the dark-eyed, dark-haired barista behind the counter. He could have half-siblings literally anywhere.

'I need to focus on this call-back,' he said, putting his mouth to the drink again.

'I read the script last night,' Trent informed, slurping at his coffee.

'You did?' Seth asked. 'What did you think?' He really wanted his friend to see what he saw in the heart-warming story.

Trent raised his hand and tipped it left and right like he was unsure. 'I think it's gonna go one of two ways. It's either gonna be the surprise box office smash of the year or it's gonna go the way of *The Chronicles of Riddick* and bomb.'

Seth shook his head. 'It's not gonna bomb. I feel it.'

'That sounds suspiciously like superstition speaking.' Trent laughed. 'Wow, I can't believe I actually got that sentence out. All those freaking "S" words.'

'What did you think of the character of Sam?' Seth asked him.

'I thought you'd be perfect for it.'

'Really?'

'He's good – most of the time – but he's also strong and determined, yet vulnerable. He's complex but relatable … and you, buddy, are gonna smash the audition.'

'Yeah,' Seth said, with a less than convincing nod.

'Come on, man, where's the positivity? You were personally invited back by Toby Jackson, you're ticking all the boxes of "what to do when you're invited for a call-back", wearing the outfit you wore when he last saw you, gonna give it as much passion as you did at Cafe Cluny, not be intimidated if Brad Pitt is there. Embrace your individuality, and don't fuck it up.'

'Thanks, I think.'

Trent's phone beeped, and he looked at it, immediately tutting and raising his eyes to the cafe ceiling.

'What is it?' Seth asked.

'It's Carlson, again. He's got a visit from some inspectorate at the Christmas world this morning.'

'Listen,' Seth began. 'I'm really sorry about the opening but—'

'Hey, I know what Carlson's like. You turned up like I asked you. You and the animal crusader stole the reindeer, we're all good,' Trent insisted. 'Plus, a couple of people tweeted photos of you and laraweekend leading Rudolph down Sixth Avenue. How is that going with her? Or has she got too needy? I haven't seen many heart-warming photos on your profile. We really need to ramp that up if we're gonna make a good angle out of it.'

'Well, I ...'

'Come on, man, raising your profile, Stand for Wildlife, repairing a Brit girl's broken heart, your mom's shelter ...' He exhaled loudly, then pointed at Seth. 'Is there an opportunity to serve the poor people some dinner or something? The press really lap that shit up.'

'The next event is the fundraiser. It's all would-be aldermen and people with money.'

'We could get some homeless people to stand outside the fundraiser and you could go out there and give them some of the leftover food. That would be golden!'

'Trent,' Seth said. 'Stop. That's completely contrived and I'm having no part of anything like that.'

'What about your mother?' Trent asked. 'Yes! You find your mother on Facebook and we have a whole emotional reunion. If you get that part today, it's gonna be amazing promotion for the film and—'

'Trent! Stop!' Seth snapped. Now it was *his* voice that was way louder than the coffee machine and the general hubbub of the chat from the customers surrounding them. He felt like he ought to apologise but instead he looked harshly at his friend. 'Listen, I know you think you're trying to do your best for me but none of this is me. This is someone who craves attention, needs fame ... I've never been like that and I don't want to be like that. I act because I love it. I act because it's all I know. And yes, I act because it pays the bills but, the fame game – I hate that.'

'I know you do,' Trent replied. 'But it's a fact of life. Everybody's competing for that spotlight and I don't want you being trampled over because you're too nice.'

'I'm not too nice. I'm just ...' He had wanted to say 'I'm just me' but he still wasn't sure who that person was when his real heritage was so up in the air. 'I'm just not ... Katy Perry.'

'OK ...' Trent said, looking a little bewildered. 'Let's get that ridiculous frappé down you and get you to that call-back ... before you start singing "Swish Swish".'

Forty

Battery Park

'The prince had his hair lacquered in a balm that contained liquid gold,' Susie announced as she and Lara stepped on the boat that was going to take them up New York's most famous river to visit one of its most famous icons, the Statue of Liberty. 'Liquid *gold*! David said a tub of it could probably buy a small country in Africa.'

Lara looked at her watch before stepping off the gangplank onto their boat and getting out of the snowy wind buffeting her every part. They had looked around Castle Clinton first before heading to the dock. Battery Park was a real mish-mash of history from the castle-cum-former immigration station to the modern skyscrapers that surrounded everything. And her watch was telling her that Seth would be at his audition right now. She really hoped it was going well. She was a little nervous for him. And she also couldn't believe that last night she had agreed to go on a date with him … When she had got back to the Airbnb apartment the previous night, she had checked Dan's Facebook page and there was … nothing. No update. No being tagged in anything. Just that last post from when he had visited the Salisbury Christmas Market. She didn't know whether that was a good or a bad thing or whether it meant anything at all to her any more.

'Did you hear what I said?' Susie asked, nudging her arm with her elbow.

'Expensive hair balm,' Lara answered. 'I didn't even know it was a thing.'

'Maybe that's what I should get David for Christmas, not the leather satchel,' Susie mused, leaning up against the rail at the side of the boat. 'Shall we go and sit inside? It's freezing out here and you're still only dressed for autumn.'

'No,' Lara answered. 'If we sit inside we won't get the best view of everything. And it's not that cold.' She tried to stop her teeth-chattering from giving her away.

'Well,' Susie said, pulling the belt on her thick coat a little tighter then moving her hands to the elaborate top-knot on her head and stretching the band containing her hair as if that would produce heat. 'What do you think about the hair balm for David? For Christmas.'

Lara looked at her friend. 'Do you really have enough money to buy a small African country? Because when we were pooling our funds to come here it didn't seem that way.'

'I have credit cards,' Susie announced. 'That's almost the same thing.'

'Are you really asking my opinion on what to buy David for Christmas?'

'Yes,' Susie said.

'You really want to know.'

'Yes!'

'Well, I would go for something a little more personal than hair products.'

'Like a diamante thong?'

'Eww! No! I didn't know they were a thing either!' Lara closed her eyes then opened them again. 'Please tell me he doesn't have any of those already.'

'Now I know your opinion on them I don't think I should say any more.'

Lara looked out over the waves of the tidal river, the water swelling up and around the boat. She had started looking for a Christmas present for Dan back in mid-November. She had spent so much time looking for the perfect gifts for him that spelt out memories of things they had done together. He had always bought her expensive perfume she never wore. Why wasn't that a warning signal? Just how long hadn't he been as into her as she had been into him?

'Where did you first meet David?' Lara asked Susie as other passengers joined them at the rail, taking photos of the scene, wrapped up, chatting excitedly.

'You know where I met him! I went to a training session in London and I sat next to him. He offered me a Tic-Tac in Spanish and couldn't believe I understood him.'

'And you said you hadn't understood a word, but he was shaking the box at you.'

Susie laughed hard, as if remembering the moment with all the meet-cute pleasure it had given her at the time. 'Yes. I thought he was so sweet. And now I think he's *really sexy* and still just as sweet.'

Lara smiled at her friend. 'There's your Christmas gift inspiration.' She sucked in some of the cold New York air. 'Right there.'

Forty-One

Statue of Liberty, Liberty Island

Lara couldn't believe she was standing underneath one of the world's most famous landmarks. The Statue of Liberty. A beacon of freedom. An inspiring monument to independence. If someone had said to her a few months ago that this December she would be on the other side of the world seeing this sight, she would never have believed them. It was almost surreal, but for the fact that light snowflakes were kissing her face and tourists were snapping a million photos and Susie was tracking the moves of a guide leading a large party around the island.

'Ceremony of Dedication 1886, she said,' Susie pulled at Lara's arm. 'Come on or we'll miss the end of the tour line.'

'I didn't know you were so interested in history,' Lara answered, walking along with her. 'I thought we were only here for the selfies with Lady Liberty not the whole story.'

'David likes history,' Susie answered. 'And when I tell him some of the facts later he might—'

'OK,' Lara answered. 'Don't say any more. I get it.' She wanted some of the history too, if she was honest, but more important than the facts of how the monument came to be, Lara wanted to drink in the symbolism and that really simply meant putting her feet to the ground and being in this moment.

Miss Freedom – just like the name of the boat that brought them over to the island. And that was how she was beginning to feel. Free.

'It wasn't until 1924 that it became a national monument,' Susie said to Lara. 'Are you keeping up with the facts in case I can't remember them later for David?'

'Seth asked me on a date.'

Susie drew in a breath that made her hiccup really loudly and the tour guide way ahead of them stopped her speech for a moment. Susie put a hand over her mouth, eyes bulging. The guide continued on.

'Are you serious?' Susie eventually managed to get out.

Lara nodded. 'Yes.'

'When did this happen?'

'Last night. After the show. Halfway through my burrito.'

'And what did you say?'

Lara took a restorative breath, thinking back to the moment she had made her decision. How Seth had reacted to her answer. How her response had seemed like one of the most important answers he had ever been waiting for. 'I said yes.'

'Oh my God! Lara! Oh my God! I can't believe it! You and Dr Mike! Dr Mike!'

'Seth,' Lara reminded her friend. 'His name is Seth.'

'I know but ... oh, wow, this is the best news ever!'

'Is it?' Lara said hesitantly.

'Yes! You're not having second thoughts, are you?'

'Well, no ... I don't think so ... it's just ... Dan.' Saying his name, she hoped, would explain everything.

'Listen to me. That dickhead is currently getting ready to go on a Christmas holiday with Chloe.'

Lara swallowed. It still hurt. All that time together. Time she thought had meant something and now suddenly didn't.

'What he is doing is not cool,' Susie continued. 'And whatever sort of break or break-up this is, you are not passing up an opportunity to go out with a lovely, lovely, gorgeous guy when Dan is tramping around on Facebook tagging himself with a … skank.' Susie let out a frustrated sigh. 'There is no way I am going to carry on doing her hair no matter how much she pays. In fact, I might set one of the Saturday twins on her.'

Lara linked arms with her friend, leaning her head on Susie's shoulder. 'Thanks, Susie.'

'What for?'

'For getting me out of Appleshaw. For giving me the opportunity to see all of this.' She breathed in, relishing everything about the scene from the flakes of snow falling through the air to the swaying river lapping at the shore of the island. Across the water the towers rose high, like slim spindles in a slightly frosty mist.

'Not missing Appleshaw at all?'

'I didn't say that,' Lara replied as they strolled, now completely broken apart from the tour guide. 'I mean anyone who's had Flora's mince-pie whisky and Mrs Fitch's Christmas cake would be missing out a little bit.' She sniffed. 'And Aldo will be getting excited about Christmas by now.'

'Lara, Aldo is excited about Christmas every day from Boxing Day.'

Lara laughed. 'I know.'

'And we're going to be back for Christmas. Doing all those things you love.'

She knew that. And Dan wouldn't be there. He would be in Scotland. She was coming to terms with that and she knew that Seth was helping. Perhaps this accepting a date with him was just a rebound reaction. Was that wrong? It was simply capturing a moment, wasn't it? Enjoying each other's company while it lasted ...

Her phone began to trill, and she rushed to get it out of the pocket of her coat. 'It's Aldo,' she told Susie.

'I don't believe it,' Susie said. 'He's psychic.'

Lara pressed to accept the FaceTime call. 'Hi, Aldo! Listen, guess where I am.'

'China?' came Aldo's reply.

Lara laughed. 'I'm in New York, Aldo.'

'I know that already,' he answered, grinning, curly hair bouncing. 'So, where are you now?'

Susie rolled her eyes and walked on ahead.

'I'm actually standing here with the Statue of Liberty.' She pulled in another breath. 'And she's beautiful.'

Forty-Two

The Chapel Shelter, W 40th Street

As Seth strode through the doors it felt like everything was suddenly different. He had never felt this way after any audition in the past. When he had got to the call-back he hadn't been surprised to see a number of really famous names alongside his, but he hadn't let it faze him. He had focused on Sam, who Sam was, who Seth *knew* he was, because he felt it inside himself, and then he had performed the requested scenes just like he had at Cafe Cluny. Only even better. When he had finished he was shaking and he had felt the atmosphere shift in the room. A woman, introduced as only Angela, had a Kleenex at her eyes. The panel had all very quickly acted business as usual, but his gut told him this part was his. Perhaps it was a little overconfident to assume but he was quietly hopeful – and he had made a decision. And that's why he was here.

'Maggie, please, if you don't get down from the tree I'm gonna have to call the fire department,' Kossy said in exasperation.

Seth came into the main room to see Mad Maggie halfway up a giant spruce, even her minuscule weight making the branches bend and bow dangerously. Tinsel was tangled up in

Maggie's hair and wrapped around her wrists were the bags she always refused to put down.

'Don't tell her that!' Felice answered with a tut. 'Why d'you think she's up the tree in the first place?'

'I don't know, Felice,' Kossy retorted. 'I kinda thought she might be off her meds.'

'Is she ever actually *on* her meds?' Felice replied.

Seth stepped forward and put a hand to both sides of his mouth. 'Hey, Maggie!'

'Not getting down,' Maggie muttered. 'Not getting down. Christmas. Christmas.'

'Seth!' Kossy let go of the tree, making it wobble all the more.

Seth reached out and grabbed the trunk, steadying it.

'It's my fault,' Kossy said. 'I got the trees too big this year. Some of them are treating them like gym apparatus. Maggie's not the first.'

'Well, let's make her the last,' Seth suggested. He held his hand up as far as he could reach. 'Hey, Maggie, what say you come down and you have another dance with me.'

'Hell, I'll dance with you,' Felice stated eagerly. 'Seeing as the Brit girl's not around.'

'Not helping, Felice,' Seth answered, trying to get Maggie's attention. 'Maggie!'

'There's something about you and people getting up trees just lately,' Felice continued, sucking on the bottom of one of her dreadlocks.

Seth ignored her and looked back up to Maggie who had recommenced muttering. 'Maggie, come on, you fall out of that tree you're gonna hurt yourself, or drop one of your bags.'

'My bags!' Maggie took a hand off the spruce, slipping a little. 'They are *my* bags!'

'Honey,' Kossy began. 'Nobody is gonna take your bags but, you know, if you stay up there something is gonna spill.'

Maggie seemed to take this latest suggestion on board, looking slightly less edgy.

'Come on, Maggie,' Seth continued. 'Don't leave me hanging here. I'm waiting for my dance.' He looked to Felice. 'Put some music on?'

'Oh, right, so let me just pull out my iPhone and slip into Spotify!' Felice shook her head. 'Jeez! You and your first world life!'

Seth took his phone from his pocket and handed it to her, still maintaining a grip on the fir tree. 'Here.'

'Wow!' Felice remarked. 'Do I get to keep it?'

'I think you know the answer to that one.'

In a whirl of Bing Crosby, golden baubles, trailing tinsel and around thirty-eight copies of the *New York Times* and a confetti of food coupons, Maggie finally arrived at the foot of the tree and clapped Seth into a bear hug of epic proportions.

'This was when gentlemen were gentlemen,' Maggie said, her head planted firmly to Seth's chest as they began a waltz to the music.

'Are you saying I'm not a gentleman, Maggie?' Seth asked her, a wry grin on his mouth.

'I'm saying they're a rare breed these days.' Maggie started to sing, very loudly and out of tune and Seth watched Felice clap her hands to her ears.

'Jeez!' the younger girl exclaimed. 'I liked her better when she was up the tree!' She headed off in the direction of the kitchen.

'Mom,' Seth called to Kossy who was straightening branches and refixing tinsel and ornaments.

'Do you think your dad could shave a metre off the top?' Kossy replied, stepping closer but eyes firmly fixed on the pine. 'Or is letting him in here with a chainsaw gonna cause me all sorts of other problems?'

'I don't know,' Seth admitted. 'Mom, I had my call-back today. For the part I told you about.'

'You did!' Kossy exclaimed, wild with excitement. Then he watched her face fall back down to contained and she cleared her throat as if trying to temper her enthusiasm. 'So how did it go? Any indication that maybe ...'

'It went real well,' Seth admitted, smiling.

'Swell-well?' Kossy said, daring to return his smile a little bit.

'Swell-well,' he answered a bit louder over Maggie's voice hitting Bing's higher range. 'I don't know for sure but ... I've gotta feeling.'

'*You've* gotta feeling! I get feelings all the time and mostly they mean nothing but when *you* get a feeling ... well!' She took a breath. 'I'm getting a feeling about your feeling!'

'We're meant to be dancing!' Maggie piped up, lifting her head from Seth's chest. 'You ain't dancing if you ain't moving!'

'Sorry,' Seth answered, recommencing shifting his feet in time to the song. 'Mom,' he said tentatively. 'There's something else.'

'There is?' Kossy said, her voice tinged with reticence.

'Yeah.' He swallowed, most of his earlier conviction seeming to drain away as quickly as the first bottle of wine at the Christmas dinner table. He wanted this. The call-back audition had told him so. The pep talk to himself on the ride over here on the subway had confirmed it. He just needed to say the words. 'I want to try and find my birth—' He checked himself. 'Candice Garcia.'

Maggie blasted out the chorus of 'I'll Be Home for Christmas' as Seth watched for Kossy's reaction. The mother who had raised him was someone he did not want to hurt with this need. And, he knew, although she had been supportive, had *always* been supportive, this was going to rock her, despite the impression she might give off.

He watched her nod, eyes glistening with tears, and he wanted to let go of Maggie and go to her, but the homeless woman was gripping him tighter than she held her bags full of her worldly possessions.

'Mom, listen, I know how you must feel but ...' Seth began, turning in his dance until he was facing Kossy.

'Seth, I need to tell you something,' Kossy said, patting down her body and seeming a little confused. 'Bernadette! Have you seen my phone?'

'No, Kossy!' came the reply from across the room.

'Mom, I've really thought about this. I want you to know that.'

'I do know that, Seth. All you've done your whole life is think. Right from the second you picked fruit over arrowroot cookies I knew you were a thinker ... oh my God, why is it in my bra? I never put it in my bra!' She pulled her cell phone out and started pressing the screen. 'When I started doing this I couldn't do it. And then I tried to get your dad to do it but he flat-out refused and in the end I did most of it with my eyes shut ...'

Kossy's breathing was getting a little erratic now so Seth tried to ease himself out of Maggie's grasp. The homeless woman only hung on tighter. He turned his head as Maggie made them circle in time. 'Mom, what are you talking about?'

'I couldn't help it. Lara said – and I thought she was right and now, you coming here telling me what you've just told me, I *know* it was the right thing to do.' She stuck out the hand containing her phone, shaking it at him.

'What is this?' Seth asked, taking her cell from her hand and staring at it.

'There's barely any battery left. Press the screen!' she urged him.

'Don't you stop waltzing!' Maggie warned and then coughed like her chest was going to crack open.

Seth pressed the screen and saw that the Facebook app was open. And there was a profile photo looking back at him. It was a profile photo belonging to Candy Garcia. She was perhaps mid-forties, mid-length dark hair, cafe-au-lait skin and with eyes he knew so well. *His* eyes. The pull inside himself was overwhelming.

'That's her,' Kossy breathed. 'That's Candice.' She swallowed. 'That's your birth mom.'

Forty-Three

East Village

'Lara, look! There are literally a million Santas over there!'

The only thing Lara was looking at was her phone. Should she have messaged Seth this morning to say good luck for the audition? She had thought about it. She had thought about it so much she had actually started composing a message but then worried, as she didn't know the time of the audition, that his phone might not be on silent and it might go off in the middle of the audition and that her good luck message might just be the thing that ruined the whole thing and she deleted it. But now she hadn't heard from him at all and it was the afternoon and she was thinking all sorts. Maybe her half-crushed burrito was on his coat and he had realised what an absolute liability she was ... maybe when he said he would message her he hadn't really meant it ...

'Lara! Look! Millions of Father Christmases!' Susie exclaimed, grabbing her arm and pointing.

This time Lara looked up. 'God! There really is,' she answered. Perhaps not millions of them, but there were certainly scores of men and women dressed up in bright red and white Santa suits and they were jogging. People on the pavements were clapping as they passed. It seemed strange, rampant festive parcel-deliverers bouncing through the snowy tree-lined streets past the brownstones and bistros and independent shops.

'Maybe it's for a film,' Susie said, tracking the runners and applauding too.

'It's a race.' Lara pointed to a sign. 'And apparently also a pub crawl. Maybe we should join in, with the pub-crawling bit, not the dressing up as Santa and running bit.'

'Ooo!' Susie pulled her phone from her handbag. 'I just got a text from David.'

'How do you know?' Lara asked.

'He has his own special noise.'

'Wish I hadn't asked.'

'I don't mean he has a special noise. I meant I chose a special tone for him ... he's asked if I want to go Christmas shopping with him tonight. Oh my God! Do you think he means somewhere like ... Tiffany's? Do you think he's going to buy me jewellery ... like a ring? Like one of those special rings you give to girls you've been dating for a while to make things a little more permanent?'

'If you say the words "engagement ring", I don't think it curses you,' Lara answered.

'No,' Susie said, nearly hitting a running Santa with her handbag as they continued up the street. 'No, it wouldn't be that. I mean, why would it be that? We haven't been going out *that* long and he's been away here for so long and ... do you think he *is* going to buy me a ring?'

Lara smiled. 'I don't know. Do you want him to buy you a ring?'

'I don't know,' Susie admitted.

'That was some high level of excitement for someone who doesn't know.'

'I'm just trying to manage my expectations, that's all. I mean, if I get all hyper and thinking about rings when he's only said the words "Christmas shopping" then I might be disappointed.'

'Ah!' Lara said, pointing a finger. 'You just admitted you would be disappointed if it's *not* shopping for a ring.'

'Did I?'

Lara nodded.

'Oh God! Is he going to propose? Do I want him to propose?'

'Quick,' Lara said, getting her phone out of her pocket. 'Let's capture this moment and the sprinting Santas with an Insta pic.' She held up her camera ready for a selfie, waiting for the Clauses to be in prime position with all the delights of their East Village neighbourhood too. 'Smile.'

Lara's phone took the photo then immediately started to ring. She looked at the screen.

'It's Seth.'

Her stomach was already performing a dirty, sexy samba just from looking at his name.

'Answer it!' Susie ordered. 'Maybe he's going to invite you Christmas shopping too!'

Before she could think about it, she pressed the button to answer and put the phone to her ear. 'Hello.'

'Hi, Lara, it's Seth. Hunt. Seth Hunt.'

She smiled. His whole manner was so sweet yet undeniably sexy and she suspected he had no idea what it did to a girl. 'I know. Since you gave me your number it tells me who you are. I thought about rejecting the call because I'm currently surrounded by hundreds of really gorgeous guys – and girls, actually – all exceedingly well dressed with beautifully groomed beards and it's really, really mesmerising.'

'I have no idea where you are, but I kinda wanna see for myself.'

'I'm in East Village, just going back to our apartment, and there's a Santa race going on.'

'Do not join in,' Seth warned her. 'It's an annual thing. Those guys are heavy drinkers, you'll be drunk before sunset.'

'What about the girls?' Lara asked. 'I'm hoping they're even worse.'

He laughed, and it made her skin tingle and instinctively hold the phone closer to her ear. She liked feeling that way.

'So, I'm going now,' she told him. 'To have drinks with the Santa Girls.'

'Oh well, that's a shame because if you're drunk before sunset you might not fully appreciate the date I was hoping you'd join me on tonight.'

Tonight. He wanted to take her on a date *tonight.* She wasn't a girlie girl who needed a whole day of mani-pedi and facials, but she might need a couple of hours to pull together an outfit she was happy with from her suitcase full of creased clothes she still hadn't hung up.

'I ... er ...' She looked to Susie. Her friend was raising her eyes and hopping from one foot to the other shaking both hands like she was doing a children's entertainer dance teaching about how to stay warm in cold weather.

'Too soon?' Seth asked. 'I'm sorry, I just ... you haven't told me how long you're here for and—'

'No,' Lara said quickly and loudly. 'No, it's not too soon.'

'You don't have other plans? I'll understand if you have other plans.'

'No … no other plans.' She swallowed, the bubbles of anticipation growing in her stomach like she had downed a whole bottle of Fairy Liquid. 'And Susie and David are going shopping at Tiffany's.'

'No one said Tiffany's!' Susie shouted. Lara muffled her mouth with her hand and they both almost fell into the path of another bunch of Father Christmas joggers.

'Great. So, shall I come to your place? Pick you up?'

'I …' Lara began. Why couldn't she just answer in a normal way? Susie grunted from behind Lara's hand, desperately trying to get free.

'Or we could meet somewhere.'

'No, my place is fine,' she said, releasing Susie finally. 'I'll text you the address.'

'Cool,' Seth answered. 'Say, seven thirty?'

'I'll be somewhere near ready.'

'Great. I'll see you then.'

'Wait! Seth!' Lara called as if he was right there with her and she was hailing him back.

'Yeah?'

'How did the call-back go?'

There was a pause, but somehow she sensed he was smiling. A strange sensation ran up inside her, like a dancing cat was breaking out the pompoms and leading a cheer squad. She felt … gooey – not in a gross way – in a warm-hot-chocolate-with-marshmallows-by-the-fire way.

'It went great,' Seth answered. 'Really great. I'll tell you tonight.'

'I'm so pleased,' Lara said, feeling so proud of him.

'Me too,' he said. 'And I have something else to tell you too.'

'What?' Lara asked.

'I found my mom.'

Forty-Four

Lara and Susie's Airbnb apartment, East Village

'For the third time, Lara, *not* jeans!'

'I don't really have anything else,' Lara exclaimed, throwing another T-shirt to the floor of her room to join the rest of the clothes already discarded. 'No, I take that back. I *completely* don't have anything else.'

'What about your nice black trousers?' Susie asked, searching through Lara's suitcase and scrutinising everything.

'Ripped them getting over a barbed wire fence chasing a goat.'

Susie shook her head. 'If it was anyone else telling that story I wouldn't believe it.' She held something up in the air. 'What about this?'

'That isn't mine,' Lara said, screwing up her eyes as if trying to bring the item into focus. 'What is that?'

'It's a navy-blue dress, plain with a little lace detail around the neckline and shoulders.'

Then Lara understood. 'Did you just put that in my case?'

'No,' Susie said in the most unconvincing voice ever.

'Then it must belong to whoever owns this apartment,' Lara concluded. 'And it must have fallen right out of the wardrobe into my case.'

'Yes!' Susie pointed dramatically and almost dropped the item of clothing. 'That must be it … but it's nice, don't you think? And no one would know that you borrowed it. And you could wear some of my tights.'

'No!' Lara exclaimed. 'Not tights. They almost killed me that last time. I came out in hives. And, if Seth sees me in a dress again he's going to think I'm a girl who dresses up in dresses and I'm not a girl who dresses up in dresses. I'm a girl who … who … dresses way down … usually in some form of denim.'

'But the New York Lara could do something different,' Susie suggested, holding the dress up and almost making it move like it had come to life and was shimmying towards her.

Lara sighed. This break was supposed to be about embracing new things and striding towards the exciting and unknown. But there were also thoughts in the back of her mind telling her that she had done quite a lot of compromising in her relationship with Dan without really being aware of it. She didn't want that again – not that one date with Seth was in any way like what she had had with Dan. Not that she really knew just what she *had* had with Dan … She looked again at the dress Susie was still holding out like she was a sales assistant in a fancy boutique.

'Can we modify it somehow?' Lara asked, leaning her head to the left as she stared at the dress.

'Which parts?'

'I don't like the lace,' Lara told her. 'And I'm not sure about the way the skirt flares out like that.'

'But, Lara, that's most of the dress and I'm not exactly great with needlework or anything like that.'

Lara smiled at her. 'Do you think the woman who it belongs to would mind if we cut it?' She watched Susie's expression.

'I was thinking, if she had left it here then she can't be missing it and if we alter it and take it she probably won't mind ...'

'Well,' Susie began. 'I looked at the label and it's from a boutique I've heard of in London and it's quite expensive.'

'That's settled then,' Lara said, reaching for her suitcase. 'I'm wearing jeans.'

'Wait! No! I ... suppose we could, unpick the lace parts and, maybe pin up the skirt somehow.'

'Susie, I'm not going to wreck your dress!'

Susie sighed. 'You know it's mine.'

Lara laughed. 'Of course I know it's yours!' She slipped her phone out of her pocket and pressed the home button.

'What are you doing?' Susie asked. 'Who are you calling?'

'Aldo,' Lara answered.

'For fashion advice?'

'Don't sound so surprised. Who do you think picks out my dad's business dinner ties?' She nodded knowingly at her friend then sat down on the bed, waiting for FaceTime to connect.

'But I've never seen Aldo wearing a pair of socks that match.'

'Ah,' Lara said. 'Because that's a fashion *statement* and nothing to do with him not being able to coordinate.'

'I'll go and find some scissors,' Susie said, heading towards the door.

'Hello,' came Aldo's voice. On the screen was a sheep wearing a string of bells around its neck who started sniffing at the camera.

'Aldo! Why is there a sheep using your phone?'

'Get down, Burkini! Get down!'

'What did you just call the sheep?' Lara asked, observing the wet tongue of the animal and wondering if Aldo's phone was going to survive the saliva.

'Lamb Burkini. That's what the farmer's called this one.' Finally, Aldo's face came into shot, grinning.

'I think it's probably Lamborghini, you know, like the car.'

'Oh! Do you think so? I'd better tell the school. I'm taking some sheep there for a nativity service.'

'I'm sure they won't mind what they're called ... listen, Aldo, I need your help. I'm going out on a date tonight and I don't know what to wear and—'

'On a date?'

She hadn't meant to say the 'date' word to Aldo. She hadn't meant to say it to anyone from anywhere near her life back in Appleshaw. Seth and everything here in New York was like a delicious escapism bubble she didn't want to get out of until she had to pop it and return on the heavy, hopefully well-engineered plane.

'On a date with no dojo Seth?'

'No, yes, I mean ...'

'Dan was in the pub last night,' Aldo continued, tying another string of bells around a sheep he had just sat astride. No mean feat when he was also holding a phone.

'Oh,' Lara said. She had wanted to sound like she was feigning uninterest but her interest *was* piqued, no matter what she was trying to tell herself.

'He was with Chloe and the horrible hot-tub men,' Aldo continued.

'Oh,' Lara said again. What else was there to say?

'He asked me if I had heard from you.'

Had he? Why? What did he care?

'I said you were catching animals for the zoo like you do at the farm here and you were visiting all the places we've only seen on TV and ... I said you were laughing all the time and buying Christmas presents, but not for him.'

Lara swallowed. Poor Aldo. Stuck in the middle of her stupid relationship situation.

'Then Dad came over,' Aldo continued. 'Told Dan that he owed nineteen pounds ninety-five for the Weeks Haulage Christmas dinner he didn't come to.'

Lara smiled and shook her head. That was typical of her dad, making a point. 'Did he pay?'

Aldo shook his head, grabbing sheep number three and straddling it. 'Chloe gave Dad twenty pounds and told him to keep the change.'

Of course she did. Because that seemed to be Chloe's job now. Being by Dan's side. This was good. This was definitive proof that Dan was moving swiftly out of her life and she needed to stand strong and drive her own sleigh.

'Aldo,' she started, watching her brother fasten the bells on the sheep that was bleating its disapproval. 'I *am* going on a date with Seth and I need your help. What can I wear that isn't jeans or a dress?'

He smiled at once, getting off the last of the sheep due for embellishment. 'Have you got your unicorn onesie?'

'No!' came Susie's scream from the lounge. 'There is no way you're wearing a onesie on a date!'

Forty-Five

East Village

'You know, I've never dated a unicorn before,' Seth told Lara as they walked up the street away from the apartment. It was snowing lightly, mere kisses of flakes, touching everything and everyone out that evening. Festive lights were glowing from office blocks, restaurants and cafes and there was a relaxed buzz in the air. People carried shopping bags, briefcases, pushed bicycles, strapped Christmas trees to roofs of cars as the endless stream of yellow taxis honked in pleasure or displeasure – no one really knew.

'You're disappointed, aren't you? I can tell.' Lara smiled and fastened the zip of her jacket over the dress Susie had modified. It was now two inches shorter, minus the lace and teamed with thick, long socks coming up from her Dr Martens boots. It was a look she was happy with. It wasn't jeans, but it was still very much her.

'Maybe you could wear the onesie on our next date,' Seth suggested.

'Ah, that's very presumptuous of you. That seems to insinuate that the first date is going to go so well that there will be a repeat performance.'

'What can I say?' Seth said, looking at her. 'I'm feeling optimistic today.'

Lara smiled. 'So is Susie, and I really hope she doesn't get her heart crushed.'

'Tiffany's?' Seth guessed.

'Yes,' Lara said. 'David invited her Christmas shopping and she thinks it's Tiffany's, although he hasn't mentioned Tiffany's … but in her mind, despite what she says, I think she's already been into the shop, chosen the ring and booked Meghan Markle's preacher to do the service.'

'OK,' Seth said. 'Got it.'

Lara slipped her arm inside his. 'But anyway, enough of rings and preachers. I want to hear about your mom. I can't believe you found her! *How* did you find her?'

'Actually, I think it had a lot to do with you.'

Seth went on to tell her how Kossy had found Candy Garcia on Facebook and how he and his adopted mum had spent the afternoon trying to find out where she lived. They had drawn an absolute blank leaving him with only one option …

'If I want to meet her,' Seth said with a sigh. 'I have to message her.' He took a breath. 'I have to just pluck up the courage to send her a message. I have to tell her who I am, and hope that she wants to know me.'

'A leap of faith,' Lara answered. 'Like me getting on a plane that is impossibly heavy.'

'Just like that.'

'And you're scared.'

'Scared and a little nervous, but also excited.'

'It could be the start of something brand new,' Lara said. 'Getting to know who your mom is and where she's from and all the things she's done since …' She stopped herself, wanting not to say the wrong thing. 'Since your other mom and dad took over.'

'I know.'

'So, will you?' Lara asked as he slowed their pace then stopped walking altogether. 'Message her?'

'I did it,' Seth admitted with the widest smile. 'I was sitting in the park by my apartment, a little before I came to meet you and I thought about the audition today and Sam's story and all these secrets and missed opportunities and heartache and ... I knew I had to do it.'

'You pressed send!' Lara exclaimed, her heart pumping. 'You didn't just draft it or discard it? You sent her a message?'

'I did!'

'Oh my God! Seth! I don't know what to say!' She threw her arms around him, holding him close and breathing in the exhilarating yet calming scent of him. It was like lying in a meadow of the sweetest summer flowers and breathing in the sunshine and the warmth mixed with a hint of exciting pre-thunderstorm.

'You don't have to say anything,' Seth said softly. 'Somehow, you knew me better than I knew myself. Is that even possible?'

'I don't know,' Lara admitted. But she felt it too. Seth was close to becoming her most precious confidant ... and dangerously close to being even more than that. She held onto him, closing her eyes and just being in the moment. 'Are you a little bit mad though? That I spoke to Kossy?'

She felt him shake his head and then he answered: 'No. Because I needed the push. I'm a lifelong procrastinator, even about the big stuff. Trent says that's why I'm not Russell Crowe.' He smiled. 'Although I prefer to think it's just because I'm not that great at keeping a beard.'

Lara laughed and finally let him go, dropping herself back down to the pavement and meeting his gaze. His eyes locked with hers and she could feel herself *feeling* ...

'So, has she replied?' Lara asked quickly, dissipating the moment.

He shook his head. 'No. Not yet. Last phone check she hadn't even read it yet, so ...'

'She might not be a Facebook addict.'

'Yeah, her last post I could see was a week ago.'

'She might not have the Messenger app.'

'Lara, it's OK,' Seth said. 'I've done my part. I'm good about having done my part. I can't do anything about the rest.'

She nodded. 'You're right.'

'So,' he said, smiling. 'We're here.'

'We're where?' Lara asked, looking away from him now to the street they were standing in.

'Well, Lemur Girl, when I thought about where to take you out tonight I had to think big ...'

'I said nothing fancy,' Lara reminded him. 'I could have chosen to wear the onesie.'

'Who said anything about fancy?'

'OK, I'm intrigued by the reference to "big".' She swallowed and directed her gaze to the streetlamps hung with stars. Why did everything sound like an invitation to the screening of a porn premiere tonight?

'I give you ... Zabb Elee.'

Lara looked to where Seth was indicating, taking in a glass frontage, Christmas wreaths hanging inside but shining out to the street, a welcoming red sign displaying the restaurant name.

'Thai,' Lara remarked.

'You like Thai food?' Seth asked.

'I like food,' Lara reminded him. 'I've never tried Thai before.'

'And that was what I was hoping. Because, Lara, tonight we are going on a culinary voyage,' Seth said, putting his arm around her shoulders and moving her towards the restaurant door. 'My New York gift to you, someone who has never travelled before is … Around the World With Food and Beer … starting with Thailand. Now, you can have absolutely whatever you want, but I really recommend the Namtok pork.'

She was unable to believe what she was hearing. This was no ordinary night out. This had required a lot of thought and planning and he'd just told her he'd spent his afternoon trying to find his birth mother too. She wanted to cry as a myriad of emotions washed over her. She was here in New York because of Dan. And now she was here with Seth Hunt and he seemed to know her so crazily well … and she liked it. More than that, she wanted to love it without concern for what it meant for anything else other than the now.

'Are you OK?' he asked, his face a picture of concern, perhaps at her reticence to move.

She nodded, sniffing desperately like winter hay fever was somehow a thing. 'Tell me about the Thai beer. Is there more than one brand?'

'Two served here,' Seth answered. 'Singha and Chang.'

'Let's get one of each and share,' Lara replied.

Forty-Six

Caffe Napoli, Little Italy

As they arrived outside the next venue, Seth could still taste the spiced pork on his tongue, together with the beers and an ice tea the waitress had given them for free. He had mainly watched Lara enjoying everything about the Thai restaurant from its intricately tiled floor to the white leather banquette seating and the Christmas crafts hanging from the walls. Her excitement made it as if it was his first time experiencing the restaurant too.

'Italian!' Lara announced, stopping alongside him and slipping her arm through his so easily. Every time she did that he felt so comfortable, so perfectly happy with it he almost had to admonish himself for feeling that way. Caffe Napoli looked just like something out of a film set where gangsters ruled their turf and rolled around with the windows down and their tommy guns out. With its black frontage, gold lettering and tables on the street complete with patio heaters to stave off the cold, it could easily have been in an Italian piazza instead of here in NYC. And that's the night he wanted to give Lara. A piece of the world. Some of the things she hadn't yet discovered.

'I love pizza,' she added excitedly.

'Ah, but there's one rule in this restaurant,' Seth told her.

'A date with rules?' Lara asked. 'I'm not sure that sounds like fun.'

'You haven't heard me out yet.'

'So bossy!'

Seth smiled. 'We both have to try something we haven't tried before. New experiences, right?'

'Hmm,' Lara mused, looking up at him. 'How do I know that what you order isn't going to be your very favourite dish on the menu?'

'Well, how do I know that you're not gonna order what you always have in your favourite Italian restaurant in the UK?'

'I only ever order pizza.'

'OK. So, my favourite dish here is the veal in the lemon and garlic sauce.'

'You could just be saying that.'

'How about a little trust?' Seth suggested.

'Trust?' Lara asked. 'What's in *that* dish?'

'Very funny.' He pulled her into him a little, their arms still joined, enjoying the connection.

'Are we allowed beer here too?' Lara asked him.

'Birra Moretti? Peroni?'

'One of each?'

'Let's go.'

Lara took a sip from the bottle of Peroni and washed down the gorgeous, slightly chilli-hot Bucatini all'Amatriciana pasta dish she had been served. They were sitting outside, at a tiny table for two at the very edge of the sidewalk where passers-by had to breathe in to navigate around them. But it was perfect. It was cold, yet toasty warm under the canopy, a glowing heater keeping the chill off their eating cocoon. There were sparkling lights in the trees and chilled-out Christmas Sinatra coming from somewhere, plus a few staggering Santas who could possibly be part of the same run/bar crawl she and Susie had seen earlier.

'How's your food?' Seth asked her.

Lara smiled, passing the beer bottle over to him. 'It's one of the best things I've ever tasted.'

'Honestly?' he said, taking the bottle from her.

'Really. It's something I would never usually have gone for, but it's so good.' She put some more pasta on her fork and offered it over the table. 'You want to try some?'

'You want to try some of this?' he replied.

'I don't even know what an eggplant is,' she admitted.

'You call it something different ... give me a second ...' He held his finger in the air as if thinking. 'Aubergine.' He smiled. 'It's aubergine.'

'And all I really know about that vegetable is people use the emoji of it when they want to reference a penis.'

'What?' Seth exclaimed, laughter bursting out.

'You didn't know that? And now I've said "penis" on a first date.' She leaned a little forward, still holding her forkful of pasta. 'And those two women across from us now *really* want to listen in to the rest of our conversation.' She proffered her fork. 'Try the pasta.'

He opened his mouth to accept the food and she watched him eating it, each movement of his lips making her think about their almost-kiss ... and how wonderful tonight was. It was all so relaxed, so simple, so much fun. She couldn't remember the last time she had felt that way, if ever.

'It's good,' Seth said, nodding. 'It's real good.' He speared some aubergine with his fork and offered it to her. 'Your turn.'

'I'm not really a purple vegetable person.'

'Don't disappoint the ladies at the table over there,' Seth teased.

She opened her mouth and seconds later her tongue was tasting a warm, soft, deliciously mellow flavour that was enhanced only with olive oil and a slight seasoning she couldn't quite work out. 'This is ...' she spoke through her mouthful. 'Really good. I didn't know it was going to taste like that.'

'Now the women are turning in their chairs to make sure you're eating actual food.'

Lara laughed, putting a hand over her lips. 'Don't make me laugh or it won't stay in my mouth.'

'God, Lara, those women are going to stroke out any second ...'

'Seth! Stop!'

'I'm not doing a thing,' he answered. 'It's all you ... and their wild imagination.' He took a swig of the Peroni and passed the bottle back to her.

'Give me that,' Lara said, swiping up the Birra Moretti from his side of the table and drinking some of that down.

'So, I've given you Thai and Italian. What d'you think is next?'

'Me in a food coma, probably.'

'Oh, come on!' Seth said. 'I've seen you eat barbecue, remember?'

'Rude!'

'Well, what's a country on your bucket list? There must be one place you've always wanted to go that you haven't been.'

Lara shrugged. 'Not really.'

'No? Really? Not one country you've seen on TV or in magazines and thought, one day I really wanna go to that one place, if nowhere else?'

She thought about it for a second before answering him. '*Everywhere* seemed so far away. I'd see places and think they looked cool and interesting, but they were literally all out of my reach. I've never really had that much money, you know, to take holidays or even think about taking holidays so I didn't dream too big.'

'Lara, I didn't mean to—'

'No, it's OK. I am what I am. And I'm happy with who I am most of the time. Happier in jeans, if I'm honest, but Susie wasn't going to let me out of the apartment until I got changed and she practically blacked out when I said was wearing socks not tights.' She took a sip of the Peroni and handed it over to Seth. 'What's your one country you want to go to but haven't been.'

He sucked in a long, slow breath, his eyes on her, making her sit up a little straighter in response.

'Honestly?' he asked.

'Nothing less than,' Lara answered.

Seth looked suddenly serious and she really wondered what he was going to say. Did he want to head off to the depths of Peru or Cambodia? Or was he perhaps more into Scandinavia and the fjords?

'I've never been to the UK,' Seth said. 'I'd really like to go there.'

She was stunned but she knew she had to respond. Because the UK wasn't Appleshaw. The UK was a big country with lots of exciting things in it and him saying that had nothing to do with this date, this first, very loosely named date. *She* was not the only UK attraction. She was not the Queen or Stonehenge.

'You should definitely visit the UK,' Lara began, knowing she was going to start gabbling at high speed and also knowing

there was nothing she could do about it. 'It's nice. It has ...
flowers and ... rivers ... and lots of old, old things to see, like,
Dame Maggie Smith and ... St Paul's Cathedral and there's
... red buses and black cabs and, where I'm from, there's fields
of wheat and combine harvesters and Morris dancing.' She
poked a forkful of pasta into her mouth to stop herself saying
anything else. Then she hurriedly ground up the food and
stated: 'Brazilian,' she said loudly.

She noticed the women at the table across from them raise
eyebrows before nestling into a clique of conversation. Lara
looked back to Seth. 'Brazil,' she said. 'I'd like to go to Brazil.
You know, the beaches, the sunshine, the fiestas, the dancing
on the sand, the animals and ... the coffee.'

Seth smiled, nodding. 'Great choice.'

'Have you been already?'

'No,' he replied. 'But, let's finish our food and go.'

'What?' Lara said with a laugh.

'You can go virtually anywhere in New York,' Seth told her.
'Let's go to Brazil.'

'You're serious?'

'Absolutely,' he said with a smile. 'And, for the record, I'm
really digging your socks.'

And suddenly it was like a whole salsa beat *carnaval* was
parading around her heart.

Forty-Seven

Brazil Brazil, West 46th Street

It was a total contradiction, the snow layered on the sidewalk, the ice-cold air, the city decked out for the approaching holidays, then the samba beat and Brazilian vibe spilling out of the Brazil Brazil restaurant. The two trees outside were swirled with lights like the Brazilian flag – green, white, yellow and blue – and the wooden planters that framed the outside area were filled with a mix of winter foliage and festive sparkle. And Lara was holding his hand. He wasn't sure how it had happened but, when they had got up out of their seats at Caffe Napoli, heading for the subway, they had kinda brushed arms like they had been the whole night. But, this time, instead of offering his arm to her, he had held out his hand and suggested they run in pursuit of a jogging Santa Claus carrying a six-pack of beer. She had put her hand in his and they had laughed, a little buzzed from the beer, heading up the street singing 'Jingle Bells'. And neither of them had let go. She had held his hand on the train, up the steps from the train, down the street and now, outside the restaurant, she was still holding his hand. And he really *really* liked it.

'Oh my God, Seth!' Lara exclaimed, eyes looking through the doors to inside. 'This really is like Brazil.'

'I told you,' Seth replied, adoring her thrill. 'You can travel anywhere in NYC.' He squeezed her hand. 'Wanna get dessert?'

She turned to face him. 'I don't even know what Brazilians eat for dessert.'

'Shall we find out?' he suggested.

She nodded enthusiastically, and he led the way.

Lara took in everything. The varnished, bare-board floor, the beaded ceiling, the Brazilian flag pinned in the middle. Wooden chairs, tables with plain white cloths and low cage-style lighting set the atmosphere. It was lively, the bar busy, and diners seemed to have moved on from eating formally and were just sitting with drinks, the remains of desserts or coffees. There were musicians at one end of the room – a man singing and playing guitar, another on a keyboard – one couple were dancing, swaying their hips in time to the sultry rhythm.

'Beer?' Seth asked her.

'Yes please,' she answered, then laughed. 'I'll have a Brazilian.'

'You know that joke's old already, right?' he replied.

'Oh, aubergine!' she said dismissing him with a wave of her hand. She went back to watching the couple dancing, suddenly struck by the fact that she had never actually danced like that with someone else. Dan didn't dance. Not even slow smooches when he was drunk. In the beginning she had always asked. In the end she had given up. *In the end.* She guessed that's exactly where they were now. She swallowed. And there he was invading her thoughts again like an ever-present time-suck.

'Lara,' Seth said. Suddenly she felt her hand being tugged. It took her a second to realise she was still holding on to him tighter than ever. She immediately let go.

'Sorry,' she apologised, feeling stupid.

'Hey, no, don't be sorry. It's just, I've gotta get my wallet out and pay and get beers and I need two hands, just for a second.'

'I'll find somewhere to sit,' she said quickly.

By the time he had joined her, at a table next to potted palms on the edge of the dance floor, she had regrouped a little.

'Brahma,' Seth said, holding the bottle out to her. 'And a dessert menu.' He put the menu down on the table.

'Thanks,' Lara said, immediately taking a large gulp of beer. Brazilian courage, if that was a thing.

'You want to look at the menu?' Seth asked, sitting down next to her, facing the slow-dancing couple and the band.

'In a bit,' she answered. Ugh. What was she doing? She was letting Dan creep into this night and it was absolutely the last thing she wanted to do. Everything had been so wonderful, so completely right, so natural. Seth had offered her his hand and she had taken it, like it was something they did all the time, like it wasn't a first date, like they were already an established couple and it had made her feel like she was starring in some sort of rom-com where the world might not be perfect but that she was zorbing in a couple's bubble where nothing ugly could touch her. It had to be the beer. Perhaps beer from multiple countries wasn't a good mix ...

'For the record, I didn't want to let go of your hand,' Seth said over the music. 'It really was a wallet and paying thing.'

She nodded. She really didn't want him to talk about the hand-holding right now. 'So, has your mom replied yet?'

'I don't know,' he answered. 'I haven't looked.'

'You need to look,' Lara said. 'If you don't then you won't know.'

'I know.'

When he moved his head, his hair shifted just a little bit, strands tickling his forehead. It made him sexier. And he *was* sexy. *Quietly* sexy, like he didn't know it at all, like it was wrapped up for the most part then revealed, slowly, piece by piece, tantalisingly …

'I'll look later,' he told her. 'She might not have seen it yet or …'

'She might have seen it and replied straight away and be wanting to meet you right now.'

'I'm with *you* right now,' he reminded her.

'I know, but it's your birth mother. If your birth mother has replied and wants to meet you then you should go. Right now, if you have to.' What was she saying? What was this all about?

'Lara, have I done something wrong?'

'No.' She shook her head. Why was this happening now? He was too special to be the rebound guy. Why couldn't Susie have suggested a January or February break to New York when she had had time?

'Then … dance with me?' Seth asked.

He had asked *her* to dance. This was not the first time he had literally opened up a door to her thoughts. And he had gone one better. He had asked her something she had never been asked before. The band began to play a song she was familiar with. It was a soft, slow Brazilian version of The Doors' 'Light My Fire'. And there was his hand again, just waiting for her to clasp his fingers. A shock, a mix of heat, realisation and longing trod over rational thought and she reacted with her heart and complete free will. She put her hand in his.

Seth's heart was lost somewhere between Brazil, Italy, Thailand and … Appleshaw. Tonight was one of the best nights he had

had in his entire life and he didn't want it to end. He didn't step too far into the open space, just far enough away from their table to be able to move. And then Lara was standing facing him, looking so incredibly beautiful, he felt his whole body melt. He was nervous, yet suddenly driven by all the feelings that were gathering speed inside him, feelings he didn't want to dismiss ... He drew her tenderly towards him, his arms around her waist, their torsos tight together. He held her close as the music filled the room.

He wanted to talk because *not* talking felt too intimate, even though he knew this *was* intimate and that he very much wanted it to be. Talking was his get-out. It was almost an acting technique. Flood the situation with words, move it on. Except here and now he didn't quite know what to say, apart from maybe to tell her exactly what he was feeling. But his mouth was dry and all he could feel was her body moving with his ...

Lara was shaking on the inside and it was taking all her strength to not let that show on the outside. She was a burning ball of sexual tension, midriff to midriff with a man she was finding more irresistible by the day. And here she was, in the middle of a Brazilian restaurant in New York, slow-dancing to one of the most erotic songs ever created, with Seth Hunt, a man she had once admired on her TV screen but now *knew* ... and knew so well in so short a time. She wanted to relax into this moment. She wanted to be cool with it, but cool was the last thing she felt. One half of her was saying if she didn't snog his face off on this dance floor she was going to regret it for the rest of her life. The other part was saying if she *did* kiss Seth then her whole world was going to change. She needed to decide which one of those she couldn't handle. She moved her hands upwards, circling his neck, stepping back a little to look at him.

'Seth,' she whispered.

'Lara.'

'I didn't ever want to stop holding your hand.'

She watched his reaction to her words, her stomach tense, as if waiting to receive some sort of rejection. She was speaking in the moment from a place she wasn't quite yet familiar with.

'I meant it when I said I didn't want to let you go either,' he said.

She shivered then, and when he cupped her chin with his hand she knew he had felt it. 'Sorry,' she whispered, dropping her eyes.

'Please, Lara, you don't need to be sorry. Not for anything.'

'I can't help it,' she said, moving to his rhythm as they still danced. 'Coming here wasn't meant to be like this. I wasn't meant to come here and ... find someone ... find you. I was supposed to come here and shop-till-I-dropped with Susie and look inwardly and feel sorry for myself away from Appleshaw and—'

'Now you're dancing in a Brazilian bar with Dr Mike.' He smiled. 'It sounds like quite the mind-bend.'

'Not Dr Mike,' Lara said immediately. 'Seth Hunt. I'm dancing with Seth Hunt.'

'Yes, you are,' he said softly.

'And, that's where I want to be,' Lara carried on, emotion taking over any form of rationality. 'I want to be here, dancing with you, almost in Brazil ... having seen France and Italy and Thailand and met a lemur and a reindeer and watched a musical about pie ...'

He smiled, his fingers gently caressing her hair.

'And I can't stop thinking … what do you taste like? What would your lips feel like on mine? And maybe that's wrong. Maybe I shouldn't feel like that. But I do. I really do. And I ran away last night, with burritos, looking for napkins I didn't really want and—'

'Lara?'

'Yes?'

'Please, stop talking.'

'OK,' she answered with a swallow.

'Because I want to find out what you taste like too.'

Lara didn't have time to think or move or backtrack even if she wanted to. Her mouth was, all at once, caught up with his and it was everything she had expected and so much more. His full, gorgeous lips were exploring hers with so much raw passion she almost expected the band to stop playing but, in truth, all she could hear was her own heartbeat in her ears, telling her that this kiss, without a doubt, was something special. This was no rebound reaction. This was real.

Lara tasted like sunrise, or maybe that was just the way kissing her was making him feel. It was like dawn breaking, a new day, something brilliant and better, opening up right in front of him. He couldn't get any closer to her, their lips were locked, mouths open, breath stolen, the rest of the world unimportant and frankly invisible. If he could have stopped time and kissed her for all of eternity, then he would have. Except he wasn't in charge of any wormholes and when the music changed from slow and sexy to fiesta and 'Samba De Janiero' he was forced to take a step back as diners flooded the dance space.

'You OK?' Seth asked, holding her hand and shouting a little as the volume of the music increased.

'Yes!' she called back. 'So?'

'So, what?' he asked, with a smile.

'What did I taste of?' Lara enquired. 'Apart from beer.'

He drew her close to him again, padding her face with his thumb. 'If I told you sunrise and literally every beautiful thing in the whole wide world, would you believe me?'

She laughed. 'No.'

'Well,' Seth said. 'I'm just gonna have to kiss you again to double check on that.'

'Oh no,' Lara said, holding his hand but dancing backwards a little. 'Kisses have to be earned in Brazil.'

'So, you're an expert on Brazilian custom now?'

'I believe we have to drink tequila and dance before we kiss again ... or our souls will never rest.'

Seth shook his head, laughing. And then, before she could do anything else, he spun her around until she fell against him and his hands clasped both sides of her waist. 'We can samba,' he told her. 'And, in Brazil, they actually drink cachaça.'

'Then make mine a double,' Lara replied, putting her arms around his neck and moving to the music.

Forty-Eight

Lara and Susie's Airbnb apartment, East Village

'I don't believe that man gave me his hat,' Lara announced, her hands touching the brim of a newly acquired Panama.

'You were wearing it way more than him and I guess he figured if he didn't say you could keep it, it was basically theft on your part and no one wants to report anyone for hat theft this close to Christmas.'

Lara took her hat off and swiped at him with it, almost slipping on the fresh snow that had fallen while they were in Brazil Brazil. They had danced until their feet were sore, sang words they didn't know to songs they didn't know, drank cachaça and lime and watched a dog in an elf costume dance the bossa nova on his hind legs while the whole restaurant clapped.

'It's almost two a.m.' Lara stated, putting the hat back on her head, then looking at her watch. 'Does that really say two a.m.?' She put her wrist to Seth's face, a little off balance due to the beer.

'It does say two a.m. and I have kept you out too late. I apologise.'

'No,' Lara said softly. 'Don't apologise. I had the best night. It was like around the world in ... six and a half hours, or so.'

'I wish it could be longer,' Seth replied. He enveloped her in his arms, gazing into her eyes as they stood just outside the apartment building. The night was dark and, for New York, quiet. The only sound was the buzz of traffic from the main street and a dog barking in the distance.

'You could come in,' Lara blurted out. 'For coffee.'

'Coffee,' Seth replied, as if the word were foreign to him.

'I don't know why I said "coffee",' Lara admitted. 'We both know I meant sex.'

'Yeah,' Seth answered. 'I got that.'

'And you're not picking me up and racing up the steps to get into the apartment to have sex with me so I'm guessing that's a no.'

'God, Lara, there's nothing I want to do more but ... I'm inherently a good guy. And good guys don't have sex on the first date, even when the girl they've taken out is the most incredible person they've ever met.'

'Really?' Lara asked.

'You are incredible,' he said again.

'No, I meant, good guys don't have sex on the first date? How about Season Four of *Manhattan Med* when Dr Mike saved that blond woman from the fire?' She nodded with authority. 'Unless you're saying that Dr Mike wasn't a good guy.'

'I'm saying, as we discussed earlier, I'm Seth Hunt. Seth Hunt doesn't have sex on a first date.'

'But rules are made to be broken, aren't they? New experiences, you said. Living in the moment ...'

'Lara, my resolve is already weak, but I am sticking to being a gentleman ... for now.' He smiled at her. 'And, in the morning, when the international beer buzz has caught up with you, you're gonna thank me for it.'

All she could focus on was how gorgeous he was underneath the glow of the streetlamp. His dark hair was a little damp from the exertions of their dancing, his eyes alive, those lips looking like they were waiting to be kissed. She wasn't going to thank him for it. She was going to wish that mouth was working its way down her entire body – but, if she was truthful to herself it *was* too soon. If she slowed her mind down and dismissed the après-beer excitement and really thought about it … he was right.

'Hey,' he whispered. 'Are you pissed with me?'

'Yes,' she replied. 'No girl wants a respectful guy.' She laughed at her own comment. 'OK, I lied. We all want a respectful guy. I'm just trying not to think about you going home and me greeting Ron, Harry and Hermione glowing through the blinds, then getting into that warm, cosy, *huge* bed in the apartment *alone* …'

'You're killing me with the glowing snowmen right now.'

'They're right there!' Lara said, pointing to the window box on the wall of the building. 'You can wave if you like.'

'I'd rather kiss you again.' He leaned in, whipping the hat from her head and delivering another heart-stopping touch of his lips. Lara clung on to him, relishing every sensation as his tongue came alive with hers and their bodies melded together, not wanting to be separate even by a centimetre.

He kissed her lips lightly and edged back. 'I ought to go … before I stay.'

'Sure,' Lara said with a swallow. 'You've got to go.'

'Can I see you tomorrow?'

'Well, depending on how Susie and David's shopping trip went, I'll either be wedding planning or mopping up tears, so if we can meet somewhere in between that.'

'I'll call you,' Seth said.

'Please, Seth, please, before you go, check your phone,' Lara begged as he replaced her hat. 'I want to know if your mum's replied.'

He smiled, a little apprehensively, then breathed out. 'OK.'

She watched him draw out his mobile phone from the pocket of his jeans. Her heart was beating in a low panic and she could only imagine what his was doing. She couldn't read his face and she waited, anxious for him to say something.

'No reply,' he answered slowly. 'But she's read the message.'

Lara smiled. 'Oh my God, Seth, she's read the message. That's something! I mean, that's huge! It makes it real, doesn't it? It makes *her* real.'

'Yeah,' he agreed, nodding. 'It makes her real.'

Lara threw her arms around him, holding him close, wanting him to know she knew how much this meant to him. 'She's going to reply,' she assured him.

'You don't know that,' Seth said, matter-of-factly. 'And, you know, if she doesn't, that's her choice.'

'She's going to reply. You have to believe that your nice came from her nice.'

'Is that right?'

'I believe it,' Lara said firmly. 'Have some faith.'

'OK, then, Lemur Girl, I'll take your word for it and believe in the power of a Christmas miracle.'

'Well, some people think Mark Zuckerberg can do anything, so a more divine sort of miracle should be quite possible.'

'Goodnight, Lara.

'Goodnight, Seth.'

He kissed her once more and then he smiled and pulled the brim of the hat down over her eyes as he turned to walk away.

'Hey!'

'I'll see you tomorrow,' he called, waving a hand. And then she heard the opening bars of 'Light My Fire' being whistled on the wind and her heart soared like Santa's sleigh.

Forty-Nine

Union Square Christmas Market

'Excuse me, could I have a closer look at that large photo of graffiti?' Susie asked, pointing at a canvas on an alternative art stall.

It was the following morning and the two women were working through Susie's list of go-to shopping venues, interspersed with coffee shop stops, after Lara had claimed no sane person could manage that many shops in one morning. It was cold and crisp, last night's snow set to ice, but the red-and-white topped Christmas stalls were a haven of hot chocolate steam, sugary doughnut smells and kitsch gift ideas for all.

The couples' Christmas shopping trip the night before *had* ended up in Tiffany's but not for engagement rings. David had wanted Susie's opinion on a very expensive brooch for his grandmother. Lara couldn't see the problem with this, in fact, she had thought it was nice that David wanted to include Susie in a family present decision. But every time she went to suggest this was a relationship plus point, Susie countered it with every other slightly irritating thing David had done in the course of their relationship ... from taking too long in the bathroom one Saturday in June to dropping a fork at the Spanish restaurant they went to a few days ago wiping it on his napkin and reusing it. After that, Lara had kept quiet.

'Who are you thinking of buying the photo for?' Lara asked. 'Because I'm not sure it's going to fit in your suitcase.'

'Oh, it isn't for anyone at home,' Susie stated as the stall owner went to get the photograph. 'It's for David.'

'Does David like modern photography like this?' Lara asked.

'No,' Susie said. 'He hates it.'

The stallholder returned with the photograph and Susie nodded her approval. 'I really like it. How much is it?'

'Hang on, just a second,' Lara said to both her friend and the man on the stall. 'Susie, you don't want to get David this. No offence,' she said, looking to the seller holding the picture. 'It's really good, but my friend here is wanting to buy it as some sort of revenge gift and I don't think she should.' She swallowed, looking at the beanie-hatted man who seemed like he would now rather be anywhere other than talking to them. And she couldn't say that she blamed him. 'Do you?' Had she really just looked at the stall-owner for solidarity?

'Well,' Susie began. 'Last night, my boyfriend took me to Tiffany's and made me look at a diamond brooch for his grand-mother. We were in there for what felt like hours, *right next to* the engagement rings, and his gaze did not shift for the entire time, not even when I said "ooo that's pretty" three times and interspersed it with a few "I really like that's".' She eyeballed the stallholder who looked like a tortoise ready to shrink back into its shell. 'That is mental cruelty, isn't it? To take your girlfriend to Tiffany's, *the* iconic store for engagement rings the world over, and *not* look at engagement rings.' She pointed a finger at the seller. 'You wouldn't do that, would you? I mean *no one* would do that!' Her hair, today curled like she had a giant pretzel on her head, bobbed a little as she got all accusing and Lara took hold of her arm.

'Susie, come on, I think it's time we got some coffee.' She mouthed a sorry to the stallholder and steered Susie out from under his canopy to the crowded marketplace that was a shopaholic's delight. When her friend got like this there was really only one thing to do and that was distraction.

'How about I let you suggest a bag for me.' Lara still didn't want a bag, but Susie needed the delight of finding one for her. And bags in the market were hopefully going to be a lot cheaper than designer brands at Macy's.

'You don't want a bag,' Susie scoffed. 'You're just saying that in the hope I'll stop going on about David's *weak* and *pathetic* display last night.'

'I'm not.'

'Lara, you didn't want the perfect bag the other day. You don't want one now.'

'I—'

'You just want me to shut up about David *not looking* at engagement rings and *looking at* crazy-expensive brooches for his ninety-year-old grandmother. I mean, where exactly is she going to go to warrant wearing a brooch that costs over five hundred dollars?'

'Well—'

'Five hundred dollars for a brooch! That's like half the amount of money I would expect him to spend on an engagement ring!'

'Half!' Lara exclaimed before she could stop herself. She had no idea how much engagement rings were, obviously. But a thousand dollars seemed like a vast sum. Her car cost less than that.

'What? You think I'm being materialistic? Well, I only plan on doing it once. It has to mean something, and no one really means something if they spend less than a grand.'

'Whoa!' Lara said. 'Who took my best friend in the night and replaced her with a … *an* … engagement-zilla.' She had no idea if that was even a type of person but, at the moment, it sounded exactly right.

'Oh my God!' Susie said, clapping her hands to her cheeks as they came to a halt at a German stall selling all manner of Christmas delights. There were gingerbread houses and men, winter drinks with spices, gift boxes filled with chocolate-coated nutcracker soldiers. 'I've gone all materialistic and label-loving. I'm turning into my mother!'

'No,' Lara said. 'No, you're not, well, maybe a bit, but I get it. This isn't Appleshaw. It's like London, but better. It's New York and you're getting carried away with the city life and seeing David again and ... I almost had sex with Seth last night.'

'What?'

Lara hadn't meant to say those exact words, or any words, but out they had come. She nodded.

'But when I asked you how the date had gone this morning you just said "fine". You didn't say anything about almost-sex.'

'I went to elaborate, but you launched into a tirade about David not knowing you at all and how you were going to blunt his best scissors.'

'I ...' Susie started. 'I did say that, didn't I! God, I'm an awful person. I don't even know if I want to marry him. I just wanted to think that he might want to marry me!' She gasped. 'Back to the almost-sex, please!'

This stallholder who had seemed like he was going to offer them a gingerbread gift box selection to look at, withdrew the tin box as rapidly as she had offered it.

'Can we go and get coffee?' Lara suggested.

They sat inside one of the stalls on stools at a whole bar of different coffees. There was every flavour you could imagine from creamy caramel and hazelnut to maple bacon and taco ... Lara had opted for something slightly more regular than savoury foods, although it was a flavour she hadn't tried before. Chocolate coconut. It smelt so good and the cream on top was divine.

'So, you kissed,' Susie said, slurping at her oatmeal cookie drink.

'Several times, actually ... and we held hands.' She flushed when she said the words 'we held hands' like she'd said 'and we did it doggy style'. Somehow, the hand-holding had felt even more intimate than the kissing.

'Does that make me a slut?' Lara asked. 'A two-timer. A cheat. A ... douchebag?'

'You are *not* a douchebag. Or any of those other things. You have done nothing wrong. Dan said he wanted a break. Dan is with Chloe. You are in New York and you've met Seth.'

'I shouldn't feel guilty? I shouldn't stop seeing him? I mean I came here to try and win Dan back and now ...'

'You've finally woken up and seen what else is out there? Reached out and discovered more than Mrs Fitch's afternoon teas and cut-price compost?'

'You make it sound like I spent half my life in the garden centre.' Lara sipped at her coffee, the flavours waking up her taste buds.

'I think you might have spent half your life with your eyes shut,' Susie admitted. 'And now you've had them opened you're staring at ... Seth Hunt.'

She shivered, and Susie caught it straight off, despite Lara trying to shift on her stool and make out it was nothing but the slight winter wind.

'And if he makes you feel like that I don't know why you *didn't* have sex with him.'

'He said no.'

'What? *You* asked *him*.'

'See, I'm a slut.'

'Stop saying that. I'm surprised he said no, that's all.'

'He said no because he's a nice guy, and he was right. It wouldn't have been right to do it that soon, if at all.'

'So, you're saying that's it? You're not going to have sex with him?'

'I don't know,' Lara said. 'I don't want to *plan* it. Who does that? It should happen, you know, organically, like it does—'

'In the movies?' Susie interrupted, her eyes rolling like two eggs trying to escape a boiling pan of water. 'You might be waiting a long time in that case. The first time David and I had sex it took him six minutes to get the costumes out of the Amazon packaging and—'

'Susie! No! Once I hear it I can't unhear it!' She clamped her hands over her ears.

'I'm just saying, a little bit of pre-planning doesn't hurt.'

'Maybe I should call Dan.'

'What? No! What for? To ask his permission to sleep with Seth?'

'Well …' Asking permission was a little over the top but she still felt a little bit like she was one foot in the relationship and the other outside it. It would be good to get some closure.

'You are not going to call Dan. Did he ask your permission to take Chloe to the Salisbury Christmas Market? Did he get your approval for him to share the mulled wine and local bands *you* love with her?'

Lara shook her head.

'Or how about the other hot-tub morons? Do you want to ask them what they think too?'

'OK, I get it. It was a stupid idea.'

'Yes,' Susie said. 'It was. Because the only person you need approval from is yourself, and me, obviously. And I give you permission. I give you permission to get Seth Hunt in every position imaginable and—'

'Shh!' Lara waved her hands in front of Susie's mouth in a bid to quieten her.

'This is *your* time now, Lara. *Your* Christmas in New York, in your ...' Susie looked down at Lara's feet. 'Vagabond boots ... getting right to the very heart of it, here, in old New York.'

She couldn't help but think about how she and Seth had shouted from the top of the Empire State Building. 'Please don't sing,' Lara begged.

'So, when are you going to have sex with Seth?' Susie asked, like her coffee had induced hyperactivity all of a sudden. 'David and I can go out – not to Tiffany's again – we can romance up your room at the apartment, put on some bedroom jams from Spotify, mood lighting, food you can smear—'

'OK, stop,' Lara said, half amused, half terrified. 'I know we've not got long left here but I still need to be sure.'

'Ugh! Well, when are you seeing him next? Tonight?'

'He said he'd call. Last night he said something about having interviews today for the film premiere tomorrow.'

'I can't believe you're dating a movie star!'

'I can't believe the first time you had sex with David you wore a costume.'

'To be honest, I've never been able to watch *Frozen* since.'

'Susie! Noooooo!'

Fifty

Four Seasons Hotel,
East 57th Street

Seth had finished his second glass of water and his mouth was still dry. He and Trent were sitting in the room outside the main suite, waiting for his turn to be grilled by the city's press. There were bright red poinsettia plants and bowls of Christmas berries everywhere. When they'd arrived, he'd been offered red and white striped candy and a cranberry juice box by a festively dressed receptionist. He had barely thought of Christmas this week, but it was coming, and it was all over the city.

He wasn't nervous about this set of interviews for *The End of Us* because he had had a relatively small character role in the set-to-be blockbuster and all eyes were on the stars of the show. It was his job to ensure he promoted the movie's themes and talked about his character. Garth had been a great role to play – he'd had his first ever male/male kiss – and the reviewers had already been more than excited about the film as a whole. But he was apprehensive about the one-way Messenger conversation with his mother. There her profile photo sat on his phone, to the right of his original message, no bubbles of a reply pending, no nothing. She had seen his words and had not answered.

'You good, bud?' Trent asked, looking up from his mobile.

'Yeah,' Seth answered. 'I'm good.'

'Because you look a little pale, you know, for a half-Hispanic or whatever you are now.'

'It's the New York winter.'

'Maybe you need one of those lamps for people who miss the summer, or a tanning session. You must have great tanning genes under there somewhere, right?'

Seth smiled and shook his head. 'I don't think anything you said is politically correct in any way.'

'What?' Trent asked, bemused.

'Nothing,' Seth said, looking at the empty water glass in his hands.

'You want some more water?'

'No, if I have more water I'll wanna pee.'

'OK, so listen, before you go in there I wanna give you a heads up about a few things that might come up.'

'OK,' Seth answered, eyeing his friend suspiciously.

'So, I might have, you know, mentioned the Twitter thing with laraweekend when I spoke to publicity so it's a possibility you might get a few questions about that.'

'What?' Seth exclaimed. 'Why would you do that? What did you say?'

'Whoa! Keep your pants on,' Trent said, looking to the other waiting actors and sending them a smile.

'What did you say, Trent?'

'I just said that Lemur Girl had made a heartfelt plea to you on social media and you were showing her a good time in New York to help her mend her broken heart.'

'I told you I didn't want that sort of publicity,' Seth said through gritted teeth.

'And I told you I need to build up your brand, especially if you get the role of Sam. We need to make you first choice for these deep and meaningfuls, Seth. We don't want them going to Christian Bale or Eddie Redmayne all the time, do we?'

'Listen, about Lara—'

'Is she a real pain in the ass? Because, if she's turned all cray-cray, wanting-to-wipe-her-ass-with-the-napkin-you-used-at-lunch cray, then I could possibly try another angle. I was thinking of you hooking up with Mira Jackson for the premiere tomorrow.'

'I think I'm falling in love with her.'

'Hey, anybody with eyes in their head is in love with Mira Jackson. Male, female, non-binary …'

'Not Mira Jackson,' Seth said, annoyed. 'Lara. I'm falling in love with Lara.'

And this time he hadn't said 'I think'. Because he knew. Whatever connection they had, it was a real one and a strong one and he wanted to explore every part of it.

'That's a joke, right?' Trent had a small smile on his lips like he was waiting for the punchline. 'I mean, that's you fucking with me, right? Nice one! Hilarious!' He punched Seth's shoulder.

'No, Trent, it isn't me fucking with you. I'm serious.' He let out a breath. 'Last night, I took Lara on a date and—'

'What? No. No, no, no … a date? Like a real date? Not just photos for her Instagram? Are you out of your mind?'

Seth didn't remember them taking photos at all. They were too involved with each other. Conversation and eating and dancing all around the world …

'This whole laraweekend thing was a godsend because it painted you as the good guy, you know, restoring her self-esteem after she got dumped. It's you, putting a comforting arm around her shoulders and saying, "you go, girl, girl power, girls are strong, girls can take rejection on the chin and then pick themselves up again and get on with their lives". That does not work if you're moving on in there a few weeks after she's meant to be heartbroken by the love of her life!'

Had Lara said Dan was the love of her life? If she had, he didn't remember it. But she had said she hadn't had any other boyfriend so, he guessed, Dan had been the love of her life ... That didn't feel so nice.

'God, you didn't sleep with her, did you?' Trent hissed.

'Will you keep your voice down?' Seth begged.

'This *is* me keeping my voice down. Which is kinda hard when what I really wanna do is ramp it up to announcer at the baseball game level and hit your sorry ass for a home run!'

'I'm taking Lara to the premiere tomorrow night.'

'No,' Trent stated. 'That's not gonna work. Laraweekend should be used for light coffee chats, feeding the pigeons in the park, maybe a little break-up outfit shopping, not potential career-changing premiere red carpet events where she will have no clue what she's doing.'

'Did you just say the word "used". She's a person, Trent. Not a vacuum cleaner! And I'm taking her to the premiere as my date.'

'Seth, you need to think carefully about this. You're moving from nice, decent, Hallmark movie guy to slut-dropping guy from Magic Mike Live!'

The door of the suite opened and a woman called to Seth. He got up from his seat then turned back to Trent. 'I'm asking Lara to the premiere. She might not even wanna go. I don't think the red carpet stuff will really be her thing. But, if she doesn't wanna come, I don't want you setting me up with anyone else. Have you got that?'

Trent ducked his head down into a copy of *Time Out*.

Fifty-One

Chrysler Building, Lexington Avenue

'Everything is so tall!' Aldo's voice echoed from Lara's phone. She had her almost-brother and her dad on FaceTime and was panning around trying to capture a little of the snow-covered streets and some of NYC's iconic buildings for them to see.

'It's three hundred and nineteen metres. But you can't get to the top because it's privately owned.'

'When I was a lad,' Gerry stated. 'I used to think that Culver Street in Salisbury was like New York.' He laughed then cleared his throat. 'That was a long time ago. Before I'd been to London.'

'Susie,' Lara said. 'Show my dad and Aldo your hot dog.' She moved the camera to Susie's traditional wiener she had just purchased – smoked sausage covered in brown mustard and sauerkraut.

'I'm so hungry,' Aldo responded immediately.

'That does look good,' Gerry agreed. 'Not like those sausages Reg Mundy did on the barbecue for the fete last summer. There was nothing of them. One bite and they were done.'

Lara turned the camera back round so she could see her dad and Aldo. It felt strange standing on the busy streets of

New York while they were standing in the yard of the haulage company next to Tina. Here she was, close to one of the biggest Christmas trees in the world at the Rockefeller Center, and there they were, the small fake office tree just visible in the background.

'So, how are things in Appleshaw?' Lara asked, earning an elbow nudge from Susie.

'Mrs Fitch got into a fight with Flora,' Aldo said.

'It wasn't a fight,' Gerry interrupted. 'It was more of a …'

'Face-off?' Lara offered.

'Bitch-slapping?' Susie suggested through a mouthful of sausage.

'A verbal discussion with … a bit of almost throttling,' Gerry said.

'With a string of angel bunting,' Aldo added.

'No!' Lara exclaimed, trying hard not to laugh. 'Are they all right?'

'The angels?' Aldo asked, eyebrow raising quizzically.

'No, Mrs Fitch and Flora.'

'Yes, they're fine,' Gerry answered. 'It was Mrs Fitch and that ancient pricing gun again. She'd tagged one set of the angels at ninety-nine p and the others were three ninety-nine. Flora always has a nose for a bargain.'

Susie shook her head in despair and mouthed 'Appleshaw' with another eye roll.

'Dan kissed Chloe at the social club,' Aldo blurted out.

'Aldo!' Gerry admonished. 'I thought I told you that was not something we were going to share today.'

Lara didn't know what to say. This phone call had been a catch-up with her family, but, under Susie's instruction, it had also been a fact-finding mission to see if any trace amounts of guilt were at all warranted. And now she had her definitive answer. Just like she had moved on – or a little bit sideways – kissing Seth, Dan was moving on with Chloe.

'Sorry, Lara,' Aldo said immediately.

'No, Aldo, don't be sorry. It's fine,' Lara said, as Susie put an arm around her shoulders and hugged her close.

'Sweetheart, that bloke isn't worth another second of your time,' Gerry stated. She could see her dad was a little emotional. Always the one there to dry her tears, put on her plasters, tell her just how to land the best punch on the older Baxter brother at school …

'Dad, it's OK. It was actually what I needed to hear,' Lara admitted. It did pain her a little to say it, but it was the truth. It was official. As black and white as it ever could be. She and Dan were over.

'And you have no dojo Seth,' Aldo said.

'Seth?' Gerry queried. 'Who's Seth?'

'You'll love him, Mr Weeks!' Susie shouted, getting her face in the frame. 'He's a real gentleman. Loves trucks and drinks beer and he likes football too, Aldo!' Susie had made all that up, apart from the drinking beer part.

'Can he get me the stickers I'm missing?' Aldo called.

'I don't know, Aldo, listen, I've got to go now but I'll call you tomorrow and Aldo, if you got it on video, send me the Fitch versus Flora showdown.'

'Henry Grove put it on YouTube,' Aldo replied.

'Bye!' Lara said, waving. 'Bye, Aldo, bye, Dad.'

'Bye, love,' Gerry said, waving back.

'Bye, Lara,' Aldo shouted.

Lara ended the call and took a deep breath of the freezing air. 'Well, I guess I found my facts. Dan and Chloe at the social club.'

'Some venue for a first kiss,' Susie said with a tut. 'Not quite a Brazilian restaurant, is it?'

'And maybe I did the half-cheating first,' Lara said with a sigh. 'I should have asked Aldo what time it was.'

'We are not having a who did what first conversation are we? Because I do not expect Dan is giving one thought to that right now. In fact, I suspect he's in the nineteenth hole with Chloe's double Ds.' She patted Lara's shoulder. 'He ended things. Break. Break-up. Whatever. He was the one who walked away first.'

Lara tapped at her phone screen.

'What are you doing?' Susie asked.

'I'm messaging Dan,' Lara informed.

'What?! Don't give him the time of day, Lara!'

'I'm not,' Lara insisted. 'I'm making things final. I'm breaking up with him.'

Fifty-Two

The Chapel Shelter, W 40th Street

Seth, I really wanted to reply right away but I took the night and half of today to think about what I wanted to say. What I want to say first is ... I might have given you up, but I never forgot you, not for a second. And knowing who you were and where you were and what a wonderful person you seemed to have grown into has made it easier to stay away, if you can understand that at all. What I'm trying to say is, I did the right thing. Kossy raised you right, as I knew she would. She gave you the kind of life I wanted for you. The kind of life I would never have been able to give you. I am not ashamed of leaving you at the shelter, I'm only ashamed of who I was then. Keeping you, making you part of that life would have been selfish and cruel, I hope you see that. And now, you've contacted me – something I thought I could only dream about. I've seen you, Seth, and not just on film, at the shelter, when I got too curious and a little bit brave. I was checking in, I guess, standing across the street, watching my boy growing so tall and looking so strong and sounding so educated. I am so proud of you, if pride in you is something moms like me are allowed to have … and I am so glad to hear from you! But what happens next is up to you. I want nothing more than to hold you in my arms again like I did in the first moments of your life, but that's entirely your choice, Seth. And if you choose to know who I am and where I am and not ever meet me, like I did all these years, then I will of course accept that. But if you want to meet then I think that would probably be life-changing, for both of us. Candy x

'You're here so much these days they're gonna end up giving you a bed.'

As Seth entered the shelter he was greeted by Felice who was holding a spanner for a handyman who seemed to be doing something with the radiator.

'Hey, Felice, is my mom around?'

'Did you take Lara on a date yet?'

'I … is my mom here?'

'Did you go on the date already?'

'I went on the date, OK? Is my mom here?'

'You went on a date with Lara?' The handyman stood up and turned around.

'Hey, Dad, I had no idea that was you. I didn't recognise your—'

'Butt?' Felice suggested. 'I think that's a good thing or I might be calling welfare.'

'Your mother is in her office on the phone to guys who can fix the heating if *I* can't fix the heating,' Ted said. 'I know … great show of faith in my skills. But, seeing as I can't even seem to bleed these ancient radiators, perhaps it's completely founded.'

'I …' The words were itching to come out, but he had to quell his excitement just a little.

'You're gonna ask Lara to marry you!' Felice exclaimed.

'What?' Ted said, staring at Seth. 'You're going to ask Lara to marry you?'

'No! Don't listen to her!'

'Don't listen to her isn't saying "I'm not going to ask Lara to marry me". What's going on, son?'

'I had a message from my mom,' Seth said. 'My birth mom,' he corrected quickly.

'Whoa!' Felice dropped the spanner.

'Well,' Ted began. 'That's ...' He cleared his throat. 'I mean, that's great, Seth, really great.' He put his arm around Seth's shoulders. 'Let's go and tell your mom.' Then he smiled. 'Your *other* mom.'

Kossy cried when she read the message, like Seth knew she would. He had got emotional too, reading it while Trent tried to debrief him about the questions he had been asked about *The End of Us*. In the end, he had had to escape to the bathroom just to get some space and time to digest the message.

'It's beautiful,' Kossy said, getting up from her chair and coming around her desk, tears flowing down her cheeks. 'It's just beautiful.' She put her arms around him, pulling him into an embrace.

'Group hug,' Ted said, joining them in the huddle.

It was a good few seconds before they all resurfaced, wiping at their eyes with their fingers and sniffing away the obvious emotion.

'So,' Seth said. 'What shall I do?'

'Seth, honey, you know what you should do. You know what you want to do,' Kossy said. 'You message her back and you tell her you can't wait to meet her.'

'Yeah,' Seth said. That *was* what he wanted to do. But it still wasn't easy. He had been a long time adopted.

'What's holding you back, son?' Ted asked, softly in his slightly obvious but well-meaning high-school counsellor way.

Seth swallowed and raised his eyes to look at Kossy. 'Would you come with me, Mom?'

Kossy let out a sob and hurriedly nodded her head. 'Sure, honey. If that's what you want, I'll be right there with you.'

Seth nodded, letting go of a breath, together with a lot of apprehension.

Ted cleared his throat. 'Isn't there something else we have to tell your mom?'

Seth looked at him, a little blank. 'I don't think so.'

'Seth's getting married,' Ted informed. 'To Lara. Felice just announced it.'

Kossy clapped her hands to her mouth and Seth jumped in before anything else was misconstrued. 'No – Mom, Dad is messing with you. I'm not getting married, but ...'

'But?' Ted said.

'But?' Kossy repeated.

'But I did take Lara out last night,' Seth admitted. 'On a date.'

'I like her,' Kossy said, nodding enthusiastically. 'I really like her, Seth.'

'I like her too,' Ted added. 'Where did you take her?'

'I, er ...' He wasn't really sure he wanted to share all the details of their date with his parents. 'We went to Zabb Elee ... and Caffe Napoli ... and Brazil Brazil.'

'In one night!' Kossy exclaimed. 'I'm surprised you're not in a food coma!'

Seth smiled. 'That was actually something that Lara said.'

'So,' Kossy said. 'When can we meet her?'

Seth was confused. 'You've already met her.'

'As your "friend",' Kossy said. 'Not as your girlfriend.'

'She's not my girlfriend.'

'Don't tell me there's a new urban dictionary word for it now,' Ted said. 'Go on, what is it? Surprise me.'

'I …' Seth said, feeling a little awkward he didn't have any cool words for his dad to work with.

'You'll make sure she's coming to the shelter fundraiser, and her friend, Susie, and whoever she wants to bring. I've managed to squeeze in a couple of extra tables this year for supporters of the shelter who aren't bankrolled.'

'OK,' Seth said.

'Good, that's settled,' Kossy said before pinching his cheeks. 'Right, well, what are you waiting for. Reply to … your mom.'

Fifty-Three

Chinatown

'This is so amazing!' Lara exclaimed as she and Seth walked down the middle of Chinatown, following the path of an ornate, dancing dragon, musicians with drums creating the beat. It was how Lara imagined being in the very centre of Beijing would be. Restaurants lit up in red and gold, strings of lights hanging from every frontage, large, bright red lanterns zig-zagging across the road together with displays of icicles, snowflakes and Merry Christmas symbols in English and Chinese type.

'And tonight, we'll drink Tsingtao beer,' Seth told her, squeezing her hand. 'But first, I need to ask you a couple of things.'

She swallowed as they stopped under the canopy of one of the eateries. She looked up at him, waiting for the inevitable. Something was wrong. Now she was completely free from Dan – not that he had responded to her break-up text – now she was absolutely in the moment, something had to upset things. It was like gravity. What went up would eventually come down.

'You know I got a message from my mom ...'

'And you know I think that is so amazing.' He had called her, sounding even more elated than he had that night at Cafe Cluny.

'It is,' he agreed. 'Well, I'm gonna meet her. Tomorrow.'

'Oh my God! Seth, that is huge!'

'I know, I can hardly believe it, but ... it's happening.'

Lara put a hand to her chest. 'I thought ... you were going to tell me something bad.'

'Something bad? No, why did you think that?'

'I don't know. Go on,' she urged.

'I kinda wanted you to come with me,' Seth said. 'To see my mom, but I thought it might be too much – for you maybe, and for her – so I asked Kossy to come with me.'

Lara smiled at him, squeezing her hands in his. 'Of course. Why were you worried about telling me that?'

'I guess, cos I value your opinion and ... I care what you think.'

She swallowed, drowning in his gorgeous dark eyes. He was so special. She wanted to kiss him. She leaned forward a little—

'No,' Seth said, edging back. 'I mean, I really want to, but not yet.'

'Are we scaling back because I mentioned sex last night? Is kissing too soon now too?'

'No,' Seth said again. 'Not at all. Come on,' he said, tugging at her hand and heading back into the throng of the street.

Seth knew exactly where he wanted to kiss Lara in Chinatown. This part of the city didn't have a permanent Chinese friendship gate, but they *had* put in a temporary one for Christmas. It was every colour of the rainbow with intricate patterns and a tiled green roof as if it had been imported direct from Shanghai.

He manoeuvred them around other walkers, some carrying closed takeout boxes, others eating from theirs already, it was a hub of evening frivolity that felt warm and inviting against the cold of the winter night. He finally stopped when they were right underneath the middle of the archway.

'I know it's not really China but ...' Seth said softly.

'You want me to kiss you here?'

'Is it stupid? It's not even a real gate, I know ...'

'It's not stupid,' Lara replied. 'It's nice.'

This time it was him who leaned forward, wanting to connect them again. Her lips were cold, but the sensations that had flowed over him last night were, tonight, hotter than ever. He held onto her, not wanting the kiss to end. But end it did, when a man in traditional Chinese dress nudged his arm, wanting him to pay attention to his juggling of lucky Chinese cat ornaments.

Lara laughed as they separated and spent a few moments watching the display. Seth put a couple of dollars in the man's money belt then turned back to Lara. 'There's something else.'

'God, Seth, are we going to get beer and rice rolls soon? I'm thirsty and starving.'

He took a breath. 'Do you wanna go to a movie premiere with me tomorrow night?'

'I don't suppose you mean getting some popcorn and watching something I haven't seen before.'

'No,' Seth said. 'I mean the whole red carpet, photo call outside the theatre and reception before the movie kind of thing. I'm in the film,' he said. 'I play Garth, he's gay. I kiss a great actor called Cole Fielder.'

'Wow!' Lara remarked.

Her tone said excitement, perhaps with a hint of nervousness. He couldn't really blame her, movie premieres weren't your average night out. They weren't even *his* average night out, but at least he had *had* the experience. For someone who had never even flown before he was guessing this was another life-changing 'first'.

'Cole'll be there too. You can, I don't know, joke about my kissing technique or something.'

Lara laughed. 'It sounds like fun.'

'It does?'

'Well, I'm trying to play it down, but inside my mind I'm running the scenario where a rough and ready country girl, who spends her days unloading animal feed from the back of a truck, meets gorgeous, epilated and, of course, supremely talented actresses who are smoother than ... smooth peanut butter ... and that orange juice without the bits in.' She suddenly looked anxious. 'Do I have to wear tights?'

'You can wear whatever you want.'

'Even jeans?' She swallowed then. 'No, because I don't have Victoria Beckham's arse and there will be photographers doing arse shots won't there? Victoria won't be there, will she?'

Seth looked at her. She was so beautiful, inside and out. He didn't care if she turned up naked or wearing a nineteenth-century crinoline just as long as she came with him.

'OK,' Lara answered. 'Ignoring my dressing-up almost-phobia and body issues, I'll come. If only to meet someone called Cole and talk about your lips.'

Seth smiled and kissed her lightly.

'Now can we have beer?'

'There's just one more thing,' Seth said.

'God!'

'Mom really does want you to come to the shelter fundraiser next week. You and Susie and whoever you want to bring. It's a good night. There's food and dancing and the shelter gets a lot of donations from rich people who need their conscience easing.'

'It's nice to know you're in no way cynical about good deeds.'

'Like it or not, everyone seems to do something for a reason these days.' His mind went to Trent. 'So, can you come? Because she'll ask me to confirm. At least every couple of hours until she has a definite answer.'

'I go back to England next week,' Lara reminded.

'You do?'

'Next Saturday.'

'The fundraiser is Friday night. How early is your start?'

'We have to leave the apartment at midday to head to the airport.'

'So ... it's a maybe?'

Lara nodded. 'It's a definite maybe.'

'OK,' Seth said. 'That will have to be enough for my mom.'

'Now, can we get beer?'

'Yes, Lemur Girl, now we can get beer.' He squeezed her hand. 'Come on.'

Fifty-Four

5th Avenue

'OK, I can't believe I'm saying this,' Lara started, eyes closed to the street full of shops opposite, around and beyond the next morning. 'But, take me shopping.'

Susie inhaled like a Buddhist about to enter a deep meditation for at least a thousand years, and then she smiled, serenely and a little creepily, before responding. 'I've been waiting *years* for you to say those words to me.'

'No going mad though,' Lara insisted. 'I only need one dress. A great dress though.'

'And a coat,' Susie added. 'And a handbag. And a few tasteful accessories.'

'What? No. No accessories.'

'I'm talking about earrings and a necklace, not ugly, really expensive brooches a nana might wear to a *bodega*.'

'Things with you and David still a little chilly?' Lara asked.

'Let's just say that while it was monsoon season when I first arrived here, I've now made it a two-day drought.'

'Oh, Susie, do you think you might be being a little harsh? Maybe if you tell him how you feel then—'

'We've been dating over a year. He should instinctively *know* how I feel.'

'But you have been apart for six months of that year. Maybe the Atlantic has numbed his intuition a bit.'

Susie inhaled again, her messy bun rising up on her head like a celestial doughnut. 'Did someone say something about shopping?'

'Yeah,' Lara responded. 'Apparently someone did. Let's find a shop before I change my mind.'

Lara had no idea what you wore to a film premiere when you weren't a stunningly good-looking actress, but Susie seemed to know exactly what to google.

Lara was currently wearing a copper-coloured sequinned dress that made her look like a boiler tank. It didn't matter which way she turned towards the mirror she just looked terrible.

'You see, you could go full-on festive. There's Kelly Rowland in this all-colours ruffled number that makes her look slightly like a Christmas tree ... or you could go classic like Jennifer Aniston ... or maybe trendsetting and be like that woman who wore multi-coloured plastic play balls to the Grammys.'

'Can I not just find a nice dress that's multi-purpose? Something I could wear a second time, you know, in Appleshaw, for my dad's next work function or for next Christmas?'

'So, you're not looking for show-stopping, more show-slowing-down.'

'Just a nice dress,' Lara said again. 'Something that doesn't make me look like one of those people who pretend to be statues in the street and scare the hell out of people when they move.' She sucked in a breath. 'But something that doesn't look like "girl from the farm trying too hard".'

'I'll be back,' Susie said, leaping up and heading out of the changing rooms for the shop floor.

Lara slumped down onto the small, round pouffe of a seat and took her phone out of her jacket pocket. It was likely her friend was going to be ages scouring the dress racks, probably finding some other items she couldn't do without – like a popcorn-holder or a tissue-grip. She clicked on to Twitter. She'd posted a photo of Chinatown last night, the dancing dragon and some acrobats they had seen on their way back from delicious dim sum. Seth had been in the photo too, just at the corner, clapping in appreciation. The first thing she saw was that she had several notifications, more than several, probably the most notifications she had ever had. She pressed on the bell icon and began to read:

Seth Hunt says he and the woman everyone is calling Lemur Girl, after that dramatic tree rescue at Central Park Zoo, are nothing more than just good friends. The former *Manhattan Med* star strongly denied rumours of any romance on the eve of the premiere of Gemstone Pictures, *The End of Us*. Seth, who plays gay writer Garth Mandelson in the movie, is also hotly tipped to take the lead role in an upcoming Universal picture about a man searching for the truth about his parentage …

She was tagged in the tweet, as was Seth. *Just good friends.* She felt sick. Was this real? Last night they had spent over an hour saying goodnight. The kisses had been hotter than the Szechuan sauce they'd eaten. What was going on?

Fifty-Five

Norma's Corner Coffee Shop, Queens

'You OK?' Kossy asked, putting her hand over Seth's. He had stopped sipping from his double espresso a while back, as every time he lifted it to his mouth his hands were shaking so much he was in danger of spilling coffee all over his shirt.

'Yeah,' he replied. 'And no.'

'I hear you,' Kossy answered. 'I know I can't be feeling exactly the same way as you, but I haven't seen Candice for ...'

'Twenty-eight years,' Seth offered.

Kossy nodded.

The coffee shop had been Candice's choice. She said it was quite close to her home. That maybe it was better to meet somewhere that wasn't her place or their place. Neutral ground. Not that Seth envisaged any sort of battle in this cosy eatery decked out with as much festive flavour as could fit into its confines. The red awning out front with the symbol of a hummingbird as its insignia didn't signal hostility but perhaps was almost a symbol of peace.

'Is this her?' Kossy asked as a woman in her mid-forties pushed at the glass front door.

'Mom, you're asking me like I'm gonna know. I don't know her. I've never seen her. You've seen her.'

'Twenty-eight years ago,' Kossy said again.

The woman was wearing smart dark trousers and a light pink silk blouse underneath a thick dark woollen coat. Her dark hair was short, tucked behind both ears, her cafe-au-lait skin virtually unlined. But then Seth took a closer look, her stance, something in the lilt of her walk and then, her eyes … He stood up, making his presence known. Clearing his throat, he spoke. 'Candy?'

The woman turned then, facing their table and she smiled, a beautiful smile, as her eyes filled up with tears. 'Seth,' she breathed.

Somehow, between the hugs and the kisses and the crying and the amazed looks from all parties, they had managed to order more coffees and the waitress had also delivered a selection of sandwiches they hadn't requested. Kossy was nibbling at them and Seth knew that was because she didn't want to talk too much and filling her mouth with food was the only way to stop words from coming out.

'You have questions,' Candice said softly. 'I mean, I know that, Seth. I know you're gonna have a lot of questions for me and …'

'Listen,' he replied. 'We don't have to talk about anything you feel uncomfortable with today … Candy.' It felt odd using her name like that. His *mother's* name.

She smiled at him. 'You've been brought up so well. I knew you would do that for him, Kossy. I knew that from the moment I first met you. I'd been to other shelters, you know, while I was pregnant, but it was like, when I met you, I just knew … I knew you were gonna be the woman I left my baby with.'

Seth heard Kossy swallow, knew every emotion would be swirling around inside of her. He watched her take another triangle of sandwich.

'Seth,' Candice said, drawing his attention back to her. 'I want you to ask me whatever you want to ask me. I mean it. You deserve to know whatever I can tell you. I want to do that for you.'

Seth swallowed. He had at least a million questions to ask her, about her life on the streets back then, about her life now, whether she was married, if she had children, but there were only two questions that were burning to be asked above all others.

'So, was I a twin?' he blurted out.

'A twin?' Candice looked completely bewildered, as if she didn't even understand the concept.

'Um,' Kossy said, trying to swallow away the sandwich. 'Seth is asking because, when you ... left him ... at the shelter, there was another hat next to him, in the box.'

'Another hat?' Candice queried.

'I ... tried to find you, Candice,' Kossy continued. 'I looked for you, all over, I asked Earl and others at the shelter at the time to look for you, I called child protection services, but there was no sign of you. It was like you'd vanished.'

'And there was no Facebook back then,' Candice sighed. 'Well, if there was, the whole world certainly didn't use it.' She shook her head then looked at Seth. 'No, sweet boy, you weren't a twin. I just left everything I had for you with you. There was a blanket someone had made for me, a couple of hats, some mittens and the clothes you had on ... nothing else. Kossy, you know how things were for me.'

'If I could have found you, Candice, I would have helped you, you know that. We might have found a way to work things out somehow.'

Candice smiled at his adopted mother. 'And that's why I didn't stick around. That's why I never *asked* you to take my son, just left him for you.' She sighed. 'Because, if I had, you would have tried to make me keep the baby ...' She stopped, looked to him. 'Keep Seth ... and you would've signed me up to some programme I wouldn't have been able to stick to.' She took a breath. 'Because you are a good person. And you would have thought that me being with my son was the best thing, no matter what my circumstances. But I know, in my heart, that life would have been nothing but shit for him if he'd stayed with me. And he deserved more.'

'Who's my father?' Seth interrupted.

He watched her expression carefully. He didn't know her at all. He had to try and work out from her face whether she was being honest. But, why wouldn't she be truthful? She didn't even have to be here ...

'I don't know,' Candice said quietly.

Seth swallowed, then quickly followed it up with a nod. It was what he had expected, given her lifestyle and her job.

'I'm sorry, Seth. I wasn't a great person back then. The life I led, the job I had ... you know what I did for a job, right?' Tears were falling from her eyes now. Full of regrets, shame maybe. He didn't want her to feel that way.

'I know,' he whispered. 'It's fine.'

Kossy reached for another sandwich, pushing it between her lips.

'It's not fine. None of my life was fine. It was shit. Just like I said.' Candice wiped at her eyes with the back of her hand, then wrapped her fingers around her coffee cup. 'Your father could be anyone – from another homeless bum like I was, to my pimp, or any of the fancy businessmen I used to see regularly, although they were always pretty careful.'

'It's OK.' Seth reached across the table for her hand. Her fingers were small and slender, her skin darker than his ... she seemed a little frail, like someone who had spent her days on earth battling through her life and was now completely exhausted.

'Your eyes,' Candice said, emotion coating her voice. 'I knew they were like mine but, seeing them now, with you here, this close …' She didn't finish the end of her sentence, maybe she couldn't, and Seth quickly got up and went across the other side of the table to put his arms around her.

'It's OK. I feel the same.' He held her close and glanced to Kossy who was nodding and looking like she had never been prouder.

Fifty-Six

5th Avenue

Lara couldn't believe the reflection looking back at her from the mirror was her own.

'Wow!' Susie commented. 'I mean, seriously, wow … like full-blown Kardashian-wow.'

The dress was bright red with a scalloped neckline and it smoothed over Lara's curves before dropping down to the floor in a full skirt. But what gave it the X-factor was the slit up one side that revealed just enough leg to make it sultry, rather than full-on sexy. She had never imagined herself being able to look this way. It was both invigorating and sad, because she couldn't get the online article out of her mind.

'Is this all pointless?' she asked Susie.

'Buying a beautiful dress to wear to a film premiere with the most gorgeous man imaginable, apart from my David, that is. If he is still going to be *my* David, you know, as he obviously wants to throw away potential apartment deposits on presents for his *abuela*.'

'The article! All over Twitter! Just good friends!'

Lara had shown the news to Susie when she'd come back into the dressing room with a dress ripe for Helena Bonham Carter or Princess Eugenie but not for her, and Susie had immediately dismissed it as 'crap'. The report, not the dress. Susie had actually liked that dress ...

'Lara, he's a celebrity! Don't you know the rules of celebrity?'

'Apparently not,' Lara answered, turning herself sideways and flattening the fabric with her hand as if she was ironing out body creases. She didn't know anything about celebrity apart from the fact that you apparently got the green light to call yourself one if you'd been on a reality TV show ...

'Well, let me enlighten you. The bare facts are: what a celebrity says on social media is *the exact opposite* of what they mean.'

'How does that work?' Lara asked, looking at her friend with confusion. 'So, when they say they support worthy causes ... they *don't* support worthy causes?'

'No! Don't be stupid! Not like that! News about *them*. Like when Bill Clinton went all "I did not have sex with that woman", he was literally saying "yeah, I shagged her".'

'Well, why would he do that?'

'Bill Clinton?'

'No, Seth.'

'Duh! To protect you. If everyone thinks you're "just good friends", then people aren't going to be following you around or wondering what you're getting up to with your hot Chinese sauce kisses and your almost-sex.'

Lara let out a heavy sigh, going back to looking at herself in the mirror. 'I don't know. Maybe this is a sign that I'm moving on too quickly.'

'Come on, Lara, you didn't come here to bag a rebound guy. You came here to get away from Dan and his terrible treatment of you. Meeting Seth and getting to know him, it wasn't planned—'

'It sort of was. The tweets and the messages, remember?'

'I know but then it was just over-the-top resilience and sucking it to Dan. Somewhere between a lemur and a burrito on Broadway things really changed.'

Yes, they had. She felt that every time she looked at Seth. Her heart literally packed its case and headed for the stars. Susie had to be right about this, didn't she?

'Have you called him?' Susie asked.

'No, I can't,' Lara said. 'Not yet, anyway. He's meeting his birth mother today in Queens. It's a huge deal for him.'

'See,' Susie said. 'You know everything about his life. He's sharing all that with you. Ignore this online bullshit because that's exactly what it is … the poop of a *toro*.'

'Susie, you do know you've said two Spanish words in a matter of seconds, right?'

'Have I?' Her friend looked a little sheepish.

'Please sort things out with David. He's a good guy. He's *your* guy. Don't throw things away just because he wants to treat his granny. Men who are nice to their grandmothers should be celebrated not … threatened with scissor-sabotage.'

As she finished her sentence Lara's phone made a bleep from her jacket pocket.

'See!' Susie exclaimed. 'That will be Seth worrying that you've seen the bull-poo article and wanting to reassure you.'

Lara bent down, the dress skirt almost covering the entire floor like she was Cinderella, and pulled her phone from the pocket of her jacket on the ground.

'What does he say? What time is the limo coming to pick you up? You are getting a limo, aren't you?'

Lara looked up from the phone, a sick feeling invading her gut. 'It's not from Seth,' she said, the words almost sticking to her lips. 'It's from Dan.'

'Well what the fuck does he want?!'

Lara swallowed. 'He says he's made a really big mistake.'

Fifty-Seven

Seth Hunt and Trent Davenport's apartment, West Village

'What the fuck have you done?!' Seth yelled the minute he saw his friend-cum-agent as he banged through the apartment door and into the kitchen-diner.

'Whoa, there, hey, buddy, how did things go with your mom?'

'Answer the fucking question, Trent!' Seth shouted, thumping him on the shoulder.

Trent recoiled. 'What the fuck, man! That's my old baseball injury right there and you know that!'

'Yeah I know that. Stand still and I'll hit the same spot a second time, only harder!'

'Is this some sort of method acting rehearsal for a new part I don't know about or what?' Trent asked. 'Because you're channelling the perfect psycho right now, so I hope that's the vibe you were going for.'

'You know I hardly ever check my Twitter, right? Except this time, today, after I met my mom and I turn my phone back on there's all these bells and notifications, so I look, and I see this!' Seth held up the screen of his phone, showing one of the articles that were declaring he had told the world that he and Lara were just good friends.

'Wow!' Trent said, staring at the screen and seeming to speed-read. 'How many websites is this on? Whoa! They actually used my phrase "hotly tipped".'

'So, this *was* you!'

'Yeah, it was me,' Trent answered, unperturbed.

'Why would you do that? I told you how I felt about Lara!'

'And I told you that could crucify this set-up I've built. You can't be the new man in her life. You have to be the gallant knight teaching her to love herself first, you know, females running the world stuff and ... "all foods before dudes".'

'This is not a game, Trent,' Seth said through gritted teeth. 'This is my life. And Lara's life.'

'And I'm doing this for both of you,' Trent insisted, picking up an apple from the fruit bowl and biting into it. 'I mean, seriously, the chick lives on the other side of the world, how far can this "falling in love" go?'

'She's coming with me to the premiere tonight, if she's still talking to me.'

'You made that clear. But, this way, with "platonic" on everybody's minds, she can go back to being the cute Brit girl you're coaching through a difficult time and I can make things work with *Ellen* or Jimmy Fallon or James Corden ... hey, that guy is British, he would love that UK angle. Everyone loves a male best friend, Seth. They don't love someone who's swooped in minutes after the last guy.'

'Minutes? Seriously?' And it wasn't like that. He got that everything had happened fast, but he really believed that Fate was turning the wheel, not him.

'I'm doing this for you. Putting your professional interests before anything else.'

'Well, I don't want you to do that any more,' Seth told him.

'Oh, OK, well, I'll just sit back and put my feet up then, shall I? Watch your career burn.' He chewed up a mouthful of apple.

'My career isn't *everything*, Trent. I've discovered that over the last couple of weeks. I'm not just an actor, I'm not just the next character. I'm a person and I'm a son. And today I found out I'm half Puerto Rican.' He laughed. 'My birth mother is Puerto Rican, which means I have a whole lot of heritage I want to find out about.' He took a breath, feeling both angry and empowered. 'And I've met Lara. And she is one of the most amazing people I have ever met. The first woman I've spent time with that just gets me without any explanation. It's like we've always known each other.' His breathing was shallow now and he could feel himself becoming more and more touched by what he was saying. 'And I can't let you take that from me because of some PR spin you think will get me parts over … Ralph Fiennes.'

'Seth—'

'No, I value our friendship, Trent. But, this isn't working.'

'Come on, man, what are you saying here?'

'I'm saying, I'm sorry but you're fired.'

Fifty-Eight

5th Avenue

'Hi, Dan.'

Just saying his name, to his face, sounded way weirder than it should. And on the phone screen, the face of the only man she had dated before Christmas time in New York looked strangely unfamiliar. Lara swallowed.

'Lara, you got my message.'

'Yes. I did.'

'God, I feel sick,' Dan admitted with a nervous-sounding cough.

There was something so honest in his expression, but looking at him now, Lara didn't feel much of anything, except maybe a tinge of regret.

'Are you wearing a dress?' Dan asked, his face moving a little closer to the screen as if it would help.

'Yes,' Lara admitted, looking down at the red premiere-destined gown she still had on. 'Quite a lot has changed here.'

'Listen, let me say. I have been ...'

'An arsehole?'

'I was going to say ...'

'A dickhead?'

'Well ...'

'Honest?'

'No, but, Lara, you can choose any word you want to tell me what an idiot I've been.'

Was he really about to say sorry? To tell her that he wanted her back? Hadn't this been what Lara had longed to happen since the minute he broke her heart? Except now it didn't feel right at all.

'You have been an idiot,' Lara said. 'But, I think, so have I.'

'No, Lara, you haven't. You've just been you and ...'

'And I'm not the person you want to spend any more time with.' She breathed out, a pent-up, hard burst of air it felt like she had been unknowingly carrying around inside her for so long.

'What?' Dan sounded really shocked. Like she had been when he'd told her he wanted a break. But this wasn't a case of getting her own back. This was something else completely.

'Listen, Dan, I think we both need to be honest with each other. Things between us, they haven't been quite how a relationship should be, have they?'

'What do you mean?'

'Well ... you hate the Appleshaw events now,' Lara said. 'And to begin with, you enjoyed them, either because you thought things like the welly-throwing were crazily funny or because you knew I enjoyed them. And I'm not criticising now, really I'm not. But you stopped caring and you stopped coming.'

'Lara, we can start again. A clean slate, a new ...'

She adjusted herself on the changing room pouffe. 'I made excuses not to come to Spa South's events.' She swallowed. 'And I never admitted that even to myself.' She took another breath. 'And I don't like most of your friends and I know the feeling is mutual. It's no wonder you didn't invite me to Scotland.'

'Lara, please, it wasn't quite like that.'

'Dan, we both need to tell the truth. No judgement.'

There was silence then and Lara looked at Dan's furrowed brow, the slight droop of his mouth as if he was considering what she had said.

'I did love you and I know that you loved me but, I think, we've really been each other's comfort blankets. You were someone I had that was outside of my family, the only person I had outside of my family, and you helped me make my first steps out of that unit.' She smiled now. 'You were the first non-Weeks I trusted.'

'And I destroyed that.'

'We both deserve more though, Dan. Don't we?'

'I hate myself for how I ended things.'

'But things have ended. I think we both need to agree on that.' Lara took another breath. 'For good.'

There was another silence, Dan's eyes meeting hers over the connection and the distance. 'I thought we could try again,' he said.

'But, I think you only thought that because it felt safe,' Lara said softly. 'Because we were easy and it was routine. Comfortable.'

'Are you really seeing that guy who played Dr Mike in *Manhattan Med*?' Dan bit.

'Are you really seeing Chloe?'

He sighed. 'I don't know yet.'

'Neither do I,' Lara said. 'But this isn't about either of them. This is about us. What we were … what we had … it was good, wasn't it?'

She watched Dan nod. 'Yes, it was good.'

'But, if we're talking about forever, I don't think it was ever going to be good enough.'

And, at that moment, tears began to fall from Lara's eyes. She knew saying goodbye to her relationship with Dan was the right thing to do, but that didn't mean it didn't hurt. She sniffed away the emotion and forced a smile.

'We have to say goodbye, Dan. You know we do.'

He nodded a little soberly. 'Yeah, I know.'

'But, will you do me one last thing?' Lara asked.

'Of course, anything,' Dan said.

'Can you find Aldo those missing stickers for his football book? It might mean searching eBay or somewhere and I'll pay ... when I get my money next month but ...'

'Lara,' Dan said. 'I'll get the stickers. I promise.'

Lara sighed and looked at the boyfriend who had broken her heart, seeing only all the good things that had made her fall for him in the first place.

'Goodbye, Dan.'

'Goodbye, Lara.'

Fifty-Nine

Lara and Susie's Airbnb apartment, East Village

'You look stunning,' Susie commented as Lara entered the main room dressed in the red, floor-sweeping dress that had put a large dent in her credit card. She felt different. Still her, just a slightly more exotic version of herself.

'Not like a contestant from *Ru-Paul's Drag Race*?'

'The only sashaying you should be doing tonight is *towards* Seth, not away from him.'

Lara held her breath. Seth had phoned her, told her about the articles she already knew about, assured her they were not direct comments from him, that Trent was responsible. And he'd sounded so worried, so truly apologetic, that she didn't have the heart to tell him she'd already seen them and had gone through a mini-crisis. She asked him about meeting his mum and he had told her how scary it had been at first, but how great it had ended up and how he was half Puerto Rican. He said it was another place to add to their Around the World list and they needed to find a great Puerto Rican restaurant to go to, with the best authentic beer.

She hadn't told Seth about her conversation with Dan but she would. Because having spent this time in New York, away from everything she'd known, including the cosy confines of Appleshaw, experiencing the build up to Christmas in another country, she knew that nothing would ever be the same again. Without knowing it, she had been coasting in life. It wasn't that she wasn't happy with her lot, she was, in lots of ways, but unless she broke her patterns, did things outside of her comfort zone, beyond her self-made borders, how would she ever know what made her happiest? And the truth was, her relationship with Dan wasn't what made her happiest.

'Well, I didn't see my going to a New York movie premiere in my future when we were trialling the vicar's festive pork pies a few weeks ago.'

'Oh, the rancid jelly stuff. It was worse this year, wasn't it?' Susie said.

'Yes,' Lara answered. 'It really was. And no one tells him.'

'Not even us.'

A car horn beeped from outside and Susie rushed to the window, pulling up the blinds. Ron, Harry and Hermione's faint glow filtered into the room. 'It's a large black car. Not quite a limo but definitely smarter than your bog-standard Uber.'

'I should go.' Lara picked up the small clutch bag Susie had insisted she buy. It was pearlescent and tiny, to be fair, snugly fitting in her phone, key to the apartment and wallet. But she had already decided she wasn't going to keep it. When tonight was over she was going to give it to Susie. 'Listen, call David, and go and practice making Spanish babies with him in an outfit of your choosing.'

'Hmm,' Susie responded.

'I really like him, Susie, I've always liked him. He's fun and he's kind and he's full of life, and he adores you.'

'He didn't adore me enough to buy me a ring from Tiffany's.'

'Not yet,' Lara said. 'But give it a New York minute. I mean, you said yourself, you don't even know whether you're ready to get engaged really.'

'But it would be super-romantic at Christmas.'

'And that isn't the best reason I've ever heard for a step towards forever.'

Seth stood outside the car, catching his breath beneath the glow of the streetlights that made the snow on the sidewalks seem like a layer of white glitter. Further down the block kids were playing in the street, rolling up snowballs and chasing each other, a man was clearing paths, then stopping to join in with the battle. Seth smiled at the display of December New York life going on like normal. Whereas, for him, today had been the kind of day that didn't come along all that often, a game-changer of a day, a day where so much had gone right and equally so much had been challenging. Meeting his birth mother was something he had never really believed would happen and it had all happened so fast. Two hours had sprinted by while they tried to fill each other in on what had happened over the past twenty-eight years. But the most important highlights were that Candice was no longer a prostitute, she worked cooking meals at a local high school and she was married, to a landscape gardener called Dwight. She was happy. They were comfortable. She had no other children. They had tried, but it hadn't happened. And another highlight was Seth was going to meet up with her again, soon, when they had both had time to take a breath and settle in to the fact that they had found each other.

When they had left Candice, Seth had held Kossy for the longest time before they headed back to the subway. He had so much to thank his mother for. Taking on someone's child, making him nothing but her own and supporting him every step of the way with every hope and dream, and now this. Helping him discover another part of his life and being more at peace with it then he had any right to expect. And the culmination of the day was now, tonight, taking Lara to this event. He felt like the luckiest person alive.

He headed towards the steps, but, as he did so, the door opened and there was Lara, looking nothing like she had ever looked before. She took his breath away, partly because he had convinced himself she would be wearing jeans, and partly because the dress fitted her so perfectly. He had been an admirer of her curves since the day they met halfway up a tree, but this outfit seemed only to highlight every beautiful inch of her.

He rushed up the steps before she could make her descent, holding out his hand to her. 'May I escort you to the car?'

'You may.' She took his hand and let him lead her slowly down each step, the snow crunching beneath their feet.

'You look incredible,' he said, his voice wavering a little.

'You,' she said, in low sultry tones. 'Look incredibly hot.'

'I think there's a possibility we're gonna set that red carpet on fire tonight.'

'Are you promising me an evening of carpet burns' Lara asked him. 'Because I am expecting to watch this film.'

'Whoa, keep that talk up and we might not even make the theatre.'

'We do get to watch the film, don't we? It isn't all just holding in my stomach for the paparazzi and smiling until the Aquafresh shine drops off my teeth?'

He stopped at the car door and looked at her again, drinking in the way her hair framed her face, her beautiful eyes, her perfect neckline down to the rounded edge of the dress ...

'And don't look at my feet,' she whispered.

'Your feet.'

'Susie wanted me to buy toe-squashing shoes and I wouldn't. We compromised on this bag. I'm still wearing my boots.' She moved the slash of the dress a little and held up a foot. 'But I told Susie that Agyness Deyn has definitely rocked boots on a red carpet before and, I also said that I thought you would rather I wore these and be able to walk and not fall over than I wear the skinny shoes and *not* be able to walk *and* fall over.'

'You were right,' Seth told her. 'Absolutely right.' He leaned forward, not wanting to wait any longer to kiss her mouth.

'Hey, Lara. Are you going out?'

He felt Lara extricate herself from his kiss and suddenly there was David.

'Oh, hello, David.' She looked down at her dress. 'Um, yeah, we're going out.'

'Is Susie inside?'

'Yes, she is.'

'Do you know if she's eaten?'

'I … we had something at lunchtime. I'm hanging on for an after-show diner visit.'

'You are?' Seth asked her.

'Is that cool?'

'Yeah, that's cool,' Seth replied.

'Do you know why Susie's pissed with me?' David asked bluntly.

'Um … I think maybe you should talk to her.'

'I'm talking to you. Come on, Lara, catch me a break here. I know there is something wrong. There were no messages today, no emojis of giraffes or—'

'Eggplant?' Seth offered. Lara shot him a look and shook her head. 'Sorry,' he said.

'We went shopping the other night and then—'

'Diamonds,' Lara blurted out. 'That's all I'm going to say. Think about the diamonds.'

'And, on that note, we'd better go,' Seth said, pulling open the back door of the car. 'Don't worry, when we get to the theatre the driver will open our door. I just felt a bit stupid getting him to do that now while only those three snowmen up there are watching.'

'Diamonds?' David said, as if still mulling over Lara's answer.

'Diamonds,' Lara repeated. 'And ... it's not a Rihanna perfume.' She ducked down into the car and Seth closed the door and walked around the opposite side.

'Diamonds,' David said again, then his expression seemed to say that he had had some sort of realisation. 'Oh, *bueno*! The brooch! Susie, she wants a brooch!'

Sixty

Beacon Theatre, Tribeca

Lara had focused on every festive decoration on every building as they had travelled in the car to the Beacon Theatre for the première. There had been all colours of stars, animatronic reindeer, a terrible sign advertising Walt's Winter Wonderland that reminded her of Carlson's Christmas World and a flashing hula girl whose grass skirt was missing some LEDs. She was trying to distract herself from the fact that she was about to step out of a car like someone she'd watch on TV, *with* someone she used to watch on TV. Who was going to be there? Was there anyone in the world who was going to stick out like a sore thumb more than her? This was so out of her haulage yard. And in the time she had spent in New York – granted, Seth had been for auditions and been an ambassador for the zoo – but the rest of the time his life had seemed pretty normal. He wasn't trailed by the paparazzi, there wasn't a fleet of screaming fans on every corner but one day there might be, and tonight was part of his world too and his world was Hollywood. She wasn't sure how a girl from Appleshaw fitted into that. She wasn't the kind of woman who shaped her eyebrows or ate fist-sized portions. Would she had to conform somehow? Change? *Shrink*?

'Are you OK?' Seth asked her as the car drew to a stop.

'I'm thinking the boots might have been a mistake,' Lara said, nose pressed against the blacked-out window. No one standing on the red carpet posing for the dozens of photographers were wearing anything on their feet sturdier than two toothpicks ... except the men. *You are not Cheryl Cole ... not Cole, something French-sounding ... no, Payne ... no, they weren't married and they were split up too now ... Nicole Scherzinger. You are not Nicole Scherzinger. You should not be here. You should be in the apartment talking to three fake snowmen.* She pressed her forehead to the glass.

The theatre was whimsical, just like the US theatres from movies she had seen about small towns and homecoming queens. There was a black sign with bright lights spelling out 'World Premiere: *The End of Us*' and, right now, Lara hoped it wasn't some sort of premonition.

'Hey,' Seth said, taking her hand in his. 'Don't be nervous. We're gonna get out. We're gonna stand and smile for some photos and then we're gonna go inside, meet a few people, then watch the film. That's it.'

'That's it,' Lara said. 'It's not shopping for baked beans though, is it?' She suspected no one on the red carpet under the lights had even ever eaten baked beans.

'No,' Seth agreed. 'But think of it as ... the trailers before the main event. We're there, enduring it, because once it's all done we get to watch a great movie and when we've watched the great movie we get to go and eat the best all-American diner food you've ever tasted.'

She couldn't help but smile as the thought of all those comforting carbs hit each and every sense all at once.

'Come on,' Seth said as the driver left his seat and went outside. 'The sooner we get out, the sooner we can go in and the sooner we get in, the sooner the movie will start.'

'You don't like this part of your job?' Lara asked him.

'I hate this part of my job,' he admitted. 'But, if Ryan Reynolds can do it ...' He squeezed her hand. 'Just follow my lead.'

The driver opened the door and, as well as the cold wind of the night, there was almost a roar from the crowd that took Lara's breath away. Seth left the car and immediately there were cameras flashing, shouts of his name, it was all so disorientating and she felt stranded. Until ...

'Come on,' Seth said, smiling, ducking his head back into the car and holding his hand out to her. 'You get out, we get in, right?'

'Right,' she answered with a nod. She took his hand and thought 'elegant'. After all, she had jumped down from many a lorry, how hard could it be to get out of the back of a car? Except what she was wearing was not jeans and was as big and cumbersome as a wedding gown. She stepped out and up onto the kerb, lifting her dress as she moved. Was this how actresses rolled almost every day of their lives? And on needle-thin stilettos? She swallowed as she straightened her frame, eyes going to the doors of the theatre. Was that Mark Wahlberg? Right there? Was she about to step on the same carpet as Mark Wahlberg? This was insane! But she had to stay composed, not run up and ask for a selfie ...

'Seth! This way! Seth!'

'Seth, Martin Faulton from *The Scene* magazine. Tell us about your character, Garth.'

Seth looked at Lara. 'I'll answer a couple of questions. I won't let go of your hand.'

She nodded, feeling a little bit sick and a lot overwhelmed. 'OK.' What else could she say? She was here, in the limelight, being snapped by a million lenses.

Because the streets weren't just lined with snow, they were lined with people, all so excited to see the stars of this movie Seth had a part in. Despite playing down his role, everyone seemed keen to talk to him for his thoughts and opinions on the movie and the world in general. Lara meanwhile felt a little bit like a wonky slice of Mrs Fitch's Christmas cake in the middle of the *MasterChef* final.

'Lemur Girl! Jackie Fox from *The Heart of the Big Apple*. Tell me, is it a dream come true being at a movie premiere with the man that's healing your broken heart?'

Someone was talking to *her*, a blonde-haired woman with a microphone stuck literally in her face. And her throat felt as dry as burnt roast potatoes.

'I—'

'First, he rescues you and Jax the lemur from a tree at Central Park Zoo, then you both rescue Santa's reindeer. I'm asking, is this the cutest Christmas love story of the year?'

'Hey, Jackie Fox,' Seth said, turning away from Martin Faulton and squeezing Lara's hand. 'How are you doing?'

'I'm very well, I was just asking your "just good friend" here about how you first met. The rumour is it was something of a social-media conversation across the Atlantic.'

'That's true,' Seth replied. 'You know how Twitter is. Lara sent me a tweet and here we are.'

Lara swallowed. That wasn't quite all it had been, but he was doing what Susie had said. Giving limited information and trying to be chivalrous.

'So, what did you chat about? Tonight's film maybe?' Jackie asked, all teeth.

'I ...' Seth began. 'It wasn't really chatting.'

Lara swallowed and forced a smile at the reporter. 'We direct messaged about star signs, actually. Seth is a Gemini and I suggested that was good for being an actor because it sort of means he should be able to adapt to lots of different roles. He accused me of saying he had a split personality.'

'You guys are too cute!' Jackie said. 'And what star sign is Lara, Seth?'

'Seth! Look this way please!'

Direct messages? He suddenly felt completely December cold all over. There were *direct messages* between them, between Lara and Trent *posing* as him?! Why hadn't Trent said anything about that? Why hadn't he *looked* at his direct messages? Because, he *never* read them. Seth realised then, as he felt his stomach hit the floor, that there was no easy way out of this. And he should have done something about the situation much, much sooner. Here on the red carpet, it was all going to come out and Lara was going to hate him for it.

'Thanks, Jackie,' Seth said. 'Thank you so much, but we have to move on now.' He held Lara's hand tight and they walked on up the line, everyone taking their photo too slowly, too excruciatingly, agonisingly slowly, the theatre doors taking an age to be any closer.

'You forgot my star sign?' Lara asked, just like he knew she would.

'Lara …' Seth began.

'I mean, obviously I'm crushed that you didn't remember but, don't worry, I can put the actual date on your phone, so you never forget.' She smiled. 'I mean, it's in the summer, so ages away, but you could send me a card, maybe, or a tweet or something.'

'Lara! This way, please. Hold out your dress! Beautiful!'

Seth watched her obey the instruction, a little awkwardly but with the most genuine smile. *Genuine.* Just like the way she approached everything.

'I didn't forget,' Seth admitted with a swallow. He couldn't hate himself more right now. 'I never knew.'

'You did,' Lara stated lightly. 'I told you, maybe in my third message or something. When we were talking about Christmas and parties and then you asked what my star sign was.'

'Lara, listen, there's something I have to tell you and I should have said something before ...' He didn't want to smile at any cameras now and he definitely didn't want to talk about the film. He wanted to take Lara away somewhere quiet, sit her down with a beer and be honest. He wanted her to know that this raw, unconventional beginning didn't matter in the slightest now ... because he had fallen for her. Deeply. Completely.

'What?' Lara asked, standing still, as the crowd furore went on around them.

'The tweets and the messages ...' This wasn't going to sound good no matter what he said or how he said it. He just had to get it out. 'The whole Twitter connection ...' He swallowed. 'The thing is ...'

'Seth! This way please! Seth!' a photographer called.

He tried to ignore everything else, focus on this beautiful woman right in front of him who meant so much ...

'It was Trent. Trent wrote everything on Twitter.' He carried on speedily, hoping more words would take the sting out of it. 'I don't go on social media very much. I told you I'm not a fan of that side of my job and—'

'*Trent* replied to me?' Lara asked. 'And wrote the messages.'

'He had just become my agent, on a trial basis. I wasn't doing so great with my other agent and he offered and ... he likes that stuff so ...'

'*Trent* wrote the messages to me,' Lara said again. He really wanted her to say something else.

'Yes,' Seth admitted with a sigh.

'All of them?'

He nodded. He hadn't even known the messages were there, let alone read them. He was pretty sure Trent had changed his login details too. He needed to take that ownership back. After he had tried to repair this damage. He could see the hurt and disappointment in Lara's eyes. She was looking at him like she didn't know him at all. He needed to do more. 'Lara, listen to me, chatting to girls ... to women ... on social media isn't something I've ever done. Something I would never do. You must know now, getting to know me, that that isn't my style and—'

'I need to leave,' Lara said, letting go of his hand.

'No, wait, hear me out,' Seth begged. 'Please.'

'If I'm honest, tonight, it felt too much too soon. Me, Lara Weeks, truck driver, dressing up for a film premiere.' She drew in a shaky breath. 'Even Disney wouldn't touch it.'

'Lara, don't,' Seth pleaded.

'But part of me wanted ...' She swallowed. 'A bit of the magic.'

'We can still have that. Listen, I met a beautiful, strong, super-funny and intelligent woman halfway up a tree. I might not have known what star sign you were and I didn't know things like ... how much you love your village, or that you hate tights and haven't ever gotten on an airplane before, or that saving animals just seems to come real natural to you, or that you have this amazing almost-brother ... but I know all that now and so much more. And I've had the absolute best time discovering it.'

'I'm sorry, Seth, I really need to go.' She turned around and began walking back down the line, cameras clicking and flashing as she moved.

'Then,' he said with determination. 'I'm coming with you.'

Lara had to keep rational. She had been right all along. Celebrities didn't respond to direct messages on Twitter, their staff did. She should have kept that in her head before getting on the plane. She didn't regret coming to New York for one second, but she did regret not keeping her feet on the ground. It wasn't just the messages, it was the whole situation. She had come to America to strike out on her own, forge a new identity as a singleton, and here she was, only a few weeks on from Dan's bombshell, with someone else by her side. She wasn't allowing herself time and space to adjust to her new status. She'd only really said a proper goodbye to Dan this afternoon!

'Seth, go in to the film. This is your job,' she reminded.

'*This* is more important.' He cleared his throat. '*You* are more important.

'How can you say that?' she asked, pushing apart the metal barriers as another luxury car pulled up to the kerb ready to dispatch more premiere guests. 'We've known each other such a short time.'

'And it's been the best time of my whole life,' he stated thunderously.

A woman in a long, figure-skimming silver dress had emerged from the limousine and stepped onto the red carpet, hands on her hips and pouting … and no one was looking. It was like a hush had descended over the hubbub and the whole world was watching Lara. And she hated it.

She pushed harder at the barrier, making a gap wide enough to move through and stepped out onto the street.

Sixty-One

Lafayette Street, Tribeca

'I've known Trent since drama school. His parents literally worked six jobs between them to pay for him to go and he's still trying to get that break to pay them back.'

Lara was walking through the snow, as fast as she could in the dress, trudging along streets that led who knew where and Seth was alongside her, spilling out stories when he should have been at the theatre.

'Go back to the premiere, Seth, please,' she begged for what felt like the thousandth time.

'I don't think he should have given up his dream, but I think he was confident that commission from me would earn him enough to pay back his parents.'

'Go back to the theatre,' Lara said again.

'But now I've fired him I guess he'll have to think again.'

'You fired him!'

'You know he told the press we were just good friends. I didn't want that. I wanted to be honest.' He sighed. 'I always want to be honest.'

'Except when it comes to social-media messages,' Lara retorted.

'Well, you told me Susie helped compose that first tweet and … I wasn't the only celebrity choice, was I?'

'Come on! That's not fair.'

'Neither is this, Lara,' Seth said. He caught her arm. 'Hear me out, please.'

She let out a sigh and looked up into those dark, heavenly eyes. This wasn't just about him. It was about her and how she had changed since she had been here. And then, suddenly, a loud shout broke the night, sending her attention to the building across the street.

'You're a fake and I don't like fakes! You make your way around the city, taking food from people who need it. You ought to be ashamed of yourself, d'you hear me?'

At once, Lara recognised the voice and the figure in the long, shabby coat. 'Seth, that's Earl.' And Earl seemed to be having an altercation with another man.

'There's a shelter just there,' Seth answered.

'Give me back the Christmas cake!' Earl shouted.

'We should do something,' Lara said. She picked her dress up a little then rushed off the pavement and across the road.

'Lara, wait!' Seth called.

Now Lara really wished she'd been wearing jeans. She'd never had to step into the middle of an altercation in a dress before, actually she couldn't remember the last dress she'd worn before NYC.

'I said, give me the goddamn cake!' Earl rasped, leaning into the other man's close orbit.

'Hello, Earl, it's Lara.'

Earl span around, his eyes a little crazed for a second until recognition arrived. 'Kid ... this is him! The one I was telling you about. The shelter-crasher.' He pointed, heavy, hard and accusing, his wooden cake-eating spork making contact with the other man's chest.

'I'm not. I have every right to be here. Just like him,' the man declared.

'Listen to that!' Earl exclaimed, nodding as if everything had now been laid bare. 'That's an Ivy League college accent. He's not from the streets!'

'Hey, Earl, it's Seth, Kossy's son. Why don't you put the spork down and we can go and sort this all out with the shelter manager, right?'

'You wanna know what the shelter manager is doing right now?' Earl asked, turning to Seth.

'I'm not sure, but shoot.'

'She's finding *him* a bed for the night. But, I told the guy, *he* don't need a bed! Not here! He's educated!' The spork was raised again.

'Educated people can fall on hard times too,' the man responded.

'Bullshit!' Earl retorted. 'They're always gonna have Mommy and Daddy to bail them out of trouble or if they ain't got Mommy and Daddy, they've got Mommy and Daddy's inheritance.'

'Earl, please, let's go inside and I'll make sure you get some more cake, or I'll buy you something else instead. What do you fancy? A hot dog or a burger?' Lara suggested. There was a small crowd gathering nearby, people filming on their mobile phones.

'I don't want nothing. I want *him* to have nothing and be exposed as a fraud!' Earl poked the man with the spork again.

'That's assault!' the man exclaimed. 'I want him arrested.'

'Fine by me, I'll get a bed for the night,' Earl responded. 'But if you're gonna get me banged up I may as well make it really worth my while.' He lunged at the man and Lara jumped into Earl's path. She cried out then put a hand to her arm.

'I'm OK,' she said quickly, backing up to the brickwork of the building and taking a chance to lean against it.

'Jesus!' Seth said, stepping forward. 'Earl, you stuck the spork in her arm.'

'No, I ... didn't mean to,' Earl spluttered. 'I'm sorry, kid. I'm sorry.'

The whine of a police car accompanied by flashing lights hailed the arrival of law enforcement.

'Lara,' Seth said, taking off his jacket and putting it around her shoulders. 'Listen to me, we're gonna get you to the hospital and get it taken out.'

'I'm fine,' Lara answered. 'Honestly.' It hurt, reasonably significantly if she was really truthful, but it was nothing compared to some of the scrapes she had been in. 'I could probably just pull it out myself.'

'No,' Seth ordered. 'No way. We're getting this done right.'

'I'm sorry, kid,' Earl said again, looking truly regretful.

Lara eyed the policemen, making their way over from their car and she looked up at Seth. 'I'll go to the hospital just as soon as we've told the police it was an accident. That I slipped on the snow and that's all.' She looked at the man Earl had been having his disagreement with. 'Can we do that, please?'

Sixty-Two

Lower Manhattan Hospital, William Street

Seth sat in the waiting area, watching the whole spread of New York life come in and out of the hospital doors. From car accidents and minor burns to an electrocution by steam iron and someone dressed as a snowman who had a rash, the characters – and the poor selection of magazines – had passed the time. But it had been over an hour since he'd seen Lara and he'd been a little sore that she had asked him not to go in with her. Though he understood. Before the spork incident she had been running from him, wanting to put an end to what they had begun together. And he doubted that anything had changed.

'Four stitches,' Lara announced. 'No other damage that they can see, and I might have a small scar I can talk about at parties.'

He turned around, not having seen her come up behind him, then immediately got to his feet. 'Jeez, Lara, four stitches and a scar—'

'A maybe-scar. They don't know. No one knows, do they, until the wound is better and it's all grown over.' She swallowed, like she was actually talking about something else and not the mark on her arm.

'Are you OK?' he asked her, his eyes on her wound. It was cleaned up now, the protrusion gone, just four neat-ish lines holding the skin together.

'I'm fine,' she answered. 'Did you phone your mum?'

He nodded. 'Yeah, she's got Earl. And the other guy. Who claims to be a reporter for a magazine who has been working undercover writing about the homelessness in the city for the past few months.'

Lara clapped her hands over her mouth. 'Oh my God! That's why Earl kept seeing him at different shelters and not blending in.'

'I don't know why he didn't just tell us this before Earl got all … sporky.'

'You know that isn't a real word, don't you?'

'I'm not sure the thing is even a real thing,' Seth admitted.

'Oh, it's real all right,' Lara stated. 'I can attest to that.'

'So, do you wanna get out of here?' Seth asked. 'We can get a cab and go get some of that diner food I promised you.'

He watched her take a long, slow breath. 'I think I'd rather just go back to the apartment.'

'Sure,' he said quickly. 'I'll … arrange a cab.' He took his phone from the pocket of his pants and strode towards the large Christmas tree in the corner near the nurses' station. He could have made the call in front of her but that wouldn't have given him the moment he needed to realise that things had altered. That, after tonight, he may never get the chance to see Lara again.

The home screen of his cell told him he had two messages, both from Trent. He'd already had a couple of 'I'm sorry' messages earlier in the evening he had yet to respond to. He didn't know what to do. He knew that there had been no malice behind what Trent had done, that he was just acting like the slight megalomaniac that he was, but being his agent wasn't going to work if they were going to maintain their friendship.

He pressed on the messages.

I am real, real sorry, bud. REAL SORRY!!

Then there was a bitmoji of a cartoon Trent, his head hanging low and holding a banner that said, 'I suck'.

The second message started the same way but had something else:

I'm sorry. You didn't get the Hoff part.

Sixty-Three

Lara and Susie's Airbnb apartment, East Village

'Holy guacamole, what is going on, *chica*?' David asked, stepping into the living area where Lara was bending spruce branches like she was in a one woman combat with the tree.

'I'll second that,' Susie chimed in. 'What are you doing out of bed, manhandling a Christmas tree, when you've had four stitches in your arm? Where did you even get a Christmas tree from? How did you drag it up all the steps? You have decorations too? Lara, you do know we're only here for a few more days.'

'Yes, I know,' she answered. 'All of that and the guy who sold me the tree delivered the tree and helped me carry it up all the steps, and in here, while you two lay sleeping ... well, you know, not sleeping exactly but ...'

'It's a great tree,' David remarked, stepping up to the pine bush and fondling a finger of needles. 'It smells real good.'

'And you two are talking, and doing other things with your mouths again, so it's all fine with you, right?' Lara said, watching the bare boards turn a little more rustic as needles hit the floor and certain boughs didn't do as they were told.

'It's all *bueno*,' David replied.

'It's the day, isn't it?' Susie remarked. 'The day you always put your tree up in the barnpartment.'

Her best friend had got it. She had tried hard not to dwell on all the Christmas preparation she usually did in Appleshaw while she was here but, after last night, after Seth had dropped her home and she had left him without a kiss or even a promise to call, she needed a distraction … and the Christmas tree was it.

'I have to go,' David said, leaping at Susie and winding around her like he was taking part in a hot scene from an adult movie. 'I will see you later.'

'You will,' Susie said, kissing him tenderly.

'Bye, Lara!' David said … and then he was gone.

'Right,' Lara said, getting to her feet and wiping pine needles from her fingers. 'Now he's gone I can run through our itinerary for the day.'

'Our what?' Susie asked.

'Our plan. You know, sightseeing, shopping, lots of shopping, coffee, bagels because we can't come to New York and only go to *one* bagel place—'

'Aren't you seeing Seth today?'

'No, not today,' Lara answered, picking a string of blue tinsel out of the bag of delights she had purchased earlier.

'Tonight?'

'No.'

'Tomorrow?'

'I don't think so.'

'Is he working?'

'I don't know.'

'Lara, what's going on?'

'Nothing.'

'Don't give me that. Last night I sent you out of here looking like a beauty queen ready to storm the red carpet, I get you had an unplanned trip to the hospital but now you're not going to see Seth? What's happened?'

Lara sighed. 'The messages he sent me on Twitter. They weren't from him. They were from Trent.'

Susie laughed. 'Is that it? You did keep saying that celebrities have social-media managers. You were right.'

'I know, but, it's not right, is it? I thought I was talking to him once we started properly talking. I assumed everything I was saying I was saying to him, not his agent friend.'

'So, what, you're not going to see him again now?' Susie asked. 'You're going to end things? Even though you've been practically inseparable since the day we got here, and I've never seen you happier?'

'It's for the best.'

'The best for who?'

'It's too soon,' Lara stated, dipping to pick up a silvery star. She hung it in the middle of the tree then changed her mind and put it somewhere else.

'Too soon for what?'

'To … fall in love with someone.'

'You're in love with Seth.'

Susie looked like she might want to start flossing with excitement. Lara hadn't meant to say those words out loud. Because they were ludicrous.

'But enough of that,' Lara said, changing the subject. 'We have a fun-packed day ahead of us, just as soon as we've decorated this tree.'

'Oh no,' Susie said, stepping closer to her. 'I'm not letting you drop that sentence and emotionally backtrack on me.'

'It's hopeless,' Lara insisted. 'We're from two different worlds.'

'That sounds like the beginning of a film trailer.' Susie cleared her throat and started husky. 'They were from two different worlds but when they met, life and love just seemed to fall into place.'

'Stop it,' Lara said, unable not to laugh. Her arm hurt a bit when she laughed, and when she used her left hand.

'I won't,' Susie said. 'I won't stop making up trailers until you fix another date with Seth. I know you think it's too soon but that kind of depends what you're looking for. You make the rules now.' She was looking at her seriously. 'So, Lara, do *you* think it's too soon to meet a gorgeous guy and have the time of your life?'

Sixty-Four

The Chapel Shelter, W 40th Street

'Lara is totally bad-ass,' Felice remarked as she and Seth packed food boxes that were going in the back of a van Ted was taking out into the city to some of the homeless camps and squats. It was something they did once a month and twice a few weeks before Christmas. Christmas wasn't always full of festive cheer for everyone. Some needed help to make it even halfway close to special.

'I mean she gets in between Earl and that shelter-crasher ...' Felice carried on.

'He was a reporter. The police suggested he writes up what he has and doesn't go undercover like that again.'

'Undercover or not, he's still been taking our food,' Felice said. Seth saw her slip some sachets of coffee into the pocket of her coat. 'But, Lara, she's like some sort of superhero. Always doing good stuff, you know.'

Yeah, he did know. He had thought about it all night while watching the video footage from the red carpet. There he and Lara were, holding hands, smiling, looking happy and then he could see things change, the second they started to talk about Trent's use of *his* social media ...

'Put the coffee back, Felice,' he said to her.

'What?' Felice asked, all innocence.

'Listen, I know you've got nothing, but I also know my mom thinks you're one of the best ones, that you're gonna make something of yourself. She gives you privileges, swings the bed raffle most nights, don't let her down.' He looked up. 'Do it now. My dad's coming.'

Felice slipped the coffee packets back into the box and recommenced filling the parcels with goods.

'How's it going you guys?' Ted asked, joining them.

'Good,' Seth answered. 'We've got a pile of almost fifty by the door already and we're almost done with these.'

'Fantastic work,' Ted said. 'You too, Felice.'

Seth watched her blush then shrug.

'Dad, have you got a second?'

'Sure, Seth.'

'Felice, are you good here?' Seth asked.

'One thing of each thing goes in each box.' She tutted. 'I don't think I need my graduation certificate to manage that.'

Seth led the way to the corner of the main room, just behind the ping pong table where two women – both with strings of tinsel around their heads like sweatbands – were playing what looked like a hotly contested game.

'Do you wanna sit?' Ted asked, indicating the chairs.

'No,' Seth said. 'I … just wanna ask you something.'

'As a father? Or as a counsellor?' He smiled. 'Or as my twenty-eight-year-old self?'

'Maybe a little of all three?'

'OK,' Ted responded.

'OK,' Seth said. Why was he so nervous? He felt like one of his dad's high-school students about to confess to smoking weed. 'So, I just want to know what you think about … about love.'

'Love.' Ted said the word like it was poetic. And he'd made the four letters sound a whole lot longer and more meaningful than Seth had. 'What do I think about love?'

'Yeah, I know, odd question.'

'Well, I believe in it. Wholly and completely. And I believe it takes many forms. It's also absolutely different to any other form of emotion I've read about or encountered.'

'How so?'

'So, let's take hate. Love's opposite. Hate can grow, over a long period of time and it can be fast too, but hate usually stems from an incident or a chain of events that led the person to feel that dark emotion. Often hate is misunderstood. When we say we hate somebody, what we really mean is we hate certain things that person has done.' He smiled. 'And we have to remember that those things only make up a tiny part of that person and that person might have been acting that way or doing those things for a whole set of reasons we have no knowledge of. Believe it or not, it's actually really hard to truly hate a person.'

'And love?' Seth asked.

'Love is more complicated than hate. Love can grow too, but love can also be instant, like a mother's love, the moment their child is born ... is this about Candice?' Ted enquired.

Seth shook his head. 'No.'

'OK ... so love, it's instinctive and knowledgeable and love is felt by the entire body – honestly, even the tips of your toes respond to love – *and* the love emotion really does almost neutralise every other feeling.'

'But, how do you know if it's right? I mean, right place, wrong time, wrong place, right time ...' He trailed off not knowing what to say next.

'I think you're talking about *true* love now, Seth,' Ted said.

'I don't know,' Seth responded. 'That's the problem.'

'I think you *do* know,' Ted said, patting him on the shoulder. 'Or you wouldn't be here asking me about it.' He smiled. 'Remember, we don't always choose love, Seth. Sometimes love chooses us.'

Seth nodded, feeling like he had enough of the answers he needed. 'Dad.'

'Yes, son?'

'Is there any way you can get me a really cool truck by tonight?'

Sixty-Five

Madison Avenue

'What store is next?' Lara asked enthusiastically. 'I know, how about Ralph Lauren? You ought to be able to pick up something nice for David for Christmas in there, right?'

'OK, this has to stop now,' Susie said, halting in the middle of the pavement so people had to walk around her. 'At first, I thought this might work to my advantage, having you *finally* interested in shopping. But it's like a shell of you! You don't give real opinions! You say you like everything! And, believe me, I have held up and admired the biggest pieces of shit this city has to offer over the past couple of hours.'

'Oh,' Lara said with a sigh. 'You noticed. I thought I was doing so well.'

'No,' Susie said. 'You are not doing well. And you are not doing well because you are sad about not seeing Seth. I know your arm is injured, but right now, you're acting like it's been severed off. Like a part of you is gone. You were not like this after Dan. You were sad, yes, but you were angry and disappointed more. Now it's like the sun has been kidnapped and Jesus has cancelled Christmas forever.'

'I definitely wasn't doing so well then.'

'I don't care what you say,' Susie shouted, passers-by listening, the busker stopping his rendition of 'Driving Home for Christmas'. 'I don't care if you've known him a week or a lifetime. You love him! You need to tell him you love him! It doesn't mean you have to live together or even be together, or get married, or get pregnant, just meet up with him again. Tell him you love him!'

The busker clapped his hands in applause and whistled and Lara felt something burst inside her ... and it wasn't the stitches in her arm. Was it really that simple? Did it really not matter than Seth had arrived in her life at the most inconvenient of times, that she had been flung into this relationship at break-neck speed straight after the loss of a man she had wasted too much time on? Surely, if she wanted to, she could be with Seth and still maintain that spirit of adventure he'd helped her to find while she had been here. Maybe it didn't have to be a case of one thing or the other ...

From the pocket of her jacket her phone made a noise and she slipped it out to look.

'It's him, isn't it! You're so in sync with each other you just have to think about him and he's on the other end of the phone!' Susie exclaimed.

'Kind of,' Lara answered. 'It's Trent.'

'Ugh. What does he want?'

She began to read the message.

Hi Lara, so, just so we're clear. This is TRENT. Sending probably my last ever communication as Seth Hunt Actor. Lara, I wanted to say I'm sorry for the confusion. Yes, at first, I thought you were a great angle with your bleeding heart and celebrity bent to try and get over your break-up but ... Seth had nothing to do with that and, if you know the guy as well as I think you do, you'll know that too. Now for the part that, as a best friend,

I definitely should not be telling you because it breaks down the whole bro-code thing, but, as crazy as I think this all is, Seth's in love with you. I mean, I seriously don't think he will eat or sleep or even drink beer if you break his heart here. He's totally sweet on you. Gone. *makes plane noise* Head over heels. Almost-had-me-in-a-headlock-Beyoncé-Crazy-in-Love crazy in love with you. So please, I'm begging you, call him, go out with him, please God sleep with him, because I have to live with him and I am a far worse heartbreak healer than I was an agent. TRENT

'Not just a three-word message then,' Susie remarked.

'I need to call him,' Lara stated, her fingers now appearing to work properly. 'I need to call Seth.'

Sixty-Six

Lara and Susie's Airbnb apartment, East Village

'Wait!' Seth greeted, grabbing hold of the door handle. 'Don't open the door yet.'

'Why not?' Lara asked, wrestling for ownership of the pull.

'Please, I promise, you'll like it. Just close your eyes.'

'So, I can't open the door and now I have to close my eyes?'

'Close your eyes,' Seth begged.

Lara took a breath and did as he asked. This felt better. She was wearing jeans, a Fall Out Boy jumper over her Truckfest T-shirt and they weren't on their way to something cinematic, she hoped. She hadn't said anything to Seth about Trent's message. Hearing that Seth loved her had turned her into a gooey mess on Madison Avenue, but she really wanted to hear it from Seth himself before she admitted how she felt to him. It was all unchartered territory for her. This kind of love she hadn't known existed.

'OK,' Seth said, taking her hand. 'Take the steps real slow. I don't want you falling on the snow and splitting your stitches.'

'I have four stitches. Not a back full of them like I did when I got stuck in barbed wire with a peacock.'

'Last couple of steps,' Seth directed as they moved down. 'OK.' Her feet landed on the sidewalk. 'Open your eyes.'

Lara snapped open her eyes and her jaw dropped. Inside she was screaming but outwardly she was so stunned she couldn't make a single sound.

'It's a … it's a …'

'You probably know all the names and numbers of it. I just call it a truck.'

'Is this our transport?' Lara asked. 'To the date.'

'Lemur Girl, this *is* our date.'

'It's so beautiful,' Lara said, going up to the truck and touching its bright blue paintwork and chrome fixtures like she was caressing a horse. She knew exactly what it was. It was a Western Star and, as much as she loved Tina, this truck was something else. 'Wait, did you drive this here?'

'No!' Seth said, holding his hands up and looking a little bit scared. 'My dad made me promise I would not even start the engine. His pal, Stan, works somewhere like you work, and he dropped me and her … is it a her?' Seth asked, looking at the vehicle as if he might be able to tell.

Lara laughed. 'This is a boy.'

'Why? Because he's painted blue? That's a little bit judge-y.'

'No,' Lara answered. 'I just know. Don't I … Austin.'

'Wow, you've named him already,' Seth stated. 'And given him the gayest truck name I have ever heard.'

'Because that's not judge-y at all,' Lara answered. She stopped running her hand along the truck's paintwork and looked at Seth. 'Can *I* drive him?'

'Well,' Seth began. 'I assured Stan … and my dad … that you really do do this for a job and …'

'I do,' Lara said excitedly. 'So, can we go?' She was already pulling at the handle but then she stopped.

'What's up?' Seth asked. 'We can go. I'm excited to go.'

'I might need some help getting up,' Lara admitted. 'Because of my arm.'

'God, yeah, I'm sorry, sure.' He opened the door for her. 'Listen, I saw Earl earlier. He couldn't be sorrier.'

'I know,' Lara said. 'It wasn't really his fault.'

'Well, he *was* holding the spork,' Seth reminded.

'And when I tell the story at parties I am definitely going to say it was a screwdriver because a spork just sounds so pathetic.'

'I'm glad it wasn't a screwdriver,' Seth stated. He was looking at her now, like he didn't know what came next.

'Just, give my bum a boost,' Lara said, putting one hand on the rail and her foot on the first step.

'OK,' Seth said, still sounding unsure.

'Come on, Seth, this is a valid invitation to touch my arse. Get on with it!'

She felt him hold her bottom, then push and with a bit of a scramble she was up and settling herself into the driver's seat. It was amazing. She felt so at home, but it was also quite different from being in the familiarity of Tina. There was the longest gear stick in the world for a start and the whole sitting on the other side of the cab …

'It's so high up here, isn't it?' Seth remarked. 'I thought that, when I got up earlier, you know, after the fourth attempt, without my dad boosting my butt, how high it is and how you can see everything so much better.'

'Where should I take us?' Lara asked. She started the engine and closed her eyes as she pressed down on the accelerator and listened to the roar of the moving parts.

'Let's get out of the centre,' Seth suggested. 'And go over some bridges.'

'Can I sound the horn?' Lara asked him.

'Yes, you can sound the horn,' Seth answered. 'Come on, Austin, let's hear what you got.'

An air-horn noise of epic proportions had even Lara jumping in her seat. 'Oh my God, I want this truck!'

'I'm sorry it's only a loan for one night. I think, to buy it, would probably cost almost as much as my parents' house.'

'One night is better than nothing,' Lara said, smiling at him. 'Thank you, Seth. This is the best almost-Christmas gift I've ever had.'

Sixty-Seven

Greenpoint Diner, Greenpoint

Lara had made sure to get the egg yolk all over everything on her plate and dotted the sausage, bacon, sourdough toast and steak with ketchup. 'You've taken me to America tonight, Seth.' They were in a simple diner with booths and cheaply uphol-stered banquette seating around Formica tables, an old-fashioned jukebox playing country Christmas songs.

'Yeah,' Seth answered, sipping from his bottle of Bud. 'All this country-hopping was getting a bit out there, right?'

Lara smiled and sipped her Coke. No alcohol for her while she was in charge of the beautiful Austin with his super-large gearstick ...

Driving the truck through New York had been an experi-ence like no other. Heavy traffic and going at minus miles per hour through the Manhattan streets had given her time to really look at NYC in detail. It was so cosmopolitan. Everyone knew its towers and skyscrapers, the landmarks shown on movies – Times Square, the Chrysler Building, Central Park, Grand Central Station – but there was a whole lot more to it than that. Every area of the city offered something singular. There was dirty and rough but there was also quaint nestling beside modern. Bright lights of theatres mixing with the soft glow of brasseries; smoky, gas-guzzling cars alongside bicycles and roller skates; designer dresses and suits mingling with authentic ripped jeans and tattered rags. It was like every corner of the world was inside this metropolis. And add Christmas to that, the scenes had been incredible. There were lights and displays literally everywhere. Now, only a week until the big day, no home, office, or store was without a homage to the season. Every shop had a display, from giant penguins to tiny mice circling around ornate sleighs piled high with gifts. There were ice-white Christmas trees, trees with every colour of the rainbow swirled around them, trees entirely made of Hershey's chocolate and probably enough Santa images to fly-post the whole height of the Empire State Building. And after the congestion of the city, they had swung out onto the Williamsburg Bridge and crossed the East River. Eight lanes flowing across a steel suspension bridge and Lara had felt like she was in a movie scene. Except it was real. And she *was* the starring role in the film of her now. There was no doubt about that.

'You didn't have to have breakfast in a diner, you know,' Seth remarked as Lara bit into her toast.

'I did. I haven't had a full all-American breakfast since I've been here and I'm running out of days.'

'Yeah,' Seth said, putting down his beer and rubbing at his eyes with his fingers.

'Where are your glasses?' Lara asked him.

'In my apartment,' he answered.

'You haven't worn them for a while now.'

'No, well, I don't usually wear them at all, you know, only when my eyes are tired, but I had some issues with my lenses so …'

'I like your glasses,' Lara admitted.

'You do?'

'Yeah, I always thought Dr Mike should wear glasses. All those clipboards he had to read.'

'God, Dr Mike did so much of that, didn't he? I know I used my glasses a whole lot more when I got home from filming on that show.'

'Have you heard?' Lara asked. 'About *A Soul's Song*?'

Seth shook his head, hair springing a little. 'No. Not yet. But I'm still hopeful.' He smiled. 'I didn't get the part of David Hasselhoff though.'

'Should we commiserate?' Lara said. 'Because I might have quite liked to see you in tiny red shorts.'

'We might be commiserating if I don't get the part of Sam. West Village isn't the most economical place to live.'

'And that's why I'm lucky to live in a barn,' Lara mused. 'Well, a barnpartment.'

'I really want to know more about this,' Seth admitted with a smile.

'When my dad bought the house, the barn used to house horses. And it's right next to our yard with a farm on the other side. There are stairs at the entrance and it goes up to an open plan room with everything I need right there. I've got a kitchen, a bathroom, a double bedroom and a lounge.'

'It sounds great,' Seth said, just watching her light up as she spoke about her village.

'It's totally not ready for Christmas though,' she admitted. 'Usually I'm highly organised with a schedule of events including the optimum time to watch *Elf* and *Die Hard*.'

'You know *Die Hard* isn't a Christmas film, right?'

'Wash your mouth out!' Lara ordered, her face turning serious.

Seth laughed and spooned some mashed potatoes between his lips.

'So, the holidays are coming, as Coca-Cola says,' Lara commented.

'Should I have got you the whole Coca-Cola trailer to go on the back of Austin?'

'Oh no,' Lara replied. 'I think we might have then been followed by marching bands and cheerleaders.'

'It hasn't taken long, has it,' Seth remarked wistfully. 'For Christmas to be almost here.'

'No,' Lara replied. He saw the reticence in her expression, mirroring what he was feeling himself. The closer Christmas got, the nearer they were to Lara leaving for the UK.

'Big turkey feast in your barnpartment?' Seth asked, trying to keep the mood upbeat.

'Oh no,' Lara said. 'I love my place but it's too small for a whole gang.'

'A gang?' Seth said, almost spitting out his beer.

'Me, Aldo, my dad, Mrs Fitch, sometimes Flora pops in for tea and Susie, if she isn't visiting relatives in London.'

'I guess, this year, I have to think about my other mom and Dwight.' He smiled. 'I have a stepdad as well as a birth mom.' He put down his beer bottle. 'If they haven't already made plans.'

'Listen,' Lara said, inching a hand across the table.

Seth looked at her fingers, there was a little hesitation in her movement, as if she wasn't quite sure she was doing the right thing. He waited for her to continue. Didn't want to push things. He had done a little too much of that already …

'Your mom sounds so nice. I think she's going to want to spend as much time with you as she can.'

'She's gonna come to the shelter fundraiser so you'll get to meet her,' Seth informed. 'Kossy invited her.'

'Your Kossy-mum is amazing too,' Lara stated.

'Yeah,' Seth agreed. 'She is.' Lara still hadn't moved her hand any further and her fingers were now just a few short centimetres from his on the slightly scuffed and beaten-up Formica diner table. He really wanted to make the connection. She was looking at him now, a tiny spot of ketchup at the corner of her mouth ...

He cleared his throat. 'You have a little ketchup, just there.' Seth pointed to the spot on the edge of his own lips.

'I do?' Lara said, not making a move for a napkin.

'Yeah,' he replied, his voice sticking a little.

'Well,' Lara said quietly. 'You could just ... kiss it away.'

Here was his opportunity. She was letting him in again, giving him permission to get closer, rekindle the relationship, like he hoped she would.

He didn't waste any time, leaning over the table, uncaring for his plate of food or the condiments that were set between them. He reached for her, his hand cupping her face and drawing her towards him. She was looking at him, eyes so full of affection and desire it was all he could do to hold back, but hold back he did, just for a moment, his tongue catching the spot of sauce. 'There,' he whispered.

Then, suddenly, he was jolted back, as her lips crashed against his and they began making out like the world was going to implode. God, he loved her. He loved her so much and whether she was going home in a few days or not, whether it lasted, that love was more important than anything.

He broke off, needing to breathe, one jumper sleeve getting in the black bean taco on his plate. 'I've got dessert,' he said, eyes not leaving hers. 'In Austin, the truck, not the state.' He swallowed.

'Let's go,' Lara said.

Sixty-Eight

East River State Park

With shaking hands – and trembling other body parts – Lara had driven Austin, under Seth's directional guidance, to the almost sandy edge of the East River. Parking up, no one else anywhere around, there was the most wonderful view of the city across the water. Tall smoke-stacks emitted funnels of grey into the night, bricks, glass and steel rising up into the stars, their pinpricks of light white, orange and gold. The Empire State's pinnacle flashing red, white and blue in turn.

'I got us something Puerto Rican.' Seth broke the tense silence by reaching to bring something out from the bunk behind. He began to pull at the wrapping over a bowl. 'It's called *tembleque* and it's a creamy coconut pudding.'

'It sounds nice,' Lara said, inhaling the scent as the dessert was revealed.

'I'm told, by the Puerto Rican lady who works at the restaurant near my apartment who made it, that *tembleque* means "wobbly".'

'We might need a spork,' Lara said, smiling.

Seth produced two spoons. 'Spoon?'

'I thought you'd never ask,' she answered with a grin.

He handed one of the spoons to her and she dug in, quick to bring the delicious-looking pudding to her lips. It tasted of the coconut Seth had told her about but also cinnamon, vanilla and nutmeg. 'It's so good,' she said, enjoying all the flavours.

She watched Seth take a mouthful and he nodded in agreement. 'It's real good.'

'You've never tasted it before?' Lara asked.

'I'm a very new half Puerto Rican.'

Lara put her spoon in the bowl he was holding and took a breath. 'It's a great pudding,' she said. 'But I don't want to eat any more.'

'No?' Seth said, looking up from the dessert and meeting her eyes.

Her gaze moved just a fraction, to the space behind where they were sitting. To the cabin bed, covered by a cheap blanket, before looking back to him. 'No,' she answered. 'I want to, climb onto the bed and ... take off my clothes.'

Seth wanted not to be holding a Puerto Rican pudding right now. He wanted to be holding her. He leant forward in his seat, jamming the container and spoons between dashboard and windscreen.

'Is it too forward?' Lara asked, her voice catching a bit. 'To say that?'

Seth shook his head. 'No.' He swallowed. 'Because I feel exactly the same way.'

'I keep thinking,' Lara said, slipping out of the driver's seat and manoeuvring herself onto the bed. 'That I shouldn't be feeling this way, you know, being fresh out of a break-up and only here for a little bit longer and a hundred other reasons but ...'

'But?' Seth replied. He really wanted to know what the hundred other reasons were, but he definitely wanted to hear about the 'but'.

'But as hard as I try to tell myself I can't feel real feelings for you, my heart is telling me something very different.'

'It is?' Seth said, watching her remove her jumper, his heart close to high-level palpitation.

'Yeah, it is,' she answered. 'And I think you feel the same way too.' Her fingers were at the hem of her T-shirt now, easing the fabric upwards, a little teasingly. Even if the teasing wasn't deliberate it was certainly hitting the spot with him.

'Lara,' he said, the emotion in his own voice surprising even him. 'You have no idea how I feel about you.'

'Oh,' Lara answered, her T-shirt coming up and over her head. 'I think I might.'

God, she wasn't wearing a bra! And the sight of her naked upper body was doing crazy things to his already heightened arousal.

'I never wear a bra,' Lara said with a shrug. 'Not since I was suspended from the top of a fork-lift.'

'You ... seem to get in a lot of scrapes,' he said, unable to look at anything but her soft, beautifully rounded, perfect breasts.

'What can I say?' she said, shrugging. 'I'm a little incident-prone.'

'So it would seem,' Seth answered. He was stripping himself of his jumper now, then his fingers were at the buttons of his shirt.

'But, what can happen to me here?' Lara asked. 'In this small cab?'

'Oh,' Seth answered, removing his shirt. 'I think you'd be surprised.'

Lara was trembling as she unfastened her jeans and shed them, letting them pool on the floor of the lorry. She was trembling, not because she was in any way nervous about the decision she had made, but because she was watching him, watching Seth remove his clothes, and anticipating what was going to happen next. What she so desperately wanted to happen next.

'Is this OK?' he whispered, his fingers poised at the fly of his dark jeans.

She nodded, sure. 'Yes.'

She swallowed, watched him shift in the limited space they had, edging the denim from his form. Then his underwear came off with the jeans. Lara bit her lip. He was perfect, in every way, no body double required here. From his gorgeous dark eyes and those full lips, down over his muscular chest and defined torso to lean athletic legs. And what lay between those legs was looking pretty amazing from where she was sitting.

He moved to sit next to her, his hands in her hair, smoothing it back from her face, fingers shaking a little. 'You are so beautiful, Lara,' he whispered. 'I thought that from the minute I saw you.' He kissed her cheek. 'Then, when I started to get to know you, I realised that that beauty on the outside was nothing compared to the beauty on the inside.' He kissed her lips, the lightest of touches, when really she wanted so much more.

'I wanted the timing to be better,' Lara breathed, her hand finding his, squeezing hard. 'I thought that, to be right, every-thing had to be in place and, I don't know ... conventional, I suppose.'

He kissed her neck, his lips finding her pulse point and applying the most sensual pressure with the tip of his tongue. 'And now?'

'Now I'm thinking ... and feeling ... and remembering that ... life doesn't really work that way, like ever.' She closed her eyes as his mouth explored, lowering, leaving her neck, tracing the line of her collarbone and dipping down onto her chest.

'And you're not conventional,' Seth reminded her. 'At all.'

'I hope that's a compliment,' she replied, a smile on her lips as he turned his head slightly and met her gaze.

'The highest of compliments,' he reassured her. 'I think you're the most amazing person I've ever met.'

She swallowed, his words wrapping themselves around her heart. 'Seth,' she whispered. 'I *know* you're the most amazing person I've ever met.'

He moved to kiss her then and it was a kiss filled with heat and passion. The sensation of his mouth on hers, the scent of his skin, the touch of his fingers as they wound a trail lower, slipping under the fabric of her underwear, was making her head spin.

'I need to tell you something,' he whispered, his fingers starting a delicious slow dance over her labia.

'Make it quick,' she breathed. 'I have better things for you to do with your mouth other than talk.'

'Open your eyes,' Seth said.

She did as he asked and when she lifted up her eyelids, there he was, admiring her, looking at her like no one had ever looked at her in her whole life. It was as if she was being honoured, inside and out, by his gaze.

'I'm in love with you,' he said, his voice sounding close to breaking.

A sound rose up in her throat and she had to clamp her lips together to stop an audible outpouring. Trent had told her. She had wanted to believe it, and here it was, from his own heart.

'I know, how that's gonna sound to you,' he breathed. 'After so short a time, after Dan ...'

Lara palmed his face, needing to touch skin on skin. 'Don't say his name,' she begged. 'Because he isn't part of this.' She swallowed. 'He has never, really, been part of this at all.' She brushed her thumb over his bottom lip, her insides frothing like mulled wine left to boil. 'What started out as a mission to show him what I could do without him, turned into a holiday where I showed myself what I could do without him.' She smiled. 'And then there was you. Part of the plan but equally *not* part of the plan. And I tried really hard to tell myself that these feelings I was having were rebound rumbles, that it wasn't possible for there to be anything genuine between us but ...' She stopped talking, just gazed at him, this gorgeous man with the sweetest soul.

'But?' Seth asked.

'I was missing the point,' Lara admitted. She took a breath. 'Because, I think, with love, you don't get to choose when it happens. It just takes over, and happens all by itself.'

Seth shook his head, a smile on his lips and tears in his eyes. 'Someone else told me that today,' he replied. 'And I believe that too.'

'I love you, Seth,' Lara told him, without any further hesitation. 'I really love you.'

He kissed her then, full and hard, edging her back down onto the bed of the truck and Lara suddenly felt like she was exactly where she was meant to be at this moment in time. Not in Appleshaw, but in New York, at Christmas, with the absolute love of her life.

Sixty-Nine

Seth spooned some *tembleque* into Lara's mouth and she closed her eyes, savouring all the delicious tastes as it hit her tongue. They had just watched the sunrise over the city – a clear blue sky overhead, frosty snow on the ground, blankets around them – and she knew they would have to leave this truck sanctuary soon before the whole of New York came to life and the park got filled up with walkers and cyclists and people minding their own business not expecting to see a lorry with a naked couple inside. Last night had been filled with the most erotic experiences of her entire life, but not in a Christian Grey way, in a deep, intense, soul-touching way. When Seth had moved inside her she had felt it absolutely everywhere and, when she had crawled on top of him, he was there, strong and hard and sexy, his gaze and his whispered words empowering her to be her, to do what she wanted to do, to be who she wanted to be. It had been such the biggest turn-on she had come without any warning and screamed like a barn owl.

'Johnny Depp or Matthew McConaughey?' Lara asked.

'Whoa, seriously? They're both such awesome actors,' Seth replied.

'Seth!' Lara exclaimed. 'I told you the rules. You have to pick one on gut feeling alone.'

'God! Matthew McConaughey because I really love *True Detective*.'

'And you're not supposed to tell me why, you have to leave it to my intuition to work that out later! Are you even paying attention?' she admonished.

'It's a little hard when you're sitting next to me wearing nothing but a blanket.'

'And the blanket smells a bit like cheese balls,' Lara admitted.

'That has nothing to do with me,' Seth replied, eating some of the pudding.

'OK, how about, Mark Wahlberg or Ryan Philippe?'

'So now we're having a *Shooter* the film versus *Shooter* the series thing?'

'No asking questions!'

'Man,' Seth said, breathing out and really considering it. 'Ryan, but do not tell Mark if you ever get to meet him.'

'Do you think Mark is pissed off I ran out of his premiere?' Lara asked. She still felt bad about that.

'Well, according to Trent, someone at the after party got very drunk and started naming and shaming half of LA. We were pushed way down the news feed.'

'I'm sorry,' Lara said, dropping her head a little.

'Hey,' he said, lifting her chin with his finger. 'No apologies needed. Besides, I can't be mad at someone who saved one of my mom's crazy guys and got sporked in the arm.'

'Remember, at parties, it was a screwdriver.'

Seth smiled, then put the pudding bowl onto the passenger seat. 'I've got one for you.'

'Oh, really?' Lara said, adjusting the blanket over her body as she shifted position a little.

'Yeah,' Seth said, nodding.

'Bring it on.'

He took a deep breath. 'Appleshaw or New York.'

He watched her expression fill with so many conflicting emotions. He hadn't done it as any sort of test, was highly expecting her to say the name of her beloved village, he just wanted to see if *his* city had made a little headway. If travel was something she would do more of now she had been on that very first plane.

'That's so not fair,' Lara stated.

'No pausing,' Seth replied. 'No hesitation.'

'You know I'm going to say Appleshaw, don't you,' Lara said seriously.

He nodded, smiling. 'Sure, I knew that.'

'But it doesn't mean that New York isn't up there as, like, the best other place I've been.'

'Lara,' Seth said.

'Yeah?'

'It's the only other place you've ever been.'

She doffed him on the shoulder with her fist. 'That is not actually true. New York is the only place I've been *overseas*. I've had some cool times at caravan parks in West Sussex and Dorset with Rory the Tiger and Bradley Bear.'

He scoffed. 'Come on, I really *don't* wanna hear about any more of your exes.'

She laughed, then moved closer to him, so their blankets and bare bodies were tight together as they sat on the bed, Austin's windscreen providing all the cinematic Big Apple scenery they needed. 'You know, I'd like to stay here longer, if I could.'

'Can't you?' Seth asked, sweeping a strand of her short hair behind her ear.

'I had to count change from my jar of coins to buy dollars to come here. I'm living on my credit card. I have a return ticket.'

'I know,' Seth answered, putting an arm around her shoulders and pulling her in tight.

'I really need a rich, successful actor to sweep me off my feet and loan me his personal jet every now and then.'

'And we're back to Mark Wahlberg ...'

'I'm joking, about the rich bit. Not the successful bit, because you are already but ...'

'It's coming,' Seth said with a confident nod. 'Not enough to buy a jet, but, if I get the part of Sam and I play him the way I know I can play him, then more parts are gonna open up for me. And more parts mean more money and ... maybe I'll get to visit the UK.'

'Really?' Lara asked him. He could almost see her heart picking up pace at the thought of him coming to England, seeing her beloved Appleshaw.

'I don't know when, Lara,' he admitted. 'There'll be filming if I get the role, for months, and if I don't get the part then I'm gonna have to think again and chase other parts and ... I don't currently have an agent.'

'Don't be too hard on Trent,' Lara blurted out.

Seth shook his head. 'We are two very different people at the total opposite end of this industry in terms of how we want to work things.'

'I know,' Lara said. 'But he's your friend and he really cares about you. He's actually a bit like Shirt.'

'Shirt?'

'Shirt's the bull at the farm next door.'

Seth laughed. 'Bull shirt?'

'What can I say? I watch *The Good Place*.' She smiled. 'Shirt spends his days trying to get the cows to do what he wants them to do.'

'I think that's a nature thing, not a personality thing.'

'And maybe that's the same for Trent.'

'I should let him make me do what he wants?' Seth asked, a bit confused.

Lara shook her head. 'No. You see, those cows ignore Shirt for most of the day and that makes him cross but then, *on their terms*, when *they're* ready, they're mooing for him come tea time and everyone gets what they want.'

'I should ... take away his power?'

'He wants immediate action on everything. Just slow his pace. He wants to talk about something now, you say you'll talk about it later that night. Don't just say "later", you'll need to give him specifics, so he can compartmentalise. But I think it could work.'

'And how did you become so knowledgeable about the Trent psyche?'

'I told you,' Lara said. 'We're all animals really.'

'In that case,' Seth said, stripping her of her blanket in one swift move. 'I think we ought to get back to basics right here and now.'

She fell back onto the bed, laughing as he moved over her, her nakedness now familiar and, in the dawn light, even more tantalising. 'Just, one more question,' she said as he lowered his face towards her, lips coming in for a kiss.

'Seriously?'

She nodded. 'Last one. I promise.'

'OK,' he said, fingers tracing over her breastbone.

She paused for affect. 'So ... Yanny or Laurel?'

She roared with laughter before him and then his fingers found her ribs, tickling the spots that he found out made her squirm then completely left her at his mercy.

'You, Lemur Girl, are gonna pay for that one,' Seth said, as she tried to curl up and escape his touch.

'No hesitation, remember?' she breathed, twisting away.

'Yeah,' Seth said. 'I remember … and don't worry, I don't plan on waiting a second longer.' He stopped tickling and caught her mouth up in his.

Seventy

The Chapel Shelter
Benefit Night, Hotel Edison,
W 47th Street

'You're gonna be in so much trouble,' Felice said, jogging along next to Lara as they powered up the street, Earl and Mad Maggie in tow.

'If we miss the start then yes,' Lara agreed. She had already had half a dozen messages from Susie and two from Seth, none of which she had had time to respond to.

'Oh no, I mean for bringing us to the benefit,' Felice continued. 'You know, when the rich people see us.'

'She means for bringing us to the benefit, for the rich people to see us,' Mad Maggie repeated, holding on to all eight or so of her bags. Lara hadn't actually worked out how many bags there were because they all seemed to morph in to one another.

'Will there be pie?' Earl asked, limping a little with the pace. 'You promised pie, kid.'

'Yes, there's pie,' Lara said, a little out of breath. 'As far as I know.' She stopped for a second and turned to face Earl. 'But if there's been a sudden menu change and there's cake instead of pie you really must not stick a spork or any other implement into anyone, Earl. Have you got that?'

'Jeez, sister, he said he was sorry,' Felice answered with an eye roll.

'I am sorry,' Earl said, tears appearing in his heavily wrinkled eyes.

Lara sighed. 'I know you are. I know. I'm sorry, it's just, I've never had to sneak in three homeless people to an event before without anyone knowing anything about it.'

And this was all down to Ted. Unbeknown to Kossy, she was receiving an award for her services to the city at the benefit and he had enlisted Lara and Seth to bring some of the people she had helped the most to speak about her. It had taken a few afternoons of failed coaching on what they should say for Lara to realise that Felice, Earl and Mad Maggie didn't need a script to work from. They all loved Kossy Hunt and whatever they said onstage tonight would come from the heart.

'We're here!' Lara exclaimed. 'Here it is, the Edison Hotel.'

'It's beautiful!' Maggie announced, eyes all over the art deco signage and the miniature Christmas trees in pots either side of the double doors.

'I used to play in places like this when I was in my band,' Earl stated.

'It's OK, I guess,' Felice said with a shrug. Lara detected a ripple of excitement before she shoved her hands in the pockets of her coat.

'Now, listen, you wait in the foyer, while I go in and check that Kossy is sitting down and not going to move and then I'll come and get you and we'll go and sit at our table at the back.'

'I want to sit at the front,' Maggie informed with a frown. 'You said there was a dance floor.'

'There is,' Lara said. 'And you can dance to the band later. But, for now, you need to be sitting where Kossy can't see you so it's a surprise.'

'I'll keep an eye on her,' Felice said, grabbing hold of one of Maggie's bags.

'OK,' Lara said. 'Let's go in.'

'My God,' Kossy said, teasing her hair a little as she gazed around the magnificent ballroom. 'They're all here. I can't see anyone that should be here that isn't here.'

'That's great, Mom,' Seth replied. It really was a fantastic venue. An old ballroom that used to host swing bands in the thirties and forties that had been sympathetically brought back to its former glory. A parquet floor held round white-clothed tables all set for dinner with bright white glitter Christmas tree branches at their centre, spraying out from tulip-shaped vases like fronds of winter blossom. From the ceiling a curtain of fairy lights hung over the dance floor like glowing snowflakes.

'I mean, most years, some of them say they're gonna come and then they don't. They just send money. Which is fine. But, it would be nice, just once, for everyone who says they're gonna come, to come, and then, hopefully, I don't have to get your father to start the bidding on every single one of the silent auction items,' Kossy continued.

'Will you try and relax?' Seth suggested. 'This is your night. One of the highlights of your year. You've sold the tickets, you've got the people here, everything is done, the food is gonna be great, it's time to enjoy it.'

'Yes,' Kossy said, a little bit more upbeat. 'You're right, you're right.'

'Kossy!' Ted called. 'Charles Barker would like to speak to you.' He beckoned with his hand to the table he was standing at.

'He'll be complaining about the beef again. He always complains if I can't get sirloin on my budget.'

'He might not,' Seth suggested. 'He's smiling.'

'I'm going,' Kossy said, stepping forward. 'And smiling back.'

Seth watched his mom approach the table, arms outstretched in appreciation. And then his focus moved to his other mom who had spent most of the day helping them get the room ready for tonight's function. Candy was sitting at a table on her own, looking back at him. Dressed in another silk blouse – this one jade green – and a plain but smart black skirt with low heels, he felt a deeper pull of connection towards her, something he had been experiencing since they had started getting to know each other better. Every meet-up taught him something else about where he had come from and he was no longer reticent about hearing it, more excited. He went towards her.

'Candy,' he said. 'I'm sorry I've not been able to talk that much tonight.'

'Seth, we spent the whole afternoon together. And this is an important night for your mom. You have people to see and other things to think about.' She smiled. 'I never want you to worry about me.'

'I don't think it quite works that way,' he admitted with a smile.

'Where's Lara?' Candice asked.

'She's gonna be here soon, I hope … unless she's found an animal to rescue or got herself looped up on fencing or something.'

'You really have something special, the two of you,' Candice told him. 'I saw it today, the moment I met her and when I saw you two together, the way you just *are* with each other. It's rare, Seth, to have that.'

He nodded, his birth mother's words hitting him hard. He knew that, which was why, over the past couple of days, he had been so determined to hold on to every moment they had here in New York and make it count. They'd gone back to the zoo to check in on Jax and make sure the reindeer had been rehoused somewhere more appropriate than Carlson's Christmas World, they'd ice-skated again, this time at the Rockefeller Center, where Lara had narrowly avoided having her finger sliced open, and they'd gone to the Top of the Rock, at night, to drink in the city in the dark, stealing midnight kisses that had ended up becoming more than kisses on the 69th floor.

'She's going home tomorrow,' he informed. 'Back to England.'

'And I can guess how you feel about that.'

'Yeah,' he breathed. 'But there's nothing I can do about it.'

'Seth,' Candice said. 'You should know, from how we found each other, there's always something you can do about it.'

Seventy-One

'… So tonight, we are here to honour the wonderful, talented, highly organised, magician with budgets, whirlwind of a woman that is … Mrs Katherine Hunt … Kossy Hunt everybody!'

Lara watched Kossy put her hands to her face in shock as the whole room erupted into applause.

'Do we go now?' Felice whispered the question.

'You have to wait for the announcement, *chica*,' David informed her.

'Who are you calling *chica*, *hombre*?' Felice retorted.

'He doesn't mean anything by it,' Susie said, her hair wound into a candy cane shape on top of her head. 'It's just his way.' She looked into David's eyes. 'His really, totally sexy way.'

'Shh!' Lara hissed. 'Or we won't hear our cue.'

'You can call me *chica* anytime,' Maggie informed David with a toothless grin.

'Earl,' Lara said. 'Put down the spoon and get ready to go up.'

'I think it's real silver,' Earl remarked.

'… But before we hear from the woman herself, let's hear from some of the people she's made a difference to,' the speaker announced.

'This is us, come on,' Lara said. 'Off you go to the stage.'

'You're coming, right?' Felice asked. 'I'm not gonna stand up there on my own.'

'You won't be on your own,' Lara said. 'Earl and Maggie will be with you.'

'Come on, darling,' Maggie said, bags in both hands but still managing to clamp a vice-like grip on Lara's bad arm. She grimaced and attempted to shift Maggie's fingers off her stitches. It seemed like she had no choice.

'She makes the best pie,' Earl stated loudly into the microphone.

'And she always tries to make the shelter look nice,' Maggie added. 'Not just tidy, I mean like a home. You should see our Christmas trees this year.' She whistled through her teeth.

'She's like a mom to me,' Felice said softly. 'Not, like my mom, because my mom was an addict and she would have sold me for her next score if she could.' She swallowed. 'She's like a proper mom, who makes sure we're safe and we're fed and we're ... kind of ... loved.'

Seth looked at Kossy. She was a crumpled wreck, mascara running down her cheeks, eyeliner bleeding, tears snaking the foundation from her face, but he knew how happy she would be inside. Happy that she was making a difference. He looked at Lara then. She had gone up to the stage, ushering the three of them on, then stood in the wings, encouraging them with smiles and gestures every time they looked for direction. She had become such a part of his life already, he wasn't sure how he was going to be able to say goodbye.

'Ladies and gentlemen, please, put your hands together for Kossy Hunt as we honour all her hard work and dedication to this city.'

Seth rose to his feet, as did everybody in the ballroom, applauding the woman who had so selflessly raised him.

'I feel like I haven't seen you the whole night,' Lara admitted, clinging to Seth as they swayed on the dance floor to a Dean Martin number.

'You were in charge of covert operations. I couldn't blow the cover,' Seth reminded.

'She was surprised though, wasn't she?' Lara said. She looked up at him and smiled.

'Yeah, we got her good,' Seth admitted. 'Nothing often gets past my mom, but this did, and it was perfect.'

'It was a perfect night,' Lara said with a contented sigh. Except this perfect night was going to end with a departure back to the UK the next day. And she knew Susie was feeling the same. So much so, Susie had investigated how much it would be to change their tickets, and the answer was a small fortune this close to Christmas.

'Hey,' Seth said. 'It's not over yet.' He held her tight, his hands running down her back.

'I know,' she replied. 'We have a whole night of trying to make love louder than Susie and David, so we don't have to listen to *their* carnal noises.'

'Oh no we don't,' Seth answered. 'And I'm not sure I can ever do that again.'

'You're not staying the night with me?' Lara said, stepping away and staring up at him like he'd just announced The Foo Fighters were breaking up.

'I meant the noises and no,' he said. 'I'm not staying the night with you in that apartment where the walls are so thin.'

'But the bed at your apartment is lumpy,' Lara reminded. 'And Trent forgets I might be there and somehow is naked in the bathroom every time I get up in the night to pee.' She could attest to this after two stays at his West Village place.

'We're not staying at my apartment either,' Seth said.

'The shelter? I'm pretty sure that would be wrong.'

He smiled. 'We're staying here. At the Edison.'

She opened her mouth then closed it again then opened it once more. 'But, Seth, money …'

'I know, but, I didn't book the Presidential Suite or anything and … this is important,' he said. 'Isn't it?'

'Yes,' she agreed. 'Yes, it is.' She settled back into his arms, letting him move them slowly in a circular motion. 'And I bet this place has chocolates on the pillow and everything.'

'It serves great beer, I know that much,' Seth answered.

'Then maybe we should get a couple … to take away,' Lara suggested. 'For our room.'

'I like your thinking,' Seth said, kissing her lips.

'Excuse me! Excuse me everyone!'

'Oh my God,' Lara exclaimed, looking to the stage where Susie was addressing the room through the microphone. 'What is she doing?'

'S-sorry for interrupting the dancing and the party and everything but there's s-something I have to say … and I have to say it tonight because I can't say it any other time … because tomorrow, I leave!' Susie spread her arms out wide, with drama, and almost toppled over.

'Oh no,' Lara remarked. 'She's drunk too much red wine. This is what she gets like when she's drunk too much red wine.'

'And … before anyone tries to get me down … Lara, I'm looking at you … I haven't had too much red wine.'

'Says the woman who's definitely had too much red wine,' Lara muttered to Seth.

'What do we do?' Seth asked her.

'I don't know,' Lara admitted. Then: 'Pray?'

'David! David, come up here! Come right up here, stand right down there, where I can see you.' Susie hiccuped.

Lara side-eyed the crowd, watching from their tables, other couples on the dance floor, Earl on about his fifth dessert, Maggie standing on a chair. Then David came into view, his turquoise suit making him easy to pick out.

'Susie,' he called. 'Come on, you haven't given me a dance yet. Why don't we do that now?' He looked to the band, as if seeking help with the situation.

'Don't you play!' Susie said, spinning around and pointing at the singer as if warning him that making any sound at all was going to end in his demise. 'David,' Susie purred. 'I know I'm going home tomorrow and I know we live so far apart at the moment but I want you to know that … I love you.' She blubbed, tears slipping from her eyes like ice dripping off a defrosting car windscreen. 'I love you so much. Being here in New York with you, spending time with you, around the demands of the prince … and, the foils and the feathering … it's just made me realise that we're meant to be together. And it doesn't matter to me that you're on this side of the world and I'm … not … because it won't always be that w-way.' She fell off her shoe, then very quickly recovered. 'But it matters to me that you know just how committed I am to you and that I'm committed to you … even though you're going to blow a month's wages and more on a brooch for your grandmother … because that's nice! That's because that's you … my sweet, sexy David.'

'Oh my God,' Lara exclaimed, hands going to her mouth. 'I know what she's going to do.'

'David, I love you,' Susie said, the volume of her declaration causing a squealing feedback on the microphone. She paused a beat, as if she was waiting for everyone's ears to recover. 'David, will you marry me?'

A hush descended and every person in the room was looking at the diminutive Spaniard in the brightly coloured suit with the perfectly quiffed hair.

'Susie,' David said, striding forward. 'You are the most irritating *chica* I have ever met, you know this, right?'

'Uh oh,' Lara commented, letting go of Seth. 'This doesn't sound good.'

'I ...' Susie began, wobbling again on her shoes.

David was marching up onto the stage now, each footstep making a thudding impact. 'Always you have to be the one in control. Well, I cannot take this any more.' He stopped walking only when he was right in front of her. 'I will not take this any more. I am a traditional man. You ask me a question that strips me of my masculinity and I will not stand for this.'

Where was Susie's relationship know-how now? It seemed her friend was breaking every single relationship protocol in one fell swoop. And now she looked like she was going to burst into drunken tears. That never went well. It usually led to ugly crying and more red wine. Lara picked up the skirt of her outfit-repeat red dress and prepared to rescue her friend. Seth caught her arm.

'Wait,' he said. 'Just a minute.'

'I have been carrying this around for the past two days waiting for the right moment, wondering if I should really do this before you leave, thinking that you might not feel the same, but never thinking for one moment that you would do this!' David whipped a blue box out of his trouser pocket and

Lara watched as her friend let out an almighty gasp of shock. It wasn't just any blue box. It was a turquoise blue box ... a Tiffany's box.

'If that's a brooch *I'm* going to murder him,' Lara remarked.

'Susie,' David said, sinking down onto one knee in an effortless move. 'I ask ... will *you* marry *me*?' He popped the top off the box and even from her position on the dance floor, Lara could see that it was not a brooch, it was a ring and its diamond was of epic proportions.

The guests all gasped now and waited in anticipation for what was going to happen next.

'Get up!' Susie ordered, using appropriate hand gestures. 'Get up and get that ring on my finger and hold me like I'm your sexy giraffe!' She grinned. 'Yes! The answer is yes!'

Seth put his fingers to his lips and whistled loudly and Lara clapped as hard as her injured arm would allow, tears forming in her eyes. She couldn't have been more pleased for her very best friend.

'Lara!'

Lara stood stock still, like someone had walked over her grave. It was all Susie's shouting over the microphone, it was affecting her ears.

'Lara!'

What the hell was wrong with her? Why was she hearing Aldo's voice? The tiny clutch bag was on her table, not with her, she couldn't accidentally have called him.

'Lara! New York is so big!'

She span around then, the voice closer and came face to grinning face with her almost-brother. Aldo was standing right there, in New York, on the ballroom floor, sporting an I Heart NYC baseball cap. She could not believe it. She opened and closed her mouth, she looked to Seth, then back to Aldo, then finally she spoke.

'Aldo, please, please tell me you did not just get on a plane and leave Appleshaw without telling Dad where you were going.'

'Don't I get hugs?' Aldo asked, still grinning. 'I haven't seen you for weeks.'

'It hasn't been that long,' she protested, but her heart was jumping joyfully at the sight of him. She threw her arms around him holding him close, breathing in that Aldo scent of sticker books mixed with engine oil and the Lynx she always bought for him. She let him go then and made a serious face. 'Dad does know you're here, doesn't he? Or have I got sixty-five missed calls on my phone?'

'Yes, Dad knows he's here.' It was Gerry's voice. 'Because Dad came with him.'

And there was her dad, dressed in his best clothes, plaid shirt and smart grey trousers, smiling at her like being in New York a few days before Christmas was completely normal. It wasn't. It was so far from normal for all of them that it was nearly surreal.

'I ... don't understand,' Lara stated, shock kicking in.

'Oh, Lara,' Aldo said shaking his head. 'Dad and Mrs Fitch got on the internet and found this cool site with all these cheap deals for flights, and we sold the old piano no one played, and Mr Jones finally paid his invoices, and then we got Silas to take us to the airport and we flew ...' He made appropriate whooshing noises and swayed his hand around like a plane. 'And I ate all the plane food, even the dry bits and then we landed – eventually – and then we came here. We're staying at this hotel because you showed me the pictures and Dad said it wasn't too expensive, and then I took photos of the tall buildings and the cars and—'

'You sounded so happy in your calls, Lara,' Gerry told her. 'And all the things you were talking about ... Aldo didn't stop going on about the food and the beer and the Statue of Liberty and the Christmas markets and the reindeer and—'

'The stitches in her arm from the fight,' Aldo added.

'What?!' Gerry exclaimed, looking at his nearly son.

'Oh, didn't I tell you about that bit? Sorry.'

'I'm fine, Dad, really,' Lara answered.

'I just thought, why have you come home for Christmas and do the same thing we do every year, when Aldo and I can come here too, and we can do something different, something none of us have done before. Spend Christmas in New York.'

'But, Dad, the haulage yard ...'

'Closed for Christmas,' Gerry said, folding his arms across his chest. 'First time in twenty-five years.'

'But, my flight back tomorrow ...'

'You'll never guess how much I got for that piano,' Gerry said. 'We can change it.'

'Oh, Dad!' Lara gushed, flinging her arms around him and hugging him hard.

Seth couldn't believe it. Her family had flown across the world to be with her, so they could spend a Christmas like no other before. He really hoped he could be a part of that.

'Oh, Dad, Aldo, I want you to meet ...' Lara began.

'You must be Seth,' Gerry said, extending his hand.

'No dojo, Seth,' Aldo said with a grin.

'It's a pleasure to meet you, sir,' Seth said, shaking his hand. 'You too, Aldo.'

'I've heard a lot about you from Lara,' Gerry continued. 'I hope she hasn't got you into too much trouble already.'

'Hey, Dad!' Lara exclaimed.

Seth slipped an arm around Lara's waist and held her close. 'Ah, Mr Weeks, it's nothing I can't handle.'

'He's funny,' Aldo remarked, pointing at Seth. 'You're funny. I like you.'

Seventy-Two

Christmas Day, Kossy and Ted's home, Gramercy

'Did you make the thick gravy?' Aldo asked Kossy. 'I like the thick gravy.'

'Aldo, don't be rude,' Lara said. 'We're in America now, sometimes things are a bit different.'

'Like everything is so tall,' Aldo said, putting his hand up to the sky. 'And everything is wider too ...' He almost knocked a row of Kossy's ornaments off the dresser. 'And it's colder and snowier and Father Christmas sounds funny when he talks.'

'Aldo still believes in Father Christmas,' Lara whispered to Seth. They were all preparing to sit around the family dinner table for a turkey feast of monstrous proportions. There was a giant turkey – the size of a fat ostrich – sitting on a platter in the middle of the table, its skin tanned and glistening, and it was surrounded by all the trimmings in mismatched crockery collected over many years. There were peas, carrots, sprouts, puréed cauliflower, mashed potatoes and sweetcorn and Lara's stomach was rumbling at the thought of being able to tuck in at any minute.

'I made the thick gravy, Aldo,' Kossy informed him, bustling from the oven with a beef Wellington on another platter.

'That looks awesome,' Ted declared, helping his wife make room on the table.

Seth stole a kiss before pulling a chair out for Lara. 'I still can't believe you're here for Christmas.'

'Neither can I,' Lara admitted.

It had been a busy few days since Gerry and Aldo had come to town. Keen to explore and visit all the places Lara had told them about in their across-the-Atlantic communications, she had taken it upon herself to be their guide and it had been such fun being the New York aficionado. Who would have thought it – the girl who had never flown before being the expert on all things NYC.

And Susie was back in England for Christmas, but with David. The prince had needed reassuring that his star stylist was going to be back before New Year's Eve to attend to his follicles but, after that, David had taken ownership of Lara's ticket home, so he and his new fiancée could spend some quality time together sharing the news with both their families … and his *abuela* via Skype.

'It's a shame Candy and Dwight couldn't be here,' Lara remarked as everyone began passing the bowls of food left and right and filling their plates. She could smell the turkey Ted was carving and it was making her mouth water.

After hearing about Seth's mission to find his real mother Gerry had asked Lara if she ever thought about her own mother and if she wanted to find out where she was. Lara had thought about it, for maybe thirty seconds, and then told her dad no. Her mum knew exactly where she was, where she had always been, in Appleshaw. And, unlike with Seth, there was no adoption red tape stopping her from making contact.

Gerry also shared that her mum had struggled with motherhood from the outset. Just the sheer being responsible for another person aspect. Then their marriage had fallen apart because of their differences in respect of family and the future. Gerry wanted more children, a home and his business to provide them with a comfortable living. Her mum had wanted lavish nights out and a penthouse apartment in the city. Their opposites that had attracted had finally been what pushed them apart. But he had never closed the door on her keeping contact with Lara, in fact he had tried hard to encourage it ... until one day he had a note from someone at her address saying she had moved and left no forwarding address. It was now Lara's opinion that sometimes, for whatever reason, people just weren't supposed to be part of your life forever.

'It's OK,' Seth said, handing her the peas. 'They already had plans with Dwight's sister. Most people aren't like us, planning Christmas in the last few days.'

'That's true,' Lara said with a nod. She gave herself five peas. Any more and there wouldn't be enough room for the better stuff, like the mound of mashed potato she needed.

'But we'll see her tomorrow. At the annual shelter basketball game.'

Lara shook her head. 'Oh no, Dr Mike, you really are getting competitive about this game, aren't you? Was it you who suggested that street kid storyline in the script?'

'You're damn right, it's competitive,' Ted replied, putting delicious-looking slivers of meat onto a plate. 'And don't think we go easy on the shelter guests.' Again, homeless people were made to sound like boarders at a bed and breakfast. 'They give it to us hard and they get it back just the same.'

'I think I might sit that one out,' Gerry remarked. 'I'm more of a darts man myself.'

'No, Gerry,' Ted said. 'You have to play. It's American law.'

'Is it?' Aldo asked, all wide-eyed, peas slipping from his lips.

'Do not listen to my husband, Aldo,' Kossy told him. 'He's insane. Particularly at Christmas.'

'Lara, five peas?' Seth remarked, eyeing up her plate.

'You haven't seen how many pieces of turkey I'm going to have.'

'Never been shy of food, my Lara,' Gerry said fondly. 'That's why she can shift hay bales better than most of the lads in the yard.'

'Not better than me,' Aldo insisted.

'Do I smell competition, Aldo?' Lara asked.

'I think that's the sprouts,' Aldo answered.

'Christmas music!' Kossy exclaimed, leaping up from her chair. As she got up she knocked into one of the giant Christmas trees and it started a dangerous stray. The lights flickered, and a few baubles fell to the floor and Ted, turkey fork in one hand, had to reach out and stop it from tumbling into the dinner table.

'Sorry, Ted,' Kossy said, leaning in close to the sideboard. 'Alexa, play Michael Bublé Christmas.'

'Kossy, come on, there are other people who have sung wonderful Christmas songs.'

'Cliff Richard's done a few,' Gerry remarked.

'I like the one about the war with the trumpets,' Aldo stated, gravy on his chin, having already filled his plate with food.

'Playing songs by Michael Jackson on Kossy's Spotify,' the machine answered.

'No!' Kossy exclaimed, hands in her hair. 'Not Michael Jackson! Michael Bublé!' The opening bars of 'Thriller' sounded out.

'Alexa! Stop!' Kossy shouted.

'So,' Seth said. 'Before we start eating and we get to the Christmas music.' He cleared his throat. 'I've an announcement to make.'

A quiet descended except for Aldo scraping every soupcon of gravy off his plate and onto his fork. Lara held her breath, wondering what he was going to say.

'I found out yesterday ... I got the role of Sam in *A Soul's Song*.'

'Oh my God!' Kossy exclaimed, leaping again, this time hitting the other side of the tree, an angel flying down to the wood floor.

'That's fantastic news, son,' Ted replied.

Lara threw her arms around him, tears in her eyes as she held him close. 'I don't know what to say,' she breathed. 'You wanted that part so much. I know how much it means to you. Not just for the money and the better parts coming maybe, but because that was the part that made you want to find Candice.'

'Yeah,' Seth replied, his voice thick with emotion too. 'And it was a part you helped me get. That night in Cafe Cluny.'

'I'll never forget it,' Lara said. 'Mussolini and tights.'

'Alexa, play Michael Bublé,' Kossy commanded.

'Playing Michael Bublé from Kossy's Spotify.'

At last the dulcet tones of the King of Croon sounded out and Kossy sat back down, satisfied.

'I got you something,' Seth said. He leaned back in his chair and produced a parcel from the bookcase.

'Seth,' Lara said, taking the beautifully wrapped, rather heavy package. 'We said no presents. We said that me being here for Christmas was enough of a present for both of us.'

'I know,' he answered. 'And it is. It definitely is.' He put his hand in hers, squeezing it tightly.

'So, this is?' Lara asked, looking at the gift.

'This is … a promise, if you like,' Seth told her.

Lara swallowed, his words making her feel the kind of special she always seemed to feel when he was around. The type of special she had been feeling literally from the moment they first met. She looked up from the parcel to Aldo, her brother taking seconds of everything before she had even had firsts, her dad sampling the wine Ted was pouring for them, then opting for beer, Kossy encouraging Aldo to take even more food. Being here, being part of this new mix of family, had been so unexpected, but she was loving every second of it.

'Open the gift,' Seth urged her.

'I don't have anything for you,' she moaned.

'This is for me too, I hope.'

She slipped her fingers underneath the wrapping, beginning to carefully peel away the mistletoe-embossed paper … and then she gave up doing that and started to tear like a desperate lemur. Finally, free of the paper, there were guide books. The first one she saw was France. The next was Korea, Thailand followed then, Italy, Brazil, China and lastly, Puerto Rico.

'You're just starting your travelling adventure,' Seth told her, his voice low and soft. 'I want you to make lots of plans.'

Lara couldn't stop herself from crying out loud. It was the most thoughtful, lovely gift she had ever been given and it said everything about how their relationship had come to be. She was looking forward to seeing Appleshaw again when this holiday was over, but she also knew she was excited about exploring so much else. And, while she could do all this on her own, strong and independent, she really had other plans.

'You know I can see myself in Rio, on the beach, sipping a caipirinha while I dance a little samba.'

'Me too,' Seth admitted.

'But drinking on your own is the first step towards having a problem, and you've seen those Brazilians dance, haven't you? I'm going to need someone to do that sexy sway with.'

'I guess you might,' Seth agreed.

'You'll come with me, won't you? Have these adventures too?'

'Filming doesn't start until the end of February,' Seth told her. 'How are you fixed for Valentine's Day?'

She kissed him then, full and slow, uncaring that they were sitting at Christmas dinner and Aldo had eaten almost all the turkey. But then she broke away, wanting to just look into his eyes and be still in this flawless moment together.

'I love you, Lara,' Seth told her, reaching for her hand.

'I love you too,' she answered, her heart skipping a beat.

'Merry Christmas, Lemur Girl.'

@TrentDavenport101: Breaking News: It's official! You shipped them and ... it's love! @SethHuntActor and @laraweekend are a couple. You heard it here first! Merry Christmas everyone!

Letter from Mandy

Thank you so much for reading *One New York Christmas* and for choosing to spend some time in New York with Lara and Seth ... and not forgetting Susie, David, Kossy, Ted, Felice, Earl, Mad Maggie and Trent. Plus, the lovable Aldo and the not-so-lovable Dan!

I hope you enjoyed this festive story. I had so much fun writing it and getting to know these characters ... especially Seth! I would love to hear who your favourite character was. Did you enjoy unconventional heroine Lara? Or did you just fall in love with the Big Apple itself in this run-up to Christmas?

I do love connecting with my readers so please do tweet or Facebook me, or maybe share some photos of you with your copy of *One New York Christmas* on Instagram wherever you're reading it!

Twitter: @mandybaggot
Facebook: @mandybaggotauthor
Instagram: @mandybaggot

Reviews mean so much to writers so, if you enjoyed this Christmas story, please leave a review where you usually hang out – Amazon, Kobo, iTunes, Goodreads etc.

And, if you want to find even more of my romantic reads, why not head over to my website. You can even sign up to my monthly newsletter for exclusive prizes!

Website: www.mandybaggot.com

Thank you so much for choosing *One New York Christmas* to read this winter and … here's to every ever-after being a happy one!

Mandy xx

Acknowledgements

Thank you so much to everyone who has supported me and my writing over the past six months. The list would be endless, but thanks go especially to ...

Tanera Simons
Ebury Publishing
My brilliant street team, The Bagg Ladies
Rachel Lyndhurst
Sue Fortin
Zara Stoneley
Carrie Elks
Chris Edwin
Matt Bates
Lynne Rose
Mr Big

Enjoyed *One New York Christmas*? Enjoy another festive romance from Mandy Baggot

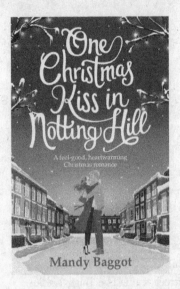

Imagine the perfect Christmas Kiss…

His strong arms around her waist, her hands on his face, the snow slowly starts to fall…

It's enough to make Isla Winters cringe! While her sister can't get enough of this – increasingly common – sight on the streets of London, Isla's too busy trying to stop Hannah's wheelchair from slipping on the ice, and making sure she's not too late to her dream job at Breekers International.

But everything changes with the arrival of Chase Bryan, fresh from the New York office. He's eager to learn everything about Isla's beloved Notting Hill, but as the nights get colder, will cosying up to him come at a price?